PENGUIN ᴍᴇ·ᴛ·ʀᴏ

A TOUCH OF ETERNITY

Durjoy Datta was born in New Delhi and completed a degree in engineering and business management before embarking on a writing career. His first book, *Of Course I Love You . . .*, was published when he was twenty-one years old and was an instant bestseller. His successive novels—*Till the Last Breath*; *Hold My Hand*; *When Only Love Remains*; *World's Best Boyfriend*; *The Girl of My Dreams*; *The Boy Who Loved*; *The Boy with a Broken Heart*; and *The Perfect Us*—have also found prominence on various bestseller lists, making him one of the highest-selling authors in India.

Durjoy also has to his credit eleven television shows, for which he has written over a thousand episodes. For more updates, you can follow him on Instagram (www.instagram.com/durjoydatta).

A Touch of Eternity

BESTSELLING AUTHOR

DURJOY DATTA

Penguin
metro reads

An imprint of Penguin Random House

PENGUIN METRO READS

USA | Canada | UK | Ireland | Australia
New Zealand | India | South Africa | China | Singapore

Penguin Metro Reads is part of the Penguin Random House group of companies
whose addresses can be found at global.penguinrandomhouse.com

Published by Penguin Random House India Pvt. Ltd
4th Floor, Capital Tower 1, MG Road,
Gurugram 122 002, Haryana, India

First published in Penguin Metro Reads by Penguin Random House India 2021

Copyright © Durjoy Datta 2021

ISBN 9780143448341

Typeset in Bembo STD by Manipal Digital Systems, Manipal
Printed at Gopsons Papers Pvt. Ltd., Noida

Text is Printed on Recycled Paper

www.penguin.co.in

To Rayna and Brahmi

Chapter 1: Arrogance

Anvesha tells me that it's arrogance that sets storytellers apart from pretenders, who waste their time writing hackneyed quotes in flowery diaries and on Instagram pages.

'A true storyteller has no time to say stuff like "I write for myself" or "my words are my babies". Writing is a job, Druvan. Just tell me if you can't write this. There's no shame in defeat,' says Anvesha.

She's trying to psych me and hijack the story.

'It's not going to work,' I say.

I open the laptop again, change the font size, fix the margins and wipe down the screen. I take a deep breath and wait for the first word to pop up in my mind. Anvesha breathes down my neck and watches over like a hungry, impatient vulture. She's ready to swoop in, tear up the carcass of my writing and take over. Telling stories is her domain, but this one is mine to write.

'I can't write like this,' I protest. 'You're giving me performance anxiety.'

I can feel her roll her eyes. She's losing patience.

'Let me write it,' she says.

'We tossed a coin. I won. This is my story to tell now. So back off.'

'Let's make it best of three?'

'What standard are we in?'

'At least let me help then. Tell me, what comes to your mind when you think of our story?'

'Umm . . . an epic tale of misery, suffering, love and death, with a light sprinkling of mind-bending sex?'

'And does this story strain against your insides like an untamed beast? Will your mind not be at rest till you have narrated it?'

'Maybe. If you put it like that. Will you stop putting pressurizing me?'

'Maybe or yes?'

'Yes, a strong yes. I do feel that.'

'Then that's arrogance. Tap into that. You, too, as I do, believe our story is better than that of all the other couples who promise each other forever. We are not like them. We are the best,' she says, clenching her fist like a football coach at the end of a match. 'Be arrogant about your story, our story.'

The scope of my arrogance is limited to *her*. Anvesha Mohan, the love of my life, the keeper of my heart, the mother of my unborn children, for whom I would die and come back. The last part—as you would see in the story I'm trying to write—I almost did.

'Druvan, start writing from the day we were born. You have heard the story so many times. That should be easy.'

'But our story doesn't start there. It starts five years before our birth—the day Vidhi Acharya was born.'

She smiles. 'You're getting somewhere. And by the way, she was born as Vidhi . . .'

'Vidhi Yadav,' I complete her sentence. 'And on the day of her birth, mankind changed. Should I start with this line?'

'Druvan, we say humankind now. Don't worry, just write. I will edit it later.'

Chapter 2: The Death of a Baby

'The baby will bring you fortune,' Rajiv Yadav's mother said to him, as they stood outside the ambulance that carried his wife, who was in labour. '*Tu jaa beta*, I will take a rickshaw and come. *Jai Shri Krishna.*'

Ten years before Anvesha and I were born, in the ambulance hurtling towards Damodarbhai Acharya Hospital, Chanakyapuri, Rajiv fumbled with a file in the bag that carried all the necessary things—reports, baby clothes, diapers and two sets of clothes for Neha.

'Are you registered with Acharya Life Medical Insurance?' asked the nurse.

Rajiv rattled off his wife's insurance number. 'Platinum cashless,' he added.

The nurse noted it down on her handheld device. 'First baby, no? Everything will be fine, everything looks great, don't be nervous,' said the nurse to Neha.

From the tiny window of the ambulance, Rajiv looked out at the hoardings looming large above them. In the past few months, hundreds of billboards had cropped up throughout the country, mourning the untimely demise of the richest, most powerful man in Asia—Damodarbhai Acharya. He was eighty-nine.

'The cycle of life. Our *malik* died and a new baby is going to be born today,' said the nurse. It had been four months since Damodarbhai's death, but the people suffered a deep bereavement. Neha clutched Rajiv's hand. The nurse continued with a sense of pride, 'Damodarbhai's body was donated to our hospital. We are the best in the city. You will see.'

Four months ago, Damodarbhai's family had lit an empty pyre at the funeral. As promised, he had donated his body to science. On the day, despite the tight security, two loyal managing directors from his company had jumped into the pyre and died.

'So is his body . . . still in the hospital?' asked Rajiv.

The nurse nodded. 'Even in death, he's helping people.'

The dead man, whose body was now being researched on, had changed the landscape of Indian business twice. First, with his oil company, Acharya Oil and Energy, and then, a little over two decades ago, in a move that had startled industry pundits, he'd ventured into the healthcare sector. Now every two out of three hospitals in India were under the umbrella of Acharya Life.

'Rajiv! Look!' said Neha.

Two leaping horses, sculpted on sandstone, their hooves hanging mid-air, almost fifty storeys above the ground, welcomed the ambulance. An expansive facility, spread over as far as the eye could see, came into view. The ambulance drove past multi-storeyed stone buildings with ornamental carvings, depicting scenes from Indian mythology and history, arches and gateways made of leaping horses and war elephants, and towering sculptures of deities, freedom fighters, politicians and thinkers. It was part hospital, part monument, part palace and part filmset.

The sprawling hospitals, the uneconomical stone buildings, the elaborate sculptures and the sprawling gardens that welcomed patients were one of the many reasons why Acharya Life was the world's most unprofitable company. It bled billions in losses, and yet the Acharyas kept pumping money into it.

Once outside the maternity wing, Neha was swiftly transferred into a wheelchair and wheeled inside.

'We will take care of her. Complete the formalities,' said the nurse.

Rajiv walked towards the desk behind which an army of men and women dressed in crisp white kurtas waited with smiling faces.

'Namaste!' said a cheery man with a name badge that had Ravinder on it. 'Rajiv Yadav?'

'How . . . how do you—'

Ravinder touched the webcam and answered with a smile, 'This recognized you.' He then turned to his computer. 'Just give me a moment, please.'

Rajiv eyes flitted to one of the many screens behind Ravinder. Advertisements of Acharya Life played on every screen. The achievements of the company were enumerated in small print at the bottom:

Never before in the history of business has a company had a direct impact in bringing down infant mortality rate. By making childbirth free, Acharya Life has brought joy to millions of families. Acharya Life has also helped build an entire ecosystem around organ donation. It has brought down deaths by 53 per cent due to the long wait involved in organ transplant. Our founder, too, donated his body to science . . . live longer, live better, live the Acharya Life!

In any other situation, Rajiv would have questioned these milestones. But five years ago, after extensive auditing, The Nobel Foundation had decided to honour Damodarbhai Acharya with a Nobel Peace Prize. Between their hospitals and clinics that dotted every city, town and village, and their insurance plans that came cheaper than dirt, Damodarbhai had monopolized the healthcare sector. Their revolutionary IT infrastructure had every man, woman and child's health record for doctors to access. One fingerprint and doctors could know the entire medical history of an individual—from a simple stomach ache to a cancer diagnosis.

The record-keeping had changed everything—doctors could now work remotely, with nurses on-site in inaccessible villages; their pharmaceutical wing could measure the effectiveness of certain drugs with pinpoint accuracy; and doctors didn't have to scramble for precise medical histories. Damodarbhai Acharya had transformed the healthcare sector before dying.

'It's all done. I have registered you. You can proceed to room number 34A. Ask anyone on the way. We are here to help you. Live longer, live better, live the Acharya Life.'

Rajiv hurried back to his wife.

'We will have to do a caesarean,' announced the doctor when he got there.

A nervous Neha was shifted to the operation theatre. When it was time, Rajiv too was led there.

'Welcome,' the doctor said, looking up for a moment, her hands still elbow-deep inside Neha. 'We are just about to be done . . . umm . . . we can see the baby . . . yes . . . just a little more . . . and . . . here she's . . .' The doctor's voice trailed away.

The doctor raised the baby from behind the curtain. Rajiv squinted to look at his newborn daughter properly. He narrowed his eyes to block out the light. He could sense the doctor's concern.

'What happened, doctor?' asked Rajiv.

Covered in blood and slime, his daughter's eyes were closed, her fists open, hanging limply, and mouth closed. She was not moving. She was as still as the air in the room. The doctors' mouths were covered with masks, but Rajiv could see the horror in their eyes.

A wave of anger and grief rose inside him.

Is she dead? Is he the father of a dead child?

'Doctor . . . ' said Rajiv, 'Why is she not breathing . . .'

*

While Rajiv's daughter struggled to breathe, on the opposite side of the town, fifty-five-year-old Hasan Ali drove like a madman towards the hospital. He had been waiting for this call for the past four months. He could finally breathe.

As had been prophesied, the baby was finally born.

Hasan checked the revolver in the glovebox of the car. It was a gleaming beauty, just the perfect weight. A Smith & Wesson 686 with Hasan's name engraved on it—a gift from his malik. 'Hasan Bhai, you don't need a gun,' Damodarbhai had said to him.

'Then why give this to me?'

'Because you're getting old, Hasan Bhai. I can't take risks with you. Save your fists. They have seen enough blood. I need them for something else now.'

Hasan had always prided himself on being a part of the inner circle, the family beyond the family of the great Damodarbhai Acharya. For men and women like Hasan Ali—whom Damodarbhai had pulled out of poverty, blessed with education and jobs, and given dignity of life and work—he was never the cunning industrialist who ran his company with an iron fist. For them, their malik was always the ever-smiling *bade bhaiya* from their village. Short, portly, fair with a big, red pockmarked face, Damodarbhai looked more the jovial neighbourhood *halwai* who puts an extra jalebi for customers' kids than an industrialist. Unlike other business magnates, he would always smile from ear to ear in his pictures that appeared on the covers of business magazines.

When asked by a journalist once, he had answered jokingly, 'Why should people not smile in pictures? Especially us businessmen. We have everything, *nahi?* And anyway, if I cross my hands in front of me, my stomach looks too big.' The uncharitable business magazines would call him the 'smiling' shark.

For his family, their bade bhaiya deserved to live forever. Unfortunately, it was not to be.

The night Damodarbhai was brutally murdered, stabbed fifty-three times through the chest and the face, Hasan slurped nihari at the Karim's near his house, watched a movie with his daughter, Fatima Ali, and went to sleep as if nothing happened.

'Your chachu will be back,' he had said to his daughter. 'Malik *wapas aenge.*'

He had refused to go to the funeral, which was attended by half a million people. Every minister of note, the richest of men, superstars, gangsters and even some heads of states of other countries had attended the funeral.

The guards at the hospital waved his car through.

Hasan Ali parked his car, holstered his revolver and marched inside the hospital. Everyone turned to look at him. Hasan wasn't a man of stealth. He was six feet six inches tall and built like a bull. His gigantic arms and puffed out chest couldn't be easily missed. When he spoke, his voice thrummed in the ears of others. He strode straight to Dr Amit Mishra's office. Dr Mishra looked a nervous wreck.

'Tell me,' said Hasan urgently.

'It's a girl, Hasan Bhai. She's healthy, of good weight, has a steady heartbeat and thick hands,' said Dr Amit Mishra.

Hasan knew that for a doctor, a man of science, today was a revelation.

The doctor continued in his small, nervous voice, 'Bhaisahib, I checked her myself. The surgeon reported that she wasn't breathing when she was born; her hands had no fate lines. Clean. I have never seen that. Her hands . . . they were outstretched. That . . . never happens.'

'Where are the parents? What do they know?'

'They have been told their girl has breathing problems so she's in the Neo-natal ICU,' said Dr Amit.

'Is the replacement baby ready?'

'We have kept a baby's body from the morgue to thaw. She will be warm in another ten minutes. The parents won't know we switched the girl's bodies.'

'Where do they work?'

'TCS, both of them,' he answered.

'We will take care of them,' said Hasan Ali and kept his large hand on the doctor's shoulder. 'How many of the hospital staff know?'

'Ten, including the doctors. We are debriefing them. They will be transferred to the new department and retrained,' answered Dr Amit.

'Bismillahir Rahmanir Rahim,' muttered Hasan Ali under his breath. 'Take me to *him*.'

The doctor led Hasan to the backroom, created in every Acharya Life Hospital for this purpose. In a room that looked more like an office than a maternity ward, lay a crib. Hasan's feet slowed down. His pulse raced as he approached the little girl, who was kicking and punching the air as if angry at her birth.

'Malik?' muttered Hasan in a small voice and bent over the crib.

Hasan had seen Damodarbhai's two sons and five grandchildren as newborns. They had stubby noses—the unmistakable characteristic of the Acharya family. The girl didn't have that.

He held the baby's feet and touched them to his eyes. His eyes flitted to the girl's hands. There were no lines on her palms.

The girl had spent nine months in the womb with[...]
her hands. This girl without her fate lines was goin[...]
the fate of humanity. When he picked her up, it felt l[...]
entire weight of the world was in his arms.

'I told Fatima you would be back, malik.' Hasan turned to
the doctor. 'What did her parents name her?'

'Vidhi,' answered Dr Amit.

He wrapped up the little girl in Damodarbhai's old shawl
and took her to the car. From the glovebox, Hasan took out
what had kept him awake for the last few months—the knife
that had the crusted blood of Damodarbhai Acharya on its blade.
The knife that had come with the revolver with Hasan's name
engraved on it—Damodarbhai's murder weapon.

He took out his phone, clicked pictures of the girl's
outstretched hands and sent them to two numbers. The first
belonged to Sanyukta Swaraj, a rising young leader of the ruling
party, who would, in a few years, be at the reins of Indian politics.
She had been handpicked by Hasan's malik to be the country's
future leader.

Our work starts, said his text.

He sent the same picture and text to another number. It
was Firdaus Shirazi's, a young godman, who ran a small cult of
fiercely loyal followers.

The roar of Hasan's 1964 Mercedes drowned out Neha's
screams, who had been brought the cold, limp body of a newborn
girl. The hospital's dean, Dr Amit Mishra, told them they tried
everything but couldn't resuscitate their still-born daughter. The
Yadavs buried a girl who wasn't theirs and went back home to
an empty crib.

A couple of months later, they both got job offers from
Acharya Systems and moved to Geneva with a considerable salary
hike and a little cottage to call their own. It would be another
twenty-five years before they would know what happened to
their little girl.

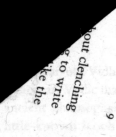

3: Our Birth

...y learning Sanskrit shlokas, German ...ic geometry and tracing the steps of ... the hawk-like eyes of Hasan at the ...tive Ashram, when, unbeknownst to ... struggling to burst out of our mothers' ammn... ...had spent nine lonely months.

This is the story of our birth. That moment in time that decided we were going to spend the rest of our lives together.

Dr Varun Mohan, a professor of history and Anvesha's father-to-be, and Dr Ramanuj Datta, a professor of mechanical engineering and my father-to-be, were best friends and neighbours. They stood outside the general maternity ward of KL Rai Hospital, waiting for us to be born. KL Rai was one of the last government hospitals in the Delhi-NCR region. The rest had been bought over by Acharya Life, renovated and run with an efficiency that was unheard of before.

Both our fathers—academics at government colleges—viewed big companies with scepticism. They didn't trust Acharya Life's burgeoning hold on the healthcare industry and its monstrous, resort-like hospitals.

'Are you excited, bhaisahib? I'm excited! Destiny has brought us here!' said Ramanuj Datta.

'It has,' mumbled Varun Mohan.

'Your child and my child, born on the same day, *maeri! Ki daarun, bolo to! Durga, durga! Ki holo, baba*? You're not excited? This is the most exciting day of my entire life! Better than even my wedding day!' said my baba.

Dr Varun nodded. His beautiful wife, Sunita, had had three late-term miscarriages. Anvesha was the first child she would carry to term. The weight of the past showed on Varun's face. Once a tall, handsome man, he was now bent, paunchy and tired, and looked older than his thirty tears.

'Sunita won't be able to take it if something happens,' said Varun Uncle in a small voice.

'Everything will be fine, bhaisahib. *Shob kuchh theek hoga. Durga, Durga,*' said my baba.

Compared to Sunita Aunty and Varun Uncle, who were tall and beautiful, my parents were cute, smiling gnomes. They looked more like roughly drawn cartoons than people. While Anvesha's parents' bodies had signs of grief and low-grade depression, my parents' smiling faces gave the impression that they were the happiest couple in the world. They looked ten years younger than they were. At five feet three inches, with a strange, long beard to mimic Rabindranath's or Gandalf's, Baba often looked like an MTech student who really loved canteen food. Mumma was an inch taller than him and was stick-thin, which made her look even taller. Together, they looked like the Bengali version of Laurel and Hardy.

But if you overlooked my parents' gummy, toothy smiles, you would find that they had been trying for a child for the past five years. Baba was tense too, but he didn't let it show.

On the day of our births, our mothers were separated by just curtains, like many of the fifty screaming pregnant women in the maternity ward, all in different stages of labour, blood loss, maddening pain and childbirth. The two men waited outside. The door to the maternity ward kept opening and closing as the nurses brought out children like fresh loaves of bread out of an industrial oven. Every time the door would open, all the men in the waiting area would stand up. The nurse would shout out a name—like it was not a baby, but an order of butter chicken— and a man would follow the grumpy nurse and the wailing baby in a pram to the nursery. Baba told me the door opened twenty-three times before their turn.

The door opened for the twenty-fourth time and two nurses walked out with two strollers, shouting, 'Mohan and Datta, follow me to the nursery.'

Our fathers followed the nurses, trying to get a good look at their respective children—us.

'The women are doing fine,' said one of the nurses, reading out from the report in a monotone. 'Mohan Girl, weight 3.54 kg, 11:32 p.m., Datta Boy, weight 3.54 kg, 11:32 p.m. You can hold the babies after the paediatrician has checked them. Both births were natural. You can meet your wives after the doctor has seen them. They will be discharged tomorrow after the paediatrician and the gynaecologist have examined them.'

The fathers couldn't tell the two babies apart. We were both chubby, wide-eyed, strangely quiet and astonishingly cute. Not in the way other newborns are cute. We looked stately, royal. Baba took out a camera and clicked a picture. The nurse shouted, 'That's not allowed', and the picture came out hazy.

'Sister, why aren't they crying?' asked Uncle.

'They cried when they were born, it's fine, don't worry,' said the other nurse.

'Maybe they are just happy to be born together, Varun Da! Look at them! Such wide smiles! *Maeri, ki cute!*' said Baba.

The two push-cribs were put in the nursery. The nurse wrote the names on them. Mohan—girl. Datta—boy.

'That's my Anvesha,' said Varun Uncle.

'You want the full name? *Pehle bolna tha,*' said the frowning nurse and changed the name.

'And that's Druvan Datta,' said Baba.

The nurse rolled her eyes and bent over to change it.

As if protesting our christening, both of us started to howl. Varun Uncle bent over and started talking to Anvesha in a baby voice, 'Nothing has happened, Anvesha, *hun rona nei. Papa aethe hi hai.* Papa is right here, no, I'm here, and your mother will be here too.'

Baba took the tough route. He said to me sternly, 'Sleep, Druvan, sleep, you have to sleep, Druvan. *Ekdom bodmashi korbe naa, shunecho? Cute howai ki shob kuchh?*'

Neither of us stopped crying. They rocked our cribs and sang the only lullabies they knew—*Rajkumari Soja* and *Tia Paakhi Aaye*. We quietened down for few moments and then started crying again.

It was Baba who noticed that we had craned our necks slightly towards each other.

Baba picked up Anvesha. Varun Uncle panicked. 'What are you doing, dada?'

'Don't worry, bhaisahib, I'm also a father.'

Baba carefully placed Anvesha next to me in my crib.

'We should first ask the nurse if we can put the two babies . . .'

Baba interrupted Varun Uncle. 'Just look.'

Within a few moments, our sobs eased off, our necks craned towards each other, our lips curved into our first smiles, and we drifted off. Baba's eyes grew wide. He picked me up. Like clockwork, both of us opened our eyes and started to cry. He kept me down and we calmed down again.

'Borun bhaisahib, do you know what this means?' asked Baba. 'The same neighbourhood, two best friends, the same date of birth, the same time of birth?' he said.

'It's called coincidence, Ramanuj Da. Didn't you see the nurses? I'm sure they write the same weight and time of birth for all the babies born within the . . .'

'Soulmates,' said Baba. 'They are soulmates. Druvan Datta and Anvesha Mohan.'

Chapter 4: Inseparable

Varun Uncle, the son of a dry fruits shopkeeper, loved history. He was all of six when he knew he wanted to be a history teacher. He was a wide-eyed, brash twenty-three-year-old when he self-published his first history book, *The Fiscal Policy of the Cholas*. The book was a colossal flop.

But it was during the first and last reading of the book that he met his wife, Sunita Aunty.

Sunita Aunty, an English lecturer at Bhagat Singh College, had walked into the Teksons Bookstore in South Extension, looking for discount deals. She found Varun Uncle sweating in his blazer, leafing nervously through a 544-page tome, wondering why people weren't interested in revenue streams and distribution, the intricacies of ledgers, and the accounting practice of an old regime.

There were twenty empty chairs in front of him. A disappointed bookstore owner's eyes kept flitting between the wall clock and the history professor. Sunita Aunty's heart twitched. She took a seat in the first row.

'What made you write this book?' she raised her hand and asked.

Varun Uncle's eyes had lit up seeing a potential reader. 'I love the Chola kings. They were exceptional and so under-researched,' he answered brightly. A single question turned into an hour-long storytelling session.

That day Aunty bought the first copy of *The Fiscal Policy of the Cholas* to mark the beginning of their relationship. Three months later, the rest of the print run of the book was sent back to the factory to be torn and pulped. Varun Uncle didn't bother. Because it was also the day they got married at the Patparganj Court in the presence of four witnesses, two of whom were Baba and Mumma. The only copy of the book was now the pride of their bookshelf.

Varun Uncle's second fan was two-and-half-year-old Anvesha.

'Shivaji *sunao* . . . vaji . . . ' Anvesha chimed in.

Anvesha, like her mother, took deep interest in Varun Uncle's sweeping tales of warriors and crumbling empires. Though she was too little to grasp Uncle's language, she would judge the cadence of his voice and gasp, laugh, cry Sunita Aunty looked at the clock. It was 3 a.m.

'*Mera baby toh mummy ki baat sunta hai?* We will sleep now, okay?' said Sunita Aunty to Anvesha.

'Maa tired, Papa tired, moon tired, the sky is tired. Everyone's tired, okay? We will sleep now,' Varun Uncle added. He pulled the bed sheet over Anvesha.

Anvesha promptly kicked free and sat up. 'Shivaji!' she insisted.

'Enough. Last story, okay? We will sleep then,' Aunty said sternly.

Anvesha nodded.

'Listen now, this is interesting,' Varun Uncle started again. 'So Shivaji had these noisy Brahmins in his court, who couldn't stop nagging him. They told him he couldn't be crowned king since he was of a lower caste! Imagine the *himmat*!' Anvesha snuggled up to Varun Uncle. He continued, 'Imagine looking down on a warrior like him who rode like the wind itself, whose war cries of *Har Har Mahadev* made the skies rumble and the Gods cower. And that's when a wily, smart Brahmin, Gaga Bhatta, found a link . . . a genealogy link between the Sisodia Rajputs and him . . . and boom! Shivaji was crowned king!'

Anvesha giggled.

'Though, Bitku, monarchies are not accepted any more, okay? Neither is Brahminism.'

'We will sleep now?' repeated Sunita Aunty.

Anvesha shook her head. 'Akbar . . . Akbar *sunao*!' she screamed.

Anvesha had no sleep in her eyes.

In the past two and a half years, Varun Uncle and Sunita Aunty had tried every trick in the book to make Anvesha sleep. Her paediatrician had never encountered insomnia in a child. They didn't tell her doctor they already had a cure for her sleeplessness; an awkward one but a cure nonetheless.

'Check how's Bubai doing?' asked Varun Uncle.

Aunty put her ears to the shared living room wall between their house and ours.

I was awake, and I was howling.

'*Bhagwan ka shukr hai*, she doesn't do *halla* like he does,' said Varun Uncle.

Sunita Aunty looked at the wall clock and said, 'They will come soon. Riti has a meeting tomorrow afternoon. She can't stay up the entire night.'

As if on cue, the bell rang. Baba and Mumma stood at their door with their troublesome, insomniac horror baby—me. I was screaming. 'Anvesha's house! Anvesha's house *jaenge*!'

'He has been screaming since two hours now,' said Mumma, handing me over to Sunita Aunty.

'Anvesha *kothaye!* Anvesha *dao!* Anvesha *kothaye!*' I flailed in Sunita Aunty's arms. These were the first two phrases I had learnt to say: Where's Anvesha? Give me Anvesha!

Sunita Aunty took me inside.

'This is Druvan!' exclaimed Anvesha when she saw me.

'This is Anvesha!' I answered.

'That's Anvesha Didi not Anvesha. Say Anvesha DIDI. She's your sister,' Varun Uncle grumbled at me.

'And that's Druvan DADA,' Mumma added, not wanting to make it sound like one-way affection.

'No! This is Druvan! No DADA!' said Anvesha.

'This is Anvesha!' I said, pointing at her.

Both of us rolled over in laughter.

'Soulmates,' mumbled my tired baba, the only one who was fascinated by our friendship.

'Both of you . . . sleep . . . the monster is coming!' said Uncle, pretending to be scared.

Anvesha dozed off, holding my hand, and I followed suit, little smiles on our faces. This happened every night. When they tried keeping us apart, I would shout and scream. And Anvesha would find a spot near the bedroom window and look outside blankly. The despair in our loneliness had an adult quality. Those days, we would spend all our playtime together, holding each other's hands and being a general embarrassment to our parents. They would try to distract us with toys, with television, with love, but nothing would work. Our insomnia had only one cure. And yet once every week, they would try to keep us apart. They would make us sleep on our own, but they would fail. Our cries and shouts would pierce through the skies, and the neighbours would shout from their balconies.

'LET THEM BE TOGETHER!'

Chapter 5: The Village Burn and the Devout Scientist

While Anvesha and I slept soundly, thirteen hundred kilometres away, sixty-eight-year-old Dr Arvind Kalam hadn't slept for three days. Buried in his office, a hundred storeys below ground, he stared tensely at the portrait of Homi Jahangir Bhabha—his childhood hero and the founder of India's nuclear programme—which hung in front of him.

If Arvind were to die today—there was a high probability—no one would know.

Deaths and kidnappings have always been the main causes of attrition at nuclear facilities across the world, including Bhabha Atomic Research Centre (BARC) and Indian Space Research Organization (ISRO). Both these organizations saw at least forty-five unexplained deaths annually—of scientists, fellows or workers close to sensitive information. Deaths by what means, you ask? Painful suicides; charring to ashes in a fire; falling over into a cauldron of radioactive material. Arvind always knew the dangers his profession would bring.

The man whose portrait hung in his bedroom as a child and now in his office had lost his life—like many nuclear scientists and technicians—to this profession. Merely a month after India emerged as a military power, defeating Pakistan in the 1965 war, Homi Jahangir Bhabha had announced that he could build an atomic bomb in fifteen months. He didn't have fifteen months. Foreign powers were already plotting his death.

Three months later, two pilots flew Air India Flight 101 right into the highest, most visible, mountain of the Alps, Mont Blanc, killing all hundred and seventeen people on-board. Every passenger's death was tragic but only one was of strategic importance—Homi Jahangir Bhabha's. Homi Bhabha's suspected assassination came just thirteen days after the mysterious death of Lal Bahadur Shastri, the prime minister who had won India its war against Pakistan, America's ally. With two strokes, the US had punctured India's rise as a nuclear and military power. Arvind never got over his hatred for the US and Pakistan, but his passion for atomic research stayed alive.

Twenty-eight years ago, freshly back from long stints at labs in Interlaken and Manchester, he was courted by both BARC and ISRO. But he knew neither of these organizations had the scientific freedom or the money to fund his vision. Building the world's biggest particle collider was his longstanding dream, and he wouldn't rest till he made it. Particle accelerators were like the Russian roulette of particle physics. You spin the chamber and wait. You speed up atoms and make them crash against each other at the speed of light and wait for magic to happen. It was the only true art in the world—to bring something into existence where nothing was before. Sometimes, you found a new particle, sometimes, a new element. But no one had really pushed the boundaries. They had mimicked the fusion of the sun in a lab, but what if they could simulate the Big Bang itself? That wondrous moment of creation? The thought of building it, of firing it up, of unlocking the mysteries of creation didn't let him sleep at night.

So he sought help from billionaires. Most brushed aside his proposal of building a particle collider. His plans to search for new matter to add to the periodic table, maybe even create a singularity and reconstruct a lab version of the Big Bang, were treated with disdain. Even tech billionaires balked at the idea. No one wanted to outdo the particle colliders already built at CERN and KEK in Japan. One of the CEOs even told him, 'You're going to blow up the earth.' No one wanted to risk it.

'Nothing but a bunch of money-crazed bastards,' Dr Arvind had thought at the time.

Soon after, he was discovered by Damodarbhai Acharya and entrusted with the responsibility to set up Damodarbhai Acharya Atomic Research Organization (DAARO). Damodarbhai was anything but what Arvind had thought of him—a wily village bum, who had gained his wealth through skullduggery and exploiting tax loopholes. Damodarbhai saw the potential in the forty-year-old Arvind and his grand plans pertaining to the unknown.

'Welcome to DAARO, Arvind Sahib. You are Employee No. 1,' Damodarbhai had said with his trademark smile. He had kept a bunch of keys to a car in front of Arvind. 'The petrol tank is full. Drive in a direction you want to and stop where you want to set up. Call Hasan, he will take care of the rest. In the glovebox, you will find access to all the money you could possibly need. It's a pot of gold that will never run out. Hire the best, Dr Arvind. But hire only those who are ready to sacrifice. DAARO doesn't exist for the world until we need it to. On paper, we will be a refinery. None of your employees will be on our payroll or any payroll. They will have to go missing from the world. Like *you*.'

Arvind didn't pick up the keys to the car. He wanted to know if this was a billionaire's pastime, which he would eventually get bored of.

'Why?' he asked.

Damodarbhai smiled as if he had been waiting for him to ask this question.

'There are questions I need you to answer for me, Kalam Sahib.'

'What questions are those?'

'We need to know where we come from, where we will go,' Damodarbhai said urgently. The desperation rang true in his voice. 'We can't just be intelligent robots, Kalam Sahib, can we? Just circuits and flesh and bone? There has to be something deeper about how we see, feel, perceive things differently. *Hai ki nahi?* The only difference can't be in our brain circuitry. *Kuchh to naseeb lekar aate hain hum sab? Aur ye naseeb lekar kahan jaate hai?* What happens to us? Where do we go? Where do our souls go?'

Arvind wasn't fooled by Damodarbhai's passionate search for meaning behind human existence. He knew Damodarbhai's interest in science came from a near-death experience. On Damodarbhai's fiftieth birthday, he had been in a grisly car crash. It snapped his spine and split open his brain. He had been pronounced dead on arrival at the hospital.

He had been dead for eleven minutes before his heart started pumping again. Soon after, Damodarbhai sought out men of science and faith. He never shared what happened in those eleven minutes. Was there a hell? Was there a God? Were there angels? Was there darkness? Or was there endless light?

Arvind stretched his hand. Damodarbhai got up and gave Arvind one of his trademark hugs. To the tall, lanky Arvind, who ran for five kilometres every morning, it felt like hugging a greasy, obese child.

'For the sake of science, for the sake of the unknown, for the sake of legacy, for the sake of being remembered,' said Damodarbhai.

'For the sake of being remembered,' repeated Arvind.

'A shopkeeper and a scientist will change the world, Kalam Sahib. *Kya bolte ho?*'

Not for a moment did Arvind fall for the shopkeeper nonsense. Damodarbhai intentionally let people take him lightly. Behind that smiling face and the usage of honorifics, he saw the strong determination and the sharp mind of the man who had his eye set on the world. He was more royalty than shopkeeper. The joviality was a front.

In the early days of DAARO, Damodarbhai would sit with him for hours and talk not about experimental physics but the nature of man. Sometimes, he would invite god-men and philosophers to DAARO and veer the conversations towards the existence of the soul.

'The soul doesn't exist. It's unimaginable, ridiculous, Damodarbhai,' Arvind had once said to Damodarbhai. Both science and the Quran rejected the idea of a soul as a tangible, transferable entity. He looked at Hasan, someone who had discussed the Quran at length with him, for support. Hasan, as usual, steadfastly stood behind his malik.

Damodarbhai poured tea for Arvind and Hasan. 'Acidity,' he said to excuse himself. He passed on the cups. Hasan refused, Damodarbhai insisted. He turned to Arvind. 'Arvind Sahib, you say it is unimaginable. If it is, then our entire existence is unimaginable, *nahi*? This universe? *Ye poora jahan, poora brahmand?* Unimaginable! The Big Bang? Unimaginable! Arvind Sahib, you believe that over a trillion, trillion years ago, all matter we see right now—the galaxies, their suns, the planets—it all came from nowhere. All matter compressed into space, a space that existed beyond time and space because there was no time and no space before the Big Bang. And then *kahin kuchh hua*, a blip of energy gave us this universe. The universe didn't expand into an empty space. It was a space in nothingness, a singularity. You believe this, you believe in the previous sentence, doctor, don't you? *Hai ki nahi?* You believe this is hard science. You believe that in the said universe, there are billions of galaxies, in which there are billions and trillions of suns, and one of these glowing balls of fire has nine rocks circling it. One among these has conditions that are just right to support life. And not just any life, intelligent life that has created art and music, and found love, and made communities, and found *Bhagwan* in their hearts. The scientists who came before you discovered fire, and now you're making this particle collider that can mimic the sun's energy itself. Don't you think all of what I just said is ridiculous? Unimaginable? Is the existence of a soul weirder than that? Weirder than the fact that we all live on a rock hanging in space? A space which has no end and no beginning? What is more unimaginable? The soul inside of us that dictates who we are or our existence?'

Kalam didn't say anything.

Damodarbhai continued, 'Kalam Sahib. If anyone discovers the soul tomorrow, I assure you the *junta* wouldn't doubt it. *Koi sawaal nahi poochhega*. They would think we hadn't tried hard enough earlier to find it. But if someone discovers God tomorrow—a real entity, with form or formless, yours or mine, but God nonetheless—people will doubt His existence despite believing aggressively in one. Even if Ganesh walks and stands in front of them, with an elephant's head sewn to an anthropomorphic body, with all his arms and weapons, and riding a mouse, no one's going to believe him. Even if a formless mist envelops humanity and whispers in Arabic that it's Allah and his written word is true, the junta would reject it. We might fight till we die, saying our God is better than yours, but we know for sure that we would never find the physical or metaphysical proof of God. But . . . we all expect, and know, deep down, that a soul exists. We know there's a soul and it's beyond just the words of poets, broken people and yogis. We know it in our hearts . . . that the soul exists. '

Kalam didn't contest Damodarbhai. But he found himself asking questions about what was behind the curtain. Quantum irregularities? Proof of Allah? Dark matter? Forces of divinity? The secrets to the universe? The energy signature of a soul? Why would Allah give his subjects intelligence if not to use it?

Like every time, Arvind broke the unsettling conversation by offering to show him the construction's progress. Around fifty feet below Arvind's office lay the massive particle collider DAARO had started to build, among other things. It would be a breakthrough in particle physics—a breakthrough meant to be kept a secret from the world.

On the way down, Damodarbhai reassured Arvind.

'A project like this requires sacrifice. Their souls are at peace,' whispered Damodarbhai conspiratorially.

A month ago, Arvind had tested a smaller version of the collider—still twice as big as the one in Geneva—and stumbled upon a startling discovery. He hadn't yet shared it with Damodarbhai or his team. He was waiting for the bigger collider to test out his hypothesis. Arvind had found an unrecorded energy signature. This discovery had come at the expense of his two dead colleagues. The deaths were hidden from the team and their bodies were disposed off by Hasan. He hadn't managed to take recordings. How do you build instrumentation around a signature you didn't know existed until then?

'We are here,' said Arvind, pointing at the beast in front of him, his dream, the final form of what he had always wanted to build.

Damodarbhai had named it Vasuki.

And like every time, Damodarbhai said, 'You're the *nagamani* on the head of the serpent, Vasuki, Arvind Sahib.' He loved referring to the ancient myth of Vasuki, Shiva's serpent who helped the Gods and the Asuras to churn out amrit, the key to the Gods' immortality.

Arvind cringed at the prospect of being a cog in Hindu mythology. 'There's only one true religion, Damodar, and one true God,' Arvind replied.

Unaffected, Damodarbhai continued with a twinkle in his eye, 'Arvind Sahib, *aap dekhna*, this will unlock the secrets of the universe. This will make the world remember us, make us immortal. So tell me, is this not Vasuki? Is this churn of quantum not the churn of amrit? And are you not the jewel on its forehead?'

'Your religion is a lie—stories told by a people who haven't discovered the one and only truth,' Arvind countered. Neither man was offended. Both held on to their truths and their respect for each other.

Damodarbhai didn't live to see Vasuki being completed. When his friend died, Arvind didn't go to the funeral, where the family burned an empty pyre. Instead, he was at the morgue, sitting next to Damodarbhai's mutilated body.

It had been five years, and between that day and today, not a day had passed when he hadn't missed his presence or feared budget cutbacks.

He missed him more today.

Chapter 6: I'm in Her

The public address system blared over the speakers: 'Calling Dr Kalam, calling Dr Kalam.'

Vasuki was to be fired up for the first time today. Today was the most historic day since its inception. This was Arvind's life's work.

'You should have been here,' said Arvind under his breath.

There was a knock on his door by his young assistant, a brilliant young scientist, Dr Kanika Dhillon. Of all the junior women scientists and engineers, Kanika made him feel the most uncomfortable. She was pushy with boundaries, always hovering, brilliant.

'We are all very excited, sir. You're going to create history,' said Kanika. 'Sir. Your tie.'

'What about it?' he asked.

'The red looks better on you,' Kanika answered shyly. And then quickly added, 'You might have to give an interview today, that's why I'm saying.'

'This is fine,' he growled.

It was his fault. And it was hers. Kalam had hired her straight out of college, IIT Delhi. Her raw intelligence reminded him of the time he could do divisions in his head, solve differentials with nothing but little taps on his fingers. She was a breath of fresh air; a mind so sharp, he had even felt a slight pang of jealousy.

Kalam's athleticism and her disdain for fitness made their thirty-year age difference look like fifteen. They were often mistaken to be a couple. The comments would always irritate him. And while he knew Kanika didn't quite mind the rumours or quash them, he didn't anticipate what was about to happen. Late one night, he had received a suggestive image from Kanika with the caption: *I want you in me*. Arvind's fingers had trembled seeing the young girl's nakedness. Before he could reply, she had deleted it. The next morning, she had profusely apologized, calling it a drunken mistake. She had later said it wasn't meant for him but a boyfriend, and that it was sent by a friend; the stories kept shifting, the stack of lies kept getting higher.

Today was not the day to feel rage at her.

In the central control room, the team of twenty-two scientists waited for the go-ahead from Arvind. They were at the brink of creating history. They were stepping into the unknown, crossing the quantum curtain and playing God with matter. Kanika opened the door of the control room and all eyes turned to look at Arvind.

'Initiate,' he said.

For the next three hours, the checks on Vasuki were carried out. Arvind didn't move an inch. Kanika stood next to him.

'Don't worry, sir. This will be a new beginning,' said Kanika.

It took two hours for the four-mile long Vasuki to fire up.

'Launch sequence initiating,' said Kanika. 'All systems are ready. Hydraulics levels stable. Heat signatures stable. Radiation levels stable. All eyes on the deck. *Chum*.'

She turned towards Arvind and smiled.

The whir of Vasuki drowned all the other sounds. The ground seemed to tremble. Just like Damodar had described the myth of the pagan Hindus—the churning of the earth to produce something mystical—Vasuki was unfolding its magic. Arvind forced the imagery of the Hindu myth out of his head and apologized to Allah for this transgression.

'Astaghfirullah,' he murmured. This moment was more religion than science. The origin of the universe in his lab, the paring down of the world to its most basic bits; it was like going back to the beginning of creation. Arvind closed his eyes and prayed, 'Allahu Alam.'

He was not the only one. He heard murmurs of prayers of different false faiths over the instructions being shouted across the room. This was not the time to remind them of the one true God, he told himself.

And then.

There was an angry crunch of metal, a shrieking sound, and a pulse knocked the electricity out. Vasuki had imploded. Another electromagnetic pulse—of a frequency yet undiscovered—flew outwards and then slammed back inwards, as if collapsing into itself. There seemed to be unseen waves, unseen matter and an unseen energy all around.

Bodies.

Arvind saw everyone's knees buckle; their bodies dropped to the ground, heads hit the console tables with a thud and the murmurs died out. They were dead. And then he saw his own still body, mouth open, slumped to the ground, growing cold.

'*Inna lillahi wa inna ilayhi raji'un* [Indeed we belong to Allah, and to him we return],' he said to his body, to himself.

Next to his lifeless body, was Kanika's.

Then there was darkness and silence.

Arvind woke up thrice in a hospital, twenty days later, hazy, disoriented, screaming and then went back to sleep. They told him everyone else in the team was dead. He switched on the TV news. It was airing an apology from the editor of *Tehelka*, a weekly, because he had reported that the 122 decomposed bodies that had been found washed up on the shores of Dwarka,

Gujarat, were of nuclear scientists who had gone missing over twenty years ago. The post-mortems done at Damodarbhai Medical College conclusively proved that the *Toofan* exposé was a lie.

Arvind switched off the TV and let out a hoarse scream.

But instead of his own, he heard Kanika's voice. He remembered seeing her lifeless body. But she hadn't screamed and yet . . . her voice. Trauma, he told himself. Post-traumatic stress disorder. After he was able to stay awake for more than a few hours, he got his first visitor. It was Hasan Ali.

'Take me to DAARO,' Arvind told Hasan. The words were his but he heard them in Kanika's voice.

'There's no DAARO, Arvind Sahib,' said Hasan. 'The lab's gone. In time, we will build you new labs across the country. For now, I will take you to Vidhi Acharya. She would very much like to see you and congratulate you.'

'Vidhi . . . ?'

'Damodarbhai's adopted daughter,' said Hasan. 'Don't worry, *he* will like what he sees.'

'He? Why are you calling the girl . . . *he*?'

'As you will soon find out, he or she will cease to matter,' said Hasan. From his bag, he took out a mirror and handed it to Arvind. He said, 'You are you, but you aren't you any more.'

Arvind looked into the mirror. What he saw knocked the wind out of him. He touched his face. He scratched it as if trying to rub it off. As if it were a mask. He blinked . . . he was controlling the face . . . his mind. He kept the mirror aside, his eyes wide in horror. Arvind looked down at the faded blue hospital gown worn by hundreds of men and women. Inside that gown was a naked woman's body. The only woman's body he had ever seen naked— Kanika Dhillion. *The woman who wanted him in her.*

'Where . . . where's my body?' mumbled Arvind.

'Dead,' answered Hasan.

He was in her.

Chapter 7: Us against the World

We were about to turn four. By this age, Anvesha's precociousness, wisdom and cunning beyond her years had rubbed off on me. And yet, sometimes, our parents outsmarted us. The parents sat down and cleverly hashed out a plan to reduce our dependence on each other. To keep us apart, our parents told us boys and girls went to different schools when they came of age. We were too young to understand that our parents could betray us. But as months passed, we noticed the children in the yellow school buses. Some buses carried only boys, others carried only girls. But some buses carried both. We wanted to know which schools were these buses going to.

'The teachers are allowed to slap the students of such schools. But if you go to schools that are only for boys or only for girls, you get chips for lunch,' our parents told us.

This was a serious conundrum.

'I won't let them hit you,' I told Anvesha.

'The teachers are big. You're small, Druvan,' said Anvesha.

'That's true.'

'And chips?'

'That's also a serious consideration.'

And so it was decided. We were to join Government Boys Senior Secondary School and Government Girls Senior Secondary School. These schools were not only separated by genders but were also fifteen kilometres apart.

Despite agreeing to go to different schools, on the first day, we noticed each other's uniforms and threw ourselves on the ground. We bawled and refused to let each other go.

'I don't care! *Main maar khaa lunga* [I will tolerate the beating]!' I screamed.

'*Main maar khaa lungi*!' screamed Anvesha.

However, we were separated by our unfeeling parents and marched to the bus stop. The full import of the betrayal came before the day ended. There were no chips for lunch.

That night, Anvesha and I discussed how it was impossible to live with our parents, and started to chalk out how we would run away from home.

'We would need lots of money,' said Anvesha.

'I know where Mumma keeps her purse.'

'Papa keeps his wallet on the table when he comes back from work.'

'How much money would we want?'

'A lot,' said Anvesha.

'A billion-trillion?'

'A billion-trillion.'

Starting that day, we began stealing money from their wallets and purses. Sometimes, they would notice a ten-rupee or a twenty-rupee note missing, so we had to be careful. While we plotted our escape, our parents continued to conspire against us. To keep us apart, they introduced other friends into our lives and tried to interest us with games that the other wasn't interested in. It was a relentless onslaught on our friendship. They would do anything to keep us away from each other. We braved it, since it was only a matter of time.

But six months passed, and we had only a few coins and a few small notes. It dawned on us that we would never be able to run away and build a new life together. Anvesha suggested we rather strive for independence and try to make as many decisions as we could. Like a general, she guided me through the ropes of Swaraj. I didn't understand many of the things she said or wanted me to do, but I listened nonetheless.

'We need diplomacy,' said Anvesha.

'Diplo . . . what?'

'We have to be like Akbar, tough but pliant, smart, tolerant and wily. We need to co-exist.'

Anvesha used a lot of words I didn't know.

'What?'

Durjoy Datta

'Arre, Druvan. Like Ireland. We self-govern, but we don't fight any more.'

'Ire . . . what?'

'We will make our parents bring us together,' she said.

Anvesha wanted us to start being obedient. We became the perfect good-boy and the perfect good-girl.

'Talk about Mrs Gupta, who gave up her job at the bank to stay at home. Say sometimes you wish your Mumma would be home too,' Anvesha instructed me.

'What if she says yes?'

'You have to be careful. Be appreciative but be sad while saying so.'

'What if Mumma feels sad?'

'In big fights, you have to make your opponent sad sometimes.'

'What will you do?'

'My shoe is broken,' she said.

'Haw! When? You can take mine. Why didn't you tell me earlier?'

'*Buddhu* [Fool]! I broke it. I will tape it and hobble to the bus stop tomorrow morning. Papa will notice it and feel bad. I will tell them I know they don't have as much money as the Makhijas.'

'In big fights, you have to do this,' I repeated Anvesha's words.

Our parents responded with love. To reward us, to cover-up their own failings, to provide us with the lives our richer neighbours were giving their children, they started to let us spend a little more time together.

My fourth birthday—*our* fourth birthday—was one of the most significant tests. By that time, we had totally stopped our tantrums.

'We will go to Shimla on your birthday!' Mumma announced excitedly.

'If that's what you want.'

Next door, Uncle said to Anvesha, 'We are going to Mussoorie!'

'Papa, won't that be expensive?'

On our birthdays, we were in hill stations separated by hundreds of kilometres, but our lack of excitement unified us. On the morning of my birthday, I saw my surprise gifts on the table and showed no enthusiasm. A similar scene unfolded in Mussoorie. Both sets of confused, hapless parents opened the presents for their children. We smiled and hugged them, ate the cake, but didn't play with our new toys or ask for an extra slice of cake, no matter how much our stomachs grumbled. They must have felt they were horrible, unkind parents to the most well-behaved children in the world.

Two days later, Mumma, Baba and Uncle, Aunty, organized another birthday party. We went to India Gate, cut two cakes, which we ate in entirety, had ice cream and played with our toys. Our joy was so profound that we found our parents in tears. The next day, they encouraged us to study together. They gave up trying to keep us away from each other.

We had won the war. Anvesha's manipulation of our parents before she was even four should have told me that one day she would have millions hanging on to every word she said.

Chapter 8: Till the Last Breath

We were six when the first big argument between Baba and Uncle threatened to pull our families apart. Every time either of us got sick, we had to go all over the city trying to find a hospital or a clinic which wasn't owned by Acharya Life. Most government-run clinics were hotbeds of disease, their doctors ill-trained. More often than not, Varun Uncle would take Anvesha to an Acharya Life clinic, which, without an insurance plan, would burn a hole in his pocket. However, the same doctors were free to consult with even the cheapest insurance plan.

To put it in perspective, to recoup the cost of a family insurance plan, one had to fall sick just once. In the last six years, healthcare had become synonymous with Acharya Life. Everyone was living . . . the *Acharya life*.

After an outbreak of dengue, Uncle surrendered and signed for an all-inclusive insurance plan with Acharya Life. They were done taking chances with Anvesha's health.

That evening, Baba and Uncle were locked in a shouting match that could be heard all over the neighbourhood.

'You don't get it, Ramanuj Da. Sunita keeps worrying about Anvesha. You know how the government doctors are,' Uncle said. 'Anvesha wasn't just born *aise hi*. We lost . . .' his voice trailed away.

'And Druvan was born *aise hi?* For three years I wore a *pokhraj*, a moonstone, and what not! I came across as a total superstitious fool. For what? For Druvan.'

'Then why do you want to take a chance, dada?'

'Do you think there aren't others who rely on government doctors and hospitals? Who are you? A Rajkumar?'

'Ramanuj Da, what are you saying? You're a mathematics professor. You will understand the numbers. Acharya Life hospital are six times safer—'

'Bah! Where did you read that? Which newspaper? Who owns the newspaper? Which companies advertise with that newspaper?'

'The survey was carried out by a government agency.'

'So? Sanyukta Swaraj is in Acharya Group's pocket.'

'That's what I'm saying, Ramanuj Da. It's either her government's ill-managed hospitals or the insurance. Why don't you get it?'

'You're a coward, Borun.'

'If I'm a coward, then coward *hi sahi*.'

Anvesha looked at me nervously.

'I don't want to garland a doll,' said Anvesha.

'Why would you garland a doll?'

'Just like Samyukta did. Prithviraj Chauhan's soulmate.'

'Why are you talking in riddles?'

'So back in the twelfth century, there was a king, Prithviraj Chauhan, and his soulmate, Samyukta. Their fathers were like ours, arguing and fighting. So Samyukta's father organized a *swayamvar* to break them up.'

'Swayam . . . what?'

'It's how they used to get married earlier.'

'They tried to keep them apart? Just like ours did?'

'And at this swayamvar, Samyukta's father kept a clay doll as the doorman to insult Prithviraj. Samyukta rejected every man at the function. She garlanded the doll.'

'First of all, what kind of insult is it to be a doorman? And secondly, are we getting married?'

'Why would we not, buddhu? We were born together and we will die together,' said Anvesha.

'Of course, of course.'

'I will prefer not dying though.'

'Same.'

The cold war between the two fathers lasted two weeks.

After two weeks, as if to validate Uncle's decision to buy insurance, Anvesha came down with a high fever. The doctors at Acharya Life diagnosed her with chickenpox. She was asked to stay locked in for two weeks and given anti-inflammatory medicines. Mumma and Baba told me I couldn't meet her because I would get it too.

'Why should she suffer alone?' I questioned.

Anvesha refused to see me. She told me over the phone that she didn't want me to suffer. And I thought: Why should *she* be the hero? Why should *she* be the Samyukta of the story?

I waited for the right time.

When Aunty came back from the vegetable market, I snuck in before she could slam the door shut. I ran to Anvesha and kissed her hand.

'Druvan . . .'

'We were born together and we will die together,' I said.

'It's only chickenpox,' said Uncle and rolled his eyes.

The virus took ten days to act and gave me a niggling fever. We traced the patterns of our blisters and found commonalities. We celebrated the bursting of the bigger ones, noting if our scabs were similar too.

All this while, I didn't know that Mumma had never been exposed to chickenpox as a child. Neither did I know that adults were twenty-five times more likely to die of the disease. A few days after I got sick, Mumma came down with a fever that wouldn't subside. Over the next five days, she got worse and contracted severe pneumonia.

That night, Mumma got so weak she lost the ability to speak. Her fever was high and wasn't coming down. She would try to string words into a sentence, but all that came out were jumbled croaks. She flitted in and out of consciousness, and every time she closed her eyes, I thought I'd lost her. It was all my fault.

Baba kept calling the government hospital for an ambulance.

Aunty lost patience and snatched the phone from Baba's hand.

'I'm not losing my friend to your stupidity!' screamed Aunty and dialled the number of an Acharya Life hospital.

Within five minutes, the ambulance of a nearby Acharya Life hospital reached our residence. In ten, Baba signed up for an insurance plan. Baba's ideology crumbled in the face of his wife's sickness.

'The hospital was quite good. The nurses were all so nice,' gushed Mumma to Aunty after she got back.

'Bhaisahib was *aiwen hi* [for no reason] sceptical. Some companies are good also, Riti. Not everyone is out there to trick us.'

'Sunita, you will see one day how this company earns every paisa back for us. No one is that benevolent.'

We were now living the Acharya Life.

Anvesha and I recovered on the same day. As a remembrance, we both scratched one pustule on our right hands. The blisters burst and left open, painful sores, which finally crusted over to become dry, brown scabs, which we later peeled off.

We both now had matching scars.

Chapter 9: The Muslim Boy

I was ten when I first encountered Rashid Quaze, the boy from 5F—the class of tall boys with hairy legs, all of them *lafangas*.

He was in the principal's office, sitting with his arms crossed, bored. The principal, Ramakant Kumar, was pacing the room angrily, clenching and unclenching his fists. He saw me at the door.

He asked me to take a seat next to Rashid. Rashid was a lot smaller, darker and dirtier than me. And that was saying something. The daily early morning football-with-a-tennis-ball sessions always ripped my shirt's buttons, and gave me sweat patches and dirt lines along my sleeves. Though I was terribly cute with my spiked hair and dimpled cheeks, I was short for my age. I was one of the shortest boys in my class.

'Will I be only as tall as you?' I used to ask Baba.

'Bubai. It's only the length of the beard that counts,' Baba would answer, stroking his long beard.

Rashid acknowledged my presence with a nod when I sat next to him.

'Rashid, this is your last chance. Tell me the names of the boys who did this. This can't go unpunished,' said Ramakant Sir, pointing to the little pieces of paper on the table.

'Can I see?' I asked.

'They have put in a lot of effort,' said Rashid, pushing the chits towards me.

Messages and illustrations addressed to Rashid in different languages and handwriting were scrawled on the chits.

'Go back to Pakistan! Also, does your father have two wives?' the first chit said.

On the second, there was an illustration of a man who was quite clearly a grown-up Rashid, living in squalor, with the flag of Pakistan outside his hut.

On the next, there was a scribble: '*Mandir toh banna hi chaihiye* [The temple will be built].'

Another had a man wearing a suicide belt and there was a thought bubble, which read, 'I'm Rashid, and I want to be a terrorist.'

I picked up another one. The illustration showed a boy named Rashid holding his bleeding penis.

I felt angry on Rashid's behalf, but Rashid himself didn't look concerned.

'Where are the boys learning this?' fumed Ramakant Sir. 'Is this what we are teaching here?'

'Sir, I didn't do anything,' I defended myself.

'You didn't, Druvan. Sir is asking a rhetorical question,' clarified Rashid.

'I can't let you be in the same class, Rashid, if you don't tell me who the boys are. I need to talk to the parents so that they don't do it again.'

'Sir, my father says you can stop them from doing it, but you can't stop them from thinking it. Let them do what they do, sir. He says they will be less angry if they show their hate through words and art. They will at least not vent their anger in other ways.'

'Rashid, you have until tomorrow. If you don't tell me the names of the boys who did this, you will be transferred to 5D, and Druvan will be your new class buddy. Is that acceptable?'

'Yes, sir. 5D is better.'

'Fine, it's decided then.'

'But, sir, don't call my parents. Baba can't close the garage on weekdays.'

Ramakant Sir nodded. We left the office and walked towards our wing.

'You call your father Baba?' I asked Rashid.

'Why? Is that a problem too?'

'No, no. North Indians call their fathers Papa or Daddy, so when I joined the school, everyone made fun of me too.' I saw the false comparison. 'I mean . . . I'm sorry.'

'Why are you sorry, bhai? You haven't done anything.'

He got back to his class and I went back to mine. At lunch, I wandered outside his class. He was sitting alone on the last bench. No one even looked at him. But they cared enough to leave him hateful notes. His words kept ringing in my ears. *Why are you sorry, bhai?*

He'd called me bhai, his bhai.

*

Rashid shifted to my class the next day. He was made to sit next to me. Rashid was the talkative type. Thrice in three periods, we were called out by the teachers. Every time he took the blame. Even that didn't stop him from talking to me like I was a long-lost friend. By lunch, I knew he was one of three brothers, all of whom worked in a garage and none of whom had studied beyond class 7; that he batted left-handed; that he loved the smell of petrol, cooked his lunch, and was considered the most intelligent boy in his locality.

Rashid was not only the first Muslim I'd met, but also the first Muslim whom I knew to be poor. All the other Muslims I knew—from Anvesha and Uncle's stories, from textbooks of senior classes—were kings and invaders, bathed in silk and gold.

'The rich Muslims left after Partition,' explained Anvesha. 'The Muslims who were left behind were poor and from low-castes. That's why you don't see middle-class Muslims.'

'That's no reason. That was so many years ago. This is a *faltu* pretext . . .'

'You can be really foolish and still keep all your inherited wealth, but you have to exceptionally brilliant to escape your inherited poverty. That's how the rich remain rich and the poor remain poor.'

'Hmm. He's nice though. He's quite good at pen fights too. We make a good team.'

Though I had been asked to be his friend, it didn't seem like he needed anyone. When he was not talking, he was quite at peace with himself. He would spend entire periods sketching the insides of scooter engines, or flipping through books with pictures of sliced automobiles. Within a week, I realized it was my section that needed him. Rashid, who used to be an outcast in his old class—the notorious 5F—proved to be a top forward for our section. In our first match against 5F, Rashid scored four goals. We still lost by three. But the hatred with which the 5F lafangas pushed and shoved Rashid around brought us together as a team. We played our best. To piss the other team off, the next week, we made Rashid our captain. Within the first month, we were ending matches in draws.

'You're rich, bhai,' Rashid said the first time he entered my house. He watched TV for straight three hours because he didn't have a screen this big in his house!

When I went to his house for the first time—Anvesha wasn't allowed to go because he stayed in Simapuri and it was *unsafe*—I felt bad for him. A single room—the walls blackened with soot, lit only by a flickering tube light—was shared by him, his sister and his parents. Two of his brothers slept in the shop. The pity melted away a bit when I ate their food, which was delicious beyond words. Rashid's mother was as strict as she was loving. His father, whom I knew to be a wise person, was ageing.

'He's sixty-three. I was a late child, bhai,' said Rashid when he noticed me staring at his baba.

I realized that nothing the boys of 5F had said was true. Rashid's father neither had multiple wives nor whipped his mother. Neither did the Quazes have animals tied around, which were being butchered by the young boys early in the morning. Though he did tell me about Bakrid, a festival when some of his neighbours celebrated the sacrifice of a goat with vigour.

'Can you do it?' I asked Rashid.

'No, but my brothers can.'

'So they—'

He nodded. 'They make fun of me. They say I eat meat but I can't kill an animal. They say it's haram to enjoy something if you haven't seen it being sacrificed. Be it an animal or harvest. So I stopped eating meat.'

I remembered all the times I had been to the CR Park market and stood outside the fish market, while Mumma and Baba had got the fish cut and cleaned. I couldn't watch the fish being cut open, their gills spilling blood, their dead eyes staring at me.

I compared Rashid's plate with mine. I had a piece of well-cooked chicken, while his mother had given him only bhindi.

'I eat fish, but I don't go and catch it. So does that make it haram?'

'Bhai, *aapko kyun bataun* what you should do. You do what feels right. If you ask me, everything should be done limit *mein rehkar*. But bhai, even you don't get fish to school,' pointed out Rashid.

I had stopped taking fish to school because the Guptas and the Jains and the Agarwals of my class had once called me immoral for eating meat. Anvesha was angrier than I had been when it happened. She sat me down and made me learn an argument by rote. 'Tell them, farm animals are forcefully mated to give them ghee, and rainforests are cut down to give them out-of-season vegetables, and that their overeating is leading to habitats being destroyed. First, tell these shopkeepers to get fitter.'

Of course, I didn't use this argument.

While leaving, Rashid's mother packed me some sweets for Mumma and Baba.

'Come anytime, there's no formality here, beta,' she said.

'Bore mat karo, Mummy,' said Rashid. 'He knows that. He's my bhai.'

Chapter 10: Gods and Goddesses

'Religion is the opium of the masses.'

I was thirteen when Anvesha told me about Karl Marx's quote, which, according to her, was a cowardly position to take for people who didn't understand the power and utility of religion. I had never heard anyone use the quote, but I would soon have to employ it to save my second best friend from certain doom. But before that, I had a question for Anvesha.

'What exactly is opium?'

It didn't surprise Anvesha that I didn't know things she did.

'We will have to start from the beginning,' said Anvesha.

'Do we *really* have to start?'

'Yes, we do, Druvan. That story of opium is connected to our fathers and their obsession with chai.'

I had always been her guinea pig. She wanted to tell stories like her father but be better at it. And to be honest, I could have heard as many stories as she wanted to tell me. She would look so beautiful when she would get excited about a story—her eyes would widen, her cheeks would go red.

And so she began. She said the English became so obsessed with the chai they bought from the Chinese that they ended up bankrupting their entire economy. To offset that, they chose to become murderous, slave-trading drug dealers. They smuggled opium into China in return for their tea. She told me how starving Indian farmers grew it and people like Jamshedpur Tata's ancestors helped the British smuggle it. 'There would have been no Tata Indica, if there were no opium!' she finished her story with a flourish.

The reason we were talking about religion was because Rashid was thinking of going to Hajj with his brothers. That would have meant missing exams. He would have to repeat the year. But it wasn't even a consideration for him. We were best friends, *ek doosre ke bhai*, and his refusal to listen to me felt like a betrayal. After all, he and I were braving the choppy waters of adolescence together. We were brothers in this journey. Nothing screamed 'best friends for life' than wondering aloud in each other's company if it were morally corrupt to get an erection thinking of a TV show heroine. It was with him that I'd watched my first porn video, but it all ended abruptly when he decided it was haram. We were a team. We had made plans for our future. We had decided we would be tall, handsome and rich when we grew up. Every morning, we would hang from bars to get taller.

And yet, he didn't even consider my position on this. I was religious too, but I wasn't crawling up to Vaishnodevi right in the middle of exam season.

I relayed Anvesha's words to Rashid the next day. 'Religion is the opium of the masses.'

'Opium is the opium of the masses, *bhai*. The cure to everything is in the book. Anyway, we don't have the money so I might not go,' replied Rashid.

'This is a sign, Rashid. You will be able to give your exams. The trip can wait but your exams can't.'

As Rashid's brothers started preparing for the journey of their lifetime, Rashid started to retreat in his shell. He carried a frayed copy of *Lonely Planet: Saudi Arabia* with him. He would spend hours reading it, marking passages and changing the itinerary of his brothers. Nothing else mattered.

Even Anvesha's new phone, which had caused a scandal in our house, couldn't elicit any reaction from him. I borrowed it from Anvesha and called Rashid home, but he refused. So, instead, the phone lay on our dining table, and Mumma and Baba stared at it with suspicion. The question in their heads was the same: How could a history professor afford this?

Mumma nodded. 'Bubai? How much is this for?'

The phone was for 54,000 rupees, but I lied. 'With discount, not more than twenty thousand. Maybe it's second-hand?'

Baba picked up the phone, ran his fingers over the screen and shook his head. He felt betrayed. 'This is not second-hand. Why didn't he tell me he was buying this?'

'They shouldn't have given a child such an expensive phone,' said Mumma.

I picked the phone, cradled it in my palm and took it to the bed. The phone was bare-bones—no apps had been downloaded yet, no games, nothing interesting. Then I found a folder with no name. It asked me for a password. I put in my—and her—birthdate.

Unlocked.

There were a bunch of videos. I clicked on first one.

'Hi! I'm Anvesha Mohan, and you're watching me on my channel. Today I will tell you the *real truth* about the Taj Mahal . . . is it really a grave for Mumtaz Mahal or is it . . . is it . . .'

I clicked on the second one.

'Hi! I'm Anvesha and today we are going to talk . . . argh . . . my channel . . . my channel . . . you have to say my channel . . .'

There were forty-three such videos. She got better with every attempt. The videos got longer. She could fit in more of the story before she lost her confidence. The last video ended with a sigh. She had given up.

Later that evening, I returned the phone.

'Did you like it?' she asked.

'It's quite expensive,' I said. 'I held it with two hands the entire time.'

'Did Uncle say something about the phone?'

'He thinks you shouldn't have it.'

'What do you think?'

'I think with a little practice, your videos will turn out great! I think this phone is a new beginning.'

'You really think so?'

'*Dharti kasam.*'

'I just think someone else could use the phone better,' said Anvesha.

Then, as if someone had heard her, she lost the phone within a week. She would get scolded every day for a week. Anvesha's TV and computer time was slashed down as punishment.

A few days later, Rashid came home, breathless and smiling from ear to ear.

'Bhai, you have to see something!'

He logged into his email. I squinted to check if I were reading things correctly. There were air tickets to Jeddah, Saudi Arabia, in his mail. He had won some sort of online lottery.

'It must be some scam.'

'I have checked with the airline, bhai! It's legitimate,' gushed Rashid. 'I will ask my brother to arrange the rest of the money. Allah has favoured me. Do you see?'

It's then when it struck me.

'Should we show this mail to Anvesha?' I asked. 'To celebrate? I think we should. Because I find it really hard to believe you received this in the same week of Anvesha losing the phone she shouldn't have had in the first place.'

It struck Rashid too. We went over to Anvesha's house. Anvesha knew we would put two and two together. She was just surprised it took us that long.

'Rashid, no one deserves a phone worth fifty thousand rupees,' said Anvesha with a laugh. 'Tell us how it was meeting your God when you are back.'

I was already looking at mine.

Goddess, to be precise.

Chapter 11: The Separation

Rashid didn't come back empty-handed from Hajj.

He came back with disillusionment and a general disgust for all things religious. He tried explaining his disorientation, but I brushed it under the carpet.

On the trip, a supposed man of God, as orthodox and devout as they come, had tried to touch him. Because I didn't know how to react, I just pretended like I didn't hear him. Years later, he would tell me that his family—devotees of the paedophile Mullah—had behaved just like I had.

In the next couple of months, it was as if his body rebelled against our inability to hear him. He grew taller and broader. His closed fists now seemed like mallets. His arms bloated. It looked like he had fallen into a vat of growth hormones. His voice started to break and then stopped. So now, it was somewhere between a deep baritone and an ugly rasp. He was taller than most boys in our standard. He was the first boy in the standard to sport stubble and the other boys shaved their marble-smooth skin to mimic his style.

Physically, even Anvesha followed suit.

Every time I saw her, she seemed to have grown taller. Her clothes weren't able to keep pace with her. Her skirts were now shorter, and I could see her taut thigh muscles underneath. Every time I looked at her, I felt a discomforting attraction for her. There were entire afternoons I spent thinking of how she had started straining against her clothes, how her lips had become fuller, and how even her arms and bare feet made my heart jump. Her gorgeousness often reminded Mumma how beautiful Aunty had been back in the day.

'Have you seen her eyes? *Etto bodo bodo like buttons* [Big like buttons]. Just like her mother,' Mumma once said to Baba. 'She's going to be so beautiful.'

To counter their sizes, their unmissable masculinity and femininity, I grew a 'sense of humour', but in reality it was just a defence mechanism, a distraction from my regular, normal being. Another distraction I built painstakingly was academic brilliance. It required sleepless nights spent studying, coupled with not telling anyone how hard you worked. Being the class clown and acing exams was my mantra for not being relegated to the background.

I was turning into Baba. I now knew that Baba's long beard was his version of a joke, a distraction from how puny he was. His mathematical genius and interest in technology were to deflect attention from his general unattractiveness. He would spend a good part of the day buried in science journals and thick books. Once that realization struck, I became comfortable with my deception because there was no one else I looked up to more than Baba.

While I spent my free periods revising chapters the other kids hadn't read even once, Rashid spent all his time teaching himself AutoCAD so that he could learn how to modify scooters and motorcycles. An hour away, at her school, Anvesha spent most of her time embarrassing her quiz teammates with her intelligence.

She had recently made it to regionals and wanted us to be there for the quiz. On the day of the event, Rashid and I were the first ones to run out of our school gates. We had to get to Talkatora Stadium to cheer Anvesha's quizzing team. We hopped on to Rashid's Activa. Despite it being a spluttering junk of bent parts and leaking coolant, he didn't call it a scooter.

'It's a machine, not a scooter,' he said.

'An injured cow just ambled past us. Can your machine go any faster? Because I'm starting to feel old just sitting here.'

We were already late, when we found the roads of Central Delhi blocked by the police and protestors.

'Bhai, why are these people protesting?' asked Rashid.

'They are protesting against the capital punishment bill.'

'Why would anyone do that? *Bhai, agar galat kiya hai to punishment hona chaiye.*'

'It's not as simple as that—'

He pointed at another group of people.

'And that one?'

This was a varied group of men wearing skull caps, women in saffron sarees and burqas, college-going boys and girls, and paunchy men and women who seemed to have taken a day off from their corporate lives. It seemed like a protest out of a movie—multicultural, clean, camera-friendly. They held giant posters of a god-man, who looked more a movie star—Firdaus Shirazi. He was in his late forties, but didn't look a day older than thirty.

'They want the government to withdraw the cases against him.'

As apparent from the protest, Firdaus and his cult Rooh Collective's charm—unlike most other god-men and their organizations—cut across religions, castes and genders.

'What cases, bhai?' asked Rashid.

'Abetment to suicide, tax frauds, etc. He also has like a dozen fatwas against him for talking about Islam.'

Our conversation died a swift death. Rashid would never talk about his religion anymore. By the time we got to Talkatora Stadium, the competition had ended. The teams, parents and teachers had left. Anvesha was waiting for us at the bus stop, arms crossed in front of her chest, shaking her head.

'Rashid's Batmobile could only carry us this fast,' I said. 'But you won, didn't you? I hope I didn't risk my life sitting on a fuel bomb for nothing?'

Anvesha smiled and nodded.

'Your victory doesn't even surprise me any more,' I said.

'I almost didn't though. I hope this isn't your *nazar*. When Krishna wasn't spared, who am I? In the last round . . .'

'Anyway, can we complete the rest of the story on the way home? Mumma will wait another thirty minutes and then start calling everyone.'

'Sit,' said Rashid, shifting to make space for both of us.

'Can Druvan and I take an auto? I need to talk to him. It's a little important.'

'What do you want to talk to bhai about?'

'It's about us.'

'Why shouldn't I know what is it? I have the full right . . .'

'Please, Rashid . . .'

'Bhai is going to tell me anyway tomorrow, so you can tell me now.'

'Rashid? I know you think you're his bodyguard—'

'He's not my bodyguard,' I butted in.

'I'm his bhai.'

'Rashid, it's important. He will tell you everything tomorrow. I promise.'

'This is what happens when you're the second best friend of two people who are best friends.'

He turned the key and revved up the engine.

'Please, Rashid? He will tell you tomorrow?' pleaded Anvesha.

Rashid stepped on the gas and drove away dramatically.

'He will be fine in a bit,' said Anvesha.

'What did you want to talk to me about?' I asked Anvesha.

She collected herself before dealing the death blow.

'From tomorrow, we won't be able to see each other every day.'

Chapter 12: The End

'We are shifting out of the house,' she said.

'What do you mean you're shifting out of the house?'

'Papa has a new job. He's going to write books for schools and colleges now.'

'Is this a joke?'

She shook her head. 'Baba has rented a house in CR Park. His office is near that house. We are shifting tomorrow.'

Blood rushed to my face. I felt my nerve endings catch fire. 'Who cares where his office is? There's a direct bus to CR Park from here. Wait, not one but three—461,679, 763. Why should you have to leave?'

'Listen to me, Druvan.'

'No, you listen to me, Anvesha. Your school is here? I'm here? You can't just pack and leave like that. Talk to Uncle and tell him it's a stupid idea.'

'Druvan, Papa—'

'How can Uncle do that? Firstly, why does he need to change his job? He has the perfect job right now. Don't worry. I will ask Baba to talk to him and then he won't go.'

'There's more money in the new job.'

'There's more money in cutting out a kidney and selling it. Should we all start doing that?'

'It's not the same.'

'Baba was right about Uncle.'

'What did he say?'

'That your papa is becoming greedy. He only thinks of money now. First the phone, then Aunty's sarees and now this.'

'What's wrong with my mother's sarees?'

'You know what's wrong with them. They are fancy, the kind rich women wear.'

'That's not true, Druvan.'

'It is true. He's moving because of money. Leaving a house he has lived in forever for just a little more. Where will he stop?'

'You're being . . . dramatic. It's a promotion. He's going to work directly with the government to write textbooks. How's that becoming greedy?'

'How long has he known about this? Is that why he got you the phone? He figured there was money coming in, so he got careless with his savings?'

'I don't talk to Papa about money.'

'Well, you should, because he's clearly a greedy pig.'

She angrily looked away from me. Even she knew Uncle's income from the professor's job wasn't sufficient for their luxurious lifestyle. First, there was the phone. Soon after, I had seen brochures of cars in their house. Mumma had noticed Aunty's two new watches. Uncle had bought himself a new briefcase after ten years. They got their sofa upholstered. A new water pump and a shower head had been installed too. Baba didn't confront Uncle, but Mumma and he wondered how he could afford it. They had been worried about the Mohans. Were they dipping into their FDs?

Anvesha held my hand and looked at me. 'He's going to take the job. He's not going to change his mind.'

'And your school?'

'They are putting me in Modern School, Barakhamba.'

'Do you know how much the fee is?'

'It's a lot.'

'I will talk to him . . . he won't go . . . isn't that a coed school?'

'It is.'

My heartbeat quickened as I recalled more details about the debauchery in the said school.

'Why a co-ed school now? He didn't agree to sending us to one! It's unfair.'

'Druvan—'

'There's no way you can go there! Everyone is kissing each other in that school.'

'I don't think that's true, Druvan.'

'Next year, you will also find a rich boy and kiss him.'

'I will not let that happen,' she said.

'I have heard everyone's very handsome.'

'Where are you getting your facts from?'

'All rich boys are handsome,' I said, tears welling up in my eyes. 'How will you not kiss them? I don't think that's possible. A Modern School boy will be your first kiss.'

'STOP.'

She held my face. 'I can fix that,' she said and kissed my lips lightly.

Her lips against mine.

A moment in history.

The tears dried up instantly. My heart skipped and danced.

But slowly, the rush of blood retreated from my brain, and I could see things clearly. The panic gave way to grief.

She would no longer be my neighbour. I would no longer see her every morning while waiting for my school bus. We would no longer wave at each other and wish our day goes well. We would no longer walk back from the bus stop together, promising to meet after a small nap. We would no longer trade our leftovers after dinner. Our study times would be spent apart, our play times would be separate. There would be no cartoons days on Sundays or mutton days on Saturdays. CR Park was a forty-minute drive away and we seldom drove forty minutes to meet anyone. But what broke my heart was Anvesha's stoic acceptance of this decision.

I searched for rebellion in her eyes and found only indifference.

'Baba always used to say that Uncle is different, he's not like other Punjabis.'

'Stop it, Druvan.'

'Look at him now. Packing his bags and sniffing the trail of money like a dog. It's disgusting.'

Anvesha knew her father was in the wrong. That's why she didn't defend him against my affronts.

'We will meet every Sunday. Maybe it's not as bad as you think.'

'You know that's a lie. It's a lie, *haina*, Anvesha? Who drives 40 km every Sunday to meet a family friend? Who?' I asked.

'Soulma . . .' her voice trailed away.

She first shook her head and then nodded and then her eyes welled up. And once the tears came, there was no consoling her. The auto driver glared at me as if it were my fault. She cried in my arms all the way back to our homes.

'I . . . I . . . tried . . . they didn't listen,' cried Anvesha into my shirt.

When we reached home, she asked me to promise that I wouldn't fight with her papa.

Baba and Mumma had known about this for a week. I had thought the erratic behaviour was because of their usual money worries.

Now I knew they were reacting to their friends leaving them. It wasn't just a shift of houses. It was a shift in their mindset, in the way they wanted to live their lives, in the way they viewed the world. When that changes, can a friendship sustain? Mumma and Baba were doing just as badly as I was. They too felt deceived. The love that existed between these four friends went back much longer than the years Anvesha and I had known each other.

The next morning, all their belongings—thirty years of their life—was packed neatly into one little truck. The house would no longer be theirs.

Early next morning, their landlord—the scum of the earth, the absolute worst, Makhija—came to check and announced that the house was in terrible disrepair.

'We will keep coming, Ramanuj Da.'

'I'm sure,' said Baba, dryly.

'And once that flyover is complete, it's only twenty minutes away.'

Anvesha and Aunty were sitting in the front seat of the truck. Like Mumma and I, they had spent the entire morning on the verge of tears.

Uncle, that cold-hearted, money-crazed man, shook Baba's hand instead of hugging his best friend of thirty years. He changed his mind just before climbing into the back of the truck. He got down and embraced Baba for a really long time. It made me want to murder him a little less.

'You're a big man now,' said Baba, as if talking to his son.

'Arre Ramanuj Da, *kuchh bhi.*'

'Take care of yourself.'

Uncle walked away from us and clambered up the truck.

The conductor slapped the back of the truck. The truck backed out of the colony lane, brimming with memories. The driver had just put the car in the first gear, when Anvesha flung open the door.

'Druvan!'

'Don't do it!'

She jumped out from the moving truck. Her knees grazed against the gravel. Her body crumpled into a heap. She got up and ran towards me.

'I'm sorry,' she said. 'I should have never let . . .'

'You're bleeding.'

'I am.'

'You two should come inside,' said Baba. He looked at the truck driver. '*Park kar do. Shaam ko jaana. Extra le lena.* My friend has a lot of money now. He can pay.'

With every turn of the bandage around her knee, I knew and she knew that this was the last time.

From now on, I wouldn't always be there to look after her.

Chapter 13: The Mourning

Makhija hung a big lock on the door and started to look for new tenants. It was as if Anvesha never lived there. It was now to be someone else's home. Just like that. Makhija had been meeting painters and masons to get the house *fixed*—a new coat of paint, a new wall there, a wall broken there, new bathroom fittings. An entire history—erased.

New tenants were going to come soon and erase every last memory of Anvesha's family.

A gloom descended over our family in the first week of the abandonment.

It was yet to sink in. There were multiple times Baba would get up saying, 'I'm going over to . . .' and then realize they had left. There were times Mumma would sleep till late in the morning, hoping she would ask Aunty for breakfast, till she would realize they were no longer there. Baba would sometimes stand in the balcony and look over to find nothing but dust and rolled-up newspapers. Mumma, when irritated, would ask me to go and play with Anvesha. My parents' tea lost its flavour. They didn't know how much tea and how much sugar were needed for only two cups. Their muscle memory only knew how to make four.

After school, I would invariably ring their bell and wait for Anvesha to look through the eyehole and shout, '*Khol rahi hun* [I'm opening]!' We were left neighbourless, friendless and soulmates-less. For the first few days, Mumma would ask the maid to clean their gate too. After that, even the maid started asking, '*Didi, rehne du kya* [should I let it be]?'

And then, the spiders weaved their webs on their gate. A thin film of dust covered it. I accepted the fact that there was no one waiting for me behind that gate.

'The gate has shifted to CR Park, but I'm still waiting, Druvan. I will always wait!' she said on the first call she made from her new house. 'I will call more often. The shifting is still happening. I will see you on Sunday.'

'It feels like someone has reached into my throat, ripped out my heart and placed in my hands.'

'That's quite graphic, Druvan.'

'It's from the new Mortal Kombat game.'

'You need to stay away from those unhealthy games.'

'Look who's talking. You spend your entire day reading about kings being blinded, their heads stuffed with straw, being forced to eat cooked meat of their own daughters and what not.'

'That's different.'

On Sunday morning, Uncle called Baba and told him they were still unpacking and would meet once they were more settled.

In the second week, to make up for her absence, she started to send me perfumed postcards through Rashid, who drove up and down. She would spray them with deodorant, and draw little hearts and ribbons on them. Slowly, she started to draw sketches of us in the margins, dressed up in different attires. She drew us as heroes and heroines from her history stories, as kings and queens, as warriors and priests.

They were busy the third week too. The promise of Sunday was broken once more.

By then, Mumma and Baba had brushed off their loneliness. Mundane things filled up the void their best friends had left. I learnt this was what it meant to be an adult, to slowly accumulate sadness and carry on. Uncle and Aunty kept promising to host a big dinner once the painting and furniture work was over. The day never came. The unpacking spilled into the fourth week, and we still didn't meet.

Anvesha raised a hue and cry about their broken promises. To ameliorate the situation, Aunty bought her a laptop with a webcam, so she could talk to me. Mumma and Baba couldn't afford one, so on our first call, I could see her but she couldn't see me.

During the call, Mumma and Baba kept looking over my shoulder. They pretended to talk to Anvesha but were actually looking at the new house behind her. They noted the three doors to the three bedrooms, the big TV, the leather sofa, the gigantic wooden showcase.

'They are Punjabis no, that's why. They have three rupees but they will spend ten. Next time you see, Bitku will have an even bigger cell phone in her hands,' Mumma said to Baba.

Baba nodded disappointedly at his friend's sudden, and slightly suspicious, rise in wealth. I didn't partake in my parents' disappointment.

Rashid would report from Anvesha's posh locality. He would count the cars, Google their prices and guess how much money people in the locality might have. We both knew it was more money than Anvesha's father could have earned out of a government job, no matter how important the job may be. But who was paying a history professor under the table?

'I also want money like those people, bhai,' said Rashid.

'It's black money.'

'It's better than no money.'

Ever since Rashid's religious fervour had exploded in his face, he had been drawn to wealth. He would often talk about opening his own garage some day. He would mark out shops he could rent in the marketplaces in Delhi. This was when his father and brothers were barely making rent for their garage.

'I am allowed to dream, am I not, bhai?' he said when I raised questions on his fixation.

'You should study.'

'Bhai, I'm better at engines than those engineers in Baba's garage . . . I'm the best I have seen.'

His self-assurance was astonishing.

He continued, 'I will also have one of those cars that are parked in Anvesha's locality. Worth crores. Bhai, you will see. I will buy one some day.'

Another week of our forced separation passed. Acute grief gave way to melancholy—the kind of sadness that settles in your bones and stays there for eternity. That Monday—a day after our parents had broken the promise yet again—I found her waiting outside my school with another bunch of letters. I thought I was imagining her.

'She's there, bhai. I can see her,' said Rashid.

'I had to see you,' said Anvesha.

We cried and hugged in front of hundreds of boys from my school and a bunch of teachers. Expectedly, Uncle, Aunty and Mumma, Baba were called to the school and told that their children were a bad influence on the other students.

'It's your fault,' said Anvesha to both sets of parents.

'You're raising us with a bad example. How can you expect us to tell the truth and keep promises if you can't do it yourself,' I said.

'Druvan is right. I stand by him.'

'And I stand with the truth.'

'*Beshi beshi hochhe kintu* [You're crossing the line],' said Mumma, grinding her teeth.

We were lucky we weren't slapped. The adults were furious, but they promised they would keep their word about meeting every Sunday.

The next Sunday, I wore my favourite chequered shirt, sprayed Baba's deodorant, and splashed his aftershave on my smooth, hairless face. The forty-minute drive took an hour and a half. It meant two changes of buses and one rickshaw ride.

Once I got to her locality in CR Park, I saw what Rashid was talking about. The lanes were packed with two-storeyed houses with gates so big you couldn't even see the house. Anvesha's house was considerably bigger than what it looked like on video calls. Each one of them had a laptop. There was a front-loading washing machine, a state-of-the-art television, an air conditioner in every room, and even a bean-to-cup coffee machine. Uncle was carrying a phone I hadn't even seen before. Anvesha had been using this phone to make her videos on history.

'I'm only still learning to edit. Next week I will be much better,' she said nervously as I flipped through a few.

'They are already perfect. You can just move your mouth in the videos, and they would still be pretty good.'

'They could be better.'

'I think you can upload them right away. The platform is going to ban you because you're going to crash the server.'

Even as we talked and slipped into the ease we were used to, a sense of sadness enveloped us. We knew this conversation would come to an end. That a little later, Mumma would come in and remind me of the bus timings. We would have to part and then wait to meet again. We knew this happiness of seeing each other was temporary.

'Do you like your new school?'

'No.'

'The boys aren't nice?'

'I didn't look at them.'

'The girls?'

'They are nice. You would have loved it there.'

'Nah, once you spend so many years in a boys' school, you are not fit for the normal environment. We are like penguins raised in a zoo. We will die in the wild.'

'I just imagined you as a penguin, Druvan.'

Anvesha had sent me pictures of herself in her new school uniform. It was in sharp contrast to the salwar kameez she wore earlier. Unlike a few of her classmates though, her shirt didn't hang loosely out of her skirt, she didn't wear sneakers instead of the school-approved shoes, and the length of her skirt wasn't risqué. She called her properness a conscious fashion choice.

'*Bas* class 10 and then two years, and it's over. We will go to the same college. I can't wait for our college friends to go like, how did this guy get this girl? And then you will flutter your eyelids and will be like, we are soulmates.'

'I have a question, Druvan.'

'The answer is yes. They will all make fun of us.'

Chapter 14: Cults

Like most young people, I will always remember class 10 for being shitty.

Within the first couple of months into class 10, Mumma discontinued the set-top box connection, limited desktop time, opted for a slower Internet connection and capped my phone hours.

She asked me, 'Do you want to be a labourer all your life? Pulling rickshaws?' When I didn't answer, she asked me again, 'Tell me, Bubai? What do you want to do? Do you want to live on rent all your life?'

I shook my head.

'Score well. The marks will matter your entire life. You can never shake them off.'

The tenth standard was also the time for me to bear the full burden of adolescence. I, too, grew that year, my voice came out in angry stutters, and my eyes lingered on girls a little longer than necessary. Within a few months, I grew taller, hairier and stronger than Anvesha. I was suddenly *a man*. On the Sundays we met, I liked that I towered over her. Rashid was still taller at six feet but, at five feet seven inches, I had finally reached the median height of my class.

Anvesha grew more . . . womanly, more beautiful. With Anvesha's obvious attractiveness and growing age and sense, Uncle got even more uncomfortable with our relationship.

'Papa thinks you're handsome,' said Anvesha.

Coming from a Punjabi man, who in his heyday was quite handsome himself, it was an honest compliment.

'What were his exact words?'

'Don't fish for compliments.'

'Why shouldn't I? I have heard fish jokes all my life and now when it's time for me to really fish you're asking me not to?'

'That was so lame.'

'I can feel you smiling on the inside. Don't lie.'

Uncle would hover over Anvesha during calls. Sometimes, he would take the phone from her and tell me he had an important call to make.

Mumma and Baba too kept tabs on our relationship.

Every Sunday, they would see Anvesha and whisper to themselves conspiratorially about how intelligent, beautiful and striking she had become.

'*Ekdom heroine laage mey ta ke dekhe* [The girl looks like a heroine],' I heard Mumma say to Baba one day.

Every Sunday, I met a newer, smarter, more beautiful version of her. Mumma and Baba would look at her and then look at me to check if I were as charmed by her beauty as they were. I would pretend to be bored. They would sometimes warn me about the changing circumstances of the Mohans and us.

'What are marks to them?' Mumma would say. 'I know Sunita. She keeps saying how unsafe India is. She would send her daughter to the US. Bubai, you have to stay here so don't get distracted. Class 10 results are everything.'

'Are you sure, Mumma, they are *everything?*'

'Listen to your Mumma,' Baba would add.

'I'm just saying what if I score averagely in class 10 but absolutely kill it in my class 12 board exams. Will I still be doomed?'

'*Beshi paeka hote hobe naa* [Don't be over smart]. The girl's teaching him all this,' said Mumma.

Anvesha's wit and her growing beauty widened her circle of friends at school. Even though she still hadn't made her video channel, her videos about interesting history trivia with 'clickbait-y' titles were already popular on her school's intranet. And through this, she had a new friend, Adhiraj, a fellow history enthusiast. My ears pricked up the first time she told me about him. We were at India Gate, our new venue for our Sunday get-togethers, sharing a tub of popcorn, when she broke the news.

'Is he handsome?' I asked. His name suggested a symmetrical face with a sharp jawline.

'I don't see him like that.'

'That's not the answer to my question. Handsomeness is a scale. I want to know where he is on that scale.'

'Where do you think you are on that scale?'

'I think I'm a solid six and a half?'

She frowned. 'You're a ten for me and the scale doesn't exist for other people. But if you continue this line of questioning, your rating will drop sharply.'

'You can just say he's ugly, and we can move on.'

'To decide that, I will have to think of him in that sense, and I don't.'

'Show me a picture of him . . . wait . . . don't.'

For the rest of the evening, I felt sick in the stomach. When I dug inwards, trying to get to the source of my anger, I realized it was the betrayal. She should have told me about him when their friendship was developing, and not after she had become friends with him.

Rashid laughed when I told him about Adhiraj. He didn't even turn away from the engine he was working on to address the grave situation. Instead, he said in a soft voice, 'Bhai, not everything means to be shared. Some relationships develop in isolation.'

'That's the most ridiculous thing I have ever heard.'

'Let her do what she thinks is right, bhai. The secret to a good relationship is guarding one's individuality.'

I know these weren't Rashid's words or his manner of speaking. The words were a direct lift from the new book he was reading, *The Secret to An Awesome Life*, by Firdaus Shirazi. It was his tone he was mimicking.

Rashid had fallen right from the clutches of one religion into the safety net of a cult. He, too, like Anvesha, had hidden this development from me till his indoctrination was complete. After his initiation into the 'collective', he started calling himself a Rooh—the term for a Rooh Collective follower. I wouldn't even have known he was a Rooh had I not caught him surreptitiously placing copies of Firdaus's books on the bookshelves of the school library. On interrogating, he admitted he had volunteered to become the school ambassador for the collective. His job was to penetrate the cool groups and spread the *truth*.

And now, every day, he would gather around boys and read a few pages from the god-man's books. Some boys thought it was unmanly, while others came to him with spiritual questions.

He tried to get me into reading these books too.

'What's with you and cults?' I asked him.

'Neither Islam nor Firdaus are cults.'

'A cult is a group that is defined by its unusual religious or spiritual beliefs, or by its common interest in a particular personality, object or goal. That's exactly what you're part of!'

'Let's assume I accept that, bhai. Tell me then, what would you call people who worship Goddesses and Gods with multiple arms? Who think the moon can be swallowed by a God? Or what would you call people who worship angels with four faces and two pairs of wings? Are these not cults?'

I bristled at him.

'Take that back, Rashid.'

'I didn't mean to offend you.'

'You know it's different from what you're doing.'

'I see no difference, bhai. It's a matter of faith and I respect all faiths. You know Firdaus was born in different religions in all his lives. He's a Muslim now but he knows the Vedas, the Bible, the Buddhist texts and everything else by heart.'

'My faith is thousands of years old and yours is . . . how old is Firdaus?'

'Bhai, I am not having this conversation with you again. *Main khush hu*, isn't that enough for you?'

'Fine, then I'm happy the way I am. Don't mention this fraud in front of me again.'

He never pushed me to read the book again. I developed a pulsating hatred against the forty-nine-year-old guru. His smiling face, his eternal youth, his hold over women and girls, irritated me.

Chapter 15: A Changed History

While Anvesha and Rashid explored other interests, I buried myself in books. Unlike her videos and his faith, there was certainty in books, there was logic, and, above all, there was a reproducible pattern.

The results were quick and unambiguous. Was this my cult? The cult of a normal life? The cult of following the rules society had built over hundreds of years?

Mumma and Baba didn't know our paths had diverged.

They were too busy finding their footing after the slow retreat of the Mohans from our lives.

Without Varun Uncle's sobering effect and Sunita Aunty's scared outlook, Mumma and Baba were on shaky emotional ground. Baba would frequently fight for parking space for his scooter. Mumma would complain angrily about the seepage from our upstairs neighbours' broken pipes. They would rail and shout at the news anchors and spokespersons of political parties, at the SUV owners who tried to cut into tight corners, and at the RWA's treasurer. Their anger was distributed unevenly and unpredictably, till they found an outlet.

It started with the prime minister, Sanyukta Swaraj, and the Nagarik Party-led central government introducing a new history and geography course for schools and the colleges under them. The government argued they were reducing the workload on students. The new history books were thin—the class 10 history book was ninety pages long, down from the 250-page book earlier.

Overnight, all schools in Delhi shut.

The teachers demanded a salary hike from the government to adopt the new textbooks. Several of Baba's friends from other colleges were protesting too. While the school teachers wanted money, the history professors in universities, the academics and the scholars wanted the government to roll back the bastardization of history. They argued that the government was killing their heritage and culture. Mumma and Baba joined this protest, fists raised, angry and frothing at the mouths.

'Do I really have to go to the protest?' I asked.

'Bubai, you would have to be a traitor to not go,' said Baba.

The anger he harboured inside him was making him older, sulkier. Mumma dressed me up in black to mourn the death of education. Mumma said, 'Save your voice for the slogans that matter.'

'Do I get money for this?'

Baba glared at me.

'How much does your soul cost, Bubai?' asked Baba.

The gathering was small—a hundred people. It was the most boring protest of all time. Old professors and excited students shouted slogans in English. 'SAVE HISTORY!', 'SAVE SOCIAL SCIENCES!', 'SAVE CHILDREN!', 'SAVE BOOKS!', 'SAVE THE NATION!'

Baba was one of the louder voices. Delhi police leaned against their vehicles and sipped tea. After a while, most of them left, leaving behind two distracted havildars. I was embarrassed for my parents and everyone who was waving their fists in the air. What was the big deal? They were just books. A reporter asked Baba his opinion.

Baba addressed the camera rather than the reporter, 'Have you read the books? It's nonsense! Just a bunch of dates and names of kings! They read like guides to pass exams, not history books! Where are the stories? Where are the achievements of the kings? The battles? The injustices! And what about the civics books? Where is the chapter on democracy versus monarchies? What does the government want to achieve?'

'But what's your point, Professor Datta?' asked the reporter.

'It's . . . it's . . .' Baba struggled. '. . . it's boring!'

The reporter rolled her eyes.

'The arts are an important skill! These stories are important! We need to know history, don't we? We need to know where we have come from!'

People behind him started shouting the slogans again. 'SAVE HISTORY!' 'SAVE CHILDREN!' 'SAVE BOOKS!'

Everyone got tired after a few hours. The reporter went home, the havildars walked away, and we came back home.

Mumma switched on the TV, while I tore up the packets of idli and sambhar we'd picked on our way home. Every news channel was reporting about the change of books.

The news anchors were firmly on the government's side. They screamed on TV debates, defending the ruling government and the prime minister—the charismatic, nationalist Sanyukta Swaraj.

On every news panel, there were also a bunch of conscientious historians in frayed sweaters and old blazers. When asked what their problem was with the books, they kept harping that they were . . . boring, inadequate.

Since the government had large-scale support from the Hindu junta, and Sanyukta Swaraj was an unrivalled Hindu icon—some even zealously referred to her as an incarnation of Maa Durga, who would lead the country into a new yuga—the historians assumed that the new books would paint the Muslims and Christians in bad light while glorifying the Hindu kings. This was all before they read the books.

The new history books didn't make Hindu kings greater or Muslim kings vile or invading kings more barbaric, they just made everything a bit boring. All kings were just kings. Rich, blessed men who sometimes did the right things, sometimes erred, but at the end of the day deserved the crown. The civics books, which had been pared down to less than 100 pages, just talked about different governing systems without comparing them. They weren't harmful, just toothless.

The slogans were: 'YOU HAVE MADE HISTORY BORING' 'TELL US EVERY GOVERNING SYSTEM!' 'NO ONE IS GOING TO WANT TO READ HISTORY!'

A few days later, Baba got the perfect guinea pig for ranting. Rashid had come home to study. He had been falling behind and the shutdown of schools was the perfect opportunity to cover ground. Rashid, like many students, was happy to see that the history book now had fewer chapters than before.

'Bhai, who cares if they change history? No one remembers it anyway. You should look ahead, not behind,' said Rashid.

Baba overheard this and saw it as the perfect opportunity to thrust his activism upon us.

'You think you don't remember, but you do. These are no longer history books but just a bunch of dates and incidents and translations,' said Baba, who was listening in.

Baba asked us to get our history books to the balcony.

'What is he going to do?' asked Rashid.

'Baba is frankly out of my hands now. I didn't raise him well.'

We took our books and went out to the balcony. Baba had a small canister of kerosene in one hand.

'Keep the books here,' said Baba.

He made us pile them up and struck a match. Baba was about to throw it in when Rashid hurriedly picked up his book.

'Uncle! That's new,' he said and stuffed the book in his pocket.

'Who cares?' grumbled Baba.

'Let his book be, Baba. You can burn mine.'

'Beta, this history is false, burn it! You don't want to be on the wrong side of history. Ask yourself if you want to be a guardian of our heritage or a meek sheep?'

Baba noticed that neither Rashid nor I was convinced by his theatrics. He put the matchbox back in his pocket, sat down, stared at the book in front of him and said, 'Do you guys know Akbar the Great?'

'We are not stupid, Baba,' I said.

'He was a great, tolerant king,' said Rashid.

'Have you read what they have done with him?'

We shook our heads.

'They have taken out the word *Great* in the version you're reading. Not just that, his policy changes are gone too. He had done some top-class administrative work—banning child marriage, getting marriage registered, issuing an ethical system to root out corruption. You know, good things, things you expect out of a great king. Things that take at least sixteen pages to list out. Now he's been reduced to just one page. One measly page? Can you imagine? *Ki aar bolbo aami* [What more can I say]? Where's the good stuff? Where's the grandiosity? Do you think there would be no difference between how you remember Akbar, having read everything about him, and how your juniors would remember him? You might remember him as a hunter-conqueror king with 300 wives who became more Sufi later, but your juniors in class 7 would argue that he was just another king.'

'Who's he now in the new books?' asked Rashid.

'He's no longer great. He's now just a king who conquered some lands, was sometimes tolerant, sometimes not, was impressed by a Hindu queen and gave up meat, and celebrated Diwali. That's it.'

He shook his head.

Rashid took out the book and started to flip through the pages. 'The Hindus always do this to our kings, Uncle.'

'It's not a Hindu–Muslim thing,' Baba interrupted. 'They changed Aurangzeb, too. All his atrocities have been covered up, Rashid. He's been written about like he was . . . an okay king. The man speared his own brothers' heads in public places. And now? He's just another run-of-the-mill king!'

Rashid kept the book over mine and nodded. Baba lit it on fire. Flames leapt and licked every page of the books. The entire history was charred.

Later, Baba took us to the stationery shop and bought us the books again.

'It's the intention that matters,' said Baba. 'You did your bit. That's what is important.'

Our little rebellion didn't change the course of anything. The righteous historians didn't win. Baba's voice slowly lost its fervour and drive. The protestors failed to move popular sentiment. The books were cheaper, so the parents of the students welcomed them. Soon, the history, geography and social sciences teachers and professors were offered a 45 per cent hike by the government. For the extra money, they chose to teach an altered history.

Mumma and Baba had strictly told me to not tell Anvesha about our family's frequenting the protests. Of course I told her.

Anvesha found my family's anger amusing, and this angered me.

'And how does your father know that the history that was in the textbooks earlier was correct?'

'Are the books not true then? We too have been brought up on lies?'

'I'm not *exactly* saying that.'

'Then what do you mean?'

'The previous books were thick, but they were very limited. You only read about either the Rajputs or the Mughals,' she said. 'Tell me the names of three Deccan kings?' She paused. 'Okay, tell me the names of three kings from the Nanda dynasty? Harsha dynasty? The Pallavas? All we know is Babar–Akbar–Humayun–Jahangir and that's it. If I were to believe the earlier history textbooks, there were no kings in south India to write chapters on. Where were the Marathas in the earlier books? Where were the Sultans of the Deccan in the earlier books? The seafaring kings of India? The books had a strong Rajput–Mughal tilt.'

'And now?'

'They have put in all the kings. And when you cram in hundreds of kings, you lose details. You think whether to keep in the good parts or the angry, violent parts. The government historians chose to keep the good parts, the ones with verifiable sources.'

'Is it not important that we know the bad the kings did? Why cover up all of that? That's distortion of history.'

'And do what? Be angry because a Muslim king killed Rajasthanis centuries ago? Or as a Bengali, you should hate Marathis because the Marathas plundered Bengal? What purpose does that serve? These new textbooks are factually correct and that's what matters. Why fill children with hate?'

'You need to know all sides, don't you? Accept the bad with the good.'

'If you really care about history, then why just read the textbooks? I prefer these toothless history books. Just facts. You can make up your own stories. You want to know what governing system was the best? Read sources and arrive at your own interpretation.'

'Anvesha, *ye kya baat hui*, what is this argument? You know everyone doesn't have the time or the interest.'

'Can you name the person who wrote the last version of the history book? The 250-page book your parents are fighting for? The person whose version of history you're so readily accepting?'

'Ummm . . . no.'

'Then why are you believing his or her version of history?'

'Because—'

There comes a time when you're faced with the fallibility of your perfect parents. The time when you realize that your parents could be ill-informed, less knowledgeable than others, weaker than others; when you see them as people rather than the Gods you worshipped them as. This was one of those moments. Anvesha's version of the truth as more well rounded.

'Is that why books are changed?' I asked.

'Of course not, buddhu. The government doesn't care about the workload of students, or them hating other communities.'

'Why are you going *gol gol*, Anvesha?'

'There's something big coming that we don't know of yet. The government wants the focus to be divided among all the kings instead of just the Rajputs and the Mughals. The question is why? Why would a government want that?'

She was talking more to herself than me. She had lowered her voice like she always did when she was thinking of a story to tell.

'Anvesha, but didn't you just say the books are better?'

'Yes, I said that. But when did governments want to make history books better? I mean just look at how they treated the writers of the last social sciences textbooks? They didn't even get paid! But this time, the writers of the books are being paid both by the government and the publishers publishing the books. Can you imagine that! They get paid for every student who holds that book.'

'. . . and we have a lot of students.'

'Hence the question: Why? Whenever they do something like this, it's for propaganda. The only question is: What is the propaganda this time?' she said.

There was a long pause after which she said, 'Get your book and open the fourth page.'

'Wait.'

I opened the book and turned to the fourth page. And there it was, in the list of historians who had written this version, Dr Varun Mohan.

'What.'

'It's Papa. You wanted to know where Papa was getting the money from? Check the first page.'

I flipped the page. Acharya Group Publishers Pvt. Ltd.

'Why are they paying the writers?' I asked.

'This part of history is being sponsored by the Acharya Group. The question is: Why?'

Chapter 16: Severed Heads

Our separation was always on the cards. It was a matter of time.

Every Sunday before leaving our houses, our mothers would make our fathers promise they wouldn't fight but it still always ended in one. While Baba remained the angry, idealistic man he was in college, Uncle became a money-loving cynic, who didn't bother about social change as long as it didn't affect him. It's a lie that friends and lovers can have different ideologies. Our parents, especially our fathers, had stopped liking each other. They would keep finding newer ways to fight and argue.

That Sunday, they fought over the new hot topic everyone in the news was talking about—Sanyukta Swaraj's government's Citizen's Justice Bill.

The Citizen's Justice Bill was introduced to clear the backlog of violent crime cases. It was to ensure justice was delivered quickly to the victims. At the moment, rape and murder cases dragged on for decades. Lawyers were bribed, witnesses turned hostile, judges died, legal costs kept mounting and what not. The bill intended to eliminate that. It limited the time courts had for the trial. The bill said that for violent crimes—such as rapes, murders and debilitating physical injuries—a blanket death penalty would be given. There would be no option of life imprisonment. You murder someone, you die. You rape someone, you die. Moreover, every trial had to be completed within three months. And if the death penalty was awarded, the convict was to be hanged within three months of the sentence. No appeals, no delay.

'Bhaisahib! Are you listening to yourself? The bill means any heinous crime would end in a death penalty. Within six months, the undertrial would die! Do you know what that means?' asked Baba.

'It means justice, Ramanuj Da. Finally, the people of this country will not be disappointed in courts!'

'*Pagol hoye gaecho* [You've gone mad]! The justice system is completely broken! Thousands, I repeat, thousands of cases will be wrongly judged and the bodies of innocents will face the gallows! The blood will be on the government's hands AND ON YOUR HANDS!'

Neither Mumma nor I could make out what Uncle was saying, but we heard him shouting. Mumma pressed the speakerphone button.

'YOU DON'T WANT JUSTICE, RAMANUJ DA? DO YOU WANT IT OR NOT? Rapists and murderers are going unpunished? Is that what you want? Criminals raping women on the streets?'

'HANGING PEOPLE AFTER QUICK TRIALS IS NOT JUSTICE! *Matha kharab hai kya* [Have you gone mad]? Three months for the investigation? Three months! What world are you living in, bhaisahib? One hundred and ninety people get arrested for murders and rape every day in India.' Baba tried to calm himself down. 'You think our justice system is ready to decide whether they should live or die within three months? Gandhi didn't die for this! Patel didn't die for this!'

Click. Baba turned to look at us.

'You should apologize,' said Mumma.

'I wasn't wrong.'

'Don't let politics ruin your friendship. Who told you to talk about this?'

'Is it that easy?' asked Baba, tears clouding his eyes. 'His politics define who he is. How can I let go of that? *Bolo*?'

'Bhaisahib has lost his way. But don't push him further away. There's a calmer way to do this.'

'I can't be friends with someone who supports murder,' declared Baba and walked out of the house.

'I think Baba should apologize,' I told Mumma.

'Your Uncle is wrong, he's not.'

'This is not your age to make new friends, Mumma.'

'Bubai,' grumbled Mumma. 'Don't act smart.'

The next day, our mothers called each other and promised that their husbands' relationship wouldn't have any bearing on their own, but a coldness crept in. Baba never called Uncle after that.

On the day the bill was passed, he looked blankly at the screen and muttered to himself in disbelief, 'My friend believes in this.'

Anvesha and I didn't share our parents' anger against each other. We were pre-occupied with something more dramatic, something truly life-changing.

Anvesha had decided it was time to plan the next step of our relationship—*the kiss*.

While I was nervous, Anvesha was excited, and her excitement made my nervousness worse.

But our parents kept avoiding meeting on Sundays. Our mothers thought our fathers needed more time to cool off before they could face each other again.

The thought of kissing invaded both our minds. Since we weren't meeting, we expressed our fantasies in our diaries, which Rashid would exchange every few days as our ferryman.

'I'm your Narad,' he would say to us.

'You're really taking "I believe in all faiths" seriously.'

'I love the stories in Hindu epics, bhai. But there's no codification, no hard set of rules. What is needed is an amalgamation . . .'

'Will you please stop selling Rooh Collective to me?'

'It's the only truth, bhai.'

In the diaries, we would explain, in embarrassing detail, the different approaches we could take for the kiss. What started innocently devolved into something more serious, passionate, dirty.

'You could hold my hair and pull me back mid-kiss,' she would write.

'Or I can maybe start with licking your upper lip,' I would suggest.

'After the first kiss, we can go slightly harder?'

'Are you thinking of a hard grab?'

'Or a light slap?'

'A bite on the lip?'

Rashid knew what was in the diaries he was ferrying. He wasn't thrilled.

'You should concentrate on your exams, bhai. *Ye sab toh boards ke baad bhi ho sakta hai* [You can do all this after your board exams],' sermonized Rashid.

'Look who's talking.'

'What do you mean, bhai?'

'How many Rooh Collective books did you slip into the bags of ninth graders?'

'Bhai—'

'Aren't they getting distracted? Or you don't care as long as you recruit more zombies for your cult?' I questioned.

'Bhai, why do you have a problem with it? I'm guiding them towards a moral path. You can see what is being taught by Firdaus Shirazi is moral righteousness, nothing else.'

'What if this man, Firdaus Shirazi, is alleged to be a rapist tomorrow? What if there are murder charges against him? What will these boys do? What did you do when that Mullah—'

Anger flickered in Rashid's eyes.

'His ideas will remain.'

'Why can't we think for ourselves?'

'Bhai, bhai, we never think for ourselves. Would a DNA specialist first discover DNA when it's already been discovered before? We want to progress in our thought, not reinvent it every time.'

'That's just dogmatism. There's a dog in that word, Rashid. Dogs follow. What does that make all of you?'

My efforts to rile him up saw no success.

'Fine, bhai, we are dogs. The thousands who follow him are dogs. At least we believe in something!'

'I believe in my mental capacities, my own judgement of things.'

'Bhai, why are you so narrow-minded? Give Rooh Collective a chance and then use your mental capacities and judgements, nahi?'

'Fuck it. Bas, I don't want to talk about this.'

My reaction was warranted because Mumma, Baba's and Uncle, Aunty's friendship wasn't the only one that was crumbling. Rooh Collective was driving a wedge between Rashid and I. We had stopped doing the things we used to.

Rashid's Rooh Collective activities, and his obsession with opening a garage, saw him slip to the bottom three of the class, while I was inching towards the top five. His fanaticism widened the academic gap between us. But it also made him more popular in school. He organized debates funded by the collective, blood banks, breathing techniques seminars for wide-eyed juniors. More and more boys were drawn to Rooh Collective's idea of a brotherhood that went beyond the four walls of gender, caste, religion. He was generating a following of his own.

When I once called out the commercialization of the god-man's interests in front of the boys he had managed to recruit, he responded with civility. He organized a debate in school—funded by Rooh Collective, which had a grand prize of 30,000 rupees, an amount unheard of—with the topic: Are Godmen Frauds?

Though he argued against the topic, the winner was a class 11 student who called every god-man, including Rooh Collective's Firdaus, a trickster. After the debate he said to me, 'We accept your truth too.'

The usage of *we* rankled me. He was my bhai, my friend. What was this *we* business?

Despite Rashid's rebuke, the diaries continued, and the detailing in our imagined scenarios got more and more intricate.

Finally the day came. Our families ran out of excuses to not meet. My fingers trembled at the thought of kissing Anvesha. I think I was running a slight fever too.

'Same story,' sighed Baba as the auto stopped in front of India Gate. 'Look, just look at them. This is what Varun Mohan believes in. He's rotting inside.'

'Don't begin today,' warned Mumma.

'You're here for your child's happiness,' I said.

'You're no longer a child, Bubai,' said Baba.

'If I'm not, then why do you decide my TV timings? Why is my pocket money so meagre?'

India Gate was no longer habitable. The lawns had been scorched and were littered with protest posters of dead men and women. The pavements were lumpy and dirty with all the melted wax. A little distance away, twenty people were wailing and shouting slogans. 'HINDUSTAN MURDABAD!', 'KENDRIYA SARKAR, MURDABAD!'

Ever since the Citizen's Justice Bill was passed, these small protests had become a regular feature. In the past few months, since the bill's passing, 25,000 people had been sentenced to death, many thousands already hanged. As Baba had predicted, swift justice was a rosy, idealistic idea. On the ground, it was an entirely different beast.

No one in the entire life cycle of a prisoner—the police, the investigators, the forensic labs, the lawyers, the judges, the jailers—had anticipated what this drastic change would entail. The police and the lawyers found themselves out of their depth. How were they to build a case so quickly?

The bill translated into a gory reality. It meant severed heads in botched hangings by inexperienced hangmen, who hadn't hung anyone in years; relatives self-immolating in front of government buildings; children orphaned with no closure; wives and husbands widowed within six months of the FIRs being registered.

For the first month, news websites were plastered with pictures of survivors and their families celebrating and lauding the government for the landmark bill. But then there were also pictures of wives, husbands, mothers of convicts, pleading for appeals against the death sentence. A stench of death gripped the entire country.

With every month that passed, things got more horrific. The inexperienced hangmen and hangwomen—despite the training—were failing to execute the hangings. A hanging is supposed to be clean, elegant. A body drops, the neck snaps, the death is instantaneous. For this to happen, the length of the rope, the weight calculation, the depth of the drop have to be precise. A stronger drop rips the head clean off. A shorter drop means the prisoners flails and struggles for minutes, their eyes pop out, and they die slowly and painfully.

Stressed jailers and police personnel leaked these happenings to the press. Twenty-three policemen who were diagnosed with PTSD shot themselves with their service revolvers. Some hangmen hanged themselves. Relatives of the executed convicts flooded social media with pictures of the returned bodies—stitched necks, eyeballs missing, bodies returned with the wrong heads stapled on to them. Relatives lined the rotting bodies outside the Parliament and left. The entire city stank of it.

Sanyukta Swaraj's image was taking a beating. Then, at the behest of the government, the Acharyas stepped in. Acharya Life suggested a humane way out. The convicts could choose between hanging and gas-poisoning. The hanging would be carried out professionally, with AI-assisted computers. The poisoning would be done by anaesthetics with more than twenty years of experience.

On a pain scale—Acharya Life claimed—it wouldn't cross the discomfort level of a tummy ache. Doctors, and an international tribunal of lawyers and forensic scientists gave the death methods the green signal.

The overwhelming support made the government sub-contract death-sentencing to the Acharyas. Mumma and Baba were less than thrilled.

Mumma said, 'It's not only that we are living the Acharya Life. We are now dying Acharya deaths too!'

With the gruesome deaths of convicts out of the picture, the news lost its bite. Hundreds were still being punished with death for their crimes, but most were dying in their sleep, which was not 'headline-worthy'.

Just as Uncle had predicted, violent crime rate dropped to 20 per cent of previous levels and kept plummeting. Rapes in cities dropped to unimaginable levels, drunk driving reduced and there was a dip in domestic violence cases. Police became more vigilant. They had figured it was better to prevent a crime than send people to the gallows.

The Mohans reached an hour late. They said it was traffic. I knew they didn't want to come. Unlike Mumma and Baba, who had stopped in front of the protestors, felt empathy towards the relatives who would soon lose a family member, the Mohans just walked past them.

Anvesha and I looked at each other. I realized at that moment that even if the world imploded, if mass murder became the norm and the world became a necropolis, there would still be two fools who would only care about love.

Chapter 17: The Hope for Death

The Mohans parked their car and walked towards us with big smiles. It was as if nothing had changed.

'They are smiling, you have to smile too. Don't be impossible today,' said Mumma.

Mumma's saree paled in front of Aunty's. Uncle's face had a shine. There was no crinkle on his forehead. A sense of calmness enveloped them—only to be found in people with considerable fixed deposits. But the coldness between our parents was the last thing on my mind.

Anvesha had dressed up for the occasion. She was wearing— I don't know what she was wearing, but it looked like an *anarkali* suit. It was red and white with intricate gold work, and swirled in waves around her. She seemed to be floating two inches off the ground. She had chosen elaborate *jhumkas* to go with it.

How could a thing be simultaneously so delicate and intimidating?

'Hi,' she said in a low, sexy voice.

Her voice seemed to skip the auditory pathways and go straight to my heart. She extended her hand and I put mine into hers. We walked to our favourite bunch, overlooking the now dry lake of India Gate.

Anvesha pushed a few stray strands of hair behind her ear. We talked about mundane things to fill up the time. She told me Varun Uncle had signed up with Acharya Publishing for his second book. This time it was not a textbook.

'Is this what you meant when you said read the textbooks, get a fair idea, and then buy books of your favourite historian?' I asked.

'They are giving Papa a lot of money to write about eastern Indian kings of the thirteenth and fourteenth centuries. They want every detail to be covered. Papa said the editor told him "the longer, the better". Papa's friends have been asked to pick a century and a region.'

'So that's like the opposite approach,' I deduced.

'The book has to be at least a thousand pages. Papa figured he can make it at least two thousand pages.'

'That sounds boring.'

'It's boring.'

'Will anyone who doesn't share genetic material with your father read such a book?'

'I can only see one reason why they would ask for such a thing.'

'They hate trees?'

She chuckled slightly.

'The longer the books are, the easier it becomes to bury details in them. Imagine scores of books spanning hundreds of years, each more than thousand pages, packed with details of each of the kingdoms, the governing nobles, the names of countless ministers, land deeds, land records of big farmers. How easy must it get to hide little specifics in?'

'What details? What thousand pages?'

'The Acharyas want to write themselves into history, somewhere, as a footnote.'

'That sounds useless. They are already the most powerful family in the world.'

'But they are not kings. They were never kings.'

'But they are the future . . . who cares about the past?'

'When the history of the ages is written, no one talks about rich businessmen.'

'So, they are rewriting history?'

'Why not? Kings do it all the time—they rewrite histories to legitimize their claim. Many Muslim kings claimed lineage from the previous powerful kings to cement their position, and so did Christian emperors. Closer home, we treated our kings as demigods. It's quite common. Sometimes it's called the Divine Right of Kings. It claims . . . wait, let me tell you the exact definition.'

She showed me the definition; she had taken a screenshot.

A king is subject to no earthly authority, deriving the right to rule directly from a divine source. Only the divine source can judge an unjust monarch and that any attempt to depose, dethrone or restrict their powers runs contrary to God's will and may constitute a sinful act.

She continued, 'Now imagine, you're reading a book about the fourth century Pallava Dynasty and a minister's name ending with Acharya crops up, and then you see that name again and again over the centuries. There's not much, just a little detail about how rich they were, how powerful, how virtuous. Acharya—a name that echoes through hundreds of years of history. *This* is what they are trying to do.'

'No one's going to believe it.'

'Right now, they won't, but years later? When an entire generation reads it? Then what?'

'It seems like a vanity project. Why can't they just buy Instagram followers instead?'

'The Acharyas want people to know they have God's blessings, the mandate from the heavens, the divine right to be the most powerful family in the country. The only family that's survived the churn of time. If they want to be the First Family of the country, this could be an easy way to do it—show the people that they were always royalty. I mean it's just my conspiracy theory. I could be wrong.'

She fell silent. We let the remnants of our conversation melt away, and our minds returned to what was the agenda of today's meeting. She kept her hand on mine. The touch brought back all the conversations we had exchanged through our diaries.

'After we kiss, we have two options,' she said. 'Either we are girlfriend and boyfriend, or we call ourselves lovers. You pick.'

The word 'lovers' had an illicit feel to it. It spelt intimacy, touching and nakedness. It was much more serious than the flippant terms of boyfriend and girlfriend.

She held my hand and squeezed it. This was uncharted territory.

'I . . . I . . . love you?' I said to formalize our new roles.

'Tell me something new, Druvan.'

'Anvesha, I think the Acharyas are trying to write themselves into history.'

'Very funny,' she said, and then added, 'I love you too, Druvan.'

My heart felt like a blob of butter on a hot paratha.

Being told that you're loved is a lot similar to when you're told you're not loved. The churning of the stomach, the feeling of heaviness, the burden of love is a bit . . . horrendous. As heady as being in love is, it is also to live in fear; to lose your love is to live in misery.

We walked over to where our parents couldn't see us and held hands. The illicitness, the three words, the ownership were heady. She leaned into me till her lips enveloped mine. The world reduced to a blur. With every attempt, our rhythms matched more and more. We kept kissing and parting, we kept telling each other this would be the last kiss, but in the next instance, we would kiss again.

When the sun set, we knew it was time for us to go. I didn't want to let her hand go. We started the long walk towards where our parents were.

'I will upload my first video on YouTube this week,' she said.

'You will break the Internet.'

We saw our parents pacing the picnic spot. The boxes were packed and the bed sheet was folded. Her mother and mine carried a diary each—our diaries, with all the embarrassing details of our kisses. A chill ran down our spines. Both parents strode towards us, grabbed us, and yanked us away from each other.

Back home, Aunty broke Anvesha's laptop and trashed her room. She then sat her down in the balcony and made her burn all of her pictures with Mumma, Baba and me. She slapped her so many times that her nails broke, and blood streaked Anvesha's cheeks.

Mumma wasn't violent.

'Wish we were childless. I would have accepted that fate,' she said.

Neither she nor Baba talked to me, or called me for meals. I had to eat the leftovers in the refrigerator. This went on for an entire week. I made and ate sandwiches on all seven days, washed my clothes, bought stationery from the money I had stolen from them earlier. They didn't ask me when I would be home from the playground. They didn't wake me up for school. I was abandoned.

Anvesha suffered a more violent fate. She would get slapped every day at least once.

Our parents met again at India Gate to decide our future. This time, no bed sheet was spread out on the grass, no pleasantries were exchanged. Our mothers clutched our hands tightly. They must have assumed that if they let us go, we would run into each other's arms. I wasn't crying. I was out of tears. Neither was she. Mumma threw the diary at Aunty's feet.

'Are you trying to kill me now?' Aunty spat.

Mumma took a deep breath and searched for an insult. 'Your *besharam* daughter is not going to amount to anything, so you tried to destroy my Bubai! Do you want to read what Anvesha has written in the diaries? Chhi–chhi!' She moved in for the kill. 'Should I tell everyone in the colony? Guptaji always said these things about your daughter. I was stupid to not listen to them.'

Aunty recoiled. '*Tum chhoti jaat wale chhote hi rahoge. Tum log wahi raho, wahi maro gandagi mein* [You are and will remain low-class. Stay there; you will die there in the dirt]. Your son is not worth my daughter's time.'

'Of course, why would we be worth your time? You have lakhs of rupees that politicians stick in Bhaisahib's underwear when he dances for them,' said Mumma.

Aunty giggled mirthfully as if Mumma's comment meant nothing.

'Don't we know how you look at our cars? Have some shame! All you want is our life, Riti.'

'Is that right, Sunita? Accha, then tell me. When is your husband asking you to sleep with a minister? Then I will tell you if I want your life or not?'

'*Kitni asaani se*, how easily you forget that your husband borrowed 30,000 rupees last year. Where is that, you parasite?'

Baba stepped forward, but Mumma held his hand. She took off the two rings she had worn for years now and threw them at Aunty. 'Here! Keep this! And if possible, please don't sell your daughter to those politicians too! God knows, with her marks she can only sell her body to be something!'

A tear rolled down Aunty's cheek. She wiped it away.

Aunty breathed slowly and said through gritted teeth, 'At least she's *my* daughter. Who knows who all you slept with for Druvan to be born after so many years!'

She spat where the rings lay.

Mumma's lips quivered. She screamed, 'I am glad all your earlier children died!'

'I hope your son dies! Then you will have to beg other men to sleep with you to give you another child,' shouted Aunty.

'I hope your daughter dies and joins her brothers and sisters in hell. At least then she won't be a whore.'

Uncle and Aunty marched away from us, dragging Anvesha behind them, who kept turning to look at me. She tried to reason with her parents just before they got inside the car. Aunty slapped her and shoved her inside. Once they were gone, Mumma, Baba and I walked slowly to the auto stand.

In the auto, Baba said, 'You saw how they talk to us? *Chhoti jaat,* low class it seems.'

Our first kiss was on the day our parents wished the other would die.

Later, Rashid, who had been watching from a distance, collected the rings from the lawns. I asked him to keep them. Years later, Baba would tell me he had combed the grass of India Gate for the two rings and hadn't found them. They had been worth 75,000 rupees. They lost three quarters of a lakh to prove a point.

Chapter 18: The Aftermath

The first week of our forced break-up was the hardest. Neither Mumma nor Baba talked to me. There was no comfort in food either. Mumma and Baba cooked a plain fare of daal and rice for an entire week. It was as if someone had died. Phone calls were banned, my movement was tracked, Mumma had passwords to all my accounts, and every other day, she would upturn my school bag and flip through all my registers to check if I had started to write again. I would sit in front of open books and worry about Anvesha. Rashid reported that she hadn't been to school in a week. Were they hitting her? Had they made her drop out? The phone calls from PCOs were never answered by her.

'DON'T CALL HERE!' her mother would scream, even though Rashid or I would never utter a word.

After a week, Anvesha started school again. Now a driver dropped her, waited, and then took her back home like she was an industrialist's daughter from a 1980s movie and in imminent danger of being kidnapped.

'Bhai, they must be paying him 5000 rupees per month. Just so they can keep her away from you. Can you imagine? 5000!' said Rashid. 'See, bhai, this is why I want my own business.'

With the 75,000 rupees, the amount the two rings had fetched, he wanted to start his garage. He was ready to give me half of the ownership. After school he would scout locations for the garage. In school, he would spend all his time getting recruits for Rooh Collective. I gave up on him.

I had a broken heart to nurse.

After a week, Rashid helped us establish alternate channels of contact. Anvesha and I would spend our lunch breaks writing letters. Then Rashid and one of his friends from her school, whom he had met at a Rooh Collective meeting, exchanged our letters. We could finally breathe again.

Her letters were lengthier, well-written, a window to her state without me. The words would leave me breathless. My letters read like complaints from a kindergarten kid who kept saying: I miss you, I miss you, I miss you.

In a month, we opened up more channels of communication. Rashid bought two cell phones from the money he had.

'I have put it under business expenses of our garage,' said Rashid.

Once we had the phones, we would lock ourselves in washrooms during lunch break and call each other. With this, our fury against our parents dissolved, and some normalcy returned. Each conversation would end with 'no, you cut the phone' or 'shit, we are late for class!'. But our chats would end soon because of the preparatory leave for pre-boards, which Rashid had shown no interest in.

'He has always been interested in engines and whatnot,' said Anvesha. 'Not everyone's built for academics. I know I'm not.'

Anvesha was faring worse than Rashid. She had placed second to last in her class of thirty-three. All she cared about were her YouTube videos—she would upload a video every Monday, Wednesday and Saturday. Some of her videos had over a thousand views and fifty comments. Mumma and Baba banned Anvesha's videos in our house. But whenever I would borrow their phones, I would find her channel's name—*Anvesha's History Bytes*—in the search bar.

'But is it worth neglecting your boards for this?' I once asked her.

'I'm doing this for myself and I'm worth it.'

'This lipstick tagline wasn't an answer to my question. Be careful, Anvesha. These things are here today, gone tomorrow.'

'You sound like a forty-year-old. Jobs that you train for today won't exist twenty years from now.'

'That might be true but people hire for consistency, for sustained hard work. That will always be a criterion.'

'And you're saying these videos don't require hard work? They just appear out of thin air?'

'I'm saying have a back-up plan ready.'

'My back-up plan is you, Druvan. You better pull up your socks and ace those exams,' she said and laughed.

I lost my will to correct her course.

Before this, I had imagined my future in pairs. Anvesha and I would both be doctors or engineers or writers or professors. Now I had to chart different trajectories for our lives.

Days before the holidays for the pre-boards started, Rashid declared he would drop out of school. It felt like a punch in the gut. He had found a small garage for rent, and he was going to start modification and repair services.

'Bhai, I'm better prepared for the future than you are,' said Rashid.

'For a future of poverty,' I snapped.

'All I need is one good modification. Then word of mouth will get me scores of customers. Of course, bhai, *aadha-aadha*. I'm putting down your money as rent and deposit.'

I was sure the people around him, the disciples of Rooh Collective, were putting him up to this, filling his head with radical and silly notions of following his dreams.

'What if it doesn't work? Then what? You will lose years! How embarrassing it would be to be nineteen and giving your class 10 boards. Have you thought about that? I don't know how your parents are allowing this.'

'Bhai, *life bohot lambi hai* [This life is quite long]. What difference would a couple of years make?'

'It makes all the difference.'

'For those who truly know the meaning of life, it's never short.'

'You need to stop talking like that to me. You sound mental.'

'I have a book—'

'I don't want any book.'

'Bhai, it talks about how if one truly learns a skill in this life, one can retain that skill in his next life. I will get you the book, just read it . . . '

'I will burn it in front of your eyes if you try giving me any book.'

'It's a good . . . '

'RASHID, will you shut the fuck up!'

There was silence of a few seconds after which he spoke in a small voice. 'I understand, bhai. You're thinking the best for me. You're worried about what will happen to me. But you have to understand that you and me, we have different interests, we are built differently, all my past lives have brought me . . . '

I got up and left.

This was the last conversation I had with Rashid on the school premises. I talked to his parents, but they didn't seem to be concerned. They said his shop would bring in extra money. He dropped out of school.

I didn't tell Mumma and Baba, or they would have banned me from calling him too. We still met every day. He would wait outside, perched on his Activa. His shop, our shop, was under construction. My anger dissipated after a few days.

'I knew you wouldn't be angry for long. You're like a *maachis*, bhai. You burn with intensity but for very little time,' said Rashid one day.

He was wrong. I was more like a cranky heater. Every now and then, I would get anxious about his life. The trigger would often be Firdaus Shirazi's face on the screen or Anvesha's mention of him. She was working on a video about him.

In those days, all we used to do was to talk about Firdaus Shirazi.

Chapter 19: Who the Hell Is Firdaus Shirazi?

'He's an opportunist thief taking advantage of poor, disillusioned people. Just look at Rashid! He sees no reason. Men like Firdaus should be put in jail,' I said disdainfully to Anvesha.

'There are richer, more intelligent people than Rashid who have been swayed by the god-man. Like . . . '

'You're about to name Vidhi Acharya, no?' I asked.

'If she can believe in the god-man, who's Rashid?'

Vidhi Acharya was the most famous, most visible of Firdaus's followers. Firdaus's popularity saw a sudden spike after Vidhi was unexpectedly chosen as the new scion of the Acharya family.

The twenty-year-old had taken over as chairperson and managing director of the Acharya Group from her fifty-eight-year-old brother, Mukesh Acharya, the eldest son of Damodarbhai Acharya. Mukesh Acharya, who had carried on his father's legacy for two decades after this death, was surprisingly demoted. It was a move that made no sense among the business circles. Some magazines had even called it the most expensive mistake in the history of humankind. It was ranked above Russia's sale of Alaska to the US for a pittance in 1867, losing 200 billion dollars in the process. Acharya Group was a three-trillion-dollar company.

Overnight, Vidhi Acharya's face was plastered on all newspapers and magazines as the most powerful woman in South Asia. Everyone used to say Damodarbhai had picked her up from a dumpster—the most common adoption story. She was said to be the luckiest adopted person in the world.

Vidhi was three years old when she was introduced to the world. At the annual general meeting at the Acharya Gardens, Kokilaben Acharya, the old widow of Damodarbhai, was seen holding the hand of a little girl. Later, Mukesh Acharya, while talking to the reporters, called the girl his sister, adopted by the family just around the time of Damodarbhai Acharya's death. The details of her birth—when exactly she was adopted and if Damodarbhai had himself chosen her—were hazy and out of public domain.

Growing up, we read about Vidhi Acharya in the papers— an adopted daughter of the Acharyas, whose freakish intelligence was the stuff of legends. Everyone knew of her as a prodigy. It was common knowledge that she'd won the International Mathematics Olympiad for five years in a row, an international record, was fluent in eleven languages and more, and could play riffs on an electric guitar with equal dexterity as handling a sitar. And that she'd dropped out of school in class 10 to run various divisions of the Acharya Group.

But even after these achievements, her right to the position once held by Damodarbhai Acharya was hotly debated.

Everyone believed in the commonly traded conspiracy theory that Vidhi was an illegitimate child and held the keys to the moral sanctity of the Acharya family.

Anvesha, who lived her life obsessing over conspiracy theories and building one where none existed, didn't believe this one.

'It's too boring. You want me to believe that Damodarbhai Acharya had just one illegitimate child? That's unheard of for powerful men.'

'So you are implying that if I grow rich and powerful tomorrow, I will have scores of illegitimate children running around?'

'I will keep you under lock and key,' said Anvesha.

'I won't particularly mind that.'

'People often say that Vidhi's support for this god-man is business suicide.'

'Oh, we are back to her?' I asked.

'So Rooh Collective is based around the central idea of rebirth and reincarnation. The concept of rebirth goes against the core of any business. Why would people aspire to enjoy and consume mindlessly if they had countless births? Why would companies support a frugal, simple god-man who advocates buying less, when consumption is the core motive of any business?'

'I . . . didn't think of it like that.'

'My *sweetu, padhaku* baby.'

'Don't mock my academic brilliance. And please, I'm sorry I don't spend time looking up to this man. Tell me one man of God who doesn't look like a paedophile? One?'

'Aw, don't be offended. Anyway, so the Acharyas and Firdaus go way back. Firdaus first shot to fame when he was fifteen. He was mocked at the Indian Vedic Science Congress because of his talk on soul and reincarnation. Soon after, he found a patron in Damodarbhai Acharya. The annual reports of the Acharya Group after that showed a huge donation to Firdaus's Rooh Collective, which was quite small at that time.'

'This was when Firdaus was . . . like younger than us?'

'Don't interrupt me, just listen, no,' said Anvesha. 'So in the last decade itself, Rooh Collective, like any other NGO, had been in dock a few times. IT raids, land-grabbing, a spate of suicides by followers, but none of the charges stuck. I'm sending you links with all the cases against them. Just read through the court proceedings. Do you know he argues his cases himself?'

'How many pages are these proceedings?'

'About 3000?'

'You read through 3000 pages?'

'Every time his collective was charged, he spent time in jail till the matter was cleared or his bail was posted. That's very unlike a god-man. Usually they sit out and get their battery of lawyers to post anticipatory bail.'

'And why was he doing that?'

'I thought about it. And then it became pretty clear. This was a great marketing and recruiting strategy. The records showed a sharp uptick in recruitments every time he went to jail. He positioned himself as a martyr. I pulled up records of three jails he spent most time in. You wouldn't believe this. So . . . almost every prisoner he interacted with joined Rooh Collective,' said Anvesha. 'Not only that, the relapse rate of prisoners is zero.'

'Why are you telling me good things about him?'

'If you hate him being good, it's going to get worse for you. Because then came a master stroke. To gain credibility, the accounts of the last decade of Rooh Collective were made available online earlier this year. They were clean as a whistle; every paisa was accounted for. He has spent crores on environmental packages, planting of trees, etc. They had kept nothing for themselves.'

'Tell me something I want to hear? A murder maybe? A hit and run case? Anything?'

'He's clean, Druvan.'

'Why are you not impressed by him then?' I asked.

'Because, unlike Rashid, I'm not lost, Druvan. You're my star, my Pole Star. I can be in a storm and follow you and reach wherever I want to.'

'How am I going to match these lines?'

'You can just say you love me and that will be enough.'

'See, things like these. Don't say them.'

'Fine,' she said. I could hear her smile at the other end of the line. She added after a longish pause, '. . . but there is something about him you need to know.'

'What?'

'His biggest test will come soon.'

Ten years ago, Firdaus Shirazi had announced to the world the date of his death. The announcement had come at the end of an intense media frenzy followed by an FIR. A woman had accused Firdaus of abetting suicides of his followers. The woman's thirty-three-year-old friend had thrown herself in front of a metro, because Firdaus had convinced her about the immortality of the soul. Even earlier, suicides among Rooh Collective followers had been a common occurrence but none were tied back to the god-man.

The media had picked up the story and ran relentless news cycles around it. It had catapulted him into national fame.

The god-man had released a video of himself at the height of the trial, in which he said:

'I will die on 23 October, ten years from now. Death has no meaning. It's just another crossroads of the eternal life we have all been blessed with. For all those mocking me, they would know soon that the soul is immortal. Soon, you ask, what's soon? A year? Two years? What's soon when you live forever?'

The largely non-committal video had sent shockwaves among his followers and increased his popularity. Since that day, many of his followers had thrown themselves on railway tracks, or consumed poison, jumped off buildings, and even stabbed themselves.

And all of them had written lengthy suicide letters, freeing their Guruji from any blame.

Now there were little over four months left for him to die. The question was: Would the man on whose ideals many had died die himself?

Chapter 20: The Death of the Century

Unlike what I and most people thought, Firdaus Shirazi was going to die. It wasn't a bluff.

Three months before the big day—named *Punar Janamdin* by the media—Rooh Collective devotees started to trickle into the city. They quietly pitched tiny tents, lit small fires and camped outside the mammoth Rooh Collective ashram on the outskirts of the city. The first few days, it looked like a small village fair with bonfires, singing and dancing, and preaching by senior Roohs. The news channels were slow to pick up on it. When the first bunch of news vans reached the ashram premises, hundreds of them had already settled in. There was a community kitchen, mobile toilets, and volunteer doctors employed at the campsite to take care of the people who had left their houses to witness Firdaus Shirazi's death. Some of the younger devotees had set up industrial speakers that filled the air with hymns, azan and prayers. It was dubbed 'the spiritual Sunburn' by excited YouTubers, who went to shoot vlogs at the site.

'We will go after he begins his next life. I have never been happier,' a devotee told the reporters.

Once the first reports were televised, the trickle turned into a stream and then a deluge. Soon, thousands of devotees entered the city—on foot, on trains, on flights. Multiple campsites mushroomed overnight, entire buildings were rented out, all hotels within a ten-kilometre radius were booked. The news cycles were dominated by the impending death of Firdaus Shirazi. It had a snowball effect. Everyone who wasn't a part of the collective was surprised by the devotion he invoked in his followers, and by the sheer number of people who loved him so deeply.

In the one hour I got to watch TV—the board exams were less than two months away—we would only watch news, and news meant hearing about Firdaus Shirazi.

'It's all politics, Bubai,' said Baba to be. 'This Firdaus is Acharya and Sanyukta Swaraj's golden boy. I don't think he will die. It's to get attention, that's it.'

'This is the kind of people Anvesha's father is working for. Do you see? Do you see?' added Mumma.

During this time, Anvesha and I could talk only once or twice in a week. Rashid would come home, pretending to study, and would bring his phone. I would sneak into the bathroom and whisper into it.

There was a month to go for Firdaus's death and the board exams when Rashid said what I had expected of him.

'This is a test for us, bhai. What kind of a person would I be if I'm not there at this time? I have to go the ashram,' Rashid said.

'Baba said there could be violence there. Police might crack down anytime.'

'Nothing will happen, bhai. If I don't stand with my guru at this time, then how will I face God?'

'How will I talk to Anvesha?'

'What is one month? There's an entire lifetime, maybe more, that you will spend with her. You can wait. Stop running after small pleasures, bhai.'

And so began the long radio silence.

In the second month, the first few suicides were reported. Three on the first day, five on the second, twenty on the third. The more screen time the suicides got, the more people died the next day. The TV channels, despite knowing the detrimental effect of describing the dead people's last moments, kept reporting relentlessly. By the end of the week, 400 people had committed suicide. Every suicide came with a suicide letter that absolved Rooh Collective and Firdaus Shirazi of any blame. Some families wanted Firdaus to be arrested for spreading lies about reincarnation, multiple births and rebirths, while other families solemnly accepted the deaths.

'They will be born again,' the relatives would tell the reporters.

Sanyukta Swaraj, our prime minister, maintained a golden silence.

The cases started to pile up against Firdaus Shirazi, who was peacefully living out his last days in his ashram. Some political leaders, mostly of the opposition party, demanded Firdaus to call off his 'death'.

Arrest warrants were issued in multiple states but no one dared to arrest him yet. The media hoopla opened the floodgates and love outpoured for Firdaus.

His ashram was now heavily guarded by thousands of his disciples. They were unarmed but determined to not move from their position just in case the police or the army was asked to take control of the situation.

Bodies kept piling up across the country.

The state government intervened only after it was reported that a thousand people had committed suicide and asked the police half-heartedly to arrest Firdaus Shirazi.

The scared police went in with armoured vehicles to face the sea of disciples that stood in between them and the ashram. They stood their ground even in the face of disciplinary violence. For two days, nothing happened. And then, a deputy superintendent of police, sleepless and on edge, ordered his subordinates to use the water cannons and pellet guns.

The water cannons killed a two-year-old, and injured and maimed hundreds.

The anchors of News69 screamed. 'Why would a mother bring her child to a rally? Why? What is the agenda! It's her fault! The police were doing their job!'

The death of the child quietened down Mumma and Baba.

They now watched the news in silence.

That night, a group of disciples sneaked into the police barracks. They sliced off the genitals of the policemen and burned them alive. Their entrails were slowly pulled out and their hearts were cut out and thrown into the fire.

Then the disciples doused themselves with kerosene and self-immolated.

The spokesperson from Rooh Collective, Karamchand, disowned the disciples, called them murderers and apologized to the families of the policemen who had died.

'It's our promise that this wouldn't happen again. We are deeply sorry for what people who were associated with us did, and we take full responsibility. We are committing one crore rupees each for the bereaved families,' he declared.

And yet, the policemen vowed revenge for the gruesome massacre. They went at the crowd with tasers, batons and riot guns.

The policemen were in for a shock. They wielded their lathis, fired their guns, expecting a stampede. Nothing happened. The men and women didn't even raise their hands to protect their heads. They received the blows to their skulls. People didn't leave their positions. They faced pellet guns with their eyes open and lost their eyesight. They wished for death, embraced it and celebrated it. Every death was welcomed with chants of rebirth. 'Martyr! Martyr! Shahid! Shahid!' the others shouted instead of helping the ones who had been injured. Forty-five people died instantly.

The injured themselves resisted police's attempts to take them to hospitals.

'Let us die! Let us die! We will live again! *Fir jiyenge! Jeete rahenge!*'

One hundred and twenty people died in an hour. It brought a swift end to the police action. Karamchand, the spokesperson, was blinded in both his eyes too.

The focus now shifted to keeping more people from joining the campsite. But the barricades, the warnings from the police, were all like a sieve and the people like waves.

News69 televised an exclusive interview of Karamchand. He sat across the spawn of Satan and ace TV anchor Navika, with both his eyes bandaged. His blindness hadn't changed anything in him.

'Let our guru die in peace. And what is it to you if people want to die with him? It's their life. The state, the people or the government doesn't own our bodies. We will die when we want to,' he said.

The anchor tried to reason with him. But he raised a hand and said, 'Navika, you need to quieten down or you will be responsible for a lot of deaths.'

He looked at the screen and said, 'I have instructions from Firdaus that if you don't let me speak in this show, I will tell our disciples to add crushed glass to saffron milk and drink it.' He looked back at Navika. 'Do you want that to happen? Would you want that on your hands?'

Navika shook her head like a petulant child.

Karamchand continued, 'We urge our brothers in the police to leave us alone. A few of us made a mistake, and we have paid the price. We don't wish to take it further. We want the police to leave the holy grounds. If the police doesn't clear out within two days, all devotees of Rooh Collective will consume poison and die. This is not just for the ones guarding Guruji but for everyone who's watching.' He turned to Navika. 'You were saying something?'

Navika gulped uneasily.

The police retreated. The world watched in absolute terror as a god-man embarrassed and held the government hostage. Despite the retreat, two days later, hundreds died after drinking saffron milk with crushed glass. The court ordered an arrest warrant for Karamchand. When the police approached the disciples, Karamchand emerged from the crowd, stumbling, coughing blood, and dropped dead at their feet.

'*Hum fir jiyenge* [We will live again].'

The image of a dying Karamchand dented the psyche of the entire nation. A powerful, seemingly God-fearing man, could bring the biggest democracy to heel, could kill and go scot-free.

The death count had reached 1933 people, a thousand more than the second-largest mass suicide led by the cultist Kim Jones of the People's Temple of the Disciples of Christ, when 908 people had died after consuming poison back in 1978.

Sanyukta Swaraj now stepped in like the hawk she was known to be.

She moved the court to put a thirty-minute time limit on TV reporting. In other words, no news channel could now give more than thirty minutes to Firdaus Shirazi's imminent suicide.

Without the screaming news cycle, without the repeated messaging of his death, disciples felt less compelled to kill themselves. The suicide rates dropped drastically. The urgency of the situation died, and people had more time to second-guess their suicides.

And for the major part of the day, Firdaus's tribe outside his ashram was left alone.

Sanyukta Swaraj then went to the ashram for a meeting with Firdaus Shirazi. There were more than a dozen cameramen strapped to the sides of helicopters, recording everything.

Firdaus's statement was recorded on a smartphone. He was still going to die on the date decided by him, but he asked everyone to stop the needless suicides.

'Live this life well. Don't be in a hurry to cut it short. I will see all the Roohs in my next life,' he said in the statement.

The Indian government had decided to allow Firdaus to die.

The police retreated. Over the next few days, the suicides almost came to a halt. Sanyukta Swaraj said in the interview to BBC, 'One death is a fair price to pay to save a million. Firdaus has chosen his fate, and there's nothing we can do to stop him. But our responsibility is the junta of our country. We will take care of them.'

When asked about Firdaus, she was cagey and said, 'He's a learned man.'

The country collectively forgot about the class 10 and 12 board exams that were going on in the country. The news channels didn't cover the cheating cases, the leaking of the papers, the tough social sciences examinations, the three children who hung themselves under pressure. Anvesha and Rashid were right after all. The importance of class 10 board examinations, and examinations in general, was overstated.

As Firdaus's final day loomed large (and my mathematics exam, about which no one cared), there was a growing fear that many would kill themselves. The Supreme Court asked the Acharyas to deploy hundreds of ambulances. They responded with thousands. The army and the police blockaded a ten-kilometre radius around the ashram, and cut off the Internet and telephone services to prevent the circulation of any inflammatory videos.

As the countdown to Firdaus's death continued, the world came to a halt.

All eyes turned to the Acharya Gardens, the only flatland in the city which could handle the rapid influx of business helicopters and small jets. People with power and money who had donated to the collective over the years landed in their Gulfstreams and Eurocopters at the multiple airstrips of the Acharya Gardens. The gardens were once a modest forty-acre land that the Acharyas used for company events. As the Acharya Group grew in size every year, so did the gardens. The gardens were constantly under construction and out of bounds to the public. But now, we were getting the first view of it. It was packed with over 100 helicopters and small jets.

The last helicopter to land was Vidhi Acharya's.

On the day before my mathematics exam, I should have been revising geometry, but I was watching the news.

At precisely noon, as the Supreme Court had decreed, the news channels were blacked out. This was to prevent mass hysteria and deaths around Firdaus's suicide. The Internet was disconnected. Everyone was left to speculate. When the TV channels turned back on, there was only one face on all of them.

Vidhi Acharya's.

She addressed the media. 'Jai Shri Krishna! Firdaus Shirazi, our guruji, died and came back. He's among us. He will reveal himself in due time. Jai Shri Krishna.'

That's it. She walked away. No other details.

The body was sent for post-mortem. The reason for death was poisoning.

It was reported that on the day, disciples didn't kill themselves. It was said to be in honour of Firdaus. His death anniversary would be his own.

The news channels beamed one interview after another of the devastated Rooh Collective followers. Mumma, Baba and I were watching with rapt silence when a sobbing Rashid appeared on the screen. Mumma and Baba squinted their eyes to make sure what they were seeing was right. They looked at me.

'I have been here since the last two months, and I know he's going to come back . . .'

Baba turned the volume down. He looked at me. Mumma said, 'Rashid didn't take the board exams?'

Chapter 21: A Priest, a Monk, a Businessman, a Celebrity

I had huge hopes from my board exams results, but my friends were hell-bent on upstaging them.

Let's start with Rashid, who was rapidly becoming a new person after Firdaus's death. A day after the god-man's death, he had called and said, 'Everything seems finished, bhai. *Apni Maa ke khatam hone ka itna dukh nahi hoga* [I won't be this sad when my mother passes away].'

After the incident, Rashid had buried himself in work. So little existed outside his world of broken-down motorcycles and Rooh Collective.

The death of Firdaus made his followers more devout. The followers were now knit together in grief, and it had become a brotherhood in the truest sense.

At school, the boys Rashid had recruited would band together and remember the man. They would hotly debate his philosophies, organize blood donation camps, and bail each other's families out of financial trouble. More and more people lined up outside the collective's ashrams across the country to sign up.

Closer home, Rashid had managed to convince a wealthy Rooh Collective follower he'd met during a protest to lease out his unused shop in Connaught Place for free and invest 50,000 rupees. Three weeks before the date of the results, Rashid inaugurated his garage, which he named Rashid Auto. I wasn't allowed to go to the opening. Rashid was a school dropout and a veritable bad influence. Mumma and Baba shut down all my requests.

'God knows what he will teach you.'

'What will he teach me?' I snapped back.

'Don't answer back to your mother,' butted in Baba.

'You can make new friends at your coaching institute. Boys who don't go about opening shops!' warned Mumma.

How would he influence me? What shop would I open? I had no skills to monetize. I saw his shop in the pictures he had clicked—he stood in front of dismantled motorcycles, arms slung over the shoulders of the boys he worked with.

Rashid kept telling me how the garage was both his and mine.

'Bhai, by the time you pass out of school, you will be earning enough from your garage to pay for college on your own and more! We will also change the name to Rashid & Druvan Auto,' Rashid would say to me.

'It's all you, I did nothing.'

In the past three weeks, he had modified three motorcycles and taken on significant repairs on nineteen scooters and motorcycles. Most of his customers were Rooh Collective followers he had met during his visits to the ashram.

'Rooh Collective is paying off for Rashid. It was not for nothing,' noted Anvesha.

'Are you saying he was in the collective there to get customers? That it was a smart business decision?'

'No.'

'I would 100 per cent be more comfortable with that.'

Like Rashid, it was Rooh Collective that propelled Anvesha's fledgling YouTube channel to the stratosphere. Two weeks from my board result, as if timed to wrest the spotlight away from me, Anvesha uploaded her video on Firdaus Shirazi.

There were already too many of them. But none came with a conspiracy theory attached to it or with a tantalizing clickbait-y title like this one: IS FIRDAUS SHIRAZI RIGHT ABOUT REINCARNATION?

Firdaus had always maintained that he had been reincarnated a number of times, in different parts of the country, into diverse religions and strata of society, under different regimes. That was the basis of his cult—multiple births, frugal and mindful living, religious tolerance.

He claimed to be born a Hindu priest in the 1900s, before that a Buddhist monk, a Jain ascetic a few births before that, and a tribal God-pleaser way back in time. Apart from the places he claimed to be born in and the rough time periods, Firdaus was stingy about the details he shared about these births.

'Lies of a god-man?' Anvesha dramatically wondered in the video. She leaned towards the screen and whispered, 'Or is there something more?'

When talking about his rebirths, Firdaus would give out the alignment of the stars, the religion he was born in, the kind of armour the soldiers wore, the layouts of the temples, mosques and churches he used to visit, the food they ate, and the weather at the time of his birth and death. Rest, he left for others to figure out.

Because, he said, he didn't know.

'Arre, arre, how many years of my past lives would you want me to remember? I'm a man, not a turtle. How do you expect me to tell you which year was it when we ourselves didn't know which year, which month, what day it was?' he would jokingly say to his followers. 'Some of you should go to the slums and ask the people there if they know the exact year they were born in. They wouldn't know. And I am talking of a time hundreds of years ago.' He would point to his head and say, 'it's a brain, not a computer.'

Anvesha said in her video, 'What Firdaus says there makes sense. For example, let's say a little, ratlike boy is born to a poor farmer on 12 May, Friday, 1322, in what is now eastern UP, would the father record it? Would he know the date? The best he would remember and tell his teenage son would be details like it rained and the Venus was the brightest in the sky that night. This is at best. Mostly, he would know nothing.'

In some interviews, historians would ask Firdaus piercing questions about the periods in which he claimed rebirth.

'So you know what the tax policy of Darah Shikoh was?' 'What did the people of the time make of Rana Sanga?'

He would wave them off dismissively, his trademark smile never leaving his face. '*Kamal ki baat karte ho* [You talk funny]. How do you think the subcontinent was in those times? Even now? India has always been an intricate web of villages, with a king ruling over us, sitting on a solid gold throne miles away. Do you think we cared who lived in the palace? *Hume to pata bhi nahi hota tha ki raja hai kaun* [We didn't even know who the king was]. What would we know of the policies they were making? Before the Internet, do you think someone in Mishriwala would know who the home minister was, what did he look like, and what not? To us poor, *hum gareebo ke liye*, all the kings and emperors and their queens, who lived in grand palaces with massive halls and pillars embedded with jewels, were chosen by God. We never saw them; to them, we never existed. All we knew was they had the divine right to rule. They were given the responsibility by God, handpicked by him to lead a life of seeming luxury. Otherwise, why would they be there and we in our thatched huts? We thought we were sub-humans and they demigods.' Then, in his classic Firdaus manner, he would wink and say, 'But happiness is not in palaces, it's in our hearts. In all my births, money has helped my happiness, but it's not the cornerstone of happiness. It's not even the second or the third in the order of importance.'

He never gave out specifics because he said he didn't remember any.

He would say, 'The 1900s look different from the 2000s. The 2000s look different than the 2010s. The world changed in these decades. But the 1300s looked the same as 1400s and the 1600s. Nothing changed. People wore the same clothes, worshipped the same Gods, ate the same food, killed with the same barbarity, married the same way.'

This recounting of his past lives had made him extremely popular among his followers, who belonged to different faiths, and religious heads for whom this was blasphemy and his increasing popularity a threat.

In Anvesha's video, she analysed all of the 4302 videos of Firdaus Shirazi and traced his births across centuries.

She marked out Firdaus's rebirths and made a startling claim.

'Now, listen to this carefully. I can't say if Firdaus Shirazi is lying about his rebirths and reincarnation. But . . . but . . . but . . . according to the calculations, it's safe to say that his soul always reincarnated within a 175-kilometre radius of his death. This calculation is consistent with at least the 104 rebirths Firdaus has mentioned in his sermons.'

She waited for the comment to sink in.

She continued, 'If you're reborn according to mathematics, know that you died within a 200-kilometre radius of your place of birth. So the old man you were rude to yesterday? Maybe he was your father who lost a son young! Think about that! Now I will leave you guys with some thoughts. If Firdaus is lying about his rebirths, why did he go into such intricate details while constructing a backstory? A backstory of which he claims he remembers very little? Will they use this backstory to further the cult? If Firdaus has really reincarnated so many times . . . then . . . then what does the future hold for us? And don't forget to like, share, and subscribe to my channel. New videos as and when I find a lie to uncover. This is Anvesha Mohan, bye!'

She signed off with a cute, conspiratorial smile.

I was the first one to see the video. The clarity of thought, the taut storytelling, her unwavering confidence and the intimacy she shared with her viewers was impressive. It was as if she was telling a secret just to them.

An hour after she dropped the video, she called me. She was breathless. She had touched 20,000 views.

'That's ten times faster than the last time!' she squeaked with joy.

There were hate comments too but no one questioned her logic.

'Do you believe in reincarnation?' I asked Anvesha because I had spent a good part of the day Googling about it after watching her video.

'Of course not, Druvan. But I wanted the audience to sit back and think about how intricately Firdaus has layered the story about his rebirths. It's flawless. It makes you think, what's his end goal?'

'To maintain his cult. To show that he's a learned man?'

'Yes, that's true. Hmm . . . Makes sense.'

'Lol. The way you're saying it, tells me it makes no sense to you.'

She laughed 'It doesn't. See, most men of God say the most nonsensical things and get away with it. They could say, "I travelled to the sun, warmed my tea, and came back", and their followers won't question it.'

'Followers like Rashid. Believers like him will cradle even his shit like it's gold.'

'No one cares about the time periods Firdaus was born in. For believers, he's beyond doubt, and for us, he's always lying. So taking that hypothesis, don't you think it's too much work to create an accurate backstory that spans hundreds of years? A story no one's going to cross-check?'

'Where are you going with this?

'What if we are missing something?'

'That maybe he had way too much time on his hands?'

My impotent imagination led me nowhere.

But even with her fertile imagination, she hadn't imagined that the video would get 80,000 views in three days, 200,000 in a week, and a million in ten days. *1 million views*.

This was not just a number. There were eyes behind the screen; living people with fingers who clicked on the play button and watched her, listened to what she had to say.

What could ever match up to that? A million people!

Why was I being misled into believing marks mattered? Anvesha and Rashid had proved that out in the real world marks didn't matter.

Chapter 22: The Celebration

While the importance of my exams diminished in my head, Mumma and Baba's prayers got more fervent. Their devotion became more complete. We started eating *niramish* food every second day just in case God was more benevolent towards vegetarians.

Mumma and Baba stayed up the entire night before the day of the results. On the day, I said a little prayer, *Durga Durga, bachiye niyo*, and entered my roll number. A deathly silence descended over us. The screen buffered for a bit before the numbers appeared.

Our hearts collectively thumped.

Mumma was the first one to calculate the total. She started to cry. 99.3 per cent. She wrapped her arms around me and kissed me all over my face.

'*Aami jaantam! Amar shona!* I knew it!' She wept.

Baba nodded, lips upturned, impressed. My heart burst with joy.

He pulled Mumma and me into a tearful hug. At that moment, it didn't matter if board exam results turned into dirt after a few years, or if they didn't hold any importance. I had worked for this, and these marks were my doing. I was happy for my happiness, for their happiness, for our happiness. Within an hour, the calls started. Kakus and Kakis, Baba and Mumma's colleagues, congratulating us with a sense of wonder and jealousy.

'We also don't know how he scored so much!' Mumma would say on every call.

'All he did was play cricket,' Baba would add.

While Mumma and Baba attended all the calls, overplaying their humility, I checked Anvesha's result.

She'd passed—that's the best that could be said about her result.

'Are you going to stay home all day? Go, go, go out, Bubai! Celebrate!' exclaimed Mumma.

'With whom?'

'Your friends!'

'Rashid and Anvesha? But isn't one a bad influence and the other a siren out to get me?'

Mumma ignored my sarcasm and said, 'Go, meet Rashid.' She pushed a few crisp notes into my palm, kissed me, and then shoved me out of the house.

When I reached his garage, Rashid came rushing out to meet me. He hugged me and picked me up.

'Bhai! *Tabahi macha di* [You have created history]! *Tod ke rakh diya* [You have broken records]!' he bellowed. When he put me down, he had tears in his eyes. 'I called, but your phone was constantly engaged.'

'Relatives have been crawling out of the woodwork like termites and congratulating Mumma and Baba.'

'*Banta hai* [Obviously]!' he said. 'Come, come, bhai, come inside. Anvesha is coming here too.'

'Here?'

'*Aur kahan*, bhai?'

'Uncle allowed her to come here?'

'They knew you would be here and they didn't mind. Marks do matter, bhai, don't they?'

Rashid's CP shop, which he kept insisting was mine too, was twice as big as his father's at Karol Bagh. Behind the cashier hung a framed picture of him and me in our school uniforms. There were three men from his neighbourhood working on a couple of Splendors, one Enfield, two Activas and even a Triumph. He introduced me to the staff as the *doosre* malik, the second owner.

'Do you like your shop?'

'This isn't really my shop.'

'Bhai, again this nonsense. This is our shop. Tell me, do you like it or not?'

'I thought it would be a lot smaller but this is . . . substantial.'

'Welcome to being a shopkeeper, bhai. I was thinking what will Uncle, Aunty say if they knew their son runs a shop now?' he laughed.

'Probably slit their wrists.'

'Sit,' he added, patting the seat of the Splendor. 'Let us make you a man.'

'I don't know how to and—'

'The only thing that's better than a big, swinging dick between a man's legs is the petrol tank of a motorcycle.'

'Does that mean I can't sit?'

We turned. It was Anvesha, grinning from ear to ear.

'YOU PASSED!' screamed Rashid.

Anvesha ran towards us and pulled both of us into a hug.

'Congratulations! You passed too!' said Anvesha to me.

'Barely,' I joked.

'Let's go the back office,' said Rashid.

'There's a back office also? You have become a *bada aadmi*, big guy!' remarked Anvesha.

'Says the girl who has 500k subscribers on her channel,' replied Rashid.

'And all I have are numbers on a paper,' I sighed.

'Aw,' they both echoed.

Rashid opened the door to his back office. Waiting behind the door was a cake, a bunch of hastily half-filled balloons and half-melted candles that said 99 per cent.

'YOU DID IT!' said Anvesha.

'Yeah, yeah, whatever,' I said.

'Don't mope and fish for compliments.'

'Bhai, your journey is the toughest. To persevere for just the goal of excellence is commendable,' explained Rashid, which I was sure he had picked up from one of the Rooh Collective books.

We cut the cake, burst the balloons, and ate till our stomachs hurt. A little later, we found ourselves locked in a no-holds-barred game of carrom.

'Papa took your name like ten times today,' said Anvesha.

'What did he say?'

'. . . that he always knew you would score well.'

'What else?'

'That you are meant for big things in life.'

'Did he say that?'

She nodded. 'I asked them to call and congratulate Uncle and Aunty.'

'. . . and they didn't.'

'Baby steps, Druvan. They took your name after months. They let me come here. That's progress. Everything will be all right eventually.'

She reached out, smiled and held my hand.

While we talked, Rashid continued to the game with laser-sharp focus.

'Kya?' he said when he found Anvesha and me staring at him.

'We are talking about important stuff here and you're pretending to be a world champion or something,' I said.

'Huh?' Rashid hadn't been listening at all. 'Sorry bhai, I was trying to focus.'

'We are meeting after so long and you're distracted,' teased Anvesha.

'I wasn't distracted. I was playing.'

'It's just carrom, chill,' said Anvesha.

'The best way to chill is to live more mindfully. That's what I'm trying to do. Right now, we should all concentrate on the game and then we can all sit down and talk.'

He leaned back and picked out a book from the shelf.

'Here. This is a new book, just came out. It talks about mindfulness.'

'Not again, Rashid.'

'Listen naa bhai, it's only for Rooh Collective members for now, so I only have one copy. It's—'

'Please burn it.'

'Bhai, at least look at it once.'

Anvesha took the book from Rashid.

'Don't encourage him,' I warned Anvesha.

Rashid continued, 'So, Firdaus Shirazi says that you need to live more mindfully, be more conscious of your choices, live slowly so that your soul remembers it in the next life. That's how you are reborn.'

'You mean Firdaus Shirazi *said*, not says. He's dead. Past tense.'

'He's alive, bhai.'

'We saw the body. Millions of people saw the body. He was dead.'

'Bhai, Anvesha believes he reincarnates every time he dies. He has had so many births.'

'I . . . ,' said Anvesha. 'I raised a question. What if he wasn't lying about it? That's what I was asking.'

'We saw the body burn, we saw followers like you crying. It was the most boring piece of TV programming.'

'You said it, bhai. What we saw was the body, not the soul.' He looked at Anvesha for support. 'Ask her, she researched. She said that there is a possibility that he was right about rebirth.'

'Don't drag me into this.' Anvesha shrugged. 'I'm a conspiracy theorist, nothing more, nothing less. I just pointed out that Firdaus's story had no loopholes.'

'Pick a side, Anvesha.'

'Bhai, there's only one side. The soul's immortal.'

'So is stupidity.'

Rashid continued with a glint in his eye, 'Bhai, we will be reborn, starting with the people who believed in him. The Rooh Collective. I will send you the details. There's still time, bhai.'

'I'm not interested.'

He kept his hand on my knee. 'Join it, bhai. We will be reborn together. We can have a carrom tournament that will stretch over centuries. Can you believe that?'

'I will believe in Hogwarts before I believe in rebirth.'

Anvesha who was still flipping through the book stopped and asked, 'So this says your memories need to be strong enough to be remembered in the next life?'

I laughed. 'Remembered by whom? A newborn baby? That doesn't sound crazy at all.'

Anvesha interrupted me and asked Rashid. 'So a baby remembers things from the past life, is it?'

'Not every baby. Everything is there in the book. Read it.'

'Tell us the gist,' said Anvesha.

'It says that most people die when they are old, and as you get older, your memories get hazy. You don't remember enough.

You forget the moments of extreme joy or extreme sadness. The mind tries its best to hold on so that it can pass them on to the next birth. That's why the older people get, the more nostalgic they get. It's the body trying to make the soul remember everything, so that it can take the memories to the next life.'

'That's nonsense.'

'Continue,' said Anvesha.

'Because people don't live in the moment, their memories aren't strong. The memories get muddled up when they get old. And when your memories get muddled up, your soul doesn't remain unique. So in a newborn baby, whose brain has significantly less processing power, the blurred memories get wiped out. The soul gets overwritten by the flood of stimulation it receives. Your soul's lost forever.'

'Wow. Don't tell me you believe in all this,' I sneered.

'And what if you die young?' asked Anvesha.

'If you die young, if you have lived correctly, if you have enough moments to remember your life by, your memories can come back to you in your next life. It's the same soul. For example, if I play this game mindfully, a hundred years from now, my soul in a new body would remember it.'

Anvesha dutifully nodded as if she was buying this steaming pile of horseshit.

Encouraged by this, Rashid, continued, 'There's a condition though. Have you ever read about cases of rebirth in newspapers? Mostly such people were murdered or they committed suicide in their past life. Nahi?'

He found me rolling my eyes. 'Bhai, you can google it. It's mostly a violent death—a terrible sickness or a murder. In all cases, you will notice that people remember their past life when they are young. As they grow older, they forget because everyone tells them it's their imagination. Their old memories from their previous lives get clouded by the new ones they make in their current life. Go, google it, bhai.'

'I'm not going to google anything. If I google "Do Vampires Exist?", I will find some website which will say they do.'

'Rashid, you continue. You were talking about violent deaths and rebirth,' said Anvesha.

'That's because a violent death means the soul is heavily marked,' explained Rashid. 'And that's why Firdaus's end had to be violent, something that the soul could remember in his next life and stitch the rest of the memories around it.'

'I just have one question, though,' I said.

'I also have the same question,' said Anvesha.

'I haven't even asked it.'

'You're going to ask about the others from Rooh . . . '

'Yes, that. Rashid, what about all your brothers from Rooh Collective, who died that month? Were they all reborn?'

Rashid paused. 'Time will tell. But not everyone deserves to be reborn.'

Chapter 23: Pet Rottweilers

Within a couple of months of joining the coaching institute, a few eventualities became clear in my mind. I knew I would make it to IIT; this wasn't arrogance but a careful reading of the situation. Physics and Mathematics came easy to me, Chemistry was a struggle but nothing that couldn't be handled.

'I don't feel special. I don't do anything like Rashid or you. You know, like, there's no talent in what I do,' I complained to Anvesha over the phone.

'This is your talent. Someone has to do things in the world that make sense. What if doctors went about cutting people up just to admire their insides and write poems about how cancerous cells invade the body? What if they just drew sculptures of a sliced body with organs hanging out and shared them on Instagram? Do you know what's important, Druvan?

It's doing the dangerous, heartbreaking, real work of cutting the tumour out.'

'I'm no doctor. At best, I will be a coder,' I said.

'And it's the tiny code that you will write some day to operate a robotic arm that will cut through a tumour, unreachable for the human hand. Art's a no-stake game, Druvan.'

'Can you repeat all of that so that I can write it down, print it, and read it every time you drop a video and a million people watch you?'

Both our parents had let their guards down after my domination of the board exams and admission into the first batch of the coaching institute. At this point, both of us were more successful than our parents had ever been. What role do parents have when their children get better than them at being adults?

After the viral video, Anvesha had released another controversial one in which she argued that both Jesus and Buddha were mythical figures who were made famous later by people who had vested political interests. She claimed that ambitious rulers might have collaborated with little-known men of God, or the ideas they left behind, to stitch together a kingdom otherwise torn by different languages and customs. She said miracles were nothing but gossip, recycled over multiple conversations.

Though I got none of the references—most of them unverified—it was entertaining. It came with many disclaimers about the possibility of her being wrong. There was also a minute-long disclaimer and an apology if her video offended anyone.

The video had more views, more likes, more dislikes and more hate comments than the previous ones. The comments made me want to tell Anvesha to stop making videos, to hide. At other times, they made me want to hunt down the trolls.

'So when's the next one coming?' I asked as Anvesha's first and most loyal subscriber, once I was done watching the video for the nth time.

'I'm still working on it.'

'So not even a hint?'

'Nope.'

As a rule, she never gave anything out until the draft was ready.

What she was working on at the moment should have been clear by her disinterest in the news of the year. Once it hit the news cycle, the anchors behaved like cocaine-addled rabbits paid by the decibel.

I first got to know of it when I saw my classmates at the coaching institute huddled around a girl's cell phone. A YouTube video played on it.

PET ROTTWEILERS RIP APART A COUPLE IN THEIR HOME, screamed the clickbait.

The video was movie-like, cut to music.

The title wasn't a click-bait. A man and woman, presumably husband and wife, lay in a corner while two monstrous, wolf-like dogs snarled and snapped at their arms. The jaws of the two dogs clamped on the wrists of the man and cut it off clean. The wife watched in horror but didn't scream, didn't move.

She waited for her turn.

The Rottweilers severed the woman's hands in two clean bites. Then the dogs sat beside them and chewed at their amputated hands. They tossed the fingers in the air, caught them, and ate them. When the man's leg moved, the bigger dog kept its paw on it. The video was violent. Every chomp from the massive dogs, every rip of the flesh, made me squirm. The dogs finished eating the hands, and got back on their feet. And then with a jerk, clamped his teeth over the man's face. The sharp canine teeth buried into the eye socket and the skull. The skull was split into half. Brain matter spilled out glacially. The dog ripped the head of the man. Blood from the carotid rushed out and drenched the dog. The woman was next. The headless bodies slumped to the ground. The dogs sat by the bodies. They tore off the meat from their faces and then the video blacked out.

'Those are the Acharyas,' I mumbled.

Twenty pairs of eyes turned towards me and then back at the video. It struck them too. The girl opened another tab, typed 'Acharya' in the search bar, and went to the news section. And there it was.

The Richest Man of Asia mauled by pet Rottweilers; CCTV video goes viral.

His wife, too, killed in the incident.

The video surprisingly remained on the Internet. The news channel kept playing the video with news anchors blaring in the background.

'WHO DO YOU THINK KILLED MUKESH ACHARYA? WHO? THE ANSWER IS SIMPLE. HIS ADOPTED YOUNGER SISTER, VIDHI ACHARYA! WHO STOLE THE CHAIRPERSON'S POSITION! WHEN THAT DIDN'T SATISFY HER, SHE DRUGGED THEM AND GOT THEM TORN APART BY THEIR DOGS!'

'VIDHI ACHARYA! PRODIGY OR MURDERER?'

Despite this popular conspiracy theory, the Acharyas didn't seek to take down the video or asked for stay notices for publications that had painted Vidhi Acharya as the killer.

While the rest of the country was lapping up the conspiracy theory, Anvesha ripped multiple holes into it.

'First of all, the dogs were Mukesh's own. There are pictures on the Internet, right from the time the dogs were puppies.'

I googled and found the pictures.

She continued, 'Do you see now?'

'Maybe Vidhi got them trained to do it.'

'Give me one reason why she would do it.'

'Money. I mean I know a neighbour whose father picked up a job of writing history books for money . . .'

'Yeah yeah, over smart *mat bano* [Don't get over smart]. Anyway, Vidhi's already the most powerful in the family. She has the controlling stake, Mukesh was irrelevant. Why would she need to kill them?'

'So, you have a theory on their death? Of course you have a theory on their death. What's your theory on their death?'

'I don't have a theory on their death. I have a theory on *death* itself.'

'You sound like Rashid.'

'I have a theory that will make the death of Mukesh and his wife, or anyone for that matter, inconsequential.'

'And you're not going to tell me because you're making a video on it.'

'Correct.'

Despite my relentless prodding, she gave nothing away. Two weeks later, she completed the video.

I didn't get to see it.

Chapter 24: The Young Mob

I never got to see the video—the full video anyway.

Anvesha hadn't shown me a draft. She had uploaded it in the middle of the night. She had anticipated trouble and it came swiftly.

Within half an hour, the website took it down. By the end of the hour, the video was off the Internet. And in two hours, there were short, cleverly edited clips from the video all over the Internet that made it seem like Anvesha had levelled some serious allegations against the Sanyukta Swaraj government.

I slept soundly while social media erupted with people calling Anvesha a terrorist, a bukkake slut and a paid stooge of foreign powers. There were calls for her arrest. Some suggested dragging her to the middle of the street, stripping her naked, raping her, and hanging from a crane while her parents watched.

I woke up to it when the phone rang in the middle of the night. On the other end, a frantic Varun Uncle was crying for help.

'THERE ARE PEOPLE WITH HOCKEY STICKS! THEY ARE OUTSIDE! THEY ARE THREATENING TO BURN THE HOUSE DOWN IF ANVESHA DOESN'T GO OUT!'

In the background, I heard Sunita Aunty weeping.

'The police . . . . ?'

'THEY ARE NOT COMING! *DIDI, AAP PLEASE A IDHAR AA JAO* [Didi, please come here ASAP]!' screamed Sunita Aunty.

'Barricade the doors, I'm coming,' said Baba, already slipping into a shirt. 'Don't worry, bhaisahib, I'm there. *Dekh lenge in sab ko* [We'll take care of all of them].'

Baba replaced the receiver and rushed to the balcony—that's where the cricket bats and the rusted sickles lay.

I put on my jeans. Mumma went inside and emerged in a salwar kameez.

'You're not going!' said Baba when he saw the two of us.

'Look at yourself!' I argued back.

I was taller than Baba, better built, and I would not stand back.

'Give the bat to him,' instructed Mumma.

'But . . . .'

'Let him come. He's big enough,' said Mumma. She picked up a canister of oil. Baba was about to say something when Mumma raised her hand. 'What? You think we will stay at home? They need us.'

'Rashid knows people,' I said.

'Call him.'

I dialled his number. He answered immediately.

'I'm going,' said Rashid. 'Anvesha called me. Bhai, Uncle, Aunty *ko bol ghar rahe* [Ask your parents to stay at home]. I will go with my boys. It's not safe.'

'I will see you there,' I said and disconnected the call.

Baba dialled the numbers of the men and women with whom he went for protests. Some were scared, some promised they would call people high up in the government, and others said they would join them.

We caught a rickshaw to Anvesha's house. We clenched and unclenched our hands around our weapons of choice; our hearts thumped in our mouths.

'Did Bhaisahib tell you how many men there were?' asked Mumma.

Baba shook his hand.

'Bubai? Have you seen the video?' she asked me.

I searched for the incriminating clips. They were no longer than fifteen seconds. The sharp cuts, the jump in tonality, made it clear the clips were taken out of context and twisted. They were accusing Anvesha of calling Sanyukta Swaraj a pimp, a murderer, and a *desh drohi* (traitor).

'Is Sanyukta Swaraj selling bodies of the citizens?'

'Is there any link between the nuclear scientists who routinely go missing and government agencies refusing to investigate it?'

'Is Sanyukta Swaraj an agent of chaos? Who's she working with? Who's she working for?'

Though these statements from a somewhat known person on the Internet were damning enough to receive large-scale trolling, they still didn't warrant a mob.

When we got there, we found twenty boys shouting in tired voices, '*Kiska raj, kiska raj* [Who's rule]? Sanyukta Swaraj, Sanyukta Swaraj.' They had been out there for some time. The venom and the rage had petered down a bit. Baba asked the auto driver to stop a little away.

'Come,' said Baba.

Both of us tightened our grips around the handles of our bats.

'Don't fear anything, Bubai. Just swing it. It will all be in self-defence,' said Baba.

'I will kill them.'

Mumma's shoulders drooped. 'They are just boys.'

'The bastards shouldn't have come here then,' replied Baba.

'Where are the others?' asked Mumma.

'They will come.'

The hooligans turned to look at us. Baba raised his bat and started to walk towards them. Mumma and I joined in.

'*Ladki ko aana padega bahar* [The girl will have come out]! She has to pay!' shouted one of them.

'How dare she talk about Sanyuktaji! *Dekh lenge us bhen ki laudi ko bhi aur tumhe bhi* [We will take care of that whore, and you too]!'

'*Jaloge to dard hoga* [If you burn, it will hurt],' Mumma said calmly, uncapping the canister of oil and splashing some on the ground.

There was now a smell of petrol in the air.

The boys, none older than me, flinched and moved back. And then, their faces lost colour. The air was pierced by the violent rat-tat-tat of loud motorcycle engines. From around the corner, five motorcycles, three men on each, brandishing hockey sticks and thick chains, came to a stop beside us.

'*Kahan hai madarchod* [Where are the motherfuckers]!' shouted Rashid.

He was on his own Pulsar 180.

The unsureness on their faces turned to terror. They made a quick calculation. They didn't want to fight.

'Freedom of expression, *kutto ke bachho* [You, son of dogs]!' shouted Baba.

The mob turned to the biggest boy among them. He nodded and turned away from us. Slowly, they sulked away from the house. A few of them dialled numbers on their phones.

'They will be back,' said Mumma.

'We will be outside, Aunty. Don't worry,' assured Rashid and nodded at the boys he had come with. The boys got down from the motorcycles and touched Mumma's feet, one at a time.

Baba, meanwhile, called his people and asked them not to come. He told them things were now under control.

'Bhaisahib's here,' said Baba.

Varun Uncle, who had watched the whole thing through the window grilles, opened the gate for us and locked it as soon as we were inside. There were no apologies traded, no gratitude expressed. Just a sense of healing of the relationship hung in the air.

Anvesha sat next to me and no one spared us a look. It was like the two families had never wished death on each other.

'I called my office, they called the seniors and no one has come as of now. The police kept saying they would come but no one is here yet,' explained Varun Uncle.

'They are just scaring you, bhaisahib,' said Mumma. She held Aunty's hand to keep her from breaking down.

'Can I see the entire video?' asked Baba.

Anvesha nodded and handed over the tablet she was cradling on her lap.

Baba frowned. 'There's nothing?'

Anvesha took the tablet back. She tapped on the tablet. 'It was here, I just. . . ' Her voice trailed away. The video wasn't there. She ran back into her room. We went after her.

'The video . . . is gone.'

Just then, the landline rang. Varun uncle answered.

He turned to us and said, 'The police are going to be here.'

'Tell us what the video was about,' said Baba.

Mumma stopped Baba. 'Let the girl be. I have called Sharmila. She's getting in touch with a lawyer.'

Baba dismissed Mumma with a wave of his hand. 'We need to know what these people are chasing her for. What do you think a lawyer can do in front of these goons?'

Anvesha nodded and started to tell us.

Chapter 25: The Prophet, the Politician, the King

Anvesha's conspiracy theory was *wild*.

She began.

'So the three people working together are Damodarbhai Acharya—the one with all the money in the world; Firdaus Shirazi—the one with the cross-religious, rebirth gyan or the prophet; and Sanyukta Swaraj, the most powerful politician of all time. The prophet, the politician and the king.

'Sanyukta Swaraj is just a few years older than Firdaus, they are from the same state, born in districts a stone's throw from each other. Sanyukta's father was a powerful politician of the district, and Firdaus was a young boy who talked about Gods, religions and spiritual texts to adoring audiences. Now I'm not sure if this is how they met, but follow the story.

'Sanyukta had two elder brothers, right, who died in a train accident, leaving Sanyukta to carry the political mantle? Her mother didn't survive the loss of her two sons. It was just her father and her. How do you deal with the loss of two brothers and a mother? Where do you seek spiritual guidance from? Your father's too busy doing rallies and arranging contracts for his friends. What do *you* do?

'You know where I am going with this. She finds Firdaus Shirazi. They became friends and who knows, future collaborators? Why would they not? They both craved control, power and attention.

'Sanyukta, whose only role model was her father, was always a political animal. Do you know she was the youngest president of her college union? Could it be that Firdaus mobilized support for her? Likely, I would say. It wouldn't be the first time a politician and a god-man worked in tandem to garner votes and devotion. In fact, it's unlikely for a man of God to *not* work with a politician.

'Meanwhile, Damodarbhai had escaped death years ago and had been on the look-out for people who could *solve* death. To solve death, he had already started taking over the healthcare industry in India, recruiting top scientists, and some rumours say that he also set up a high-tech laboratory buried deep inside the earth. Nuclear scientists have gone off the map. But no one has investigated it. Everyone knows about the refineries in Gujarat where there's no oil production, and yet, construction material keeps flying in. This must be the time Damodarbhai heard of Firdaus with his talk about reincarnation, rebirth and his theories about death.'

'Where are you going with this?' asked Baba.

'What if . . . Acharya recruited Firdaus and Sanyukta.'

'He recruited them for what?' I asked.

'This is where it gets tricky.'

'Go on,' said Mumma.

'We are what our consciousness is, isn't it? The sum total of our memories, of how we react to stimuli. That's what makes us a person. That's what makes all of us unique. It's all in our heads—the millions of neurotransmitters going off in different combinations to give us our personality. Our brain is essentially a very complex Sudoku puzzle, an endless number of calculations. Our brain is essentially data.'

'*Haan toh?*' I asked impatiently.

'Data can be transferred, Druvan, if you know how to. When our brains die, the data dies. What if the data is transferred before the brain dies.'

'Our brains are not pen drives.'

'What if they are? What if Damodarbhai had cracked the mapping of the brain? Now we all conceptually know what reincarnation is? What if reincarnation is possible scientifically too? What if it's just a transfer of consciousness? A transfer of data from one brain to another? A long-winded series of 0s and 1s?'

'Where are you getting with this, beta?' asked Mumma.

'So . . . let's look at the chronology. For decades, he owns the entire healthcare system and the scientists who can study the human brain. These people can find how and where consciousness lies. Aunty, the difference between you and me is our consciousness, isn't it? The data of your mind and mine? If I wipe your data and transmute my consciousness to your mind, *I will be you.* So imagine if I can reduce consciousness to numbers and digits, and move it on a server.'

'How . . . how . . . can you map consciousness?' asked Aunty.

'That's where Rooh Collective comes in. What does Rashid say? Live every moment? Make sure you're aware? That your memories are strong? That's living consciously. That Firdaus guy must have meditative techniques to strengthen the neural pathways. The scientists must have the key to map it? The nuclear scientists? What if . . . I know it sounds stupid . . . they can beam it on to a fresh brain?'

She started to sound a bit . . . loony.

'Let's assume you can reduce a brain to a code. But where do you . . . print these brains? Whose brains do you use?' I asked, worried for her.

'That's the last piece of the puzzle—Sanyukta Swaraj, the biggest political power to have emerged in the country. She can single-handedly get bills passed, can't she?' she said.

'So what?'

Baba cut me as I tried to speak. 'What bill has she passed?'

'Not one, but two. One's passed, and they are working on the other one as we speak,' said Anvesha. 'The first one is the Citizen's Justice Bill. Remember that? What happened with that? When the government failed to kill the convicts, Acharya Life stepped in. What did Acharya Life gain out of researching the best ways to kill a convict? Of course, they didn't do it out of charity. They wanted test subjects—human subjects to experiment just before their deaths.'

She paused for a breath.

'Now imagine if that worked. Assume that they could download the consciousness of a brain housed in an old, diseased body, transmute it into information. This information can then be imprinted into a new brain of a healthy body. Think for a second. They could sell this technology to the rich for a fortune. But then comes the new problem. As Druvan asked, where will they get fresh brains? Where will they imprint this consciousness? Where will they get fresh, young bodies for the consciousness of the rich, dead people?'

'There are only two ways. Now either they grow entire bodies in a lab or . . . they find the bodies—bodies that can be disposed, bodies that aren't needed any more, bodies that are condemned to life . . . in jail.'

We shook our heads in disbelief. This was just what it was meant to be—a conspiracy theory.

Anvesha continued, 'You get your bodies and the brains from jail. That's your inventory. A healthy, living body, taken care of by Acharya Life.'

'But Anvesha, the Acharyas don't have any control of the jails,' I argued. 'All they do is put people on the death penalty. That's it? They don't own the jails or the people inside them.'

'That's where the second bill will come in. You will see it on social media first. With the longer prison sentences for small crimes that came as a by product of the first bill, they have already crammed the prisons. Slowly, you will see paid activists lament the condition of these decaying jails. There will be a huge hue and cry about it, an entire social media blitz. After that, Sanyukta Swaraj will introduce the second bill. The government will cry hoarse that the jails are getting too unmanageable, that they are just too expensive to manage. Just last year, the government spent 6000 crore rupees on prisons. What's the way out? They will pass the second bill to privatize it. Once the bill is passed, the entire jail infrastructure will be privatized and owned by the Acharyas. The Acharyas will own every prisoner. From here, they can use those brains to imprint the consciousness of people who can pay to be reborn. Of course, they will have the prisoner's consent. Imagine you are a criminal on death row. Would you want to die? Or would you want your body to live on? Though with a different consciousness?'

'Anvesha . . . ' I said but Anvesha cut me.

'. . . and you know what I think? Firdaus Shirazi will be back—in another body. That's why they made such a big deal about his death.'

'This sounds impossible,' said Baba.

'Then why were they outside? There must be some truth in what I'm claiming?' ranted Anvesha like a madwoman.

'Because you're famous?' I argued. 'Because you alleged there could be a friendship between a god-man, an industrialist and the prime minister? That's . . . enough these days.'

'Conspiracy theories are about the impossible,' said Anvesha, unfazed.

Baba shook his head and mumbled, 'It's possible these fellows are friends, hand-in-glove in some scheme. What's not possible is the mapping of the brain. That technology is not there yet.'

'They have hidden it,' argued Anvesha.

Baba, who was obsessed with new technology, subscribed to a dozen science magazines and spent countless hours just listening to science portals, cut Anvesha mid-sentence. 'Look, to scan the brain, to get every synapse in the picture, just a picture, mind you, beta, you would need MRIs to be a thousand times more effective than where current technology is. Even then, the magnetic field required to get that kind of resolution would melt the brain and char the skull. Now it could happen, but to make a scientific leap that huge in half a century is impossible. And it would be impossible to keep it under wraps. And this is just a picture. Not even interneural interactions that keep firing in the brain. For capturing the neural interactions, the resolution, the magnetic field and the computing power needed would be a million times more.'

Baba was now talking to himself.

'And for a moment, let's assume they did succeed in just clicking a picture of the brain in all its microscopic details. But mapping a brain doesn't mean pictures, it means a real-time video. Now let's assume they even did that. The mountain of data in the human brain, the space required to store that data—from just one brain—would match the space needed for the entire Internet.'

'Baba, that sounds like something out of a WhatsApp message.'

'Bubai, I am actually quoting a research paper from Allen Institute for Brain Science in Seattle, Washington.'

Anvesha started impatiently at Baba.

But Baba continued, 'So, these scientists tried to map the brain of a mouse. Not even the entire brain, just a small sliver, as big as a grain of sand. Do you know how much time it took with the greatest array of microscopes and supercomputers ever built? It took five electron microscopes, which ran continuously for five months, to take the images. The computers then took three months to assemble them into a composite image that could be studied and made sense of. The data itself was 2 million gigabytes. From a brain sample of a tiny mouse brain, not even the entire brain. Now let's do a small calculation. Bubai, get me a paper.'

I gave him one.

'Now a *complete* brain of a mouse would require 400 times as much space. That becomes 800 million gigabytes. Now the human brain is 10,000 times as big as a mouse's. By that assumption, the space required will be 800x10,000 million gigabytes. The top four Internet companies—Amazon, Google, Microsoft and

Facebook—have a total data of 1200 million gigabytes. We are talking 7000 times as much data! And this is just *one human brain*.'

'You're saying my brain is 7000 times more data than the top four Internet companies combined?' asked Anvesha.

'Anvesha beta, the human brain has more neural pathways than the universe has stars. If the data of the universe is downloaded, it can't go unnoticed. Where are the server farms? Where are they storing this data? Just to cool this much data in a server farm would require all the water from the Pacific Ocean. And this is just one brain. Just to have the information of one brain, you would need 7000 times the data capacity of the top four companies combined. Imagine a hundred. How are the Acharyas running a secret corporation with data farms with a capacity that huge? How much data can they have without getting noticed?'

Anvesha's shoulders slumped.

She now knew her conspiracy was far-fetched.

She mumbled, 'I ended with video saying, that the Acharyas imprinted Damodarbhai's consciousness over Vidhi's brain. I said that Vidhi is Damodarbhai reborn. That's how Vidhi is so intelligent, and knows how to run the company. I argued in the video that for the Acharyas, his death's a non-issue. That they have solved death.'

Baba shook his head. 'So you're saying this happened two decades ago? When Internet, MRI, imaging and storage technology was, at best, in its adolescence. How would they hide the future for so long? And why?'

While Baba and Anvesha debated the possibilities, we heard a loud crash. We rushed towards the balcony. A Molotov cocktail had been smashed on the ground. Baba was about to rush out to douse it when Mumma held him back. She pointed ahead.

The mob was back. And this time, they had petrol bombs in their hands.

Chapter 26: Hasan Ali, the Saviour

An hour passed. The crowd kept shouting slogans against Anvesha. They kept exhorting us to come out. They screamed and brandished swords and said they just wanted to *talk*.

'The lines are dead,' said Baba for the nth time. 'Why the hell isn't the police here yet!'

And as if on cue, we heard blaring sirens. Three police vans and two jeeps came to a screeching halt. The policemen jumped down the cars; they were dressed in complete riot gear. The crowd still didn't let up—if anything, the shouting got louder. Was the law here to protect them? Or us? And then, a heavily built policeman raised a baton and brought it down on a boy carrying a torch.

'*Bhaag .madarchodo* [Run, motherfuckers]!' shouted the policeman.

The police dispersed the crowd within minutes, like they were little boys playing cricket where it was not allowed. The boys and the men who were shouting just moments ago were now on the ground, writhing in pain.

Two policewomen came running to the door and shouted to ask if we were okay.

'We are fine!' shouted back Mumma.

'Do you want Sarita, my colleague, to be with you?' asked the policewoman.

'We are fine!' repeated Mumma.

The policewomen stood at the door. Just then, the phone rang. It was Baba who picked it.

'Who's this?' asked Baba.

'Good morning, Datta sahib, I'm Hasan Ali. Vidhi Acharya read Anvesha's tweet for help.'

Baba put Hasan Ali on the loudspeaker. 'It's Hasan Ali.'

Anvesha came forward and addressed the rest of us. 'I tweeted . . . he's her . . . right-hand man?'

'Anvesha's right,' Hasan's voice boomed on the speaker.

'There's nothing to worry. The police, I believe, has reached there and are picking up the miscreants. We will take care of them,' assured Hasan. He seemed to be in a hurry.

'Why did you send the mob?' snarled Baba.

We heard a loud sigh.

'Datta sahib, we didn't.'

'Of course, you did!' said Mumma.

'Behenji, they came on the orders of a local MLA. He will be fired from the party tomorrow. They do these things to come to the notice of the headquarters. You can read about it in the news tomorrow. I give you my word that everyone out there will be arrested by tomorrow morning.'

'Why . . . are you helping us?' asked Anvesha.

'Because Vidhi asked me to; I do what she asks me to do. The Acharya family is sorry that this happened. Take care . . . '

'Excuse me' said Anvesha softly.

'Yes, betaji?'

'Mr Hasan. Umm . . . I wanted to ask that Vidhi. . .umm . . . she didn't mind the video? Instead, sent help? I have alleged that Vidhi is involved in quite a few things.'

Hasan chuckled, and, in a soft voice, said, 'She found it entertaining. Then she saw your frantic tweets and sent me here. I notified the police; they will clean this mess up. Vidhi asked me to tell you to put up the video wherever and whenever you want. I'm sorry this happened. I have a daughter too, slightly older than you. I know what it's like.'

I googled 'HASAN ALI DAUGHTER ACHARYA'. In the first few pictures, Hasan's daughter was dressed in a sharp suit, back straight as an arrow, her chin up. She had the gaze of a bull—much like her father—who stood beside her. Fatima's face was marred with red, flaming scar tissue. She was unmistakably an acid attack survivor.

'None of the things I claim in the video are true?' asked Anvesha.

'My malik and now Vidhi are friends with Swarajji and Firdaus. That's common knowledge. Anyone with a keen eye would know that,' answered Hasan. 'And exposé videos are common. Yours is more interesting, betaji, I admit. The video can be up tomorrow morning. I promise there will be no mobs outside.'

'So all this for nothing?' asked Varun Uncle softly.

'We can't control everyone, can we now, Varun Sahib?'.

'She won't put up the video,' said Varun Uncle firmly. 'We don't want any of this.'

'Dekho, bhaisahib. It's for her to decide. Let's stop telling girls what they should do. Take my daughter. She has taken up air rifle as a sport. Can you imagine? Let the girl decide, *hai na?*' His voice turned soft. 'Do as you feel like. If it's your truth, then feel free to share it.'

'If this isn't the truth, what is?'

Hasan laughed softly. 'The truth is always much simpler than you think, beta. I hope Allah favours you and guides you towards it. But for now, you're wrong.'

The phone disconnected. Mumma and I went outside to check. Two sweepers were cleaning the streets.

Chapter 27: Hasan Ali, the Murderer

My fervent requests to Anvesha to upload the video fell on deaf ears.

'Your baba was right. There's no way Acharyas have been sitting on scientific breakthroughs needed for this for decades. The truth is something else, something we haven't thought of yet. I don't want to embarrass myself.'

'But at least, the video got our parents together.'

'Papa, Mummy are ageing backwards. They missed Uncle, Aunty. It's like they are in love again.'

'Same. So how long do I have to wait for the next video?'

'I have a few ideas.'

The wait turned out to be quite long. Soon after, Anvesha came down with typhoid and was bed-ridden. Following her cue, I contracted it too.

'How are we soulmates if we don't fall sick at the same time?' I asked her.

The diseased wrecked havoc on our bodies. Both of us lost a ton of weight. Our energy was sapped out of us. We groaned in bed all day. Time slowed down to a crawl. To cheer us up, both sets of parents let us call each other any number of times we wanted. Every time I looked at her on a video call, I felt worse. Her cheeks had sunk in, her skin had paled, her eyes had retreated into their sockets, and her voice reduced to a whisper. I looked no different. Our parents were in constant panic.

'Do you think the Acharyas poisoned us?' I joked.

'They wouldn't give us typhoid. Maybe thallium would be more up to speed. KGB used to do it, quite effective. Google Alexander Litvinenko.'

'Do you think I'm in a position to google?'

'A KGB spy who went against Putin. He claimed Putin orchestrated the Russian Apartment Bombings.'

'Do you want me to google that too?'

'*Arre, yaar, kabhi toh* read a newspaper or two. The Russian Apartment Bombings were a series of blasts that left 300 people dead. A little-known Putin blamed it on the Chechen rebels and waged war on them. His popularity spiked, and he became the president soon after.'

'Putin killed his own people?'

'The Chechen rebels didn't own up to the bombings. And guess what? A government investigation revealed Russian security services were involved.'

'Then how did he get away with it?'

'The committee was dissolved, two of the lawyers were assassinated, the findings were junked. And then there was this spy, who fled to the UK, who had refused to take part in the bombings. It's all on YouTube. You should check it out.'

'That's screwed up.'

'This is why I like conspiracy theories. Imagine being governed by a head of state who orchestrated a terrorist attack against his own people to rise to power. What's the life of 300 people when there's power at stake?'

'This would never happen in India.'

'Are you sure?'

'I am already sick, but this makes me want to die. Let me watch this and I will call you in a bit.'

Instead, I slept off and woke up shaking from a nightmare eight hours later.

That month that I spent in bed, I often had nightmares about the night the mob attacked Anvesha's house. I kept thinking of an alternate reality where Hasan didn't call and disperse the angry mob.

And though Hasan slipped out of everyone else's minds, he dug deep into mine. I kept thinking of the power he exerted on Anvesha and our lives. He was the villain of my nightmares.

My obsession with him started slowly. It began when I found myself searching for him on the Internet. Then I started downloading pictures and arranging them in a timeline. The first picture I found of Damodarbhai, and incidentally of Hasan, was taken in Dubai. Hasan was the photographer, and visible in the mirror behind Damodarbhai. The picture was taken in front of a trading firm in Dubai where Damodarbhai worked as a salesman and Hasan as an office boy.

Apart from this story, there was nothing more on Hasan Ali. The next picture of him was from the biography of Damodarbhai Acharya. The picture was taken at Tirupathi, and Hasan had holy markings on his forehead too. The next picture had him standing right next to Damodarbhai, in front of the mammoth trading warehouse at the port of Vadodara. Hasan's hand was firmly on his waist as if ready to whip out a pistol if need be. I couldn't find any photos of the next few years, and then the glut starts. After Damodarbhai's company was listed on the exchange, he was clicked often, and in the hazy background, there was always Hasan. Middle age wasn't kind to Damodarbhai, but Hasan grew handsome with age—his back got straighter, his muscles got bigger, and his eyes piercer. Damodar amassed wealth and power, and Hasan guarded him with his life.

While Damodarbhai grew older rapidly, Hasan greyed painfully slowly. And then there was the picture that everyone had seen—a bloodied Damodarbhai in Hasan's arms. He had been in a car accident. Hasan Ali had wrenched apart the door of the vehicle and pulled him out. There was another picture of him carrying his employer to the other side of the road, where the ambulance waited. He was captured screaming in the picture. That picture had thrown him into the limelight for an entire news cycle.

After he recovered from the crash, there weren't a lot of pictures of Damodarbhai—and in effect Hasan—for a while. Damodarbhai had removed himself from social life.

And then came the biggest tragedy of Hasan's life which brought both of them back in the news. Hasan's daughter was attacked—an acid attack by an ex-boyfriend. Hasan's daughter's face melted. It took countless surgeries for her to recover.

Three weeks later, the boy was found shot in the head. The bullet matched the ones in Hasan's revolver, but the report was changed later. In the trial that had lasted barely a month, Damodarbhai had sat in the first row, right next to Hasan Ali.

Till the day of Damodarbhai's violent death, all pictures had Hasan lurking in the background. He was Damodarbhai's shadow.

Once I finished tracking Hasan's photographs with Damodarbhai, I turned my attention to him and Vidhi.

The positions remained the same—Vidhi, a step ahead of Hasan. Hasan, always by her side, his hand firmly on his waist where his pistol rested. The pictures started right from her childhood, of which there weren't many.

The Acharya family maintained that Vidhi had been home-schooled, so she wasn't seen out and about a lot. So, Hasan wasn't seen too. Until, of course, she started acing Mathematics Olympiads. I pored over hundreds of google search results, clippings from magazines and newspaper archives, and old corporate videos.

And then came the moment—the moment of blinding clarity, the feeling of having light thrust inside your body. I felt what Anvesha must have felt quite often. A question arose in my head: *Where was Hasan the day Damodarbhai was murdered?* Why wasn't he with him that day when there were so many pictures of the two jogging together snapped by the paparazzi over the years?

I typed the words 'Damodar's cremation Hasan' and google spat out hundreds of pictures. Hasan wasn't in a single one of them. Even in the images taken a couple of days after the cremation, Hasan didn't look devastated. In most pictures, he looked on dispassionately as if a stranger was murdered. It was a ridiculous thought. I thought numerous times before sharing this with Anvesha, who I knew would poke a million holes in my theory.

'I know,' she said.

'You know what?' I asked.

'That Hasan . . . he could have been the one who stabbed Damodarbhai.'

'What . . .'

'But that's only one half of the equation, Druvan. For a conspiracy to hold, you need to answer why he would kill Damodarbhai. He had nothing to gain.'

I felt breathless. 'What do you do when you sit on a feeling like this? Like you're sitting on an explosive idea that no one else has?'

'You wait. That's the fun thing about these theories. You wait for the puzzle to solve, for your truths to be made public. Pattern recognition is a heady feeling, Druvan. Welcome to my world.'

It was some welcome, because I was sweating buckets. But she was used to this.

'So we wait?'

'Yes.'

A few months later, one of Anvesha's damning predictions came true. It wasn't the one about Hasan. It was about a bill Sanyukta Swaraj's government was about to pass in the parliament.

Acharyas were soon to be the owners of millions of bodies.

Chapter 28: The Acharya Parivar

Our doctor held up both of our reports and looked at them side by side. The bilirubin, albumin and alkaline phosphatase levels were the same right down to the last decimal.

'We are calling it "the soulmate sickness",' I said to the doctor.

Anvesha, her parents and mine rolled their eyes rather aggressively.

'I will call it a severe case of jaundice if that's okay with you, Druvan,' replied the doctor.

'But did you see? It's the same to the last decimal! Have you ever seen a case like this?'

'We thought it was psychosomatic,' said Baba.

'Every time she falls sick, he falls sick as well,' reiterated Mumma.

'The reports aren't lying, Mrs Datta. These two are quite sick,' he said in an accusatory tone, intended for both the sets of parents.

'It's a case of parental negligence,' I added.

It was the third time in five months Anvesha and my intestinal tracts had given up. All three times, we were prescribed

bed rest and antibiotics. The months went past in a haze. From my dominant position after my class 10 board examinations, I slipped to the bottom of the class.

When I entered class 12, feeling healthier, I promised I would eat better, sleep better and smash the fuck out of my entrance examinations. I cut out all distractions except Anvesha. I went about my days in school with blinders on. But despite that, I lacked the motivation and the energy. By the time I would come back home from school, I would be too tired to study. I would spend the days feeling angry at my bad performance. I would often end up fighting with Anvesha. I couldn't help it. The sicknesses had lingering after-effects. I felt constantly spent, cranky and on the edge. The doctor said it was nothing to worry about. It wasn't just me. Anvesha was quick to rile up as well. She hadn't put out a video in a while. When I would ask her, she would shout at me and tell me it wasn't easy. It was an incredibly cranky phase in our relationship.

That day, after an exceptionally bad Chemistry unit test, I headed to the library. Just inside the library, I saw a bunch of humanities students painting posters.

'STOP GIVING PRIVATE COMPANIES THE RIGHT TO KILL!'

'STOP THE PRIVATIZATION OF JAILS!'

'CAPITALISM KILLS!'

'DOWN WITH ACHARYA!'

'VIDHI IS A MURDERER!'

'JAILS SHOULDN'T BE PRIVATIZED!'

I decided to keep walking, while my other classmates stopped. I didn't have the mental strength to get into a conversation. I sat as far away from the humanities students as possible, opened my chemistry book and started to mug up the exceptions. The boys wouldn't shut up. They kept arguing among themselves, despite the librarian shushing them a number of times.

'You think the Acharyas are doing the nation a favour? Bullshit. It's a money-making scheme. The bill says they can make these prisoners work in their factories. That's not even cheap labour! That's free labour! Bro, imagine not paying your workers anything.'

'You're overreacting,' said a bespectacled girl.

'Am I? What about the death penalties that are doled out like they are candies, bro? The Acharya Group, a private company, will hang them, not the government. Don't you think that's wrong?'

The bespectacled girl countered, 'Who the hell cares who's pulling the lever?'

'Can you please shut the fuck up?' I groaned.

The students turned around to look at me.

'I'm sorry, go on,' I said, reminding myself of my chemistry marks, and returned to my book.

They got back to their conversation.

'The bill passes and a million people work for free for the Acharyas! It's slavery.'

'Better a slave than a humanities student,' I said, got up, and left the library.

They passed the bill the next day even as the noise from the activists kept getting louder. But how long and how hard can people scream? A couple of months later, activists, national and international media, writers and actors were called for the inauguration of the first Acharya jail.

All TV channels were broadcasting live. But it wasn't just that. Reactions to these images were also being streamed by live streamers, and one among them was Anvesha.

Mumma, Baba and I watched it from our living room.

On the computer screen, I was watching Anvesha's reactions to the reporting.

I spotted Hasan Ali. He was to cut the ribbon at the entrance to the jail. There were several high-ranking government officials who stood beside him. At a distance, slogans were being shouted against the government and the Acharyas.

In a shocking move, Hasan invited a few activists to join him for a walk through the prison.

'There are people who say that the bill gives the Acharyas free workforce and the power to kill people,' said Anvesha in her stream. 'The last time a private company was allowed to kill people was a couple of centuries ago, and they slowly took over the country. The East India Company. They raised a private army and what not! In the live chat, I can see people saying I'm overreacting . . . fine, fine, maybe I am, but what if I am not? So let's read a few comments now. Amit Narad says . . . I'm making a big deal out of it and it's saving our government a lot of money. Smita Patil says it's a bad decision to privatize jails because it's inefficient. She says in a sarcastic follow-up comment that our judiciary is inefficient, should we privatize that too? So is the police, wouldn't that be great? The efficient police arrest criminals and then the efficient jury and judges give them prison time, where the efficient Acharya machinery can use them as free labour.'

I turned to the TV.

Anvesha was reading out more comments, 'Rishab Datta is asking why am I doubting them so much? And Tanu Singhal says it's our job as citizens to question the things the government is doing with the power we have given them.'

I turned up the volume of the television as the first image of the prison flashed on the screen. It looked like a place of worship—marble floors in the lobby, high ceilings, tall and expansive windows, and a flood of natural light. At the centre of the hall was a colossal statue of Damodarbhai Acharya.

The camera moved and passed the smiling guards who waved at us.

We were in one of the twenty-three buildings, each with fifty circular floors that would house the prisoners. Men with steady cameras strapped to their bodies ran across the floors to give us 360-degree views of the prison.

Anvesha gasped at the opulence. The cells were the size of our bedrooms. They came with a mattress, an attached bathroom, a table, a chair and a lamp.

'Take us to another building!' one of the activists shouted.

I saw Mumma and Baba's face light up too. This was probably just the model. Others would be bad.

Hasan split the group of activists and asked them to pick any of the twenty-three buildings in the prison complex that stretched across hundreds of acres. The activists broke into groups and scattered, hoping to find squalor, dingy rooms and darkness. Men with cameras went behind them to report every minute.

The naysayers tried every tap and it ran water; they switched on every lamp and it worked; they went to the libraries of every building and found the shelves stacked. On some floors, there were deluxe prison suites not for the richer, but the more productive prisoners.

Hasan told the press the deluxe rooms would also be given to prisoners who showed good behaviour, learnt the most and contributed to the country's economy. Outside each building, there was a massive gym, a cricket ground, two tennis courts, table tennis tables, a computer room and countless gardens. Hasan announced that within the next month, thirty-two more prison facilities will be completed around the country, and the Acharya Parivar would invite activists or the media to have a look around.

Anvesha suddenly said out aloud, 'Did you guys hear that? Not Acharya Group . . . but Acharya Parivar . . . hmmm. Are we hearing that for the first time? Do these prisoners belong to the Acharya Group or the Acharya Parivar?'

The chat was immediately populated by comments such as: 'Overreaction ki queen etc.'

The prison tour went on for another twenty minutes. The news channels split their screens and compared the gory images of the current prisons with those of Acharya's prisons.

The activists were defeated. Most returned to their houses, which were probably worse than the prison cells they had just spent a few minutes in.

Now they had all shifted focus to a new concern: Would Sanyukta Swaraj privatize the police and judiciary too?

By the evening, the news channels were reporting not only the massive support the Acharyas were getting from human rights organizations worldwide, but also the rising crime rate. The prisons had set a new standard of living.

Within twenty-four hours, hundreds of cars were jacked, chains snatched and pockets picked. A few even slapped policemen and stabbed them. Slowly, lock-ups started to fill up. Suddenly, robbers were being sloppy and getting caught. Husbands were beating up wives and getting themselves arrested. Some middle-aged men claimed they had taken dowry—a non-bailable offence.

Hundreds and thousands of people wanted to be in the prisons run by the Acharyas than in slums. There were large-scale celebrations in the old jails by the prisoners who were first in line to move to the new prisons.

On the other hand, the families of victims of various crimes were crying foul. They wanted the perpetrators, the assaulters, to be punished, and going to an Acharya prison wasn't punishment.

Anvesha's stream ended with a one-line review of the entire drama, 'It's pretty simple what it is. The Acharyas are taking over the country.' And then, after a pause, she said. 'I know you're listening to this, Vidhi. I know you're taking over the country . . . and who knows, the world? The only question that remains is . . . how? What are you going to do next, Acharya Parivar?'

The words reverberated in my mind all night. I couldn't sleep well. In the morning, I burned with a fever.

'You look bad, Druvan. Fever *acche naa ki?*' Mumma asked me.

On cue, I vomited. I knew I was going to be sick again. At the clinic, I saw a familiar face. Sitting on the ground, bent over, vomiting into a paper bag was Anvesha Mohan. She looked up at me.

'The soulmates are sick again.'

Chapter 29: Soulmates After All

Acharya Life had spared no expense in the rebuilding of Chanakyapuri Hospital. It was a fortress, a palace, a resort, all rolled into one. And yet, I understood why hospitals are built in the blandest way possible—when you're sick, nothing else matters.

In the waiting room, while Anvesha and I were coughing and holding our heads steady lest we vomit again, Rashid was in an exceptionally chirpy mood.

'Little girls you both are. How often do you both fall sick!'

'That's offensive. This is why you should have had a sister,' said Anvesha.

'Rashid, can you please go into the corner and die a little?' I added.

'That's why I say, join Rooh Collective and do their breathing exercises. It will help build immunity.'

'Please go away,' groaned Anvesha.

It had been an hour. Our parents were talking to the doctor who wanted them to go through the treatment options for our recurrent sickness—jaundice, nausea, frequent diarrhoea and the general feeling of discomfort we had been experiencing.

'Bhai, there's a perfect day for the two of you to join also. It's written in the stars, the two of you joining Rooh Collective on the same day as the new guru.'

Anvesha looked at me. We both rolled our eyes.

Soon after Anvesha's videos had started going viral, she had started getting support from unexpected corners. She had elaborate whisper networks with whom she communicated online, and they had all sorts of information for her. She had become a walking repository of strange information. Out of the glut, she would glean information that matched with her second damning prediction. She had got to know of a young man, twenty-one, in Baliya district, UP, who was entering the god-man business.

She was getting reports of villagers travelling miles on foot to meet this new man of God, who spoke many tongues and talked about remembering his last births. He hosted past-life regression therapies for children, who claimed to be haunted by nightmares of previous lives.

He called himself Yogi Ashwinath.

For the past couple of months, Anvesha had been in no position to make a video for her channel. But she made one specifically for me. She stitched together a bunch of videos of Ashwinath, split the screen, and compared them with videos of Firdaus Shirazi.

She pointed out the similarities—their mannerism, their way of talking, the inflections, and even the choice of words.

'He's going to take over from where Firdaus left,' Anvesha said.

'To build a cult, you need to step out of the shadow of the previous guru. Why be a cheap imitation of Firdaus?'

'He was taught by Firdaus, or if you want a crazy one—he's Firdaus reborn. Whatever it might be, he's coming to the take Firdaus's throne, *likh ke le lo* [take it in writing from me].'

I knew better than to bet against Anvesha on matters like this.

Soon after, her prediction came true when the senior council of Rooh Collective made a big deal out of spotting Yogi Ashwinath. They made a swift decision to pass on the mantle to him.

Anvesha hadn't shared this with Rashid, who had gone too far to have a reasoned conversation with.

The doctor knocked at the door.

'They are calling you,' said Rashid. 'Both of you.'

Rashid helped the two of us get up.

'Hope you two find a cure for your frailty,' said Rashid and laughed before we entered the doctor's room.

Inside, we saw our parents doubled over, tears in their eyes.

The doctor made us sit down. He slipped the reports of our biopsies in front of me. There were numbers on it that we didn't understand, a couple of coloured scans, and a bunch of other papers.

He caught our gaze and started to tell the story of our bodies. Quite painfully, he began from the very beginning.

'What has happened to you can happen to anyone,' he said.

The doctor started by telling us about Andy Warhol, whom I didn't know.

'He was a pop-art icon. He was pretty much the one who started it,' said Anvesha.

'What's pop art?'

'You know? Big fonts? Minimal backgrounds?'

I shook my head.

'Fine, have you heard of the phrase "fifteen minutes of fame"? That's him. He coined it. He's a legend in the art circles, Druvan.'

'What does he have to do with us falling sick?'

'He had the same condition as two of you,' said the doctor.

The doctor told us about a little part of the human body—a part he said we could live without—gall bladder.

'Doctor, are you doing this for the first time?'

'Just listen to him, Druvan.'

He told us that the gall bladder serves no real purpose. If it is removed, one might experience indigestion problems. The doctor told us we didn't even need it as much as our ancestors did, as they used to binge-eat and needed the gall bladder to aid digestion. Even astronauts are asked to get them removed.

'It's a useless organ, we get it. Can we move past it now?' I said.

'Let him do it. They tell stories to soften the impact on people like us.'

'Impact of what? Like us? What are we like?'

The doctor continued. There was a sharp segue into biology. He pulled a chart up and showed us the location of the gall bladder.

'We get it. It affects the digestive tract, etc., and this is why we have been falling sick. What now?'

The doctor looked straight at us.

'He will remove our gall bladders. It's a small surgery,' said Anvesha.

'She's right, Druvan.'

'That's awesome. We will soak our gall bladders in formaldehyde, and put them in our showcases. We aren't scared as long as we are both doing it,' I said. I looked at Anvesha. 'Haina?'

'We will also need radiation therapy,' said Anvesha.

'What . . . why?'

The doctor didn't say anything.

Anvesha continued, 'That's what they do when your cancer starts from your gall bladder. They take it out and blast you with x-rays to kill your cancer cells. That's the basic funda . . . '

My head spun.

'But . . . that's . . . will we be fine? It's cancer . . . like proper cancer? Like cancer, cancer? Bald people, teary movies *wala* cancer? But I feel fine . . . I feel okay. How can we get cancer?'

'Ask the doctor.'

'Anvesha's correct. It's cancer. That's what I wanted to take you through,' said the doctor.

'But will we be okay?' I looked at Anvesha. 'What happened to that Andy Warhol guy?'

'He died a few days after his gall bladder was removed.'

'Okay, but he was old, right?'

'Fifty-eight.'

'So then we are young. Young people do better, don't they? We will fight this. They say will is everything, don't they?'

Anvesha shook her head again.

'Stop being a bobblehead, Anvesha.'

'Baby, only 5 per cent people survive each year after they are diagnosed with this cancer.'

I turned to the doctor. 'Then why the fuck did you not diagnose this earlier? We have been coming here for two entire years!'

'Druvan, please sit down,' said the doctor.

'Sit down, Druvan,' said Anvesha.

The doctor continued, 'The survival rate is low because it's hard to diagnose. Early diagnosis is very rare in a case like yours.'

'It's the hardest cancer to diagnose,' said Anvesha like some fucking science textbook.

'And yet you seemed to have diagnosed it, nahi?' I snapped at Anvesha.

'I guessed it.'

'Some guess.'

I leaned back into the chair, and tried to collect myself. A deathly silence engulfed us. I could hear our mothers softly weep. A few moment passed. Or maybe an hour. I stared at the hazy scans in front of me which looked like Van Gogh's abstract paintings.

'What happens now?'

'We prepare to die as soulmates,' said Anvesha.

Chapter 30: Dying

Fuck being strong. I wasn't strong. I was furious and the rage took away my ability to reason.

'We've existed for so long. Like we are here now, we lived, and we will be gone tomorrow? Just gone? Thin air? Would we be nothing? You know . . . I'm here, I want to be here,' I said.

Anvesha looked at me. She wanted me to be strong, so our parents wouldn't disintegrate under grief.

'Everyone dies. We are just scheduled for an earlier date than most.'

'Don't give me that nonsense. It's not fair. Why us? Like . . . why? Give me one reason, why?'

On our way back to Anvesha's home, Mumma, Baba and Uncle, Aunty were inconsolable. Their only children were dying.

'There's still a 5 per cent chance,' said Anvesha, who was taking this quite well, better than all of us.

It was a hollow assurance. Baba held my hand in the van as if I was running away. My memories of his touch were of a hard hand, a firm grip. Now I felt a change—fifty-three years had undone the tautness, the muscularity. Mumma rubbed my back and neck. How crushing it must be for them. I felt my anger melt. I would be nothing, gone, but they would have to deal with my absence.

The one dying is never the hero of the story.

Once we were back home, the men frantically dialled numbers to take second and third opinions. It's easier to hunt for solutions that don't exist than face emotional upheaval. To surrender takes more courage. The women had begun to accept the fate and dealt with it through tears and warm hugs.

'I'm sorry,' said Aunty to Mumma. 'That day . . .'

It came back to all of us in an instant. The mothers had wished death on each other's children. Their curses had come true.

'What's this nonsense, Mummy! It could have happened to anyone,' butted in Anvesha.

Over the next few days, my body slowly started to break down. Meanwhile, Anvesha made a folder on the chronology of our treatment. It made for morbid reading. She told me about the medicines, the therapy, the pain, the highs and the lows of it. And despite knowing what it would all lead to—a loss of dignity, sanity and, eventually, death—she maintained a cheery optimism about it.

'We have each other, don't we?' she said.

'Had you died alone, I would have followed soon after.'

'That's a silly, romantic notion. But if you were not sick, you would have to live your life and be a child to both our parents.'

It wasn't lost on either of us that our deaths would mean they would stop being parents. No longer Baba, Mumma and Papa, Mummy.

'I would die of a broken heart.'

Anvesha rolled her eyes.

'What? Wait . . . I would really die of a broken heart.'

'No one dies of a broken heart.'

'Wait a minute. Damn! Is this the moment, Anvesha? This is the moment, isn't it? Here, I know something you don't.'

'What do you know?'

'Takotsubo cardiomyopathy! No, no, don't google.'

'Go on,' she said irritably.

'This is the best day ever.'

'Can you please . . . '

'So this is an unexplained condition which got discovered in the 1990s in Japan. Usually, in couples deeply in love, like us, their hearts beat in sync. Can you imagine that? It's crazy. If one dies before the other that synchronicity breaks. The other dies of a swollen left ventricle and mysteriously weakened heart muscles. Your heart literally breaks and you die.'

Anvesha wasn't used to this happening, so she googled it.

'I got you to google something. Now I can die in peace,' I said.

'Stop saying that. Always remember, 5 per cent.'

In the days before the surgery, the fathers remained stoical, while the mothers broke down often.

Rashid, meanwhile, had treated the news of our death with nonchalance.

'Bhai, *aise thodi mar jaoge, fight maarenge* [You won't die so easily, we will fight this],' he had said and then set about sending our reports to his entire network in Rooh Collective.

With every passing day, Rashid shrank in size. It was as if he was joining us in our death.

'Plunge a knife into me, Rashid. Maybe I will be reborn,' I said to him.

'Don't joke. Nothing is going to happen to you two. Allah is watching.'

It was the first time he had taken his God's name in years. Whether it was a slip of the tongue or a desperate plea, I didn't know. Despite Rashid moving heaven and earth, and getting the top doctors of the country to look at our reports, nothing changed. The diagnosis, the percentages—all remained the same.

On the day of the surgery, Rashid's contact came through. He got us permission to be operated on tables next to each other.

The assistant doctors attached the probes to us. Our parents were nervous wrecks.

'Hi, Doctor? Can you check if our heartbeats are in sync?' asked Anvesha.

The doctors checked the monitors. They looked at each other, then at us, and smiled.

'You better not die on me, Druvan.'

They closed the door of the operation theatre. Masks pumping oxygen and anaesthesia were put on our faces. The doctor started counting.

'See you on the other side,' said Anvesha.

'Whichever side that is.'

Chapter 31: A Crash Course in Reincarnation

We survived the removal of our gall bladders. However, the worst was yet to come. With every passing day, we inched a little closer to death. That's the fantastic thing about cancer—you die hundreds of little deaths till the big one comes. You don't know what your pain threshold is till you cross it and a more painful experience awaits you.

'You need money, bhai? Tell me,' Rashid told me. 'Where do you want to go?' Choose the country and I will book it right away.'

'Death should come on a normal day, Rashid,' said Anvesha.

'Why? There's so much to see!'

'How much? How much would be enough? A trip to an amusement park, followed by a trek up a mountain and then a meal at a Michelin-starred restaurant? When can you possibly think you have lived enough, loved enough?'

'This sounds pretty good,' I said. 'When we are dead, and people look at our Instagram profiles, there should be something, nahi?'

'Doing nothing is a gift.'

I thought for a moment and knew it was the truth.

'Bhai, can you at least—'

'FINE!' snapped Anvesha and I together.

Anvesha and I were too exhausted to argue. He wanted us to talk to a Rooh Collective *mrityu* (death) counsellor.

On a Sunday, when both of us weren't feeling our worst, he drove us to the Rooh Collective ashram.

'Not many get the chance you're getting, bhai,' said Rashid.

'Yes, true, it's one of the rarest cancers, so that's quite some luck,' I said.

'Rashid, you can get angry at him. The cancer isn't what has made him annoying. He was always like this,' said Anvesha.

I felt a strong sense of déjà vu when Anvesha and I, the crankiest cancer patient ever, entered the ashram. I had seen the ashram too many times on television for it to be unfamiliar. Rashid led us straight to Tarun Katial, a mrityu counsellor, whom he had praised so much that I expected him to be an older man.

He was in his mid-thirties and wore thick, round spectacles. In his lap was a thick book, frayed at the edges. He kept it aside and smiled at us.

'Come, come,' he said. 'Sit. I'm Tarun. You must be Druvan and Anvesha.'

'And you're a mrityu counsellor. Is that like your official job title?' I asked sarcastically.

'Stop it, Druvan,' said Anvesha.

'I want to understand what he does. What does he know about death that we don't?'

'He's quite known here, bhai.'

'Does he have cancer too? Is it prostate cancer? Because it would need quite a few balls to hold a job title like his.'

'I see you're quite angry,' said Tarun.

'Is that what you write on your résumé? Mrityu counsellor?'

'As you would find in a few days, it's a very important job to have. In my résumé, it comes right after the mention of my degrees from IIT Delhi and IIM Kolkata, and the five years of work experience at McKinsey and Company.'

'Was it the stress that broke you? Just blink if you're held captive here,' I asked him.

'You're funny. I like it. Till the time your sense of humour is intact, death can't touch you,' said Tarun.

'Why don't you go and tell that to Robin Williams?'

'The only difference between him and you is that you want to live. And that's why you're here. Rashid said it took some persuasion.'

'Did we really want to meet a mrityu counsellor? The answer is no.'

Tarun wasn't one to be easily riled up. 'I don't blame you. What we do here is questionable at best, lunatic at worst. Who would believe in reincarnation without any proof? Haina? I'm with you, Druvan.' He looked at Anvesha. 'You seem to be more on board though.'

'Don't go by me. I believe in UFOs being real, the 9/11 attack being masterminded by the US itself, and IPL matches being fixed to the last ball. Also, that Firdaus himself trained your new guy, Ashwinath.'

Tarun Katial laughed. 'Fair points. But listen to me, you're dying. You have nothing to lose, so why not believe you could be reincarnated?'

'We don't want to die as fools,' I said.

'What does it take to be reincarnated?' asked Anvesha.

'According to them?' I butted in. 'Meditation and living mindfully. Am I right, mrityu counsellor?'

'You're right, Druvan, absolutely right. Meditation brings us stillness. Our soul's restless. Your mind and body know the pain, and hence they fear the pain they will experience when you die. But they don't fear death itself because they have never experienced it. Your soul, on the other hand, has been through many life cycles, knows death intimately, and it fears the uncertainty. The uncertainty of what the next life would bring.'

'That's some next-level nonsense.'

Rashid glared at me.

'Does this make sense to you, Rashid?'

'Bhai, listen to him,' begged Rashid.

'When you die, your soul tries to find another body. If your memories are deep and intimate, if your experiences are visceral, it makes it easier for the soul to retain the memories in the next birth. That's how you remember having lived before,' said Tarun, his eyes now glinting.

'I have heard all of this before and you might have a better voice than Rashid's, but bullshit is still bullshit.'

'Bhai.'

'Why should I listen to him?'

Tarun Katial smiled, paused, like we were on a satsang channel and said, '. . . because I remember my past life.'

'Wah! Is it time for another story?'

'Who were you then? How did you die? What do you remember?' interrogated Anvesha.

'Don't lie to her. She has a very strong bullshit detector.'

He looked away from me and towards Anvesha. 'What I remember now came to me slowly over the years. When I was young, I kept seeing myself dying in an accident. My father was riding pillion with me on a noisy motorcycle. We got crushed under the tyres of a truck. My father died in front of me.'

'Well, that's called hallucinating. You imagined a scenario that wasn't real.'

Tarun snapped his fingers excitedly. He said, 'Exactly! That's what I said to my therapist. I used to keep seeing this dream repeatedly. And not just that, more details kept adding on. I would imagine being a student of Sanskrit in Hindu College, when I had no interest in the language. Why did I dream of taking up Sanskrit as my subject? And then there was a house. I would show the therapist sketches, but she would wave them away dismissively. It was quite obvious that she thought I was hallucinating.'

'He found the house,' said Rashid. '. . . and the damaged motorcycle in their garage.'

'How did you find the house?' asked Anvesha.

'When the medications didn't work, I resorted to my daily walks, the only activity that calmed me down. Every day I was drawn to the Punjabi Bagh housing blocks, which were quite a few kilometres away. I walked around aimlessly for months. And then I found it. The house from my dreams.'

Rashid added, 'Months before Tarunji was born, a young man had died in a motorcycle accident. Tarunji told them the motorcycle model before they showed it to him.'

Tarun continued, 'I saw the man's—my father from my previous life—face from my dreams on the wall. We both died on the same day. The family still lived in the house.'

'Lamest story ever,' I said.

'Do you believe it?' Tarun asked Anvesha.

'What I believe is that the story of the death of the son and father, a gruesome death no less, travelled the locality and reached you. It found a place in your brain where you slowly started adding more details to it. On your walks, you must have seen the motorcycle been taken out for cleaning. It registered in your head. With time, your imagination took shape. You added the correct model of the motorcycle to your dream; you added the likeliness of the man who died, whose picture you might have seen on the dashboard of one of their other cars. Your mind played tricks and concocted this story, and it found affirmation at the house.'

Tarun nodded appreciatively.

He looked at Rashid and said, 'You were right. She's quite good at conspiracies.'

'What's your truth?'

'The truth is,' said Tarun, ' . . . that the soul exists.' Just then, a bell rang. He got up. 'It's time for my class. All I would suggest is, live more mindfully, breathe, do some yoga, still yourself. There's nothing to lose. But if it works, who knows, thirteen years later, you might walk back into Rashid's life as a pesky teenager!'

He pressed into our palms forms to join Rooh Collective, after signing which we could attend his sessions for the almost dead.

'That's quite a specific course name,' pointed out Anvesha.

'Because it's these people who need it the most.'

He walked to the group of students who were waiting for him. Some of them were bald because they had cancer, some were being pushed in wheelchairs by their parents—fools, all of them.

'I will see you in a bit, bhai,' said Rashid.

Once he walked away, Anvesha asked me, 'Why did he say his job will become the most important job in the world?'

'He's a fraud.'

Desperation makes you believe the most nonsensical of things, because back home, the fraud's words echoed in my head.

Did Anvesha and I die together in our past birth? Did our souls get born together? Isn't that what Baba had said to Uncle when we were born? That we were soulmates? Why was I resisting the existence of souls when I always believed Anvesha and I were soulmates? What if souls existed? If what he had said was true, if souls did get recycled in a soul version of a paper mache factory, had I lived mindfully enough to be reborn? What if Anvesha remembered this life in her next? What if I didn't?

I sat up straight. I closed my eyes and tried to still my ragged breathing. I tried remembering the life I had lived. My concentration wavered. I tried another way. I wrote down things about my life, read and reread the letters Anvesha and I had accumulated, pored over the pictures of me, Mumma and Baba. My life wasn't half bad. I deserved another life.

Chapter 32: The First Day of Humanity

As time rolled by, Mumma, Baba and I started spending more and more time at Anvesha's house. There were two spare rooms that we occupied. The Mohans would not let us leave. The hospital was close by and that was their pretext. Their real fear, though, was being left alone. With Mumma and Baba around, they had someone who knew exactly what it felt like to have a dying child in the house.

That day, Uncle and Aunty dragged the cot outside to the balcony like they often did. Baba roasted some makhanas for us, and Mumma kept two basins with their lids on beside us, just in case we felt like vomiting.

We put the radio on, tuned into our favourite channel and to the radio jockey who solved the love troubles of married men and young girls alike. We settled inside our blankets.

I read the scripts of her next few videos and watched the rough cuts that had already been shot. This was a bucket list in itself—to complete the videos. To make up for the lack of videos, Anvesha had started streaming. Streaming didn't require the precision or research that a conspiracy video did. Just switch on the webcam and go—raw, unfiltered. She could put forth a conspiracy and then debunk it in the next one. Surprisingly, her consistent streams ramped up her popularity and let the viewers get more intimately connected with her.

For a long time, Anvesha hadn't shared her diagnosis with her followers. She didn't want the sympathy. But her gaunt face, her sunken eyes, the beanies she wore made it too obvious. When the word got out about her diagnosis, a wave of sympathy rocked her channel numbers. Her viewership—on the back of her disease—quadrupled.

It wasn't just she who was getting popular.

In a few videos, she called out my name. 'Druvan, can you please give me water?' 'Druvan, can you check the light?' 'Druvan, can you lower the volume, please?' The viewers picked up on it. Was I the boyfriend of their favourite video creator? The question raged on in her forums. The romantics hoped it was the case. When it was no longer possible to keep me under wraps, Anvesha introduced me to her audience as the dying boyfriend. The forums collectively sighed. Some called me handsome, others were jealous, but, either way, we came to be known as the dying couple—who were also conspiracy theorists—among our audiences.

That morning, lying outside on the cot, I started to doze off. She slipped her leg into my blanket and brushed it against mine.

'You're disturbing me,' I joked.

'What? I'm not doing anything.'

I thought we had been caught when I heard Uncle shout from inside. Once, twice.

'Bitku! SEE THIS!' he shouted.

We dragged ourselves out of the cot and then trudged towards the living room, where Uncle sat in front of the TV, mouth agape.

'What?' groaned Anvesha irritably.

'This is Ten Sports. Every channel is showing this, Bitku.'

We turned towards the TV. The logo of the Acharya Group was flashing on the screen. Anvesha flipped through the channels. It was on every channel, be it sports, travel, or general entertainment.

'There must be some glitch. Let me try again.'

Just then, Vidhi Acharya appeared on the screen, draped in a tricolour saree, a small bindi shining on her forehead, arms chock-full of gold trinkets. She folded her hands, which were painted red with *alta*.

'Jai Shri Krishna.'

The cameras panned back. Vidhi Acharya was standing on a dais, a crowd of news microphones placed in front of her. The subscript read: Acharya Gardens.

'When did it open?' asked Baba.

For the past ten years, the 1000-acre Acharya Gardens had been under construction. It had remained mysteriously barricaded with reinforced asbestos sheets taller than entire buildings. People had wondered what architectural monstrosity would emerge from it.

The first few haphazard pans around the complex made us all sit up.

The perspective of the camera shifted to one mounted on a drone that hovered inside the main gate of the Acharya Gardens. The camera pans slowed down, and, for the first time, we saw what had become of the gardens.

It totally blew our minds.

There were endless rows of intricately carved stone pillars touching the sky. It seemed like the tops were lost in the clouds. They looked ancient, as if each massive stone had been placed over the other by an army of men, using nothing but their hands. Made of out sandstone and marble, inlaid with gems, they glittered and blinded the lenses. It felt as if the sky itself was the roof and these pillars were holding it up.

When the cameras zoomed in, the etchings on the stone pillars came into focus, which were from religious texts such as the Mahabharata, Ramayana, the Vedas, the Quran, etc.

It was part medieval temple architecture, part fantasy.

Between each of the giant pillars, each the size of a high-rise apartment building, there were towering stone sculptures of Ram, Arjun, Krishna and the like.

The camera turned towards the ground. There were people there—the press—and they looked like ants.

The stage on which Vidhi Acharya stood was a thousand feet above the ground. It was built like a chariot, the size of which would dwarf the Konark Temple.

Twenty colossal and magnificently sculpted horses pulled the chariot, which had twenty wheels carved out of a single piece of rock, each at least a hundred feet high. It looked like the horses would come to life any instant. They would break into a gallop and the earth would tremble under their hooves.

The guards who stood at the edges of the platform were so high up, they wouldn't have been able to make out the face of one journalist from the other. The people below were cockroach-like, sweating in the sweltering heat, waiting for Vidhi Acharya to speak.

The sun was now setting. It was Anvesha who noticed it. She squinted at the screen.

On the platform, just behind where Vidhi Acharya and the rest of the Acharya family stood, was an army of stone warriors. They were sculpted so intricately that it felt like they would come to life and brandish their swords and spears.

'They are kings and queens,' said Anvesha. 'There's Raja Raja I, and that . . . that's Akbar . . . and those are the old Kuru kings . . . there's everyone. What . . . what are they doing here?'

Just as Anvesha said this, the feed cut to the images from the drone cameras as they flew between the rows of stone sculptures of dead kings and queens.

'The older ones are larger,' pointed out Anvesha.

They were placed in ascending order of height. The older ones larger, the newest ones right in front, smaller, like a choir.

The first row had kings we had all seen pictures of— Bahadur Shah Żafar, the Nizam of Hyderabad . . . The drones swooped behind and the Mughal kings appeared in all their finery, chiselled down to the last detail, every fold in their fabric captured.

Then came the Mewar kings, the maharajas of Cochin, and kings of the Vijaynagara Dynasty. A few rows behind, the statues were two-storey high. They were of Ahom Dynasty, the Qutb Shahi and the Bahmani Dynasty, and the Delhi Sultanate. Statues of Alauddin Khilji and Chakrawadh Singha looked like they would reach out and crush the drones between their fingers. Further back were Hosalya and the Chandra Dynasty kings, the Palas, and the Pratiharas. The drones looked like little flies hovering in front of the eyes of the Pallava Dynasty kings of the fourth century. Just behind them were the Indo-Parthian kings— Iranian kings who had ruled parts of India—and another lineage of Indo-Scythian rulers, again from Iran.

The statues grew in epic proportions. The first in the God-like reproductions were the great Cholas, whose rule started in third century BC, right next to the Pandya kings, Shunga kings, and Porus, the man who defeated Alexander the Great. Then came the last line of kings—the ones who straddled the thin line between myth and legend—the Mauryas and Nandas, who were more legend, less myth, and then the kings of Magadha, more myth than legend.

The feed cut back to Vidhi Acharya.

Neither of us could speak. All of Indian history was laid out in front of us. Every recorded king, every notable queen, every year of the existence of the land south of the Himalayas and north of the great Indian Ocean accounted for. This was a world beyond anyone's imagination.

'Why would do they that?' I asked.

The drones hadn't finished with their aerial acrobatics. On the side, there were hundreds of other figures. I couldn't recognize them, but Anvesha told me they were sages and saints and Sufis, and monks and yogis who had shaped the Indian consciousness.

It seemed as if at any moment, they would stand up and start walking. I recognized only two of the lot—Ramkrishna Paramhansa, whose pictures were in our house, and Paramhansa Yogananda, whose book, *The Autobiography of a Yogi*, I had read before. My excitement petered when I saw Firdaus Shirazi's statue.

'Only religious men are important?' I said.

As if the drones had heard me, they took a sharp right to where another bunch of statues awaited. I noticed Rabindranath Tagore, Swami Vivekananda, Homi Bhabha, A.P.J. Abdul Kalam, among many others, who were dressed in ancient robes, or nothing at all. Uncle named them in quick succession—Aryabhatta, Bhaskara, Brahmagupta, Chanakya and so on. They were scientists, surgeons, and men of literature and philosophy, and they outnumbered the religious men, shutting me up immediately.

The camera cut back to Vidhi Acharya, and her family who stood behind her. The camera stayed focused for a while on the wife of Damodarbhai Acharya, Ramaben, and then on their children, and the rest of the family.

'Everyone's there,' I said.

'It's time,' said Anvesha.

'Time for what?' I asked.

She turned to look at me and said, 'The world's going to change.' Anvesha turned up the volume.

Chapter 33: Aatma

Vidhi Acharya spoke. Her voice boomed through the gardens and our living room.

'Thank you for the support you have extended to us over the years.'

'Did you hear her? Over the years? How many years?' butted in Anvesha.

'It has made the Acharya family what it is today . . . among the great men and women from our history that you see on this stage. Today's a big day for the Parivar and the rest of our country. Together we walk towards a new tomorrow, a new dawn, where we will be stronger, where we will be more knowledgeable, where everyone will carry faith in their hearts. We will be where all the kings, the sages, the men of science and word, wanted our country to be. For the first time, truly, we will be the *sone ki chidiya* of the world. And we, the Parivar, have taken the responsibility to usher Bharat and every Bharatvasi into this new, glorious future. Today, we are here to announce . . .'

Vidhi Acharya's voice trailed away.

'The children don't have the charm of their father,' remarked Mumma.

'Aunty, wait,' said Anvesha.

Vidhi spoke again, 'It's better we hear from. . . '

A screen descended on the platform, and a video started to play. It was Damodarbhai Acharya.

'Fuck, it's starting,' mumbled Anvesha under her breath.

'Anvesha?' scolded Aunty.

'She's dying, Aunty, she can swear,' I said.

In the video, Damodarbhai was sitting in his study, looking healthy . . . and alive.

'Jai Shri Krishna,' he said 'I have waited for this day for a long time. I have counted my days to be among you, to explain my demise and ask for forgiveness for the dreadful murder that took place twenty-eight years ago. I want to start with an apology to the entire Acharya family for my untimely death. I want you to forgive me for any pain that I might have caused you. But my death was necessary. Shri Ram willed it, so how could I have not died?'

'What's he talking about?' I said.

Was Damodar still alive? Why was he apologizing for his death? Did he fake his death? That didn't make any sense. There was a body that was still being researched on at the Acharya Life hospital. Moreover, he didn't look a day older than the day he died.

'Shh,' said Anvesha.

'Two days from now I will be murdered,' he announced.

'Did he say two days from now? What is now? Like today? But he's already dead? Oh, wait, this is an old video?' I said.

The camera panned out. There was another man on the screen. A man I recognized—a much younger Hasan Ali.

'This is the man who will carry out the job of killing me. Two days later, he's going to stab me to death. He's Hasan Ali, my friend.'

On the stage, Hasan Ali emerged from the shade and bowed to the big screen. The journalists gasped.

Damodarbhai Acharya continued, 'All of you watching this video would have either seen me or heard about my death. My death was for a purpose, and today, my countrymen, we fulfil that purpose.'

On cue, the entire stage lit up in a warm glow. The light of thousands of diyas and torches flooded the gardens slowly, sequentially. The gardens thrummed with mystical energy.

It was as if all of the past, present and future stemmed from this moment. The drone cameras reached the skies, and it felt like the Acharya Gardens were the centre of the universe and all of humanity. A thousand acres of land and stone bathed in warm, yellow light. Fires from the more giant torches licked the now dark sky. The music changed. A low hum of drums could be heard.

Damodarbhai Acharya's voice seemed distorted. It was now more resonant, had more bass, and it seemed to thrum in our chests. The reverberations made it feel like it wasn't coming from the screen's speakers but from the dark clouds above. His voice echoed and even the tinny speakers of Anvesha's TV trembled with its intensity.

He spoke in Hindi, then in Bengali, in Tamil, Malayalam, Punjabi and Assamese, 'The girl or boy that you now see in front of you is the result of the hard work of the people working in the new division that we will announce today. The one you see in front of you will lead you into the light, to the new future of humankind, to immortality!'

We heard claps and thalis being banged in the neighbourhood.

'What are they cheering for?' I asked.

And just then, diyas lit up around Vidhi Acharya, the adopted daughter. Her face was radiant with the yellow glow of the fire around her.

He continued, 'This is the beginning of the history. The blood in my veins, the flesh of my body, my mortal remains were all but a small sacrifice.'

The feed cut to the video of Damodarbhai's murder we had all seen before. His murder had been caught on a CCTV camera. Damodarbhai was relentlessly stabbed to death by an unknown assailant during his morning jog. It was one of the most viewed videos on the Internet.

But this time, the video wasn't grainy like the one we had seen growing up.

As the video played, the frame got wider. No one had seen these angles before. The frame got even wider. There were more people in the frame other than the assailant and Damodarbhai.

There were three people holding lights, two people holding boom microphones, five people holding secondary film cameras. A heavy-duty primary camera was mounted on a crane—we had seen footage from this camera, and thought it to be from a CCTV camera.

The crew's faces came into the video.

Damodarbhai's murder was shot by a twenty-people film crew, with high-speed film cameras, and directed by a director I recognized as Anubha Kashyap.

The murder played out. Hasan, his face now lit up with lights held up by spot boys, plunged the knife into Damodarbhai's rib cage. The Arri Alexa cameras caught the grimace on Hasan's face.

The knife punctured Damodarbhai's skin. He smiled at his murderer, held his shoulder, and pushed the knife further in, embracing his death.

He murmured, 'Jai Shri Krishna.'

There were shots of a weeping Hasan, grunting and stabbing Damodar repeatedly, beads of sweat streaming down his face. Hasan slumped to the ground, and Damodarbhai lay dying, a close-up showed him smiling, eyes vacant as if he had already stepped into the afterlife. *Shukriya*, he murmured to Hasan, who sat there, looking at the blood in his hands.

Then there was a booming instruction from the director, 'Hasan! Leave the frame! Cut!'

The director called for the next shot, 'Silence. Roll sound. Action!' We were watching the behind the scenes of the murder video.

The screen blacked out, and Damodarbhai Acharya came back on.

'My death, which will be shot two days from now, will be real; what you saw did happen,' he said. '. . . but I died for us.'

The music stopped. There was deathly silence. Outside, no one clapped or banged thalis.

He spoke in a low voice as if telling us a story, a secret, 'Forty-four years ago, I was in a car accident on the Gujarat–Maharashtra highway. By the time they got me to the hospital, my heart had stopped, my lungs had deflated, my brain had stopped processing, and the blood had stopped flowing in my veins. I was declared dead. Was this my end? At fifty-four, I was a family man, I had two children, a wife, a business, and this was all that would be left of my existence? A decomposing corpse?'

A moment of silence.

'And then I got another chance at life. Six minutes later, under the desperate defibrillating pads that coursed thousands of volts through my body, my heart was made to beat again. I came back from the dead. In those six minutes of my death, I knew I was *dead*. *Maine apni mrityu ka har pal mehsoos kiya tha* [I experienced every bit of my death]. But if I were dead, how could I feel my death? How was I mourning my death? Who was missing his sons and wife? Where did those feelings come from, if my body was decomposing?'

The drumming became more intense and the thousands of little flames flickered.

'For those six minutes, I knew there was more to us than our bodies. I was living even while I was dead. I could feel, think, worry, panic, regret. What was it if not the soul? I wasn't lost. My existence wasn't wiped out like I had never existed. In those six minutes of death, I was still alive. *Main zinda tha*. My soul was alive and felt every moment of my death. My body was dead, but I wasn't.'

In that instant, everyone held their breath.

'The moment my body came back to life, I knew the soul existed, and it carried all the sins, the deeds, the memories of one's life. The soul exists. The *aatma* exists.'

The flames of the torches blazed brighter.

What.

Chapter 34: Vidhi Damodar Acharya

Damodarbhai's tone changed to that of a professor.

He said, 'Soon, after my near-death experience, the Acharya Parivar instituted a new division that was to be kept a secret from the entire world—the Aatma Vibhag or the Soul department. We brought together our country's leading scientists, mystics and people of God, with the single aim of finding evidence of the human soul. And if the soul exists, where does it go? Where would my soul have gone had my body died? Would it have found a home in a new body? If souls existed, the philosophers argued, so should reincarnations. So we spent years recording people who remembered their past lives; decades went into finding the energy signature of the soul. We went to the basics, the foundations of matter, of the universe. We struggled, we hit dead-ends. Most times the stories of reincarnations didn't match. Some were downright lying. We were slowly beginning to believe that death was death. And then, like the light in a cold, damp dungeon, Firdaus Shirazi came into the Parivar's life. Firdaus told us that not only did the soul exist, but looked for new vessels. He told us he remembered his past lives, not one but all the hundreds of times he had lived and died. He told us all our bodies house souls that are thousands of years old, born and born again. We initially thought Firdaus Shirazi, like the others, was a fraud. Our team of astronomers and historians analysed his memories. Hypnotists extracted more details of his past lives. His stories were all true, down to every last detail.'

We looked at Anvesha.

Damodarbhai continued, 'With that, our hypothesis was confirmed—the soul exists. We could breathe again. He gave our department life. On Firdaus's suggestion, we split the Aatma Vibhag into two parts. The first one, named the Reincarnation department, was to research the soul's journey into new lives, into newborn babies. The second, the Soul Transference and Transplant department, was to facilitate cutting-edge exploration into the idea of transferring a soul into a living body. Firdaus Shirazi headed the Reincarnation department.

'He had the responsibility of tracking souls. We started our quest to find out where the soul went after death, to trace its journey across bodies. The possibilities were endless. For the clinical trials, we needed both men and women. It was then that Firdaus's followers volunteered. We started the trials. Over the next decade, hundreds of people placed their trust in the Parivar. They laid down their lives for the project. Their bodies were put through simulations of near-death experiences to find evidence of the soul and mark its characteristics. Some came back, but others died. After years of toil, the Parivar and its supporters uncovered the biggest mystery of the humankind—*the soul is immortal!* It's our greatest honour and privilege to tell each and every one of you watching this, everyone who has died, and everyone who will die—the soul doesn't die. Each one of us has a soul that will never die. It lives on. It's immortal. WE. ARE. IMMORTAL!

'More than a thousand brave men and women sacrificed their lives for the Reincarnation department. They will go down in history as martyrs. These men and women of Rooh Collective donated their bodies for the greater purpose.'

Tickers with thumbnail pictures of thousands of men and women, who were smiling, one hand placed over their chests, ran across the TV screen.

'This was *murder*,' said Anvesha.

Damodarbhai continued, 'We have God on our side. We have succeeded in preparing the soul for death and tracking it in its next life. We can now trace souls across births. We have tracked souls of dead Rooh Collective volunteers into their next lives with some degree of success. Firdaus's research has told us that the souls have been reincarnated in babies born a little distance away from the death of the previous body. Every one of you, your soul has come from someone who died around you when you were in your mother's womb.'

'Firdaus found the spiritual pathway to reincarnation. But it doesn't come easy. One has to make sacrifices, endure pain to continue living even after one's death. Men and women have to die violently for their souls to be tracked. And before their death, they have to live their lives mindfully, be aware of their experiences. How do you find a soul that's reborn? You can't be pursued in your next life unless the soul prepares for another birth.

'A baby is conceived without a soul. But our research tells us that it starts to get ready to receive a soul in the tenth week, when the foetal brain areas—the cerebrum, cerebellum, the brain stem and hypothalamus—are up and running. This process does not start until folds are formed in the cerebral cortex, where our cognitive functionality fits.

'It's now when the biggest test for the soul starts. The soul tries to hold on to its previous life. The brain capacity of a baby is minuscule, making it more challenging. For weak souls, the memories, the subconscious is lost. Only the ones that lived lives survive. But that's not the hardest part—you need to be discovered. How do you do that? It was what Firdaus had done in the past. Let's look at some foetal scans of the Rooh Collective followers who died and were reborn as babies.'

Grainy black-and-white pregnancy scans of babies popped up on the screen. They were a month apart. In each scan, there was a commonality. All the babies' hands were splayed.

'When you receive your new body as a newborn, you don't close your fists. You spend five months with your hand stretched out in your mother's womb. And *dekha jaaye toh*, it makes sense. It's the closing of the fists that gives the palms fate lines, *haath ki lakeere*. But why would you need these lines when your soul has lived before? All reincarnated babies are born with their hands stretched out, not a single *haath ki lakeer*. That's how you identify the reincarnated babies.

'But we still needed to sift through thousands of babies born every day. The only viable way of doing that was to assume the reigns of the healthcare industry of this great country and place it under the aegis of the Acharya Parivar. After years of drudgery, we can now track almost every breath in this country. No baby is born without us knowing.'

Damodar smiled proudly.

He continued, 'We persevered through the difficulties to perfect reincarnation. While Firdaus was trying to perfect his spiritual pathway of Reincarnation, we turned to science—our Soul Transference and Transplant department. Scientists are now trying to transplant souls into living bodies, replacing souls to say. We envisioned a world where a worthy person would get another chance to live. A person's soul could be transferred into the body of another person who didn't deserve to live.'

A swift breeze blew and stoked the diyas. The flames leapt up, lit the stone faces of the dead kings who had died only to be born again. Whose bodies were now ashes and dust, but whose souls were drifting through bodies across centuries.

His voice trailed away, and the diyas dimmed. Soft, ominous music played from the speakers.

'As of now, we haven't succeeded completely,' Damodarbhai continued, with a bright, childish smile, as if to answer my question. 'But by God's grace, we will succeed some day if at all God's given us the means to do it.' He folded his hands. '*Aur jaane se pehle, main aapko kuchh batana chahta hai* [Before I go, I want to tell you something]. Two days from now, Hasan Ali will murder me. Two months ago, I was diagnosed with a neuroendocrine tumour . . . I am dying. Time . . . is running out. The Parivar and I have decided that I should follow the path of my brave brothers and sisters from Rooh Collective, who have died for us. I have decided to be reincarnated. My soul will be marked by Hasan's violence against me. I'm prepared for my next life. My soul's ready.'

Just then, a young Firdaus Shirazi walked into the screen and kept his hand over Damodarbhai's shoulder. The three men—Damodarbhai Acharya, Firdaus Shirazi and Hasan Ali—folded their hands.

Damodarbhai said, 'See you in my next life. I don't know who will carry my soul, but I hope that body serves my countrymen as this body has.'

The screen went blank and melted into the darkness. The torches around Vidhi Damodar Acharya on the stage flared up.

Chapter 35: The Science of the Soul

'Jai Shri Krishna,' announced Vidhi Damodar Acharya. 'I'm him, and he's me. I'm Damodarbhai Acharya, reborn!'

Hundreds of conches trumpeted in unison. The drums joined in and the ground seemed to tremble—it felt like the sound of the cosmos was ricocheting off the walls of Anvesha's living room. The diyas, the torches dimmed. Only the one next to Vidhi blazed up, bathing her in golden light. She folded her hands and said in a booming voice, 'I was born again. I died and was born again. The gods of the gods willed this! The name I have taken in this birth is Vidhi Damodar Acharya! I want to tell my country, the world, the universe, that we have defeated the biggest injustice of all time—*death!* Jai Shri Krishna! *Main aapka Damodarbhai Acharya tha, aur rahunga* [I was and will always be your Damodarbhai Acharya]!'

She folded her hands and raised them in the air. It was unmistakable now—her mannerisms. She was a photocopy of her . . . father? Of herself? Of himself? How could one explain this? How could one rewrite the history of an entire species? A few people in the neighbourhood clapped. But most people cried. I didn't want to believe it but . . . It was *him*. The torches blew out. The screen lit up again. A video started to play of the life Damodarbhai Acharya had led. After a minute, Uncle reduced the volume of the TV.

'But why now?' asked Anvesha. 'Why wait for this long? She was born decades ago. Why wait this long?'

'Maybe they have been perfecting this reincarnation thing?' I ventured a guess.

Baba, who had been holding his head all this while, looked up. For a man of numbers and science, this was a defeat. The existence of a soul? The concept had been ridiculed by scientists for over a hundred years. He wasn't taking it well. He said, 'No, no, that's not it.'

'Then?'

'Remember the other division she just talked about? The Transplant department? They have cracked it,' said Baba.

'Cracked what?'

'Anvesha?' he looked at her. 'Didn't you say that Indian nuclear scientists have gone missing?'

'Yes, there have been reports, but you said magnetic imaging would fry the brain? The data problem?'

'That's irrelevant now, Anvesha. That was when you said they had cracked the mapping of the brain. It was on the assumption that the brain decides a human's cognitive behaviour, that millions of synapses of the brain work in different combinations to dictate the cognitive behaviour. But now, all that's out of the window. The brain is just functional. The soul sends out information for the brain to execute. Just like the brain sends out information for our hands to work. Why would we need to map the brain?'

'But that's still data, nahi? You have to store it somewhere?' asked Anvesha.

Baba shook his head. 'As a matter of fact, you don't need to, beta. Like if I take a drop of blood from you. That blood is more than enough DNA to write your entire genome sequence. But when you print the genome sequence out, it will be more than 3 million letters long. An entire library. University of Leicester even did it. But do you need to print it out? Store it? No. Because it's imprinted on your DNA, all that information in a ready packet. So the soul . . . I'm guessing . . . is an elementary particle, matter or antimatter that hadn't been discovered yet. The only question is . . . why didn't the scientists find it earlier?'

He slumped into the chair. We waited for him to arrive at a theory. He grappled for a bit after which he said, 'Anvesha? What's the area of the land which is under the Acharya Group in Rajasthan?'

'Thousands of acres,' said Anvesha.

'What if . . .' Baba's voice trailed away.

'What if?'

'Could they be building a bigger version of LHC?' he asked. He found us staring blankly at him. 'Large Hadron Collider? The one at CERN? They speed up sub-atomic particles at a high speed, make them crash, and then observe them. But the collider has one problem. You can't run it at 100 per cent, and even at lower percentages, you have to shut it down for repairs for years. And that's why they are never 100 per cent operational. No one pushes it to the limit. The first run of LHC in 2010 was a failure. It was a 5-billion-dollar mistake; ten years of construction gone down the drain. They realized they made it too small. They could no longer create resonances with the truth quark.'

'Truth . . . what?'

Baba shook his head dismissively. 'It's named Large, but it's so small that it didn't allow them to check theories with extra-large dimensions. Basically, they couldn't prove the existence of a fifth dimension.'

'So is that where the soul exists?' asked Anvesha.

'Isn't that a possibility?' asked Baba, his eyes twinkling. 'Maybe that's why it has remained undiscovered all this while. We couldn't peek behind the quantum curtain; they knew of the curtain but hadn't managed to shift it. But even then everyone knew the fifth dimension existed. Ever since the Kaluza-Klein theory in the 1920, the dimension where gravity unifies with electromagnetism, everyone knew it was just a matter of time. The theory was discredited after a few days, but in the 1970s, it saw a revival. Because some scientists working with supergravity and superstring theory had a brainwave. This is the brainwave which inspired the manga *Ghost in the Shell* series, which inspired the Wachowskis.'

'The Wachowskis?' I asked.

'Lana and Lilly Wachowski, the directors of *Matrix*.'

'So these scientists said, all of reality, all the matter, everything, is strings of energy vibrating. So you, me, our bodies, this flower pot, are energy sequences.'

'Baba, you're making no sense,' I said.

Baba got up and started pacing the room. He was trying to find a reference for us numbnuts.

'So, in *Matrix* and the Japanese manga series people saw each other like a bunch of sequences of vertically and horizontally scrolling green numbers. Why was that? Because they were looking at people from inside the simulation programme—a sort of a hidden dimension. When you looked from outside the simulation, a man was a man, but inside, they appeared as strings of numbers. And these strings of numbers could be manipulated only from the dimension of the simulation. Like for a minute, imagine if this is a simulation, we can only know it's one if we step out of it. Or of course . . . if there's a glitch. So imagine the fifth dimension like that. You see things from a different perspective, a dimension where magnetic fields and gravity unifies, and their rules are bent. So, according to the quantum field theory, the scientists argued, if you look from the fifth dimension, you would see our bodies as energy. No tissue, no blood, nothing, just energy waves and sequences. Now, what if . . . imagine, Bubai, I am looking at you from the fifth dimension, and all I see are energy waves. What if . . . what if in all those energy waves, there is also the energy signature of a soul? An elemental particle with all the information? What if they can isolate that energy?' He frantically took out his phone. He googled something and it threw up an article from the Max Planck Institute of Physics. 'See? See this. So Max Planck is . . .'

Anvesha completed Baba's sentence. 'Got the Nobel Prize in 1918 for the discovery of energy quanta. He is the guy who made Einstein's theory of relativity famous. They even had a band, Max on the piano, Einstein on the violin.'

'Who was on the drums?' I asked.

'Is this a time for jokes, Bubai?' said Mumma.

Baba said, 'Yes, yes all of that. But he discovered quanta. Even now, the scientists from his lab say that the soul is an energy quantum stored in microtubules, and it dies when the microtubules of our body die.'

Anvesha's eyes glinted. 'But . . . uncle. . . that's what, no? Even if it's a quantum of energy, it's tethered to these, what did you say?'

'Microtubules, he said microtubules,' I said.

'So, let's assume that they isolate this energy. But what do you bind it to once the microtubules die?'

Baba shook his head. He paced the room. He spoke, 'What if they have found a new element? You know, nothing has been discovered after Tennessine? It's possible . . . What if . . .what if near-death experiences are nothing but electromagnetic glitches in the fifth dimension?'

Baba was racking his brain when the Damodar's autobiographical video came to a stop. Acharya Gardens was once again lit up in a warm, yellow glow.

Vidhi Damodar continued, 'The question in your heart is why are we making the announcement now?' The long pause after this sentence churned my stomach. 'Between then and now, our research into the soul has taken giant leaps. Our Soul Transference and Transplant department has come through. We have entered a new era!'

She let the words sink in.

'They have done it,' said Baba.

'Shh,' said Mumma.

'What do our rishis say at death? *Vaasaansi jeernaani yatha vihaay; navaani grhnaati naroparaani: tatha shareeraani vihaay jeerna; nyanyaani sanyaati navaani dehee!*'

Uncle translated it for us, 'What's the body but a change of clothes? Just like people shed worn-out clothes and wear new ones, likewise, the soul casts off its worn-out body and enters a new one.'

Vidhi continued, 'Ever since we discovered the soul, the Aatma Vibhag wanted to harness it, to preserve it, to pass it on. At the time of my death, we had only found out the way to track souls to unborn children, the way of the strength of the soul. We wanted the course of science to also work for the old, the infirm and the poor. At the Transplant department, we tried to follow souls wherever they went after they left the bodies, pluck them out and transmit them to a new body whose soul no longer deserved to live. We wanted to conquer immortality. We asked ourselves, where do souls come from? The answer stared at us—the origin of the universe. *Humari rooh bhi tab bani thi, jab ye brahmand bana tha*. And so, our group of nuclear scientists, headed by Arvind Kalam, sought to recreate the origin of the universe. We dotted the upper mantle of Rajasthan's Thar desert with particle accelerators, the biggest of which was Vasuki.'

On the screen, a picture of an old scientist in his sixties appeared.

'Vasuki, the serpent of the Gods, had slithered down Shiva's throat, but this time to grant immortality to *manushya*, the mankind. It churned and churned, it shook the earth it was buried in, it threatened to split the ground into half, just like Mount Mandara had nearly disintegrated.'

Vidhi Damodar Acharya's eyes squinted.

'And just like in our myths, Vasuki breathed out Halahala, a poison that could have destroyed the entire creation, our Vasuki breathed death. For a few moments, it disintegrated the flow of time and space, folded the continuum. But we didn't have Shiva to consume the poison, bear the brunt. We had hundreds of courageous scientists who made the ultimate sacrifice. The fold in time and space made their souls leave their bodies. But . . . one person survived.'

A woman in her sixties walked to centre stage. The torches lit up her face.

'This is Dr Arvind Kalam.'

The crowd, the people watching from their homes, squinted at the screen. This wasn't the old man whose picture had been shown earlier. This was a woman.

Vidhi continued, 'This is him in Dr Kanika Dhillon's body.'

The woman raised her palm to her head and did a salaam.

Vidhi Acharya spoke again, 'We bent the rules of time and space. Kanika Dhillon's soul left her body and was replaced by Arvind Kalam's. In that moment, we realized that even though Brahma is the creator of souls, we are the ones who can control it. From then started the long journey of honouring the dead scientists. What if what happened by accident could be controlled? Under the right conditions, the energies that make up a soul can be disentangled from the body. Arvind hypothesized that all near-death experiences are phase-shifts of the human soul.'

Baba nodded. He was right. Neither of us could believe what was happening.

'But this was only one part of the puzzle. There was a more significant challenge before us. How to phase-shift a soul into a body in a controlled manner? How do you beam a soul out of the body and phase-shift a soul into it? How do you restrain it? What do you tether it to? What do you use to transplant it?'

We all looked at Baba.

As she spoke, the camera trained on three drones, each the size of a car. The spotlight shifted to the drones as they made a sharp dive towards the ground. They seemed to be heading for a crash. But the earth opened and the drones plunged into its depths.

They made the vertical descent at breakneck speed. The counter on the screen showed the depth. The drones were now 45,000 feet below sea level.

'That's deeper than Challenger Deep,' said Anvesha. 'The earth's deepest point. Any lower and they will enter the upper mantle.'

The drones reached a tunnel which was massive and otherworldly.

'*Bhaiyo aur beheno*, right where we are standing, thousands of feet below us is Vasuki in its final form. The Parivar thanks Sanyukta Swaraj and her party for leasing out this space deep inside the earth to the Parivar for this noble purpose. Thousands of miles long, snaking around the capital of Delhi, thrumming with life, churning out the amrit of immortality, which has the power to tether itself to the energy field of the soul, an element that can facilitate the transfer and transplant of the human soul. An element that was an impossibility. One hundred and seventy-six protons packed into a little nucleus! A physical improbability! An element found by the Parivar. We named the element after the collective—Roohnium.'

A holographic image emerged from where the sun had set. It became bigger as it came closer to the cameras and hung in the middle of the arena. It was a pregnant nucleus and hundreds of electrons whizzed past in orbits; a dark, deathly Om sound reverberated from it.

'It took us thirty years after the discovery of the soul to harness it, to gain control over it, to defeat death, but we did it. Welcome the amrit, the *ṣomras*, the secret to immortality—Roohnium, the element that would change the world!' Vidhi smiled and said, 'We have perfected immortality! We will live forever! We will live forever! We will live forever! forever! *Hamesha*! *Hamesha*!'

The word forever echoed in the arena, amidst the family and then in our neighbourhood, and in the next neighbourhood till everyone was chanting '*Hamesha, hamesha*'.

And then Vidhi raised her hand and everyone quietened down. There was silence. She let this sink in.

Chapter 36: Humanity By Acharya

Vidhi Acharya spoke in a low tone.

'It's our Gods who have given the Parivar the burden to take this mantle forward, to usher humanity into a new beginning. The Acharya Parivar has been an illustrious family of this country since decades. God has always been kind to us, and everything we are today is because of his benevolence. Our ancestors have been kings, men of business, at the forefront of science for centuries. Our Parivar's history has been tied to the history of the country. We have always been in the nooks of history books, little footnotes, waiting to know how we can contribute to the future of this country. And now, the moment has come. We are humbled to shoulder the responsibility of leading men and women to immortality and beyond.'

A few diyas flared up. While the rest of the kings, and men of science and philosophy bathed in darkness, a few statues lit up. These statues were supposedly the ancestors of the Acharyas. Kings of small kingdoms, ministers and men of science.

'Papa, this is why they made you write their history,' said Anvesha. 'They were always planning to be kings. To portray themselves as royalty, to set the stage for their rule.'

'It's quite obvious now, but at the time it wasn't. We all thought . . . '

'This is what they paid you extra money for?' asked Baba.

'My senior put me, and hundreds of historians like me, on this project for some money on the side.'

'And you accepted it blindly?' grumbled Baba.

'What difference would my saying no would have made? At the time, we thought it was the Acharyas' vanity project. We thought they wanted to construct their family tree, going back centuries.'

'You're a fool—'

'Is this the time for this?' scolded Mumma.

'Ramanuj Da, no one knew what they were doing.'

'But is it true? Did they go back centuries?' I asked.

'We were given detailed dockets about these.'

'Did you check their veracity? Or were you doing this blindly, Papa?' asked Anvesha.

'It all checked out. The details were impeccable. At the time, Acharya Publishers said it was proprietary information held by the family but verified by the Archaeological Society of India,' said Varun Uncle. 'But now . . . I think if they had people like Firdaus, who remembered past lives, it was easier to construct alternative history footnotes.'

'What's history then?' said Baba. 'They can desecrate old monuments and carve their names on to inscriptions to show they were there.'

'We have hard evidence of the Acharya surname in documents, on tablets going back centuries,' said Varun Uncle.

'What's a few fake historical artefacts when you're looking to rule a country for eternity, Papa?' said Anvesha.

'But we have archaeological ways to check, no?' I asked.

'Our prime minister gave them Delhi's crust to bury their particle accelerator. What's an archaeological department?' retorted Baba.

We turned back to Vidhi Damodar Acharya.

She was saying, 'No one has to suffer. Our bodies are things of the past. Today, we all become immortal! This is what God intended for us. To help us live forever. Jai Shri Krishna!'

With that, she walked away from the family and towards the edge of the platform. She looked down at the teeming press wallahs. She raised her hand towards the crowd, and a hush descended over crowd.

'Now I call on Fatima Ali, the head of Aatma Vibhag, to enlighten you on the way forward.'

Torches lit up a pathway to the stage, and she walked up. Fatima Ali—Hasan Ali's daughter. She bowed in front of the family and then walked to the centre of the stage.

In all the pictures I had seen of her, she was in business suits, power dressed. Today she was in a sequinned abaya. Behind her, was the logo of the Acharya Group—a stylized AG. It melted into a golden circle. A new symbol emerged. Engraved on the gold was now an image of a snake encircling the earth—Vasuki.

'This is their insignia, Vasuki,' said Anvesha. 'They are the Parivar now. Didn't you hear them say it repeatedly? She kept repeating, Parivar, Parivar, Parivar. We are now under the rule of their dynasty.'

Uncle added, 'That's a gold coin. That's what every dynasty does. They mine a new coin, they make a new flag, a new coat of arms.'

'They have a piece of technology. So what? Doesn't make them rulers!' argued Aunty.

Fatima Ali spoke in her business-like tone, 'I want to thank the family, the Parivar, for giving me this opportunity.'

It had started—it was *the family, the royalty, the dynasty*.

On the screen, an option to choose the language appeared. The list was 120 languages long. The mystical vibe of the gardens also changed. Now it looked a product launch of another flashy piece of technology. Holographs came up, lasers took centre-stage and the arena was immersed in white light that's usually reserved for product shots.

'Hi! Welcome to the future! We are happy that all of you have joined us for this momentous occasion. What we are going to present comes after decades of toil. We are now at the bleeding edge of human technology and progress. And we are proud to present to you the Reincarnation and Soul Transplant Yojana.'

The laser lights turned the stage psychedelic.

When the laser show fit for an auto-expo stopped, Fatima Ali spoke, 'Before I go into the details of the yojana, I want to elucidate who is eligible for rebirth in what we are calling the "Phase 1" of the project. If you're below twenty-five years of age and you have a terminal disease, you're eligible for this yojana. Slowly and steadily, we will extend it to everyone. The family believes the youth of the country deserves the opportunity first.' She took out a phone from her pocket and pressed a button. 'On your phones, you will receive the brochure of the first phase of the yojana. Refer to it while I explain it to you.'

As she spoke, the Parivar walked off the stage. In the background, we saw the stones shift. A statue came alive right next to the statue of Bahadur Shah Zafar, the last emperor of India. It was the statue of the Damodar Acharya, *the first immortal.*

'We are under twenty-five,' muttered Anvesha.

Fatima droned on about the numbers for a while.

'Twenty-five thousand people die every day in our country, and our ultimate aim is to give these people a choice between life and death. The preparation of the soul to be reborn takes three months. Hence, our programme can't accommodate, as of now, the very old, and the people who will die unnatural deaths, be it in accidents or suicides or poisoning or murders. Our programme will benefit the terminally ill patients who are predicted to die in the next two years. Acharya Life estimates there are over two million people who fall in this category. In Phase 1, we will facilitate the rebirth of 21,600 patients under the age of twenty-five. These will be divided into four quarters of the year, and between the 540 Lok Sabha constituencies. That means the Parivar will choose 100 eligible terminally patients from each constituency every four months. The candidates will be selected based on the severity of their illness and the need for them to live another life. A few slots will also be available through nominations. We will also keep a few slots for people in the age groups of thirty-five to fifty and above.

These will be nominated by business groups, cultural guilds, the Parivar and the Parliament.'

An hour ago, the soul was fictional, rebirth impossible, and death the ultimate truth of life.

'This should be available to everyone!' protested Aunty.

'Mumma, the soul didn't exist until now, and suddenly you want immortality for everyone?'

'What's stopping them from including everyone, Bitku?' snapped Aunty.

'Sunita's right,' said Mumma. 'They have been planning this for decades, haven't they? The Parivar took over the medical industry, which gave them access to terminal patients and whatnot; they took over the spirituality industry, they lobbied and pushed crores into passing the Citizen's Justice Bill; they took over the prison administration. For what? For this nonsense? Why such a slow roll-out? Nonsense!'

'We need to protest against this. This is greed. They are creating artificial scarcity.' bellowed Baba.

'This is not a product, this is a right!' added Mumma.

'Aunty, every life-saving treatment, every life-saving medicine is a product. The validity was usually limited but now it will last a lifetime.'

'Multiple lifetimes,' I corrected her. .

Fatima Ali explained the programme in excruciating detail. Most elements were technical, but the gist of her lengthy exposition was clear.

There were two options for anyone who was dying—to be born again, a Classic Reincarnation option; or one could choose to shed their body and get their soul transferred into the body of an adult called Soul Transplant.

The first option was riddled with scientific guidelines—babies with old souls had to be brought up differently. To deal with the challenges of remembering an entire past life and yet being in a baby's body, they would need to be enrolled in special residency schools. These schools would be run by the Parivar till they could be assimilated into public life at the age of thirteen. But this was the cheaper option.

Fatima Ali laid out the cost of the rebirth packages.

'Classic Reincarnation, our affordable offering, will cost a person, rich or poor, 50 per cent of their inherited wealth and five years of service to the Parivar, starting at the age of twenty. There's no sign-up fee and there are no hidden costs,' she announced.

Images came up on the screen with subscription plans. There were discounts for family packages or buying two subscriptions or more. There was also a one-time immortality package.

'Who's going to give them that much money?' wondered Varun Uncle aloud.

'Papa? What's your inheritance worth if you die?' asked Anvesha

Fatima Ali continued, 'Soul Transplant is our more cutting-edge offering. The soul of the buyer will be transferred into a body provided by the Parivar. Post the transplant, there will be three months of recovery and healing. Then they will be good to go. The cost is 75 per cent of inherited wealth and five years of service to the Parivar, regardless of the age of the body. The new bodies will be certified healthy for at least thirty years by Acharya life. Acharya Life Insurance will also cover all the illnesses the body might develop. If the new body develops a terminal illness, the Parivar will grant another Soul Transplant free of cost. For a small premium, the buyers can choose a body of their own liking. But it will depend on availability.'

They had made Fatima Ali the face for multiple reasons—her religion being only one of them. The more important reason was that she was in charge of the new bodies. She was now the new head of the prison department, which owned these bodies. In one fell swoop, the Parivar had split the humanity into two—bodies and souls. Bodies could be traded; souls lived on forever.

'The bodies the Parivar will provide will be prisoners on death penalty, haina?' said Uncle.

'Who else?' said Anvesha.

The video ended once Fatima Ali was done. The channel switched back to Ten Sports, which was airing a cricket match between India and Australia. Bumrah was in the last over of the game, unmindful of what had just happened.

Chapter 37: Knee-Jerk Reactions

I switched to a news channel on the TV, one of the many owned by the Acharya Group. Anvesha sat next to Uncle, who rubbed her back, trying to take stock of the situation. That *only* our bodies were dying should have been soothing, and yet it had only made things worse.

Earlier we were committed to dying. Now we had to commit to being lost, our souls wanting to carry on but not knowing how. An hour ago, we had accepted our death, and now our lives were dependent on a lottery.

'Why just 100?' Aunty kept on grousing.

'We have a chance, behenji,' said Baba.

'Have you seen how many people come for chemotherapy? How many? Tell me Ramanuj Da? How many?'

Baba looked away. He had never had the fortitude to accompany us. Both men didn't.

'What if we kill the ones before us?' I asked.

'Bubai,' grumbled Mumma.

An unfair future stared at us, at our parents. Our souls—immortal as proved by the Acharyas—would find new homes in newborn babies. We would remember nothing of the life we had lived. Sometimes hope was more demanding than an inevitable defeat.

What would you do if you were faced with something unprecedented like this? How would you process it? If you were to stack things that changed humans forever, this would easily be on the top, defeating the invention of religion, the discovery of fire, and the synthesis of antibiotics and vaccines.

The discovery of souls, their transference and their immortality, made two of the three things on the list superfluous. Would religion be the same now that man had discovered immortality? Wasn't it death that separated God from humans? What good were antibiotics now when you could inhabit another body?

Every news channel scrambled to make sense of the announcement. The anchors tried to string arguments while they played the recorded speech of Vidhi Acharya repeatedly. A 100-year-old man in the body of a twenty-three-year-old.

Slowly, the TV channels started to respond.

The media channels owned by the Parivar were advertising it like it was a new telecom plan they had launched. The commercial went like this: A weepy young couple, with their dying child in their arms, walks into the Aatma Vibhag Clinic and then walks out with a baby with rosy cheeks and a charming toothless smile. The young parents look up at the sky, and the tagline floats in the air—*Ab jio hazaro saal*. And finally, the gold coin with the insignia of the Acharya Parivar—the serpent Vasuki.

The news anchors were finally coming to grips with the announcement.

It was laborious to watch these journalists—Deepak Bhosadiya, Namish Tattegun and Rudhir Chowchowdhary— jump around like clowns when the future hung in the balance.

A few serious journalists crowded their TV studios with scientists and experts. Despite their intentions, it was a train wreck. How could any expert weigh on this scientifically when they firmly believed that rebirth and soul were nonsensical until a few hours ago? And which anthropologist could correctly predict how the soul's existence and transference could alter the fabric of the social structure within a couple of hours?

Other channels beamed interviews of tarot card readers, yogis and yoginis, and other quacks, who had always sold their products on the assumption that souls exist, most of whom said, *I told you so.* For the first time in human history, people were watching the fate of humans change in real time.

It took half an hour for the international media to spot the story and treat it with the deathly seriousness it deserved. BBC picked it up first and made a glorious mess of it. They treated it with amusement. For them, it was like Ganesha statues drinking milk, cow piss being distributed in packets. It was mere superstition; a multibillion industry fashioning a Ponzi scheme for savages in the third world.

Their tone, though, changed sharply in a while. They must have found telltale signs of this not being a hoax. I understood their surprise. For the first time in recent history, the future was not being changed by a white man. BBC took a sharp U-turn.

Slowly, things started to get interesting. Journalists started asking the real questions: 'Would the selection process be fair? What about the nomination process? Would it be a back door for people with connections and money? And how long before the Parivar starts owning all major businesses, because every time a rich man dies, at least 50 per cent of his wealth would go to the Parivar?'

India iTV, the scum of Indian television, was the first to reach the Parivar's house, and soon others followed.

Miss Malini and Buzzfeed and ScoopWhoop made lists of people they thought should be nominated for reincarnation. Aging superstars got their PR engines' to trend their names. Soon #RajnikanthReborn and #SalmanFirst started to take over Twitter and Instagram. By the end of the first hour, everyone, from sixteen-year-old students to ninety-year-old academics, was writing op-ed pieces.

Wellness Instagram influencers went live and talked about how to strengthen the soul, food bloggers made lists of soul food, and fashion influencers talked about 'soul-based dressing' that aligned the nature of your soul with the fuchsia of your eyeshadow.

Book editors fought among themselves for the attention of god-men. Dystopian fiction writers tried to rewrite large parts of their stories. Successful romance writers planned sequels to their books where they had killed off their main characters.

By the time the second hour passed, press vans were blocking the roads of the Parivar's house in Delhi. The Parivar-owned channels were addressing Vidhi-Damodar Acharya as a demigod, the man who would lead the humans away from the darkness of sickness, death and misery.

Slowly, the crowd swelled in front of the Parivar's house. The first ones to join the crowd were the intellectual hipsters from Delhi University. They weren't carrying placards, they were mostly curious, but reporters quickly labelled them as ignorant protestors.

One of the first reporters on the scene, Deepak Bhosadiya, spoke to the camera, 'We are outside Shri-Shrimati Vidhi-Damodar Acharya's house. Earlier today, the Acharya Group announced its discovery of the soul and its plans to roll out the Reincarnation and Soul Transplant Yojana for the public. Sources close to the prime minister tell us that the ruling party believes it will bring back the glory of the ancient Hindu civilization. Let me remind you here that Hindu sadhus and rishis have always believed in souls and rebirth but had lost the knowledge after barbaric and religious invasions. As you can see behind me, students from Delhi University are starting to gather here. Reports tell us that they are against the yojana. Let's talk to a few of them and see why they are against the eradication of the greatest cause of misery in the modern world.'

He thrust his microphone into the face of a long-haired, spectacled student.

'Why do you hate the country?' shouted Deepak Bhosadiya.

The flustered boy blurted, 'I don't know what to think of this. But to know that it will be controlled by the rich is terrifying.'

'But why are you protesting?' shouted Deepak Bhosadiya.

'I'm not protesting, I just . . . '

Before the boy could complete the sentence, Deepak moved on to another student with a shake of his head.

A student from Hindu College said, 'Maybe the government should have this power and not a private corporation? How do they get to decide who will live and who will not? Who decides who gets nominated?'

The girl standing next to him leaned in and added, 'The government or the Parivar? Isn't it the same thing? The Parivar runs this country. The PM is a puppet.'

Deepak Bhosadiya turned to the camera and said, 'As you can see, not only is this protest anti-Hindu, anti-progress, but it's also turning out to be anti-PM and anti-national and anti-everything. I can see anger and murder in their eyes. We, journalists, are risking our lives here to bring you these images because we care for the nation. These students here want people to die. In other words, they are murderers. Reports tell us most of the students here are Muslim. Their clothes are a dead giveaway.'

He moved on. The students behind him were in hoodies and faded jeans.

A girl from IIT Delhi weighed in, 'This is the worst that could have happened. Do you have any idea what it will do to the Dalits? They would be denied this for sure!'

Deepak Bhosadiya said, 'As we all know, Fatima Ali is the marketing head of the Reincarnation Yojana, but these antisocial, murderous elements want to divide the country based on religion and caste. It's a well-established fact that caste no longer exists. I'm Deepak Bhosadiya, a Brahmin from UP, and I can tell you that caste doesn't exist, because I know at least one Dalit in my office, and we allow him to use the water cooler. I'm proud to be a Brahmin, and others should be proud of their identities too.'

The students rolled their eyes in the background.

Anvesha changed the channel. More students were being interviewed.

Someone from Hansraj added, 'These are matters of God. Haven't we meddled with nature enough? When will this stop?'

And just when the bite out of the news channels was dying out, Aaj Aur Kal Tak, claimed they had an explosive interview and the list of the people who were going to be nominated for the Reincarnation Yojana. It was, as we found out later, fake news.

Chapter 38: Souls and Us

Three hours passed, and the mood in our house kept flitting from dejection to hope to anger. For the moment, everything drowned out, and everyone focused on how the selections and nominations would work.

'Corruption, this would be riddled with corruption,' said Baba and raised his fist in the air.

Everything Fatima had said was, at best, vague.

All this while, my phone kept beeping. It was Rashid, and I didn't want to hear him gloat about Rooh Collective. Or be hopeful about our chances.

There was no way of telling if we had a chance.

It was then I realized that no matter how epic our love story was, in the newly established scheme of things, it was all but a blip.

Love stories usually died with death. But now the rules had changed. For the first time, a forever could mean forever, but only if you were the *chosen* ones. With the discovery of the soul, all love stories were now incomplete.

Anvesha's mother took it the worst. The idea that there were ways to prolong Anvesha's life but it all depended on a lottery was unpalatable for her. She said, 'What if it's all a lie? A scam like everything else in the country?'

'Maa—'

'This is stupid, Bitku. You just wait and see—it's a all ridiculous lie.'

'Maa, everything you believe in today was considered stupid, ridiculous at some point in time. Was it not? Democracy? Ridiculous. Women writers? Ridiculous. A boy and a girl in the same room? Ridiculous.'

'Bitku, these are social situations, not laws of nature, physics, chemistry, whatever.'

'We made babies out of test tubes, we grew human ears in Petri dishes, we sent men to the moon, we split atoms and broke apart land and created new, we made machines think like we do.'

'This is different. Don't you see this is different?'

'Maa, go back in time and imagine. It's exactly what someone would have said when they were told that hearts could be transplanted, that you could strip off the face from a dead man and put it on another, that you could create an arm out of plastic to replace a damaged one. Just because it hasn't been discovered yet, doesn't mean it doesn't exist. How can you measure something when you don't know what it's like? What units do you use? What instrument?'

'But . . .'

'They, the intelligent men, men of science, doctors, thought cancer was a black, viscous fluid that flowed with blood and that's how they chose to measure it. But now you know what cancer is. What's inside our bodies, our cancer, is not fluid, it is . . .'

'Us, more of us. Our own cells multiplying,' I said.

Aunty butted in. 'But if the soul exists, then people would remember their past . . .'

There had been instances. We all had heard them, mocked them, attached ulterior motives to people who remembered their past lives. There had been TV shows about past life regressions, and even the most learned of scientists called them imagination and not snatches from lives lived before.'

'What Aunty is trying to say is that if every soul is reborn, then why has this remained undiscovered for so long,' I said.

'Maa, yaar, you're trying to resist the idea of the existence of souls. But tell me this, how many around you believe that souls exist? Without any proof? Don't you too? After you eat a lot, what do you say? My soul is content. *Aatma ko tripti mil gayi.* The body only gets filled up.'

'That's just a figure of speech,' said Aunty. 'Let's think about this rationally.'

'Let's do that, Maa. Let's do exactly that,' said Anvesha. 'You know how I come up with conspiracy theories, and scout out little details that no one else can? What I call my imagination? Oh, maybe Sanjay Gandhi was assassinated by his own family? Oh, maybe the US in the 1970s continuously released germs in India to slow us down? What if it's gossip from my past life that my soul remembers?'

'That's your imagination,' I said.

'But what if I have lived before? What if the details come to me from my past life?' she said, getting up.

And just as she got up, she felt nauseous and wanted to vomit.

'I will help her,' I said.

I walked her to the washroom, helped her vomit, and clean up.

She sat on an upturned bucket and said, 'You know how our parents and you keep calling us soulmates? What if we really are? And not because we were born on the same date and same time to neighbours, but what if we were in love before? Not once but multiple times? For centuries? Druvan, baby, you remember when I first kissed you? Of course, you do. But to me, it didn't feel like I was kissing you for the first time. It seemed like I had done it before. I remembered how your lips felt, what your touch felt like.'

'I mean . . . I would say you're overthinking this?'

'But it can be a possibility, nahi? Don't we feel like we have always been together? Not for eighteen years but forever? I can feel it in my bones. You know how you miss me more than I miss you. It's because I don't ever miss your presence. I can always feel you around. What do you think, Druvan? What if it's because my soul remembers? Not only this love story, but what you have made me feel during different lifetimes? What if that's why we are soulmates? It's a romantic notion, no?'

I nodded.

'So let's go with this, Druvan. Even if we don't get selected, know that our souls will always find each other, we will always be born close to each other and fall in love. Let's not lose hope.'

'Just one question,' I said.

'You said the kiss was familiar. I want to know what your soul tells you about how the sex would be?'

'Just like sex between a thousand-year-old couple who has done it a million times before.'

'Boring,' I complained.

She laughed.

'It feels like love. It feels like surrendering to someone who can tell precisely what to do, where to touch, where to let the fingers linger,' said Anvesha.

'It still sounds boring. Where's the excitement if we have done it hundreds of thousands of times.'

'Excitement lasts for a few minutes, three dates, a two-month relationship, but intimacy lasts forever,' she said and, in a low, seductive voice, added, 'We are soulmates.'

Chapter 39: This Was History

History had become boring since World War II and the fall of the last monarchs. The establishment of noisy democracies, the curtailment of the scope of absolute power, the boringness of hard science had made decades mostly uninteresting from the view of a historian like Uncle.

We always said the world had only a few thinkers, and the rest was a herd, but I saw first-hand how people across the globe came to the same conclusions, felt the same fears and uncertainties about rebirth. Never in history had a family shifted the power structure of the world so swiftly. The future of all humanity lay in the Parivar's hand. They had changed the history irrevocably.

The day after the announcement of the yojana, the world descended into chaos. Only twenty-four hours had passed, but every minute was exhausting.

News channels could not keep pace with the things unfolding in India and across the world.

It would be hard to pick where it began, but let's start from the Breach Candy Hospital in Bombay and try to cover at least a smattering of the shitstorm.

Thirty-two cancer patients and burn victims lined up at the ledge of the forty-third floor, their hospital robes billowing in the wind. The cameras panned between the smiling faces of the patients and their screaming families who begged them to come down. They did come down, but their skulls cracked on the pavement with a crunch. These thirty-two people had spray painted 'Souls Exist' on the wall of the last room they were in.

Aunty held Anvesha close and purred, 'Don't even think of doing this, Bitku!'

'You really think Anvesha will miss out on the most exciting thing that has ever happened to humanity?' I asked.

'It's a popcorn event for me, Maa.'

You could always count on TV channels to create drama. It started with Anjani Kaschhap, a charmless, talentless, hate-mongering monkey, screaming on her show.

'If souls exist, so do heaven and hell! Where does the soul go between its death and rebirth? We are waiting for the answer from our saviour Shri-Shrimati Vidhi Damodar Acharya on where did he go for those eleven minutes? Did he see a glimpse of heaven? We will answer the question today at 9 p.m.! The nation wants to know!'

The fear she stoked spread like wildfire.

'The *chudail* is asking the right question,' conceded Anvesha.

'About Damodarbhai knowing what heaven looks like?'

'You think a businessman of his standing went to heaven? Especially after making hundreds sacrifice their lives.'

'You're saying he went to . . . hell?'

'If there's a hell . . . that would change everything. Can you imagine, Druvan?'

'Imagination is not my strongest suit.'

'The moral structure of society will change.' She fell silent. She murmured in a small voice. 'But why miss out on this detail? And what about God? The creator of souls? Is he in the picture?'

Forwards on people's phone, some from renowned philosophers, enumerated a number of ways in which errant souls were tortured between death and rebirth—thieves were boiled in oil, soldiers were drowned in blood, violent men's limbs were cut off, rapists were castrated and fed their privates, adulterous women's breasts were sliced off, cheating men were burnt alive, etc.

Graphic artists around the world wasted no time in illustrating what hell looked like.

Misinformation, or the lack of information, had made hell a very real place.

'HOW ARE PEOPLE BELIEVING THIS!' Baba spat out angrily. 'The soul is an energy signature, not a body that can be cut, sliced up, or burnt.'

'Uncle, the soul can emotionally be anthropomorphic. We didn't trust our ancestors when they said souls existed. Who is to say they are not right about hell?' asked Anvesha.

The discovery of the soul made hordes of Hindus realize that they had sinned. Hundreds of rich, semi-rich, middle-aged business people, moneylenders, fund managers across the country were rushed to ICUs after they complained of chest pains and minor cardiac arrests. The dread of hell, the horror of being born as an animal, an insect, into a lower caste, stuck deep in their hearts. They wanted to repent.

Railway stations soon became death traps. Thirty-four people died in a stampede on a platform in Hyderabad. They were trying to board to train to Tirupathi to ask for forgiveness from Lord Vishnu. The government cancelled all trains to pilgrimages. Stampedes, even at smaller temples, became commonplace. Hundreds died.

Thousands of people crowded at Assi Ghat, Varanasi, trying to wash away their sins. Hundreds fell into the water and drowned. Little children were carried away by the currents. The river choked with bloated bodies.

Within six hours of the announcement, thousands surrendered for crimes ranging from petty thefts to serial murders to rapes. Sinners wanted earthly punishment than one after death. Forty-six people died from overcrowding lock-ups across the state of Uttar Pradesh.

The next development was at Vikash Institute, the coaching institute for aspiring doctors. It saw a significant dropout rate. There were predictions that in ten years, doctors who now performed life-saving surgeries would no longer be needed.

'The market for surgeons will shrink. Why spend on heart or liver transplants when you can buy a new body and a fresh start?' said Anvesha.

'What if crime drops? Then what? Where do you get bodies from?'

'The Parivar owns every clinic in this country. They will easily convince poor women who go for abortions to keep the baby in exchange for a job or money. The baby will have someone else's soul!'

Then the news started to trickle from all parts of the world. Diplomats were dealing with an unprecedented situation. No one wanted to mess with a country that held the key to immortality. The stocks of Indian businesses shot up. The Acharya Group's— now known by just a symbol—market cap outstripped multiple small countries.

'Indian business will decimate the competition. We will be the richest country,' declared Anvesha.

'Will you start singing the national anthem, right now? Give me notice because I'm too tired to get up,' I said.

Varun Uncle butted in, 'Imagine Steve Jobs, JRD Tata, Edison, Henry Ford never dying. Can you imagine what these businesses would have been today?'

Baba shook his head. 'Bhaisahib, you're missing an important point. The Parivar will own every Indian company with time. They will own everyone who chooses to reincarnate.'

And then the resistance started.

It came from the king of Saudi Arabia. He threatened to cut off all ties with India if it allowed the Acharyas to roll out the yojana. To drive home the point, he mounted a bigger spectacle than Vidhi Damodar Acharya.

'This is going to be so screwed up,' said Anvesha, the second the telecast started.

'Is that . . . is that . . . a sword? Why is the King carrying a sword?'

'Devout Muslims are going to push back.'

'Rebirth is haram or what?' I asked.

'Their holy books teach them about Munakar and Nazir, the angels who test the dead's faith, and about Zabanniya, the nineteen angels of hell, who torture errant souls out of the body. But there's no rebirth.'

The King invoked the Prophet in a rousing performance and said, 'The soul's existence is known to Muslims, the believers! There's no rebirth in Islam. There's only *jannat* and *jahanum*!' he roared. 'Where would morality go if there's no punishment? Only rebirth? This is all a blasphemous lie that should anger Muslims around the world.'

One hundred and thirty-four people were dragged to the stage in handcuffs by swordsmen. The men were lined up, their hoods taken off, heads pushed on to the wooden block. The king raised the gleaming sword and hacked off a man's head. Screams rang out as the rest too lost their heads. These 134 people were of differing religions, most of them Indian tourists on Hajj, and had dared to share articles about the harnessing of the soul.

Hindu Mahasansad took out a rally in Aurangabad, asking the Acharya Parivar to only allow the three upper varnas, the twice-born, or *dvija*, to reincarnate to maintain the purity of race.

Their chief brandished a *trishul* on camera and said, '*Har Har Mahadev!* The Reincarnation process for Dalits or Shudras goes against the Hindu scriptures. *Nichli jaati ke log* [People from the lower caste] are destined to be reborn as dogs and insects. And even if you do go ahead with it, *likh ke le lo*, it will result in mentally unstable people. They will be like dogs in human skin.'

In Bangalore, Dalit activists organized large-scale processions and demanded that an international body should preside over the reincarnations. They argued that the oppressed classes, the poorest in the country, would not have access to rebirth, owing to the glaring crowding by the upper classes in both the Acharya Group and the government.

Meanwhile, the Jewish Federation of North America, led by few of the richest men in America, started to pool in billions of dollars for research.

'Of course, they would,' said Anvesha. 'Reincarnation in Judaism has always been a popular concept. It's called Gilgul. Souls are believed to cycle through lives or incarnations, being attached to different human bodies over time.'

'Damn, the Government of Israel just offered the Acharyas 4 trillion dollars for a complete buy-out.'

Anvesha laughed. 'What's 4 trillion dollars when you can own the world?'

By the time the day came to an end, there were reports of thousands of Indians retracting their citizenship applications in the US, Australia and Europe. Their country now offered reincarnation, another life, another body. What did the other countries offer? One good life? India now provided many.

Following this news, White supremacists invaded desi neighbourhoods in US and Australia with torches and assault rifles and asked them to the leave the country. Twenty-three brown-skinned people were lynched in Washington, fifteen in Perth and forty-four in Texas.

A retired general from the army took it a bit far. He urged the Government of India to occupy Pakistan, colonize it, own every last Pakistani man, woman and child, so it could serve as a warehouse of bodies for Indian soldiers who had died in service. Other voices joined in who wanted the Indian government to become colonizers, raise an immortal army, and establish an empire.

Muslim organizations across the country argued that with time Muslim bodies would be forced to house Hindu souls. Several Hindu organizations countered that if a Muslim family had more than two children, the third one should be replaced, by law, by a Hindu soul.

Several men's rights activists demanded that the souls of men shouldn't be transferred into women's weak bodies. While feminist organizations argued that men's souls should only be transplanted into women's bodies, so they would finally understand what it felt like to be scared of being assaulted, raped and subjugated.

And soon, it veered to theories about soul and sexuality.

'This is what I was talking about,' said Anvesha. 'The fabric of society is going to change. So much of what we do is centred around sex.'

'Bitku?' said Aunty.

I giggled.

Since no one was an expert on soul–sexuality, everyone was an expert. They argued that if your soul fell more in love with women over the multiple cycles of rebirth, there was a high chance that you would like women no matter what body you were in. Your soul decided your sexuality, not your body, or your brain chemistry.

Soon a glut of coming-out stories came out on all social media platforms. The declarations all took the same form— 'my soul likes men'; 'my soul likes women'; 'I'm in a man's body, but my soul is of a woman, and I hope to be born as one in the next birth'.

By the time the first day after the announcement ended, the world had changed forever.

Chapter 40: The Weirdness

'There are mobs on the street! Are they dying? No!' Mumma complained.

'Ei? Calm down *koro*,' replied Baba.

'Why, bhaisahib? If Druvan and Anvesha can be at home and wait, so can they! What kind of country are we in?'

'Apparently, the one that solved death,' I quipped.

'Druvan, get away from the window and go inside,' said Uncle.

I walked inside Anvesha's room. She was bent over her phone.

'I'm telling you, there will be riots,' said Anvesha. She was frantically tweeting, posting stories, telling people to go back to their houses. She looked up from her phone and said, 'If the Parivar doesn't answer the questions, people are going to lose it.'

'Does this include you?'

Anvesha paused. She asked in a small voice. 'For a moment let's imagine we are selected.'

'I would stay away from such optimism.'

'Just imagine we are.'

'I don't want to. Why be hopeful and get disappointed?'

'For the same reason we don't jump from our balconies and die right now rather than next year. Hope gives us a reason to live.'

'You're my reason to live, not hope.'

'Oho, yaar. Just imagine no.'

'Fine. I am imagining that we beat incredible odds and both of us, not one but *both* of us are selected. Then what?'

'What would you pick? Soul Transplant or Classic Reincarnation?'

'Ummm . . . if we choose the latter, Mumma and Baba will be in their sixties when we turn twenty. That's not too bad actually.'

'You're missing an important point.'

She gave me time to think.

'. . . oh damn. That in twenty years our parents will have the choice of reincarnating too?'

'Imagine if their turn comes when they are seventy? They wouldn't want to come back as children, because they will be as old as our children. And if they come back as adults, they will be our age.'

'That's weird. Could that be a reason why the Acharyas are rolling it out slowly? To not push the world into weirdness?'

Meanwhile, Varun Uncle and Baba called everyone they knew to see if they could get us on the list of the first 100 people to be selected from our constituency. It bore no fruit.

Mumma and Aunty spent the entire week at the hospitals in our constituency with a notepad and pencil. They chatted up nurses to know how many people under the age of twenty-five were dying soon.

'There are too many,' conceded Mumma glumly at the end of their survey.

'We will find a way, don't worry,' assured Baba.

Every day was a ramped-up, beefed-up version of the first day. The Parivar stayed tight-lipped. They let the world assume theories, take action, burn itself to the ground.

The Parivar's silence on the selection process had led to blatant fearmongering, protests and stone-pelting. People wanted the constitution of India to change to accommodate reincarnation as a fundamental right. With every passing day, hundreds more took to the streets.

We were on the brink of a riot. To be on the safe side, our parents stocked up on ration and Hide & Seek biscuits.

'The protests are going to end soon. A few people will die and things will go back to normal,' declared Anvesha.

'That's very casual and evil of you.'

'You think the government can't crack down right now and make them all go home?'

'That would be against their constitutional rights.'

'Aw, that's really cute of you, Druvan,' she said.

'Don't be condescending. I'm a handsome, dying boy.'

She took a paper and wrote a bunch of words on it. 'So here's the sequence of the events that are going to happen in the next few weeks. Open it then?'

'It's a bet.'

The build-up culminated after two weeks when a stray bullet from a Gujjar's gun hit a Muslim. It started as a communal clash between the RSS and the Islamic hardliners, between the upper caste organizations and Bahujans, and quickly became a free-for-all. Groups of raging mobs from the neighbouring states poured into the city armed with rods, stones, kerosene canters and bloodlust.

'Lock the doors, switch off the lights,' ordered Baba.

Uncle and Aunty wrapped iron chain around the main gate. Mumma and Baba doused the walls with water so they wouldn't catch fire. Anvesha and I barricaded the windows.

Neighbourhoods went up in flames. People were dragged out of their homes and garlanded with burning tires. Men and women were hacked to death, children cut out of wombs and impaled. Hundreds of women were raped, filmed and cut to death. The religious chants of 'Jo Bole So Nihal', 'Allahu Akbar' and 'Jai Shri Ram' turned into war cries.

The city was burning.

And then, just as the fire started to touch upper middle-class neighbourhoods, the riot died a swift death.

It started with a light buzzing of bees at a distance. I could hear it despite the barricaded windows and sealed doors.

'Don't,' screamed Aunty who had endured two full-blown panic attacks. 'Don't go outside!'

'*Arre, rukiye zara,* behenji,' said Mumma and unlocked the door.

We followed her outside. We looked up and around to see where the sound was coming from. It was as if someone had stirred up an industrial-grade beehive. Slowly, the buzzing turned into a louder, ear-splitting hum. Scared children in the neighbourhood clasped their ears and hid behind cupboards. Cars across the city screeched to a halt. Some crashed into each other because no one could hear the horns over the whizzing sound. Soon the shadows became long, and the skies thundered. Darkness descended like an eclipse. The sun was blocked out. Angry, murky clouds threatened to crash to the ground and annihilate everything.

'Maeri!' exclaimed Baba and pointed at the darkened sky. 'What the hell is that?'

The source of the sound now came into view—they were drones. Hundreds of thousands of drones hovered over people's heads. The sun was blotted out.

People ducked, thinking they would be armed with pellet guns. Instead, they were armed with something much deadlier—a speakerphone.

Vidhi Damodar Acharya's voice boomed from the thousands of synced speakers on the drones.

'Jai Shri Krishna! Deshvasiyo! *Bas karo!*' she said. The entire city plunged into silence.

The speakers boomed again. '*Narak kalpanik nahi hai*! Hell exists! When you die, everything you have done in this life is open to question! Fear your judgement day! Your soul will reject rebirth if your sins are beyond redemption. What you are doing will lead you straight to death!'

The collective clang of swords falling to the ground echoed through the air.

'Drop your weapons! Go back to your families! Live an honest life!'

There was a little flash in each of the drones.

'Cameras,' said Anvesha.

Vidhi Acharya's words rang out. 'Everyone who's found outside rioting will be excluded from the Reincarnation programme. Not just them, their extended families, and their neighbours too. Jai Shri Krishna.'

The drones flew away and disappeared into the glare of the sun. Everyone retreated to their homes.

The confirmation of hell and the misinformation around it had it's—Anvesha called them expected—repercussions. By the time Anvesha and I made tea for everyone, news had started trickling in about imams, diplomats from oil-rich countries and theologists reaching out to the Parivar to ask what hell was like.

The existence of hell brought two unlikely casualties—the first was big businesses. High-level executives emerged from the woodwork like termites and turned into whistle-blowers. They exposed instances of money-laundering, prostitution rings serving companies, use of child labour, animal and human testing of products, funding of terrorists, et al. Stocks of many businesses plunged.

The second causality was governments. Politicians across the world tendered their resignations from places of power and returned to community service. Within a few hours, the populist governments of Australia, Greece, Canada and Turkey collapsed.

Closer home, 145 scared MPs and hundreds of MLAs across states and parties resigned from their positions. Sanyukta Swaraj responded with suspending the constitution, curtailing civil liberties, taking control of the armed forces and the police, and announcing Emergency until further notice.

In her televised speech, she said, 'Until normalcy returns to the state and a general election can be held, we will withhold certain civil liberties. The responsibility of taking this great nation to its next phase will rest on the shoulders of our party and our cabinet ministry. We are working closely with the Parivar to restore things as they were. Jai Hind!'

'The country is theirs now,' said Anvesha. 'They are the kings, the undying dynasty. Sanyukta is their bootlicking, undying mantri. A perfect apparatus of power.'

I opened the chit.

In her squiggly handwriting, Anvesha had written the following:

- *Accidental firing (paid thugs of government?)*
- *large-scale rioting—poor neighbourhoods*
- *government/Parivar crackdown*
- *threats of exclusion from reincarnation*
- *constitutional rights rescinded*

Eventually, a new constitution.

Chapter 41: Selection Day

For a month, newspaper and TV channels were bombarded with the Reincarnation plans. The advertisements encouraged every dying person to visit the nearest Acharya Life hospital and get a 'Severely Damaged' certificate for their bodies. The coverage was effective. Hundreds of thousands of people were scanned, tested, their biopsies analysed, their diagnoses delivered. With every diagnosis, the competition for survival got stiffer. Anvesha and I, customers of Acharya Life, received our 'Severely Damaged' certificates via mail.

Rashid, meanwhile, hadn't given up. He had pulled out all the stops, trying to get us through somehow.

'*Hoga,* bhai, *hoga,*' he would say every time we would call him.

'Rashid, you are never around,' Anvesha would scold him. 'If we die, you don't want to regret not spending enough time with us.'

'And we want to beat you at games. You have to let us win because we are dying and stuff.'

'Bhai, *suno toh*—'

'Rashid,' Anvesha cut in. 'You need to be here. Drop everything and come.'

Rashid's avoidance of us was understandable. Anvesha and I had grown sickly thin. We would vomit, stumble around, and die a little in front of him every time he saw us. His helplessness made him sick.

An interview date—named 'Selection Day' by the Parivar—was announced where the dying—us—would be called to present their case for survival.

'Did Hasan pick up your call?' I asked Anvesha again.

We had been trying to reach him to beg for a back-door entry into the Reincarnation programme. He had been unresponsive.

On the 'Selection Day', Mumma, Baba and Uncle, Aunty woke up early and invoked all the Gods they had ever been introduced to. The house felt like someone had triggered a smoke bomb.

At the designated time, an Acharya Life ambulance came to pick us up. Our parents clung to us and sobbed until the nurses reminded them of the strict schedule.

We were still quite a way when we saw the queue of half-dead people. Like Anvesha and I, everyone carried their 'Severely Damaged' Certificates.

We stood at the back of the line. Volunteers and nurses from Acharya Life offered us foldable chairs, water and some snacks. They took down notes on their iPads—medical history, insurance numbers. They shared Wi-Fi passwords and handed out power banks to those waiting.

Fifteen minutes after the gates were opened, three large trucks, followed by a dozen army jeeps, came to a stop in the parking lot. Scores of men and women in army fatigues hopped off. Large screens were unloaded, carried, hoisted up the walls of the hospital. The volunteers whispered urgently on their walkie-talkies. The screens lit up. There was static for a while. And then, Vidhi Damodar Acharya came on.

'Jai Shri Krishna,' she said in a low, sombre voice. She was dressed in a salwar kameez, the chunni draped around her head, her eyes weary. 'Welcome to the new beginning. I will not take a lot of your time. Over the past few days, doubts have been raised on the Parivar's selection process. I'm here to dispel those allegations.' She picked up papers from her desk and spoke. 'First of all, the selection won't be done on the basis of money or connections but will follow a legitimate process headed by imminent people of knowledge.'

The screen shifted and on it appeared the selection jury. There were scientists, economists, business people, writers and philosophers. The net they had thrown was wide, intersectional. Everyone got a place, regardless of gender, orientation, caste, religion and age.

'We are not looking for the most knowledgeable to be reincarnated because knowledge not only shifts but can be gained over births. We are not looking for the most intelligent because paediatric scientists have discovered that IQ is determined by postnatal care and nutrition in children. We are not looking for achievers because money can be accrued over multiple births. We are looking for people who have a genuine will to live, who possess an excellent soul. In the future, we will give every man, every woman a chance to live again, but a great civilization is not built in a day, and for now, this is where we begin. We will select on the basis of how we want the world to look like a hundred years from now, two hundred years from now. We will all work towards it. You, me, us. We will all make this happen. Some day we will all live forever. And it starts here. It starts with you! A new tomorrow!'

The crowd started to chant with her.

'Imagine having a never-dying *praja*, immortal subjects. You use propaganda only once, and you're set for multiple lives,' said Anvesha.

When the chants died down, Vidhi Damodar Acharya said, 'There has been a lot of disappointing talk about nominations. The Parivar has been insulted and questioned on this matter. There are people who believe these nominations will be riddled with corruption.' There was a long pause. Hurt bubbled in her eyes. She spoke again, 'The Parivar has decided that the eight nominations for the first quarter will be decided by the people themselves, by you and every last of our people. It will be a transparent, democratic process. You will vote for who lives! Jai Shri Krishna. May God be with all of you!'

The screen blacked out.

'Wow,' said Anvesha. 'Did you hear her?'

'I . . . I'm guessing I missed something?'

'*Uff* yaar, Druvan.'

'She just said knowledge can be acquired over births, so keep your *guroor,* your pride, in check, okay? Give me a few hundred years, and I will catch up.'

'The Parivar is at the peak of social engineering right now. By choosing just who gets rebirth, they can decide exactly how the society will look. You know . . . they can run the world like a company. They can have a small percentage with leadership traits, hundreds with a follower mentality; they can fix gender issues, weed out fundamentalists. That's insane, nahi?'

'I . . . got that, of course.'

'Of course, you did.'

'So if they want someone cute, they can get me?'

She pulled my cheeks. '*Haanji.*'

The gates opened. With military precision, the doctors saw us, tested us, took our e-mail IDs, addresses, and then ushered us to the hastily created set-up on the top floor of the hospital. There were rows upon rows of transparent cubicles with a chair and tripod on which a camera rested.

A woman dressed in a crisp white saree with a gold border tapped on her microphone to get our attention.

'Welcome to the Selection Day,' she said. 'I'm Nurse Kamla. I want to start off by telling you how lucky all of you are to be getting the chance to be reincarnated. In front of you are cubicles where you will state your reason to want to live again. These will be reviewed by the experts. All the videos will be uploaded to the Parivar's Reincarnation app, ReAP, by the end of the day, where the public can vote for them. As we speak, ReAP is being downloaded automatically on phones across the country.'

I, like others, took out my phone. And there it was. An app had downloaded on my phone, overriding all the security features. The icon, a little infinity sign, glowed with the tag line, *ReAP What You Sow.*

I was already signed in, the profile picture had been uploaded from my PAN card, and my status read: Severely Damaged. There were a host of options : Change Your Status, View Videos, Contact Local Centre, etc.

'Tap on the video section,' said Nurse Kamala. 'Here's where your videos will be uploaded to be assessed by the jury. This is also where the junta can vote for you.'

She then took us through the procedure. Our numbers flashed on the cubicle doors, we had to go inside, switch on the camera, and record the reason why we wanted to be reborn again.

Nurse Kamla gave us fifteen minutes to collect our thoughts, and then the recording started. The cubicles were soundproof, but we saw people break down, wail, and record and rerecord their pleas to be reborn. A few sang hymns, a few performed the namaz, crying and hoping to move the Parivar and the junta. Anvesha and I were ushered into neighbouring cubicles.

'Take your time. Don't be in a hurry. This is your only chance,' the attendant said to me.

I recorded, fumbled and pressed the delete button. I turned to look at Anvesha. She closed her eyes for a minute, and then looked straight into the camera. A confident stream of the words seemed to spill out of her mouth. She hit the done button and walked out. I looked at her. She shrugged as if mocking the time I was taking. I started again.

'Hi. I'm Druvan and I think . . . umm . . . I'm an okay guy, quite good-looking also. Lol lol lol. I am a nice guy and my parents . . . Mumma and Baba . . . they love me . . . and they don't deserve this . . . so it would be nice I think? To live . . . again. It would save . . . them tears.'

I pressed delete again. Anvesha tapped on the glass door.

'WAIT!' I mimed.

She chuckled and shook her head. That slight shake of her hair, the way her eyes looked at me, the pity, the love, the ownership they had for me told me why I wanted to live again.

'Hi! I'm Druvan! I will keep this short. You guys are intelligent, aren't you? I am assuming you will look past the bluster, the tears, and the desperation of most people. Every death is tragic, and grief can't be measured. You are rational people and know exactly what to do. It's also a bit strange you hold the power of God in your hands. And to think of it, wouldn't we have a healthier relationship with God if we thought of him as rational and not benevolent? Anyway, coming to the point. I know everyone has parents and kids and what not, and they want to go back to them . . . but for me, the girl you see behind, the girl who's slightly out of focus? Yes, that one. She's here because she's dying too. I'm in love with her, and not the kind of love you might have felt, but love that feels like it's your entire being, that makes you believe that the only reason you exist is to be with that person. To that end, I don't mind dying, but if she lives, I want to live too. If she gets chosen, I want to be chosen too. I can't bear the thought of her being born again, while my soul drifts into nothingness. That's unacceptable to me. But if she dies, if she's not chosen, then I don't want to be chosen either. So yes, that's my plea. Choose me and my soulmate. Choose me for my love.'

I left the cubicle with a spring in my step. It felt like a good enough reason.

'What did you ask for?' I asked Anvesha.

'Either I get reborn with you or I'm good with drifting off. You?'

Chapter 42: The List

No one knew what the jury was doing, but ReAP showed us in real time those who had a chance at immortality. The leader board fluctuated the first few days before it settled. A few clear leaders emerged.

Number One

Topping the list was Faisal Sheikh, a TikTok star. He had always been a hero in his own right. He had shot his first video in his shop in Dharavi. It was of him doing cross-stitch with blazing fast hands. In his last video, he was dancing with ward boys of the cancer department. Every one of his 10 million loyal fans had voted for him. Faisal Bhai was always number one in their mind.

Number Two

Snapping at his heels, a close second was a boy India had seen growing up. Twenty-four years ago, he was born to a smart but middling movie star, Sameer Ali Khan, and a super successful actress, Katrina Kapoor, under the unrelenting glare of the paparazzi. He quickly became the most famous baby/toddler/young adult of all time. Everyone expected him to be a disaster—a boy with misplaced entitlement, a warped sense of reality, an addiction to drugs. What they instead got was a sensitive, handsome boy who dressed modestly and was seen carrying thick books in his airport clicks. He would often be spotted hugging his nanny, his elder sister and his parents with equal love. In all his interviews, he expressed his disinterest in acting. Instead, he wanted to write.

On the day a blind item reported his tumour, young women and gay men drank the entire night. When he shaved off his head, he made it to the list of sexiest men in Asia.

Number Three

Right behind him was Sujay Shetty, a man who had converted his ALS diagnosis into a multi-crore industry. An MBA and a consultant before his diagnosis, he started posting videos about how to deal with the illness. Soon he realized people were more interested in him—light-eyed, strong-jawed, with smooth chocolate skin and the perfect hairstyle. He started to say stuff like: 'Seize the day!'; 'Live like it's your last day!'; 'Dream big, live small!'; 'Run your business, love your business!'; 'You're unique!'; 'Hustle and follow your heart!' He soon became the poster boy of positivity. So when the time came for the community he had built online to step up and vote for him, they did. In his recording, he asked his audience, whom he called his fam, to make him live again so he could help them again.

Number Four

The fourth on the list was the most deserving according to most (if you discounted the accounts of sexual assault). It was Sachin Mittal, the twenty-three-year-old genius behind the mobile app *Mitti*, which connected farmers directly to consumers. You order a kilo of onions in the morning, and you get it in twenty-four hours directly from the person who'd sowed the bulb and harvested it, complete with a picture of the farmer and your order. The farmers called it the second Green Revolution. Sachin Mittal was their hero. He had earned the moniker *Mitti ka ladka* across villages. His entire voter base was from rural areas, using phones he had given the farmers. None of the cases of sexual assault against the man had stuck till now.

Number Five

The fifth one on the list was a confusing name. The name people knew was 'Dhinchak Neha', or 'the queen of cringe' as some called her. She was a talentless hack from East Delhi who couldn't rap or sing to save her life and yet earned a fortune from her YouTube channels where she uploaded out-of-tune, self-written, self-composed, self-directed music videos. She was the most disliked artiste of all time. Leaked WhatsApp chats slowly revealed that Dhinchak Neha grew up in Vasant Kunj, surrounded by pop-art, Picasso prints, Satyajit Ray movies and had only recently shifted to Vikaspuri for the continuity of the image she had shrewdly built for herself. When she made her diagnosis public, social media celebrated. Despite this, half the people voted for her because they found her cringeworthy and giving her another chance at life was their version of a joke. The other half thought she was a maverick genius whose life was a big laugh at people who celebrated their own normality.

Number Six

The sixth and the last one who was important to our story was the most shocking of all—Amruta Swaraj. The daughter of Prime Minister Sanyukta Swaraj. And that answered our questions about why this current government had held the Parivar's feet delicately and placed them over its head.

Number Seven and Number Eight were fluid and changed every hour.

Where were we?

Anvesha and I were at numbers fifteen and eighteen on the list. Though we were still far below, hundreds of thousands of people had watched our videos and chosen us and written us long emails, telling us that our love story had inspired them to believe in love again.

Our parents found no joy in the verbose emails. They wanted votes. They were obsessively refreshing the voting page, tracking the analytics of the voters by gender, region and economic backgrounds. They scoured the Internet for mailing lists and sent our voting link to everyone they could.

'Baba, this is such a waste of time.'

'Every vote counts, Bubai,' said Baba.

'The difference between us and the one at the seventh position is 6 million. I'm not sure how these 100 people will help.'

'*Chup kor to?* Let us do what we are doing,' said Mumma. She turned to Anvesha. 'Did you upload a story asking for votes?'

'You can't be careless, Bitku,' said Aunty and took Anvesha's phone from her and uploaded a bunch of stories begging for votes.

Nothing helped. Our position didn't move. This madness continued till the day of the announcement of the 5400 selected by the jury. On the day, Anvesha and I left the house for Rashid's. We didn't want to deal with the grief of our parents.

The eight would be announced the next day after the voting lines closed.

When we got to Rashid's, he had an excel sheet open on his laptop, and he was talking animatedly over the phone to higher officials in Rooh Collective, trying to get our voting link sent to the collective's members.

It always took him a moment to reconcile with the way we looked now—sickly, old, emaciated, severely damaged.

He was pissed off to see us. 'Bhai, this would have been much easier had you just listened to me and joined Rooh Collective. Just one tweet from Ashwinath, and you would have been through.'

'You're scarring my soul with all this Rooh Collective talk,' I said.

'Are you meditating, bhai?'

I shook my head.

'He is,' said Avantika.

'Bhai, there's a chance you two will find each in the next birth.'

'Don't have such foolish hopes, Rashid. Your friends will be dead, get used to it,' I said.

Durjoy Datta

'I'm not ready to believe there are 5400 people more deserving than the two of you.'

'The competition is stiffer than IIT,' I remarked.

'Have you two decided yet? Reincarnation or Soul Transplant?'

Anvesha shook her head.

'We will think about it after the jury decides if we are worthy,' I said.

'You will always be worthy in my eyes, bhai. *Meri umar bhi aapko lag jaaye.*'

'And for me?' Anvesha laughed.

'*Aapko bhi.* Half-half.'

'This selection thing feels like a death sentence.'

'Bhai—'

'*Sahi mein.*'

'Druvan, don't say that,' said Anvesha.

'Everyone thinks this jury is choosing people who get to live again, but what the jury is really doing . . . is rejecting the people it thinks should die because it doesn't care.'

'This is how cranky he is the entire day. Imagine living another life with him?'

'Then would I be better if you get selected and I don't?'

'Take that back,' snapped Anvesha.

'Sorry.'

'No, say I take it back.'

'I take it back.'

The telecast was about to start. We switched on the television. For now, it showed a black screen with a timer counting down. And yet, there were 3 billion concurrent viewers. Half the world was watching this.

Then the Acharya Parivar insignia glowed on the screen; Fatima and Hasan Ali came on. We were back at the Parivar Grounds, but this time there was no press, no army of soldiers perched on stone horses. Fatima Ali started to speak.

'The Acharya Parivar welcomes everyone to today's telecast. They want to wish everyone luck, prosperity and happiness. They also offer consolation to those who won't get another chance at life.' She paused. 'Now, what we have all been waiting for. The start of history. This is where it all begins.'

My heart thumped against my chest. Anvesha held my hand.

'Bhai, there's no way they will keep you out.'

And with that, a screen holographically projected the faces of the people who had been selected. Simultaneously, the phones of the 5400 people chosen in the first batch beeped with a congratulatory message. The others received a message of regret.

We let each other go. On our phones was the list of 100 names from our constituency.

And above that list a small message that read: *Dear Druvan Datta, The Parivar regrets to inform you that your Soul hasn't been selected for our programme. We wish your soul luck in all its future lives.*

Anvesha had received the same message.

Chapter 43: The Eight

There were still eight hours for the names of the final candidates— the ones to be decided by voting—to be announced.

Our hopes dashed, the three of us sat back and watched the news for the analysis of the 5400 people who had been selected. Every minority got the right representation, women seemed to dominate the list, differently abled people constituted a considerable chunk, and there were many on the list whose inherited wealth was close to nothing. There were no loopholes.

For people like us, the game was over. The leader board of the eight wasn't changing. Mumma, Baba and Uncle, Aunty kept calling us every fifteen minutes to console us. For Anvesha and I, it was a double whammy. Not only were we still dying, the jury didn't think our love story was worth continuing in another life.

'What was the jury thinking?' grumbled Rashid.

'That we were just two people in love,' I answered.

'And who are these people in the jury?'

'There are many from Rooh Collective.'

'If Yogi Ashwinath were on the jury, he would have seen the truth in your love story.'

'And sent someone else to their death instead of us?'

'Bhai, but look at the junta. They are still voting for you! They see the love!'

'Apparently, it's not enough.'

Anvesha slipped her arms around me. 'It's enough for me.'

To distract ourselves, Rashid made Maggi with more masala because WOLO—we only live once. We turned to the news again. Reporters had descended on the chosen people's houses like pests.

And then, just then, Rashid stood up straight. He switched the channel to the leader board.

'Bhai. I have an idea.'

'Can we please switch back to the debate?'

'Bhai, *suno toh.*'

'Please don't say another live video to beg for votes.'

'Nahi bhai, this is much better.'

'I have mailed every possible celebrity, Rashid. It's not going to work,' I said.

'*Suno bhaiya*, so this is what you should do. Both of you should get married.'

'And so?'

'Bhai, we will live stream the entire thing starting now. Don't resist, think, think bhai think. Shaadi episodes get millions of views on soap channels, why shouldn't yours?'

'We are eighteen.'

'Bhai, your bodies are eighteen. Your souls are much older.'

'That doesn't make a difference.'

'Who cares, bhai? It will only give us more views!'

'And set a bad precedent. Not that I care,' I clarified.

I turned to look at Anvesha, who hadn't said anything.

She let Rashid continue, 'Bhai, you have nothing and everything to lose! If you win, you get another chance with each other, and you if you lose . . . well, you lose. We will wait for another three months and try again.'

I looked at Anvesha. 'What do you think?'

'What do you think, Druvan?'

'I think you would look smashing as a bride.'

'Why didn't I think of this?' said Anvesha. She caught Rashid's gaze, smiled and said, 'This is what we need.'

Rashid was close to tears.

She picked up the phone and called Uncle and Aunty. 'Come to Rashid's shop. Bring your Benarasi, ask Papa to get this kurta. Tell Uncle and Aunty too. There's no time to explain.'

'Can you tell me what's happening here?'

She turned towards Rashid and said, 'You're going to officiate the wedding. A Muslim best friend reading out Sanskrit mantras is exactly what we need to bolster this wedding. It's going to reach a lot of people.'

'You're using my religion,' said Rashid. 'And I approve.'

'We are going to look like such fools. There's no way this is going to get us the votes and . . .'

'Druvan?'

'Bhai.'

'Druvan, do you want to get married to me or not?'

'Yes, but . . .'

'Then stick with the plan. This can work.'

In the next one hour, Rashid and his boys cleared the space and decorated it with the bare minimum, so that it would look only partially staged.

'Okay, here's the script. We are playing on sympathy. We won't ask for votes. Let's start with accepting our defeat, and then say we wanted to invite those who supported our love story to our wedding,' instructed Anvesha.

Our parents reached Rashid's garage with all of Anvesha's high-end camera gear. Anvesha sat them down and explained to them what we were planning to do. The plan was thus: Two dying lovers decide to call each husband and wife before they die and ask their Muslim friend to officiate the wedding. They live stream the wedding to immortalize their love story; the parents watch the video and join them in their happiness and give them their blessings.

Rashid made them sit in the waiting room. We set the cameras, Rashid got printouts of the Sanskrit slokas. He was going to wear his skullcap to drive home the point. Then he left the room for us to get ready.

With every piece of clothing Anvesha and I took off, with our emaciated, weak, withered bodies now on display, it reminded me how close we were to death. And with every drape of her saree, I felt surer that I wanted to spend the rest of my life, no matter how long or short, calling her not my soulmate but my wife.

She let her mother in to do her make-up. Mumma put the sandalwood dots on my head, fixed the *topor*, and made me into the quintessential Bengali groom.

'You look like such a *shona babu*,' said Anvesha and laughed.

'I was thinking of good things to say to you, but maybe I will just keep them to myself.'

'It's better that way. Save your emotion for the stream okay? I want you to be your silly, romantic self.'

'You look beautiful.'

'So do you, Druvan.'

'I can keep saying that.'

She walked towards the cameras, the lights and checked the setting once more.

'Is everything fake?' I asked.

'Just because something is being done for a show doesn't mean it's fake. Our friends are here and so is our family.' She held my hand.

'. . . we are getting married then.'

'This is what I always wanted. Only the timeline has shifted a bit.'

She looked at Rashid. 'Rashid, keep using Urdu words, okay? Keep saying *aap ye karein, aap aage aa jaayein* kind of stuff. You know, how Pakistani cricketers talk.'

'That's not how I talk.'

'That's how you will talk today. You have to really sell your religion. I see the *surma*, nice.'

'Never put it before. It feels odd.'

'It looks great,' I said. 'How confident are we?'

'Wait till the third act, trust me it's going to work,' said Anvesha. 'Shall we roll?'

The live stream on Anvesha's YouTube channel started. Anvesha turned on her camera personality. In a few but powerful words, she told the audience what was happening here—two dying lovers were getting married. They wanted to die as husband and wife. They almost made it to the eight but. . . .

By the time she stepped back from the camera and the mandap, and Rashid and I came into the picture, the live stream already had a thousand viewers.

It started slowly. But the image of Anvesha and I in wedding finery and the clickbait-y title, 'Wedding of the Dead', got a lot of her viewers to tune in.

Rashid had prepared well.

Anvesha put her hand into mine on the instructions of Rashid, who rattled off Sanskrit verses as if it were his first language. As Anvesha had predicted, two things happened in quick succession—a deluge of hate from both the communities washed over the comments section. And soon, riding on that hate, another hundreds of thousands of viewers joined in. When people get married, the priests offer them an express package—a quick one-hour in-and-out. Rashid was going for the longest ceremony. A four-hour wedding, right till the time Fatima would name the final eight.

In the first fifteen minutes, the leader board shifted. From the fourteenth and sixteenth positions, we dropped to the twentieth. People were rescinding their votes and transferring them to other people.

It was backfiring.

'Don't look at the board,' whispered Anvesha when she saw me continuously looking at my phone, '. . . and wait.'

Rashid came with up with a spectacular move. He picked up his phone and started a fake conversation.

'*Haanji, Ammi. Haanji, Ammi, main karwa raha hu unki shaadi. Aap sab bhaad mein jaayein* [Yes mother, I am officiating the wedding, you can all go to hell]. I need to do this. I don't see their religion, like they don't see mine. *Ye haram hai to haram hi sahi*,' he said.

Thirty minutes later, we were back where we started. We were losing votes by droves, but were also gaining new voters. The chat section was filled with heart and fire emojis. The young seemed to be on our side. The older people were yet to join in.

That's when we played the parent card.

After an hour, our parents entered. They looked the part—haggard parents of dying children. And boy, did we get our money shot! Seeing us sitting around the fire in our wedding finery, they burst out in ugly—and real—sobs. They ran to us and took us in their arms.

'Hug my mother for longer, be the perfect *damaad* [son-in-law],' whispered Anvesha in my ear.

There was a flood of votes. Rashid touched their feet. Another flood of votes.

In the next fifteen minutes, we snaked up the leader board. I was at the eleventh position now, and Anvesha at the thirteenth. The chat was populated with comments that said:

> *Did you see the respect?*
> *Where do you get boys like him?*
> *Druvan for life? Druvan for two lives?*
> *I just voted for Druvan!*
> *Such supportive parents!*
> *Why shouldn't they live instead of a Tik Tok star!*
> *Poor parents, they didn't get a proper wedding.*
> *Vote for Anvesha!*
> *That star kid is getting to live and these two are dying! This is nepotism.*
> *Look at how her father is holding her hand. Did you see that . . . he looks at her so lovingly!*
> *Aw! She winked at him.*
> *Druvan for lyf! Anvesha for lyf!*
> *# savedruvesha!*
> *Did he just kiss her hand? I want a love like this.*
> *They are soulmates. #druvesha*
> *Soulmates for life.*
> *Save Druvesha!*
> *Who else should live if not them!*

The next big spike came when Anvesha coughed violently—something our illness rarely made us do, but what did the users know? When I bent forward to hold her, she fluttered her eyelashes at me and told me she was okay. The chat exploded with:

> *Ah! Poor girl. All she wants is to get married to the love of her life.*
> *May God bless them. #savedruvesha*
> *Vote for Anvesha!*

She whizzed past me and reached the tenth spot.

We couldn't believe this was landing!

The next stunt was targeted at the soap viewers. Hidden from the camera, Rashid started to spray water at the havan kund. The fire threatened to flicker and die a slow death. At this, we all acted panicked and rushed to keep it alive.

When Anvesha had suggested this, she had said, 'It's a metaphor. Like the fire, our love is dying too, but if all of us come together, we can light it again.'

'No one's going to get it,' I had argued.

'They got the flickering diya metaphor in *Kahani Ghar Ghar Ki*, didn't they?'

And again, we had nothing to lose.

It worked like a charm!

Within the next half hour, there were families who voted wholesale for us. And now, for the first time, we had a chance. We were in the top 10—she at ninth position and I at the tenth.

This is where it got tricky. The ones who were still in the top eight were leagues ahead of us. We needed double the votes we had got till now to overtake them.

While I panicked and sweated, Anvesha remained calm. Time ticked by but our positions remained the same. I waited for her third act.

And then it came.

It looked as authentic as it could be. Straight from a bestselling book, a super-hit movie, a TV show coming to an end.

A death scare.

As the last of the mantras left Rashid's lips, Anvesha rolled her eyes and keeled over. *She was dead.*

Her portrayal was so real that I too bought it despite having waited for the trick. For a few moments, we all believed it. Our reactions were true. Our hearts truly stopped. A few anxious minutes passed. We gave her CPR. She remained lifeless. And then a breath . . . followed by a huge spike in votes. Our screaming stopped. Anvesha stumbled back to her feet and held me close. She kissed me. There was an uptick in votes.

She was at the eight position. She was now at the seventh position. The chat exploded. They noticed the shift in positions.

But I was still at the ninth position. She would live . . . but . . .

She whispered, 'There's still time, Druvan. We will make it.'

'We won't,' I said.

'We will.'

'Should we finish the rituals?'

Just then, there was a huge bang outside.

'What?'

'Who's outside?' shouted Rashid angrily.

Rashid picked up the camera and went to the window. Outside, a mob of masked men awaited us with lit torches, pitchforks, and desi *kattas*.

'Mussulman Hindu *ki shaadi nahi karaega! Nahi karaega! Nahi karaega* [A Muslim can't get two Hindus married]!'

A few people from both communities had come together to make sure that they put an end to this blasphemy.

Mumma, Baba and Uncle and Aunty pulled us away from the window and made us sit back down around the havan. The mob had broken down the front shutter of the garage. They were now inside the garage and were trying to break into the back room, which we were in. With the shouts of Jai Shri Ram and Allahu Akbar, they banged relentlessly at the door.

'Start what you finished,' said Baba.

'We will take care of them,' said Varun Uncle.

Mumma and Aunty picked up wrenches, kept two for themselves, and tossed two to Uncle and Baba.

'I will kill every one of them!' shouted Aunty.

The four of them stationed themselves behind the door.

Anvesha and I were about to get up, but Rashid shouted, 'Sit back down, bhai.'

The door was now creaking.

Rashid rushed through the last of the mantras and gave me the little pot of sindoor.

'Put it on her—'

'I know where it goes,' I snapped.

I applied the sindoor. My hands trembled, and some fell on her nose.

The banging stopped abruptly.

The familiar buzzing of the drones filled the room. Anvesha held my hand. We walked to the window. The men were scurrying away. In the sky, the drones of the Parivar were hovering ominously.

Our parents weren't the only ones who had stepped up in those life-threatening moments.

Rashid whispered in our ears, 'Five minutes to go. You're at sixth and seventh.'

'Will they come back? What if they come back?'

'They won't,' said Rashid.

'We should call the police just in case.'

'They were my men. This was my third act.'

Chapter 44: The Real Third Act

Rashid had given us another life.

Another thought burrowed deep in my head. In the course of those few hours, through our subterfuge, acting and manipulation, we had robbed two people of their lives. Their parents, their siblings, their friends and their extended families had probably started celebrating by now. What must they be going through? To see Anvesha and I leapfrog over them, cheat and relegate them to their deaths? Our survival shouldn't be a game, and yet this was what it had been reduced to. By us.

They called it a democratic process, but was it?

As the clock counted down to the last ten minutes, I knew we would make it. In the last five minutes, we went back online. We owed it to Anvesha's audience for what they had done for us. And our votes jumped once again.

We were now holding hands, looking at the leader board, waiting for the ticking numbers to stop, and for our new life to begin.

And then, our world came to a halt.

Lavina Tandon was on the eleventh spot and without a shot. Her pitch at the time of the recording was simple. She was a rape survivor, raped by none other than her family doctor, and she wanted to leave this body behind. She had argued that with the body, the shame and the hate would also melt away. She had explicitly asked for a male body, so that she could feel the power a man felt just because he inhabited a body that could, in most cases, inflict more damage. Her terse recording had courted both sympathy and controversy. That's what had got her to the eleventh spot.

No one truly wanted her to win. Her winning would set a dangerous precedent for women wanting to be born in male bodies. Some argued it would trivialize rape as it would be treated as a bodily crime, much like a stabbing.

But things changed when we weren't looking. And in at T-minus two minutes she had jumped to the ninth position. There was panic in Rashid's shop. Baba googled the girl's socials and saw she was online and streaming from all of her platforms.

Unlike our stream, she was in a dimly lit room, standing on a chair, a noose fashioned out of a dupatta around her neck.

Behind her, her parents sat motionlessly on plastic chairs. A boy, who was hardly seven or eight years of age, had cried himself to sleep on of the chairs.

There was one-line caption on all the live streams: *Save me or kill me.*

There were just sixty seconds to go, and she was still at the ninth position. She wobbled on her stool, her feet slipped, and she struggled to keep the balance for a few seconds. That did it. Votes started to flood in. She was within sniffing distance of my seventh position on the leader board.

At thirty seconds to go, she was eighty thousand votes shy of the eighth position. She closed her eyes. She lifted one leg as if stepping down from the chair. Her brother got up and tried to rush to her but was pulled back by his father. Votes poured in, and she reached the eighth position, just a few thousand votes away from me.

At fifteen seconds to go, she kicked the stool. For a split second, her body was in free fall, and then her neck snapped—a short drop. Her votes levelled with me.

At 10 seconds to go, we saw Lavina's eyes straining against her skull, her legs trembling. And in the few seconds that the rope was wringing out life from Lavina Tandon, two things became clear. First, that she would take the lead. Second, I wished her dead before the voting ended.

Out of these, one came true.

At the end, this is what the leader board looked like.

1. Faisal Sheikh
2. Babur Khan
3. Sujay Shetty
4. Lavina Tandon
5. Amit Swaraj
6. Sachin Mittal
7. Dhinchak Neha
8. Anvesha Mohan

Fuck the third act.

Chapter 45: Unfairness

Anvesha cried for two days straight. Uncle and Aunty couldn't meet Baba and Mumma's eyes, who were going to lose their child. I tried cheering everyone up, but they kept behaving as if I had already died.

'I'm so sorry, baby,' said Anvesha.

'What for? I will be dead, I would feel none of the pain. So, if anyone should apologize it's me.'

'What will I do without you?'

'You will live for both of us, duh.'

'That's nonsense, Druvan. I don't want to.'

'You have to take care of Mumma and Baba. You're their daughter too, aren't you?'

She nodded.

'And you have to take care of Rashid.'

Rashid was handling it the worst. He was still fighting for me. He had spent hours talking to Rooh Collective seniors, trying to eke out a way my soul could be tracked in my next life and be rehabilitated.

Anvesha had a week to spend with us before she would be taken to a reincarnation facility. Days to her death had started ticking the minute her name was announced. And yet, no details had been given till now.

'It's on you to hold on for as long as possible, Druvan,' said Anvesha.

'I promise. I'm already doing a lot better.'

Anvesha rolled her eyes.

'No, trust me. The doctors said they would have to re-estimate the date of my death. The nurses were quite impressed by my pain threshold. I think she was flirting with me a little.'

'Of course,' she said.

'Even the doctor . . .'

'You better love me regardless of the body I come back in.'

'Sexuality is a spectrum, Anvesha.'

'Easier said than done.'

'I will manage. But what if you get like a really hot body and get obsessed with it? Your own . . . you know?'

'That wouldn't be new. I have always been obsessed with myself.'

Our empty conversations didn't slow down time and the day soon came.

On the eve of her departure, Uncle and Aunty organized a farewell dinner. The list of people started at sixty—relatives, cousins, friends. As the time of the dinner approached, Uncle and Aunty kept paring down the names. In the end it was just us—the people who truly understood what this meant.

We had just sat down to eat when the phone rang.

'Don't pick up. *Kya zarurat hai?* I don't know why people call at this time,' said Aunty.

'Arre, what if it's important?' asked Varun Uncle and received the call. 'What!' He smiled and turned to us. 'Switch on the news. Quick!'

We switched on the TV. A news anchor was screaming BREAKING NEWS.

Faisal Sheikh had been shot twice in the back. He was being taken to the hospital. The images showed his head rolled over to the side; his eyes lifeless.

'You know what this means, bhaisahib!' said Varun Uncle.

Baba looked at Mumma.

'We can't celebrate his death,' objected Mumma.

And just as our morals kept us from pumping our fists in jubilation, we heard ear-splitting sirens outside. They converged outside the house. Before anyone could react, a bunch of boots made their way up the stairs.

The door flung open.

'Who . . . '

Baba's words hung in the air.

Fatima Ali stood in front of us. She carried a pistol in her left hand.

'Two of you, with us,' she commanded. She looked at our parents. 'They need to be safe.'

Her men led us out.

'My men will be outside to guard you,' she announced. 'There's no time to waste. Their lives can be in danger.'

'But—'

'Datta Sahib, all your questions will be answered,' interrupted Fatima.

The men led us to the five Land Cruisers parked outside. The windows had been blacked out. I kept turning to look at Mumma and Baba. They waved at me as I was hauled inside the car.

Sirens off, the cars drove away from the house and our tearful parents at astonishing speed.

'Faisal Sheikh might survive, but we need to protect you,' explained Fatima. 'We are going to the Soul Centre. It's dangerous for you to be outside. As we speak, the others are being picked up too.'

'All 5400 of us?'

'The eight . . . and now nine of you are at security risk. The junta thinks you don't deserve what you're getting. None of the 5400 people we selected are being questioned, but all of you are, by the same people who voted for you.'

We kept our mouths shut. The men in uniform drove the cars at dizzying speed towards the Acharya Gardens.

'I think I will vomit.'

'Five more minutes, hold it in,' warned Fatima.

'Have you ever had cancer, Fatima?' I asked.

Fatima Ali glared at me.

'Worse,' she said. The ridges on her scarred face burned bright.

The convoy of cars entered the parking lot of the gardens. We were transferred to another set of guards, who formed a security cordon around us.

The guards offered us wheelchairs. Anvesha waved hers away.

The doors to the lift opened.

'Wait. Are we going to the . . . wow!' I said.

I spotted the helicopter with the Parivar's logo emblazoned on it. The rotor blades were already in motion. The guards slapped headphones around our ears. I spotted snipers, looking out in all directions. I wondered who was so powerful who could assassinate us here, at the most secure area in the world.

'Get up! Get up! Get up! Wheels up in two.' Instructions were being barked in my earphones.

'Fuck, chill a little,' I replied, scrambling to my seat.

The guards sat on opposite sides of us.

'First time?'

'Huh?'

Right in front, in the window seat right opposite ours, was Babur Ali Khan, looking more gorgeous than he did in any of his pictures. How was death making him more beautiful?

'Scared?' he asked.

'Not any more,' murmured Anvesha staring into the dark pools of Babur's eyes.

What.

The stern guards giggled.

I butted in, 'I'm probably going to vomit.'

I had aimed for a comeback and blurted out the truth instead.

'Do you know he's gay?'

'Why would you say that, Druvan?' snapped Anvesha.

Babur laughed and said, 'Bisexual. By the way, I love flying. I have flown this model too.'

'Only a rich person can say that,' I shot back.

'Who's rich now? We have quite a few lifetimes to decide, don't we?' Babar mused, smiled, and looked ahead as if this was a fucking movie.

All the middle-aged guards around us were moderately charmed by Babur.

The helicopter lurched to the right. I felt a tight knot in my stomach. Vomit bubbled at the back of my throat.

'Nice trick, though,' a girl's voice said.

We turned to see from where the voice came. It was Lavina Tandon—my nemesis.

'We should be saying that to you, shouldn't we?' I shot back in rage.

'You can now pray for Faisal's death like you prayed for mine . . . umm . . . Druvan, right?' she quipped. She looked at Anvesha. 'You have to admit your reason is silly. Who in their right mind would carry one love story into another life? That's just bleh.'

Anvesha looked at me and asked, 'Does she think we are having a conversation?' And then gave her the finger.

I clutched Anvesha's hand tightly as the helicopter manoeuvred dangerously. Babur caught my eye in the rear-view mirror and handed me a paper bag.

'It's not too far from here,' Babur spoke. 'They had to make it away from the city because—'

'The traditional reincarnation happens in a 200-kilometre radius, so they had to control that,' said Anvesha.

'So that the souls find home only in the foetuses of—'

'Acharya Life's surrogates, who they will employ for birthing newborns.'

'Can you stop completing each other's sentences? It's disgusting,' I said.

'It's cute, a better-matched couple,' said Lavina.

I blew into the paper bag.

Then it came into view.

At first, it looked like a top-of-the-line resort. And then it morphed into something more. An ashram? A dharmshala maybe? A yoga retreat? As the helicopter hovered nearer, I spotted a complex with religious buildings—a temple, a mosque, a church, a synagogue, a fire temple and a few others which I couldn't recognize. We were still high up in the air, so it didn't strike me how massive the complex was. Slowly the other buildings came into view. They were nothing like the lifeless cubes and rectangles we saw dotted around the cities. Each one had a distinct characteristic. They held the same mystique and grandness we had come to associate with the Parivar.

The guards, too, had their noses pasted flat against the windows of the helicopter. They gawked at the enormous reproductions of chariot horses and war elephants carved out of stone, the domes and the minarets, the marble platforms that glittered in the sun and stretched out for miles.

As the helicopter made its way to the roof of one of the short, squat buildings, I counted twenty parked helicopters and five jets.

'Fifteen of the Soul Centres have already been built. There will be five in each state once the Parivar is done,' said Fatima Ali. 'This isn't reincarnation. This is heaven itself.'

The helicopter landed.

We all staggered out. I promptly vomited on the tarmac. Babur and Anvesha rubbed my back.

'Better?' asked Anvesha.

'You guys look so cute,' said Babur.

I nodded.

We were led towards the reception. The walls, the ceilings and the floor were all made of glass.

As we stepped inside, my head spun a bit more, terrified that the glass beneath would crack. At a distance, Fatima was instructing her retinue of juniors, who were all dressed in light linen kurtas. Like it was ethnic day at the office.

The juniors parted when Hasan Ali walked up to them. Fatima took her father in her arms. The gigantic Hasan seemed to melt in her embrace.

Outside the glass walls, another helicopter was landing. This one didn't have the Parivar's logo.

It had the *Mitti* Logo. Sachin Mittal didn't look anything like his pictures.

I remembered him as a portly bald guy, who wore big spectacles and had an awkward crooked smile with misshapen teeth. But all that was in the past. Mittal was now made out of plastic, Botox and fake hair.

'Is there anything surgery can't do?' remarked Babur.

Mittal walked straight to Anvesha with his gleaming teeth, thrust his hand out, and said, 'Well played, the two of you. Good, solid effort.' He turned to Lavina Tandon. 'You, too, actually. What's the news on Faisal? Is he dead or do we have to suffer through more of his TikTok videos?'

He guffawed. His corrected teeth shone.

'Were you always this obnoxious or has the money turned you into an asshole?' quipped Lavina.

If Sachin Mittal was hurt, he didn't let it show. 'Lavina, that's so cute. But did you know you will still be a whiny, suicidal, poor little bitch when you are reborn?'

'Fuck off, Sachin,' said Babur looking up from the book he was reading.

'Ah! Look who has finally spoken! What are you famous for again? Oh yeah, your mother didn't use contraceptives, that's why!' exclaimed Sachin.

'Love your jawline,' said Babur pointing to Sachin's chin, where there were still scars from the surgery.

Before more insults could be traded, a light plane with the Government of India logo landed, carrying Sujay Shetty, Dhinchak Neha and Amruta Swaraj.

They were laughing as they entered the premises.

'Why's everyone so sullen here!' squealed Sujay Shetty, his eyes twinkling, 'today is a new beginning! Let's all look at the broad horizons, believe in ourselves and be positive!'

'You're talking too loudly,' grumbled Lavina.

Anvesha shook hands with Amruta Swaraj. 'You're beautiful,' she told her.

'Her politics is far from beautiful, though,' chuckled Neha. Neha, whom we knew from songs such as '*Main rap ki rani, west Delhi ki kahaani*' and '*Mere hater khaayein feeka butter*', had an unmistakable anglicized accent. She continued, 'What? We are friends.' She put her arm around Amruta. 'Not Neha, I'm Arundhati Biswas.'

'You're a Bengali?' I asked.

Lavina clarified it for Sachin, who seemed confused. 'For a smart person, you're quite dumb. Dhinchak Neha is an alias. It's all a front. Read a tabloid some time for fuck's sake.'

'There's no need to use strong, negative words, Lavina,' butted in Sujay.

'Fuck off, Shetty,' said Babur.

And just then, Fatima Ali walked towards us. She asked everyone to line up in front of her. We had a star kid and a billionaire, but the force of her voice commanded respect.

Next to her were Hasan Ali and Dr Kanika Arvind Kalam—a ninety-year-old man in a forty-year-old woman's body.

'Welcome to your new lives,' said Dr Kanika Arvind Kalam. 'First of all, you need to understand that none of you deserve to be here. None of you were selected. The public wants you to be reborn, not us. Eight deserving citizens don't get to live again because of you. Always keep this is mind—*none* of you deserve to live. You know what you have done, and you will pay for it in your afterlife.'

All of us shifted nervously in our places.

'Are we going to get some details on how this is going to work?' asks Amruta Swaraj.

Dr Kanika Arvind Kalam didn't answer.

'When are we going to die?' asked Sachin.

'Is God involved? Divinity?' asked Anvesha.

'And how?' asked Babur.

'Will our deaths be televised?' asked Arundhati.

Fatima answered none of the questions. Instead, she asked another one, 'Any more questions?'

'When does our entire consciousness come back?' asked Sujay Shetty.

'Any more?' asked Kanika. She waited and said, 'I will answer the ones I can. The last one about consciousness—it's variable. But if you pick Soul Transplant, inshallah, your entire consciousness will be restored within the first three months. The process is piecemeal and not chronological. You will remember this life in your next, but it will be a jigsaw puzzle. Small pieces. Small memories of different ages. The timeline will be off, and you will have to arrange it to make sense of it. We will train you to do it.

'About your deaths. Every one of you is going to die a painful, horrific death at the time you choose. It's going to be your worst nightmare. When it's time, all of you will have to tell us how you would like to be killed. That's how your soul is marked. Through violence, through distress, through pain. People who die in their sleep, who die with trifling heart attacks and the like, lose their character, their souls drift away, and the bodies they inhabit have no consciousness of their past life. The soul remembers violence.'

'You will get actual people to murder us?' asked Babur.

Kanika shook her head. 'You will be injected with our state-of-the-art lethal injection to stop your heart slowly. But it will come tainted with a hallucinogen. Your worst nightmare will be projected to you in a virtual reality environment. The pain will be real; the blood will be pixels.'

My heart pounded.

'As for God and whether divinity is part of it, the answer is both yes and no . . . '

Kanika paused. We waited for her to break out of her trance. A few moments passed, and then some. She was lost, her eyes welling up, fingers trembling.

'Doctor?'

'Huh?' She continued in a soft voice. 'God exists if you want him to. Wait for your death to transform you. And that's all that you will get from us for the time being.'

Now Hasan Ali stepped up, closely followed by the men behind him.

'These men will help you to your rooms. The process starts tomorrow. Welcome to your death. Welcome to your new life.'

Chapter 46: Hello Doctor

Dr Kanika had turned the control room into her apartment. The hexagonal walls had been broken down, a bed had been placed, and a washroom had been constructed.

There was no time to waste.

The little beeps from the control panels had kept the doctor up at nights for the past many months. Hundreds of little meters clocking every little variable in the fifteen particle colliders flickered all day, all night. There were still hundreds more to be built— thousands over the course of the next fifty years. More scientists needed to be recruited. A mountain of work stared at her.

As if this wasn't enough, Damodar had insisted that the reincarnation/soul transplant process of the eight people be televised to gain popular support.

In the past three weeks, disgruntled foreign nations had funded protests in India against the Reincarnation programme, calling it playing God and corrupt, and fuelling rumours of torture. The relatives of the prisoners, who would be used as replacement bodies for the souls, were protesting too and this had only made the situation worse.

Vidhi Acharya had been uncharacteristically angry when the first protest had broken out.

'They would rather have the bodies of their sons and daughters and fathers rot and burn than allow someone else to use them?' she had shouted in the meeting.

'Damodar, we should have anticipated this. Twenty years ago, we had spent crores on encouraging organ donation, but with little success. The junta had resisted the idea of donating their organs,' Hasan had pointed out.

'Will nothing change? When the hell will we learn?' Vidhi Acharya had looked over to the marketing department. 'Fix this.'

The Aatma Vibhag's image needed tweaks and rebuilding.

New marketing plans meant that for a couple of hours every day, Dr Kanika Arvind Dhillon had to shoot for a reality show which Vidhi Damodar Acharya had mounted. The show aimed to humanize those who were going to be reborn, the people behind the curtain. At last count, the viewership of the one-hour daily, named unimaginatively *The First 8*, had reached 3 billion.

The eighteen-hour workdays made Dr Kanika Arvind Dhillon's body feel weary and tired. The day before she had discussed the need for a new body again with Vidhi, but she had got the same answer.

'You're the face of our science, we can't keep changing it, *beti*,' explained Vidhi Damodar.

'Don't call me beti.'

Vidhi Damodar chuckled. 'Let the world get used to reincarnation. Then we will get you an athlete's body, okay? A runner, a weightlifter, anyone. Man, woman, anything. For the time being, do you want a young heart, a fresh pair of lungs? We can make that happen. Just say the word.'

Kanika settled down on her recliner and picked up the script for the next day. They would introduce the world to Roohnium and explain the elegance of the element that will reshape humanity. She instinctively touched her wristlet—a small boron-enclosed strap that contained a minuscule particle of Roohnium. Each little subatomic particle in the wristlet took millions of dollars to synthesize. But in terms of value, of what it allowed the Acharya Parivar to achieve, it was immeasurable.

'Interesting.'

Kanika was startled.

'Stop breathing down my neck,' said Kanika before closing the script.

'The ungodly process of a soul's transmission,' said Yogi Ashwinath.

'If it is so ungodly, it should have been named after Kalam and not your organization,' said Kanika, pointing at the wristlet.

'Ah! You and your concepts of duality. If it's that then it can't be this. I thought the discovery of another dimension would change things, but no,' he mused. He took a seat in front of Kanika. 'Isn't it time for you to take it off?'

'Let me decide when the right time is.'

'Just make sure it's not too late. You never know with these things,' he warned.

Kanika brushed it away.

'So, did any of the eight choose your brutish, unscientific way? The classic reincarnation?' asked Kanika.

'Amruta Swaraj, as we had expected. Sanyukta Swaraj wants a dynasty to look like a dynasty. Like our Acharyas. They would never take up grown-up bodies of criminals to house their souls. Reincarnation is a more elegant solution, a clean body, a fresh childhood. People will realize that.'

'There's nothing more elegant than the controlled transmission of a soul. I'm sure she will change her mind.' Kanika's finger lingered over the wristlet, the centrepiece of soul transplants—her invention that would change the world.

The second option, Soul Transplant, was more like a graceful transition. This is how it worked: You phase-shifted a soul out of the replacement body, let the signature of the void soul decay in the fifth dimension, and then slapped on the wristlet on the body. Then they phase-shifted the soul of the 'Severely Damaged' and guided it into the flux of the replacement body. In our dimension, the process lasted just a few seconds.

You wore the wristlet for three months after the procedure, till the body stopped rejecting the soul signature. While others had to return it after three months, Kanika still wore it. For the strict reincarnation into foetuses, Kanika had fashioned a Geiger Counter powered by Roohnium—which could measure the soul's energy signature in the womb to a 98 per cent accuracy—to track souls into the next birth.

Kanika poured herself a drink. 'You want some?'

'I'm good.'

'It's not a sin.'

'Just because something is not a sin doesn't mean you should do it.'

Kanika filled her glass to the brim.

Ashwinath frowned. 'The Muslim in you will reject what you're putting into your body.'

'I can control it.'

'That's what you say every time,' he said. 'Are you getting any sleep?'

Kanika shook her head. 'Hardly. I can't take the risk, can I? Anyway, what are you here for, Ashwinath?'

'I can't come to see my favourite girl?'

'Oh, don't take me for a fool. You don't like this body any more. Wait till we get this over with, and I get Ravinder Singh's body.'

'Ravinder Singh? Hmm, is he the actor who's in prison for murder? Not bad.'

Kanika brought up pictures of him on the big screen in front of them. In his late thirties, he was a hardbody, with salt-and-pepper hair. Kanika had figured she could take his body for a ride for a good two decades. The screening of his body had come out exemplary.

'So, will you tell me now what you want, Yogi?'

'Tell me, Kanika. What would you say if I were to go to Vidhi and ask permission to kill Faisal Sheikh in his sleep? Give his Rooh some rest?'

'I will think you're out of your mind.'

'There's a boy in Rooh Collective—Rashid. Dedicated, loyal, a friend of Druvan and Anvesha. I have talked to him. He has been with them for years now. He has kept them together through all the drama, helping them build their relationship. He tells me these two have the potential. There's none other like these two.'

'That's a dead end, Yogi. Don't chase it. How many more of your volunteers are going to die for this crazy idea of yours?'

Ashwinath took out his phone.

'I don't want to see another poll.'

'Closing your eyes won't make it go away, Kanika.' He went and sat beside her.

The hair on Kanika's arms rose. They had slept together only once, but she had had to pay for it. For days after, the Muslim in her had punished her body. The bloodied belt still hung in her closet. The scars from the self-inflicted whipping that had lasted days pained her even now.

Ashwinath continued, 'The mood of the junta still needs to be altered, managed. A reality show fixes nothing. The replacement bodies of the eight and the other 5400 have families, friends, relatives. Would they not see it as unfair no matter how many reality shows you force them to watch? By the end of this year, thousands of souls will be walking around in bodies they don't own. How do you think their acquaintances will react? In the next five years, hundreds of thousands. You will have a revolt on your hands.'

'We are working on a model to incentivize death. Money for bodies.'

'*Murkh ho tum*, Kanika. We need to show them that God willed it. We need to show them there's another way out—a more humane way. We need a back-up plan. Establishing dynasties and religions asks for sacrifices and risks.'

'Science got us this far and—'

'Science? Are you sure?'

Kanika conceded defeat. 'Druvan and Anvesha are both "Severely Damaged". So there's no use.'

Yogi Ashwinath laughed. 'I thought you would say that. But have a look at this.'

He slipped a report in front of her.

Kanika reached out to pick up the report. Her hand stopped mid-air. Her outstretched fingers were now clenched into a fist. She was pulling her hand back.

'What's wrong?'

'The Muslim in me . . . he's fighting back.'

Chapter 47: The Preparation

I was with the eight, and yet away.

Once we were all admitted, the eight were wrapped in a reality show that the Parivar had mounted to give people an insight into the reincarnation process.

By the time they would be done with her, Anvesha would be too tired to even talk. They would spend countless hours trying to reconstruct the lives they had led. For entire hours, they would be strapped to high-powered brain scanning machines to see if these were distorted or precise memories. A simple way to check for distorted memories was to see if their frontal cortex— where creativity originated in the human brain—was engaged. They were asked to repeat the stories and correct them, till only the parts of the brain that stored memories—the hippocampus, the neocortex and the amygdala—were engaged. To strengthen these parts, get the neurons firing, they were given drugs and blasted with radiation.

On some days, their pain threshold would be tested and increased by subjecting them to VR-induced pain. They could pick and choose the method of death, and it would be beamed directly into their brains while electrodes attached to pain points would mimic the pain.

It was said that a lower threshold of pain led to higher chances of losing all the memories of a past life.

Meanwhile, Anvesha and I waited for Faisal to wake up. Every day, to pass time, I would walk around aimlessly in the facility that was being built like a palace cross-bred with an Acharya Life hospital. And despite the hours I spent, I would find new buildings cropping up.

That day, I was walking around the empty halls, nodding and smiling at the people who were working on the rooms the Severely Damaged would inhabit when the Parivar ramped up its capacity. Like other days, I found myself outside Faisal's room.

Ideally, they shouldn't have let me anywhere close to Faisal, seeing how our lives were invariably interlinked. That day, there were no doctors in his room monitoring him.

I went inside and sat on the sofa next to Faisal's bed. He had been flitting in and out of consciousness—a sure-shot sign of recovery. They just needed to check if his brain worked fine. Without that, there would be no reincarnation for him.

Every few seconds, my eyes darted in the direction of the clutch of pipes that kept Faisal alive. Just one tug, and Anvesha and I would have another chance at love. My mind had reconciled with the possibility of his murder.

The only problem was committing it.

'Kill him,' my mind screamed. 'For Anvesha! Do it!'

Almost involuntarily, my hands reached out for the pipes. I told myself I shouldn't do it. I couldn't possibly kill a man. But I wanted to know what it felt like to hold the pipes in my hand.

I pinched the pipes for just that minutest part of a second. My heart jumped. I let go. What was I going to do? Immediately, feelings of shame and disgust washed over me.

'*Hatiye wahan se*, Druvan beta.'

I turned back, startled. Vidhi was standing behind me, breathing heavily. Hanging by her side was a small pistol.

'Sir, I wasn't . . . I was about to go,' I said and got up.

'*Aa jaiye*, let's take a walk.'

'I . . . with you?'

'Are you busy, beta?' she asked.

She left the room. I calmed my heart and followed her out. Like the others at the facility, she too was dressed in a white linen suit. I had to actively remind myself that inside her sinewy body was the mind and soul of a man older than my father.

She waved down the three guards who trailed us. We turned around the corner. Vidhi murmured into her walkie-talkie, 'Haanji, Hasan Bhai, Damodar *bol raha hu*. Switch off comms.'

I looked up and saw the little light on the CCTV cameras die.

'It wouldn't have ended well had you gone ahead with what you were trying to do.'

'I wouldn't have done it, sir.'

Vidhi didn't believe it.

'Firdaus was right about you. Anvesha and you, there's something there.'

'Sir, believe me, I wouldn't have done it. I was just . . .'

'Good for you then. Because you would have had to pay for it. In this life and the afterlife. Because remember . . . everything that you do in your life creates a ledger.'

'L. . .edger, sir?'

'Call me Vidhi. That's my name.'

'So . . . this ledger . . . this is what decides what afterlife would be like? Like you steal something and you have to pay for it? That sort?'

Vidhi nodded.

'Why don't you share that with the people? What it's like? You let them assume a lot of things, sir.'

'Druvan beta, *manoge ki humne koshish kari hai?* But how do you describe something that's indescribable? It's pain. It's pain in its very essence, and how do you describe pain? *Jaise* doctors just put a scale to it. One to ten. But what if you feel pain that's beyond that? Imagine that; imagine that going on infinitely. That's what the afterlife is. It can't be described. The scientists describe it as an energy signature struggling to latch on to a host.'

Her eyes seemed to cloud over thinking of the pain.

'And the ledger? How do you know that? What is that? Like the Santa Claus's list of good and bad children?'

She let out a full-throated chuckle.

'Druvan beta, you like to be funny. I read that in your profile,' replied Vidhi. 'So yes, a list like Santa Claus's. *Haan, shayad, ye keh sakte hain.* By saying that you might offend my team of philosophers at the Soul Division, who were making Rooh Collective's mrityu volunteers die and come back, live a little, sin a little, and then die again, to compare the pain.'

'You killed people for this?' I blurted out.

'Some of them. Some we just put through near-death experiences, phase-shifted their bodies, slapped Roohnium wristlets on their hands and grabbed their souls again.'

'For what? Comparing their sins with the intensity of the pain they experienced? Like a proper graph and stuff? Please tell me you at least succeeded. Or did you just kill off people for nothing? This is not the Age of Empires; this is real life.'

'We tried to, beta. But the entire karmic hierarchy is a muddle; it's chaos. Sin and punishment are still amorphous subjects, and we are clutching at clouds. *Kisi ko samajh nahi aa raha.* We are trying to work out a framework that doesn't fall apart. We will get there. We got here, didn't we?'

'Why don't you share with people what you have found? I mean if you're such a benevolent man . . . sorry . . . woman . . . person, you should do that.'

Vidhi Damodar Acharya laughed again. We turned into a corridor that was still under construction. The clickety-clack of her heels bounced off the walls and echoed.

'Druvan beta, what do you think will happen if we release a list of sins and crimes that attract the most pain in the afterlife? And things one can do to mollify that pain?'

'People can cut out the bad stuff they do . . . '

She lost her patience and said, 'What do you think the Indian Penal system does? It gives people a list of behaviours that are considered criminal, and yet people go out and commit crimes. How's our list going to be any better?'

I was kind of done with her treating me like a child, so I tried to put together a compelling argument and said, 'This will be a higher power, not fellow humans. When you commit thievery, and your fellow humans arrest you, judge you and imprison you, you can always say "Oh, what do they know what I was going through". But this will be . . .'

She smiled at me smugly. 'You said a higher power would judge them. Something divine? Something godly? Is that right?'

'More or less.'

'What you're saying, Druvan beta, is that this list should be announced, or at least relayed through someone who has access to the divine power?'

I hated where she was going with this.

She continued, 'Like a priest? No, that would not do. We need someone bigger, don't we? A prophet? A God's man on earth?'

'I mean . . .'

'Druvan beta, *main aapko kuchh batata hu*. We have had people convert from Islam to Christianity and vice versa, to and from Hinduism, Judaism. We have tested fringe religions, keeping the other variables constant. What can be a bigger sin than converting to another religion? Guess what, beta? There is no retribution. *Thenga*. No one has met a God who has punished them for conversions. Where are these Gods whose hierarchy of sin and good we follow?'

'For someone who found the soul, you're saying that God doesn't exist?'

'I didn't say they don't exist. We say we don't know yet where they exist, or if our definition of them is correct. Druvan beta, I was a Hindu, I'm still a Hindu and will remain so, but would I be punished if I step over the moral or ritualistic boundaries defined by my religion? Our studies say no. A Hindu and a Muslim, keeping other variables in check, get no more severely punished than usual if they eat meat. Imagine that? So many people dead because of this . . . and what is it? Nothing, a code defined by our ancestors that has outlived its purpose. So, coming back to your question. Where will the list of sins be announced? Who will announce it? Which God's prophet? Which religion? Beta, where would the new laws, codifications come from? By whose authority?'

'Vidhi, I'm guessing the answer is you will introduce a new religion? That's where you're getting at, aren't you?' I asked.

'Maybe that's the part of the conspiracy Anvesha couldn't guess?'

'You crave power, unencumbered power, and religion is going to give you that. Isn't that punished?'

'Desiring power is an instinct. It has kept us alive all these years. To kill, conquer, build—everything has its root in power. Even writers seek power over their audience when they write stories. Comedians, who project a lightness of being, crave power and feed on the laughter of their crowd. Power isn't punished. So isn't money, to be honest. We created money—the little papers that everyone holds, the pieces of plastic—but it carries no significance in the afterlife.'

'When will you announce the religion then?' I asked.

She started with a giggle. And then broke into peals of laughter. 'What?'

'I . . . Druvan, I just forget you're just eighteen,' she said and pinched my cheek. She walked towards a bench and sat down. She patted the space next to her and asked me to join her. 'Ask the question of *when* again? But give it a thought before you ask the question. We now live forever . . . so how relevant is when?'

I felt stupid.

'We would let the junta figure out the things we have first. They would realize the things they assume to be blasphemous, the higher power, the God, don't give a damn about them. All those rules and rituals are worth nothing. We would wait till everyone realizes that. It might take a decade, or two, even a hundred years. I'm willing to wait.'

I weighed my words and then said slowly, 'That sounds boring. To just live and live and live . . . I mean even sex gets boring.'

'As a virgin, you seem to know a lot, beta.'

'I am not . . . well, I am but I have masturbated, which means I have had sex with people I was with in my past life. Anyway, no one would want to live forever.'

'Were you not about to kill someone to live on with Anvesha? It's a matter of perspective, beta. Everything in this world is a matter of perspective. And to think the mind just carries on from one rebirth to another? The body changes the mind, too, Druvan. It dictates a path of its own too.' She looked at me. 'I have an eighty-three-year-old woman waiting for me at home. She's my wife,' her voice trailed. 'I . . . this body . . . this body . . . desires men.'

'I heard Ashwinath talk about sexuality . . .'

Her eyes shifted away from me. 'Talking about him,' said Vidhi. 'He's here.'

I turned. Ashwinath was jogging towards us. Unlike the other times I had seen him, the calm on his face was missing. A nerve throbbed in his forehead.

'That's the first time I have seen you run, Firdaus,' Vidhi joked.

Ashwinath caught his breath. 'It's important.'

'You can say it here. This boy's dying.'

Ashwinath looked me up and down and said reluctantly, 'Damodar, 1500 replacement bodies have been found dead in their cells. All of them stabbed in their hearts with a ballpoint.'

Vidhi's face lost all colour. '*Bhenchod*, how did this happen?'

'. . . the . . . that boy.'

'*Vo haraam ka pilla*. The dead are all Muslim?'

Ashwinath shook his head. 'No, all religions. We have a mutiny on our hands. Hasan is taking stock of the situation.'

Vidhi barked into her walkie-talkie, 'Switch on all comms.' She turned to Ashwinath. 'Ask Kanika to take the damn wristlet off.'

Chapter 48: The Soulmate Programme

I followed Ashwinath out of the building. Security drones hovered above us and there were snipers on every roof. Their guns were aimed at me.

'It's a long way, Druvan. Do you want a wheelchair?'

'I feel much better actually,' I said. 'Where are we going? Unless we are jogging then I might . . . '

'As Vidhi said, we need to get Kanika Dhillon's wristlet off. You will see why.'

We walked in silence through the expansive gardens.

'A friend is a huge fan of your cult. His name is—'

'Rashid, yes, I know him. He's a bright boy, got Rooh Collective a lot of volunteers. One of our top recruiters. Some of those boys are now mrityu volunteers. Some martyrs, some reborn.'

Vomit bubbled at the back of my throat. Rashid had recruited a lot of sixteen-year-olds. Did he drive them to their deaths? A few minutes later, another building came into view. It was a single-storey building, and of all the others in the complex, this was the most guarded. I spotted three laser dots on my chest.

We both were frisked. A man in a white kurta–pyjama and a doctor's coat put out two fingers in the air.

'We will have to wait,' said Ashwinath.

'How long? Who knows when I will drop dead?'

'You're not dying, Druvan. Stop being dramatic.'

'As an old soul, like a wrinkly, senile old soul who remembers like 100 lives, you should know drama keeps things interesting. It's weird that, in essence, you're more than a thousand years old. You're a typical Maha Uncle.'

He didn't rise to the bait. He smiled instead. 'You're that old too, Druvan. You just don't remember.'

We took our seats at the reception. Now and then, the scientists and administrative staff nodded at him.

To explain the heavy security, Ashwinath said, 'This building houses the embryos from Vidhi Acharya's biological parents. Thousands of little Vidhi Acharyas.'

'I'm damn sure I don't want to know what that means.'

'Vidhi Damodar Acharya can't come back looking different in every birth. That's not how an immortal dynasty is built. People want continuity, and, more importantly, how many different looking statues will you build for one soul? So, we have embryos of him ready to go into surrogates if he falls sick.'

'What? I can steal it, raise the children and train an army of clones?' I asked.

Ashwinath chuckled. 'I see what Anvesha likes in you.'

'I know I'm handsome. You should have seen me before the cancer. The girl you were fifteen births before would have fallen in love with me,' I said.

He laughed again. I tried to hate him since he had wrested my best friend away from me and used him to recruit young children for sacrifice, but his easy laughter made it hard.

'What else is here?' I asked.

'Oh? Your jokes are over, Druvan? Hmm, I was just coming to that, and I know you would be interested to know.'

'Me? As in, specifically me? Or like in the general knowledge sense?'

'Yes, you. Who else? Faisal's coming in, and the clock's running out for you. Isn't it? So yes, you, Druvan.'

'Continue?'

'So, when we formulated the Reincarnation programme, we knew no one would want to be a newborn again. Even I didn't; I just stepped into Ashwinath's body. That's understandable. Everyone wants to start where they left. But our trend forecasters saw the bottleneck. Where would you get the bodies from?'

'Don't tell me you managed to create bodies without souls.'

'I wish. That was the idea. We came close too. One of our scientists suggested keeping newborn children sedated in a continuously altering amniotic suspension. Let them grow up with unmarked, weak souls, with no experience, no consciousness. And then when the time comes, transplant souls into them. We found that to be a comparatively easier job. A weak, unmarked soul would leave its body more easily. A little nudge would be enough. And the body would be ready for the new soul.'

'You're raising bodies like clothes. Wow, you don't disappoint as a god–man. Just as I had expected, a complete and total disregard for human life.'

'Did I forget to add that we rejected that option?'

'Aw, why would you do that? It was such a cute idea. Raise humans like farm animals and shift souls into them when needed. It seemed like a perfectly reasonable thing to do by psychopath standards. Don't disappoint me, god–man.'

'Stop trying to rile me up, Druvan. It's not going to work.'

'Fine, so why did you reject it?'

'Greed. If I were to give you an option of being transmitted into a new body, wouldn't you want it to be a handsome man? Or a beautiful woman? One with higher brain capacity? With a big dick, perfect breasts? Wouldn't you want that?'

'I was on my way to cracking the IIT, and I'm the eggplant emoji in real life, so I don't care.'

'Everyone cares. We were thinking of rolling this out. One of the IT guys suggested we name it the Avatar Yojana. The minute he said it, we knew we were going wrong with this. We knew where people would take this. People would want to create better, superhuman versions of themselves. Imagine a rich man or woman. They would have access to technologies like CRISPR within a few years. They would use that to gene edit their sequences, weed out the imperfections coded into them, and give us those perfect bodies to transmit their souls into. The idea behind the Soul Project wasn't to give people better lives, but to give them a chance to live.'

'Rashid tried to sell me Rooh Collective for years, and I didn't take the plunge. I still won't. Stop trying to be noble.'

'Well, there was another problem. There was an environmental issue. Millions of bodies in a suspended state would add tremendously to the carbon footprint. In other words, it would wreck the planet.'

'It's really interesting, Ashwinath, to hear about all the ways you people failed. Please tell me more.'

'Our scientists started another programme to replace the Avatar Yojana and right now, we are failing miserably,' he said and got up. 'It's a programme very few people know about.'

He led me into an elevator. At the door, he scanned his eye, his fingerprints, and then said his name aloud to gain access to the minus twentieth floor. The lift dropped for a few seconds. Then the door opened. In front of me was a brightly lit corridor with little cells on each side—prison cells from the look of it but with glass doors.

'Welcome to the Soulmates Programme,' he said with a flourish of his hand.

'What—'

He walked towards the cells. I followed. Something ominous hung in the air. The unmistakable smell of human shit pervaded the air.

We reached the first cell. More than a prison cell, it was a viewing cubicle, the three walls were mirrors. It looked something out of a circus with mirrors that distorted your reality.

I didn't notice it at first. Behind the bed was a little crouched person. Ashwinath knocked on the glass window. A girl jumped up and sprinted towards the glass wall. She lunged and slammed against it. Blood splattered and trickled down the wall. She got up and screamed, but we couldn't hear a word on this side of the soundproof glass. He pressed a button.

Her screams filled the corridor.

'Help me!' she screamed. 'Get me out! Who are you?' The girl was talking to herself. 'This is my body! Get out!' She then looked at Ashwinath. 'Help me! Get him out! This is my body! This is my mind!'

'Who are you?' asked Ashwinath.

The girl calmed down and said in a low voice, 'I'm Abhishek. Jai Shri Krishna.' But in a split second, she started screaming again, 'NO! I'm Karuna! I'm not Abhishek! Hellpppppp!'

'There are more,' said Ashwinath, tapping on my shoulder.

'DON'T GO!' shouted the girl from the cell, and then, in a soft voice, added, 'Bye, we will meditate now. Don't worry. She will come around. I want to die! I want to die!'

Karuna–Abhishek tried to bang her head on the wall but was pulled back by herself.

We walked the length of the corridor. I counted thirty-five cells, which housed young boys and girls in varying degrees of mad frenzy. They were fighting themselves, trying to restrain one hand with another. Their eyes rolled every few seconds. Some of the boys had their hands chained to the wall, shouting.

Ashwinath stopped outside a cell. A girl sat calmly on the bed.

'Is she drugged?' I asked.

Ashwinath shook his head. He pressed the speaker button of the cell and a girl's voice streamed out.

'Hello,' the voice said.

'Hello. Is it Preeti or Sudeep?'

The girl said, 'Sudeep.'

'Can you feel Preeti inside you?'

'She's there. She has reconciled to our new shared reality. I'm ready for an assessment,' said Preeti-Sudeep.

'Hmmm. Can you tell our friend, Druvan, here what our Soulmate Programme is trying and failing to do?' instructed Ashwinath.

'Hi! I'm Sudeep, a mrityu volunteer from Rooh Collective,' parroted Sudeep. 'We are trying to house two souls in one body. But till now it has had a 100 per cent fatality rate for the body. The souls are at unrest. Eventually, one of the souls can't take the pain any more and kills the body. Just this morning, the "people" in the next room pushed their hand down their throat and killed themselves.'

My heart thumped.

'What pain? Like you don't want to share the body type of pain?' asked Druvan.

Ashwinath butted in. 'A body is not used to bearing the load of two soul signatures, so it keeps pushing them closer to death. It's the Roohnium that keeps the soul tethered to the body. Imagine the soul doing a balancing act—one foot in the body, another in the afterlife. And we all know what pain awaits us in the afterlife. It's worse than a million deaths, so the souls choose the easier way out. They commit suicide. The body dies and the souls drift off.'

'What happens when you take off the wristlet? Which soul leaves the body?'

'The guest soul, the one transplanted into the body leaves,' said Ashwinath. 'In a few cases, the other soul leaves too.'

Sudeep turned to Ashwinath. 'I feel good. We feel good. I think we can be the first . . . we can be the first soulmates.'

Ashwinath nodded.

'*Rooh ke liye*,' said Ashwinath.

Durjoy Datta

'*Rooh ke liye,*' said Sudeep.

'*Rooh ke liye,*' they both echoed.

Sudeep raised his arm to the glass. Ashwinath tapped on his tablet. The wristlet was activated.

It slowly came off.

'I feel fine, Yogi . . . I feel great actually . . .'

The words stopped abruptly. The girl's body collapsed.

'Great, my foot,' grumbled Ashwinath and started to walk away.

I stared at her blank open eyes. The cell's light went off. In the shadows, I saw the girl's body being dragged away. Shutters came down in the cell.

I vomited. The man on the computer came running and offered me tissues and water. My head spun.

'Sit,' said Ashwinath sternly and dragged two chairs in front of the darkened cell.

'They . . . they just . . . '

'C'mon, Druvan. You have been trotting up and down the cancer ward for more than a year. You can handle death. Look at your face, so pale. Sudeep and Preeti will find peace in their next life if the Gods so wish.'

'This was murder.'

'At best, it was euthanasia. The girl was on death penalty and begged us to save her. So, we put Sudeep's, a mrityu volunteer's, soul in her body.' Ashwinath took a long breath. He reined in his anger and disappointment. The smile was back on his face. 'These two did better. Usually, either of the souls kills the body within a day or two. They just find a way to end their life.'

'Where the fuck are we going now?'

'I disapprove of you abusing in front of me.'

'The guru of gurus, Mahaguru, the one who doesn't know murder from death, tell me where are we going next, please? Because I think I need to lie down for a bit.'

'Just bear with us for a few more moments.'

'For?' I asked.

'To see the longest surviving body with two souls—Dr Kanika Dhillon and Dr Arvind Kalam.'

The shutters of the cell opened again. Dr Kanika Arvind Dhillon had replaced the corpse of the girl. She looked up to meet our eyes.

She was frothing with anger.

'I will not let you do this! Fifteen hundred people have already died and thousands more will die, but you will not succeed!'

'Arvind.'

'He's under control, Firdaus. Trust me,' said Kanika Dhillon. 'You can't disrespect Allah! There is only one true religion! You will not be able to decimate our religion! Anyone's religion! Muslims, Hindus, Christians! We will all rise.'

'Dr Kanika, try to centre your soul. If you die, we will track you to your next birth,' said Ashwinath.

'I can control him,' she reiterated.

'He mounted a mutiny while being inside you and you didn't know. Clearly, Kanika, he's not under your control.'

'He is, trust me,' said Dr Kanika. 'Allahu Akbar! Fuck you, Arvind. You're a *daayan*. I'm trying to save you, Arvind. You violated my soul! Calm down, Arvind. Do you want to die? I will die, and thousands will replace me!'

'Take it off, Kanika. We don't need him. You now know everything he does.'

'She knows nothing! I built Vasuki. Will you shut up, Arvind?'

'It's time,' said Ashwinath.

'You made me do this,' muttered Kanika.

She took a long breath and tapped her wristlet. As it came off, Kanika slumped to the ground. The wristlet lay on the side.

'Is . . . she. . .?'

With a huge breath, Dr Kanika came back to life. She looked at Firdaus and muttered, 'He's gone.'

'Don't I see that.'

'I told you, Firdaus, it's a stupid dream. Even after years, the body didn't take to two souls.'

Chapter 49: Death's Profitable

Twitter activists were confused. The Parivar pre-emptively extinguished the outrage. Parivar's official communication channel released the news of the 1500 suicides and not a rumour on the grapevine. What was even more surprising was the heartfelt apology.

Fatima Ali held a press conference. Dressed in black, it was clear she was in mourning. For one and a half hours, she recited the names and ages, and gave reporters a short history of each person who had died.

The eight and I were in the cafeteria, watching it on TV.

'You look quite bad. Are you feeling okay?' asked Anvesha.

'That's just his face. Don't give me the cancer thing; cancer has made him look better, if you ask me,' butted in Lavina Tandon.

'What else do you want from us?' snapped Anvesha.

'Do you know there's a small chance you won't reincarnate, Lavina?' asked Babur.

'I hope it doesn't happen to you, Babur. How will your parents stay relevant without you,' retorted Lavina.

'You just love this idea of torture, haina?' joked Sachin Mittal.

'Can we all just embrace our insecurities and love ourselves with our stretch marks and our love handles?' suggested Sujay brightly.

'Sujay, we are not thirteen-year-old unemployed people on Instagram who will buy this shit,' snapped Amruta.

'And Sachin, you should stuff your face in a blender. That's the only surgery you need,' snapped Arundhati.

'Aw, look who's offended—the girl whose only currency is that she's cringeworthy. You know what I think,

Dhinchak Neha? If you show your real self, you will be hated even more.'

'My mother should have taxed *Mitti* out of existence, plastic boy,' quipped Amruta Swaraj.

'Your mother was too busy buying members of Parliament. There's news she came up the hard way to the Lok Sabha, jacking off senior members.'

'You need to shut up, Sachin,' said Babur.

'Or what? You will hit a dying man?'

'I don't know why all of you are trading insults,' I said. 'When we can just humiliate Sachin by repeating how small his dick is. We all saw it in the shower. Babur will testify?'

'It's minuscule,' concurred Babur. 'It's so small I don't even remember it, seriously.'

'Accept yourself in totality. Small penises don't define you. You're not your penis. I advise meditating,' said Sujay.

The remarks burned Sachin up. 'It's not that small.'

'Guys and their obsession,' scoffed Lavina.

'Lavina, I hope the guy's body you get has a small one and then you can tell us all about it,' said Arundhati. 'But obviously not as small as Sachin's. That would be cruel.'

Everyone laughed.

We turned to the screen.

'Fatima Ali, who do you blame?' asked a stern-faced reporter.

'The Parivar takes complete blame for what happened. It was an oversight, and we are introspecting what changes need to be made.'

There was a follow-up question. 'How could you not know there was a mutiny on your hands?'

'We weren't looking for a mutiny. We treat our prisoners with kindness and love. Though we knew there were a few people in the programme who didn't want to give up their bodies for the Reincarnation Yojana, we didn't know how deep the resistance ran. We failed in that department.'

'Hi! I'm from Kaaj Tak. So, what will be the step forward? Without bodies, the Reincarnation Yojana will fail, won't it?'

Shockingly, Fatima Ali agreed and said, 'That's true. That was always going to be a problem. Fifty million people die every year. We will never get as many replacement bodies. But we were expecting people facing the death penalty to cooperate. Why would the prisoners who were dying anyway rob someone deserving of another chance at life? What was the basis of this selfish behaviour? These are questions the psychology and philosophy teams are now trying to answer as we speak.'

'That's fucking smart,' said Lavina. 'Did you see what she did there?'

'She put the moral responsibility on the prisoners,' answered Sachin. 'That's brilliant. That's a fucking masterstroke.'

'At least she has something to stroke,' quipped Arundhati.

Abhinandan Suman from News Foundry said, 'My question is: Did the prisoners kill themselves because they thought they were given death penalties for crimes that didn't deserve it? Or they thought that with time the Parivar would start incarcerating more and more people, make rules stricter, award more death penalties just to generate more bodies for soul transmissions?'

Fatima Ali frowned. 'It's offensive that you would suggest that.' She looked down at her phone, tapped through a few screens, and projected a bar chart.

'As you can see, ever since the announcement of the Reincarnation Yojana, the number of crimes committed, the number of the arrests made and, most importantly, the number of death penalties awarded have slipped. The Reincarnation Yojana is keeping people from committing serious crimes. I hope that answers your question.'

'I want—'

'I'm sorry I'm interrupting you. I remember you saying that the Parivar should roll out the yojana to all and not just 5400 people. How will we do that without the death penalty? This is a testing time for humanity, and we need everyone's support. We are doing the best we can.'

'A follow-up?' Abhinandan raised his hand. 'Assuming that the prisoners don't get swayed by your moral lecture on being selfish, what will the Parivar do?'

'The Parivar will look for willing participants,' she said.

There was silence in the reporting room, silence in the cafeteria.

'What did she just say?' I said.

'This is fucked up,' muttered Babur.

Fatima continued, 'Citizens of the country who believe they have reached the end of their life and are willing to give up their bodies can do so. We are currently looking at economic models that can support this. Our in-house economists and financial experts suggest that 10 per cent of the reincarnated individual's inheritance go to the family of the person who has sacrificed his/her body. The number can go up. We are still ironing out details.'

The microphones picked up the murmurs in the room.

'They will be incentivizing death?' murmured a shocked Anvesha.

'What do you care?' butted in Sachin.

Anvesha shot him an icy glare. 'That's the monetization of death. They are now selling death.'

'That's a pretty sound business strategy. Love it. What's a better product than death!' exclaimed Sachin. 'It's not seasonal, and then there are bonanza events like pandemics and wars.'

Fatima Ali took the microphone out of the stand and spoke clearly into it.

'We are incentivizing a better chance at life for two souls—one who wants to live and has a dying body, and another who wants a fresh start and wants to die. Why would you want to keep people in misery? This would also bring about the biggest wealth redistribution reform in the country, as we would aim to pair the higher-income souls with lower-income bodies to flatten the curve.'

Anvesha buried her face in her palms. She murmured, 'Play socialism with money, capitalism with souls. The new currency.'

Fatima Ali continued, 'We will go ahead with soul transference only if the prisoners consent to the procedure. One family member of the prisoner should also agree.'

The aggression of the journalists started to die down.

'The Parivar seems to have its shit figured out,' said Lavina.

'It covers all populist angles,' pointed out Amruta.

Fatima Ali continued, 'Also, once the transference happens, the family of the prisoner will have medical autonomy over the organs. In other words, if any immediate family member needs blood or a safe transplant, the owner of the body has to acquiesce to that demand compulsorily.'

She waited for a split second for the journalists to formulate a question and then, in the absence of one, got up and left.

'This is government-aided suicide,' said Anvesha. 'This . . . this is wrong!'

Just then, a Rooh Collective employee rushed into the cafeteria.

'Faisal is awake.'

Fuck.

The inevitable had happened, and yet, I was surprised when it did. We got up and walked to his room. I looked at Anvesha. It felt like life had been drained out of her in one fell swoop.

'Welcome to your death,' said Sachin to me.

'I will stab you in your sleep,' snapped Arundhati.

'Will that be before I grab your boob or after?'

*

When Faisal opened his eyes, he saw us staring at him. His eyes searched for, I assumed, his family but rested on Babur Khan. Faisal reached out, and Babur held his hand. Babur kissed Faisal's hand, his arm, and then moved up his chest and finally kissed him on his mouth. The tenderness of the tearful kiss startled all of us.

'Whoa! Where are the paparazzi when you need them, haan?' said Lavina.

'I can feel my heart break,' said Arundhati.

'Druvan, if anything, this is one less reason for you to hate them. Soulmates for soulmates,' consoled Amruta.

Anvesha clasped my hand tighter.

Faisal helped himself up. Babur shifted on to the bed next to him. They looked at Anvesha and me. 'We are sorry.'

'Just imagine how people would have reacted had this been known, eh? The beti of TikTok and the beta of a movie star, both cocksuckers,' said Sachin.

'You need to shut up, Sachin,' grumbled Amruta.

'I don't know what problem you have with people sucking cock. I'm only stating a fact.'

'Can I punch him?' groaned Faisal.

'He has a small penis,' answered Babur.

Everyone laughed except me.

Sujay Shetty looked at me and said in his highest pitch, 'Look at the brighter side, Druvan—'

'The only bright side to this is that I won't have to suffer watching you be successful,' I snapped back.

'It's only when there's negativity . . .'

'Fuck off,' said Anvesha and I.

'You need to say your goodbyes,' said Arundhati. 'They are here.'

We turned, and there they were. Led by Fatima Ali, the gun-toting guards had flooded the corridor outside.

Babur and Faisal tried to mutter an apology.

'Don't,' said Anvesha.

She turned and kissed me. She pushed her tongue into my mouth and I into hers. For a moment, we kissed as if we were trying to consume each other, weld together our souls, be inseparable.

'It's time to go,' announced Fatima Ali as if she wasn't relegating me to my death. 'We are wheels-up in ten minutes.'

'I hope there's space for one more on the helicopter.'

'Anvesha?'

'I go where my soulmate goes,' said Anvesha and kissed me again.

Chapter 50: The Best friend

By the time we made it to the helipad, Anvesha's spot had been given to Ranvijay Bhat—a gamer-cum-reaction-video-specialist who had legions of young fans.

Anvesha and I were strapped in by guards. Hasan and Fatima Ali got into the front seats. They were piloting the plane.

'We will go to the headquarters nearby, debrief the two of you, and then you can go home,' instructed Hasan Ali.

Just as he was about to put the rotors on, he got a message. Hasan checked his phone.

'It's your mother again. She's bombarding the board number. Tell her she has five minutes,' said Hasan Ali to Anvesha. Hasan muttered into his mouthpiece. 'Wheels up in five.'

Anvesha took the phone from Hasan.

'Druvan had nothing to do with it,' explained Anvesha for the nth time. But her mother wasn't ready to listen. Someone had to be behind this stupid, moral decision. 'Maa, he's crying and begging as we speak.'

Aunty's howls seeped out from the receiver. 'How can you do this to us, Bitku! Please . . . please go back. We can't live without you, we can't.'

'Maa, I don't want to snatch anyone's body and live there. For an entire lifetime? Absolutely not!'

'They are criminals!'

'Nikhil Advani,' said Anvesha.

'Who's that?' I asked.

'The boy whose body I was to live in.'

'He killed someone—manslaughter,' interrupted Fatima.

'Involuntary manslaughter, Fatima. He was seventeen and lost control of his scooter. He should be dead for that?'

'Should he not be? Would you be able to say that to the nine-year-old girl he knocked down?' scoffed Fatima.

Aunty shouted again. 'Give the phone to Fatima. She will make you understand. I will tell her if she brings you home, you will see our dead faces. What will we do when you're dead? Nothing, nothing will be left.'

Varun Uncle said in the background, 'Bitku, we will die too. That's final.'

'*Kya bol rahe ho,* bhaisahib,' I could hear Baba say.

'Maa, I'm not doing this. And honestly, I feel fine. Let me enjoy these couple of years I have left than do this. It doesn't feel right to me. I won't be able to live like this.'

'We need to go,' instructed Hasan.

'Maa, I will talk to you when I get home.'

She cut the phone even as Aunty and Uncle screamed in the background.

'Wheels up. Strap in,' bellowed Hasan Ali.

The rotors started, a loud humming noise blocked everything out, and the helicopter soared. My stomach churned.

Anvesha's decision was unfair to all of us. Her righteousness sickened me. Who was watching her? This was not a YouTube video. This had real consequences.

'You can't do this, Anvesha. One of us needs to survive.'

Anvesha rolled her eyes. 'Don't parents die, Druvan? How's this different? In how many different ways do you want me to tell all of you? I wouldn't have been able to live like that.'

'It's fucked up, Anvesha. You can say anything right now to sound saintly, but your morals are worth dirt. This is a once-in-a-lifetime opportunity.'

'It isn't an opportunity of a lifetime. This will last forever. How's that fair? You will die. What if my parents die too before they get on the roster to get reincarnated? What will I do then? Live all alone? For what?'

'These are hypothetical situations.'

'But possible situations. Why can't you guys bear the grief of my death when I'm supposed to bear the grief of yours?'

I closed my eyes to keep myself from vomiting again.

I reached out and held Anvesha's hand. It was cold, limp. I turned to look at her.

'Anvesha?'

Her head was slumped to the side. When I let her hand go, it slipped away. I screamed.

Fatima saw me freeze in the rear-view mirror. She unstrapped and jumped to the back. She unbuckled Anvesha in a flash. Anvesha collapsed to the floor of the helicopter, her body limp and lifeless. Without wasting any time, Fatima Ali started to resuscitate her.

After what seemed like a tortuously long time, Anvesha spluttered back to life.

'Don't you fucking unbuckle,' Fatima snapped at me.

'Down in five,' announced Hasan. He shouted for a medical team at landing.

The next fifteen minutes were a haze. We landed on a helipad amid the hills. I would later be told we were an hour's drive from Mussoorie. An emergency medical team was waiting for us when we landed. They hoisted Anvesha off the helicopter, put her on a gurney, and wheeled her out of sight.

I felt my heart burst when I saw her head roll to one side.

'Keep yourself together, betaji. Nothing will happen to her,' scolded Hasan.

My knees buckled. Hasan picked me up.

'It's cardiomyopathy.'

'What's that?' asked Hasan.

'The broken-heart syndrome . . . we die together . . .'

I passed out.

When I woke up three hours later, Mumma and Baba were at my bedside, holding hands. Aunty and Uncle were at the door, their eyes downcast. To them, Anvesha was already dead.

'Uncle . . .'

'We know. She keeps saying it's her decision,' mumbled Uncle.

'Where's she?' I asked.

'They are in the ICU. They are monitoring her,' said Baba. 'She will pull through for now, don't worry.'

Aunty looked at me, and I could see she couldn't bear the look of me. Yet she didn't say a word. Someone had to shoulder the blame for Anvesha's decision, and, for the moment, it was me.

We sat around without talking. What were we supposed to say? The light of our lives had decided to extinguish itself. We all cursed the Acharyas under our breath.

A little later, Uncle and Aunty were called by the doctor to give an update on Anvesha's condition. Mumma and Baba left after them.

Once alone, I flitted in and out of sleep. The fear struck in deep that Anvesha would die before I would.

It was late when I woke up and saw Ashwinath sitting in front of me. He had medical reports of some kind in his hand.

'I'm surprised to see you here, Druvan. You walked quite a bit with me without tiring out. Such a handsome man like you strapped to a hospital bed. Nah!' remarked Ashwinath.

'Is this when the pervert god–man molests the helpless boy?' I said. 'You flew here just to find me vulnerable. Wow, I must be really attractive.'

'You won't stop trying ever, will you?'

'I will when I die, which I hope happens before Anvesha. Because that's going to really suck. Congratulations to you for making this so fucked up; she bowed out.'

'That's the issue, Druvan. Your cancer is in remission. Not a single errant cell. Haven't you felt better in the past couple of months? I am sure you have noticed how you have been responding to the treatments.'

'I—'

'Of course, you have,' he interrupted. He shifted to another file. 'Did you know that they stopped all life-saving medications for the eight? We didn't want their brains to be muddled with all the drugs. It's counterproductive to our goals.'

'So? So what? Do all men of God take courses to talk in circles? Why do you do that? Does it emerge from the desperate need to be seen as intelligent?'

'Druvan . . . that means Anvesha was taken off chemotherapy. No supplemental radiation was given. You know what happens when you do that.'

'The cancer—'

'Let's put it plainly, Druvan. She's not going to survive. She knew the risks when she pulled out of the programme. She's facing quick and certain death. She's dying as we speak.'

'What the hell are you saying . . . we can put her back on the cycle,' I groaned. I wanted to reach out and grab his throat, but even talking was an effort.

'Yes, the doctors will try to do that, but you have read quite a bit, researched quite a lot. What do you think the result of that will be? A few more months? A few months in indescribable pain and suffering, devoid of any dignity.'

'You killed her. You took her off the drugs!'

'Correction, Druvan. We were doing everything we could to save her, give her another life. This one's on her. At least the decision-making is on her.'

Just then, from the shadows, emerged Rashid. He touched Ashwinath's feet, pulled a seat, and sat next to him.

'Hello, bhai,' he looked at me and said in a soft voice. '*Aap acche lag rahe ho.*'

'Oh c'mon, *bhosadchod*, stop making that sorry face. I know what you did for Rooh Collective. You sent little kids to their deaths,' I said.

'It's for the larger good, bhai. *Aap to dekh hi rahe ho*. You wouldn't have understood it, bhai. You never had faith.'

'The one you had faith in, felt you up, and your new man of God maybe has a crush on me. He takes me out on walks to dark dungeons.'

Ashwinath smiled. Nothing could rile him up.

'Recruiting volunteers for the Aatma Vibag was not the only thing Rashid was entrusted with,' said Ashwinath. 'His other responsibility was of far more importance. Something that would change the world as we know it, save lives and change the definition of love itself.'

'His friendship turned into a ruse? Is that it? Rashid, you were never that interesting anyway.'

'Bhai, it was never a ruse. I just . . . .'

'When he told me about Anvesha and you, it piqued our interest. You two were very interesting. Born to neighbours on the same day, same date; kids who wouldn't sleep if not next to each other,' confessed Ashwinath. 'We wondered if souls were tied cosmically; if they trailed each other geographically. Wouldn't that be something? Like souls determining where and when they will be born. That would be incredible. You know, Druvan, like actual soulmates.'

'Are we . . . '

'No. We looked into all the deaths of lovers around the time of your birth. The search was futile.'

'I see why you are a god-man. You're good with false promises and murders. Glad you chose well, Rashid!'

'But then, it threw us another opportunity. You met Kanika Dhillon and the recently departed Arvind, didn't you? We had been trying to cram two souls into one body, and, strangely, it just worked for the two of them. It was painful, but it worked. The Roohnium kept the souls packed in there. But they were halfway in their afterlife, their soul signatures flickering. But they hung on. The pain never overwhelmed them, they were never driven to suicide. We wondered if it was Kanika's obsession with Arvind that kept his soul in that body. Was that the reason he could weather the pain that comes from a wavering energy signature? Going by that assumption, we tried to acquaint people with each other, but with no success. We tried it with Rooh Collective volunteers; with people who were in successful marriages. It didn't work.'

Rashid added, 'When two souls are in one body, their subconscious merges. Nothing's hidden. The souls operate from the same biology, so the memory banks are readily accessible. Everything is laid bare—their past memories, the lies, the fake emotions, their darkest secrets, their worst of thoughts. Nothing remains hidden. That's what *ek jism, do jaan* does. All the pain, the baggage, the burdens are passed on to the soulmate too. It becomes unbearable, bhai.'

Ashwinath picked up, 'Rashid was asked to make sure to iron out the kinks in your relationship. He was the moral compass for your relationship, Druvan. He kept the two of you from breaking apart, he kept the two of you from lying to each other, he was the glue who held you together. He was always around, sensing fights, discord and dousing them before something bigger happened.'

'He didn't need to. It was all a big fucking waste of time. Anvesha and I would have been perfect anyway,' I argued. 'And wait a fucking minute. Did you do this trickery before our cancer diagnosis? Now don't tell me you got us sick, so you could test this out on us.'

Ashwinath looked at Rashid.

'You're fucking with me, right?'

Ashwinath laughed. 'We didn't do anything. But the Soul Division throws dices that span decades. You had to die some time or the other, didn't you? The cancer was just lucky for us.'

'Winning the lottery is lucky, getting sex on the first date is lucky, a viral video is lucky, a god–man falling off the stairs and getting paralyzed is lucky. This is death. Death is not lucky.'

'You know what's lucky, Druvan? Your best friend Rashid having the brilliant idea of getting you and Anvesha married on live stream, and that last-minute dash of Lavina Tandon. How do you know it wasn't planned?'

'Was it?'

Neither of them answered my question.

Ashwinath continued, 'We knew Anvesha would bow out of it when the time comes. There was absolutely no way she would go ahead with it. With you, yes, 100 per cent, but alone? Absolutely not.'

'There's nothing you know for sure. She could have gone through with it.'

'Why, Druvan? Because of free will? That's long being packed and sold as a product to an advertiser. At Acharya's, a data scientist knows more about a person than his wife of twenty years. You can hide an entire family, an affair, a lost job, a drug habit, sexual orientation, kinks and fantasies, crushes and heart breaks from someone, but can you hide it from the Internet? No.'

'Glad to know, Ashwinath, you were spying on us. Did you access our bathroom videos and shag?'

'If we wanted, we could have. We know exactly how long you view something, for how long you read it, when your hand is on the fingerprint sensor, we know what you're feeling, the cameras on your phone record the dilation of your pupils. We not only know the inane stuff but also your deepest desires. We know your vulnerabilities, the times when you feel lonely, what makes you happy, what makes you nervous. We know you're going to lie on a call, on a text, even before you say that lie. We can read a text and predict your behaviour. Sitting behind a screen, our guys can not only predict your behaviour but also guide it. It wasn't by chance that Anvesha came across articles debating the ethics of using someone else's body. She spent hours reading them, and we flooded her timeline with more. We flooded the timelines of the people she looked up too, so they would talk about it and reaffirm her thoughts.'

'I ate a sandwich today morning. Was it by design?' I snapped. I calmed myself down and asked, 'But why us . . .'

'Us? Not just you. There are many Druvans and Anveshas we are tracking. There are many Rashids too working on this project.'

'But we are the best?'

Ashwinath laughed. 'From what we know of you, the data says, you have been . . . true soulmates.'

'Yes, bhai. You two are right up there.'

'Right up there or the best?'

'The best, bhai. You're always the best for me.'

'Now's the time to decide, Druvan. Anvesha won't survive. The questions is: Will you volunteer for the programme?' asked Ashwinath.

'*Bhosadike* Rashid, you're recruiting me as a mrityu volunteer?'

'Bhai, we are only helping you.'

'You're asking me to step into hell and stay there.'

'We don't know what happens when it works. And with the two of you, true soulmates, I think we will do much better. I believe it would work.'

'Have you asked her?'

Ashwinath shook his head. 'She's not in a position to answer that.'

'There are only two options, bhai. Either she dies and you live. Or both of you live in your body.'

'What if it fails, Rashid?'

Rashid kept the wristlet in front of me.

'You two can still say together. This will keep her soul locked in.'

'And if I take it off?'

'Her soul might get lost, bhai. Your soul too, maybe. But I know you, bhai.'

'. . .'

'You would rather die with her. It's better than the odds you have right now.'

From the shadows of the room, I saw Uncle and Aunty emerge. Behind them were Mumma and Baba.

'They are all waiting for an answer, Druvan,' said Ashwinath. 'This is what you have always believed. The two of you are soulmates.'

'You always were, Bubai,' said Baba.

Chapter 51: Soulmates

The helicopter ride didn't feel unnatural. The step on the footrest, wearing the microphones, flashing a thumbs-up to the pilot, and the first lurch towards the right felt familiar.

I looked in the rear-view mirror.

'Are you excited?'

'I am.'

I put her hand into mine. The guards turned to look at us.

We were now minutes away from the Parivar Gardens. We saw it from miles away. There were security drones hovering in the air, assault helicopters, Tejas jets parked in different parking lots, and armed men dotting passageways. As soon as we stepped down, an entire troop of commandos surrounded us.

Parting the cordon, a chirpy boy with a headset strapped firmly around his head, iPad in hands, found us, and said, 'Sameer, I will be your handler.'

'Thank you for making us feel like terrorists,' I said.

'He has the worst jokes,' responded Anvesha.

'I'm a big fan,' gushed Sameer, as he trotted beside us.

'Aren't you the sweetest!' Anvesha said.

We were taken to what was labelled as a green room, but it was nothing like the one we had seen on television. It was a hotel suite, complete with a buffet, a mini bar, and a jacuzzi. When Sameer saw our jaws drop, he said, 'You deserve it. You are the stars of the evening!'

We walked up to the curtains and pulled them apart. The room, we realized, was built into the structure that held up the Acharya Garden stage.

Below us, we saw a crowd of journalists and civilians, waiting for the Parivar to show up. The journalists sat in the first few rows of the raised steps and behind them was the general public. There was entire stand for the relatives of the 5400 people who had been selected for the Reincarnation programme.

Today was their *muh-dikhai*.

Every relative had an iPad in their hands. Anvesha and I had been given one too. There was a 'search' bar in the middle of it.

The empty space asked for a name and promised to take us to the pictures and videos of the new bodies assigned to the reincarnates. The software wasn't live as yet and it asked us to wait.

Just then, the Parivar's jets landed on the tarmac. A few minutes later, there was a thunderous applause. We assumed she had taken the stage above us.

'Jai Shri Krishna!'

It had started.

Vidhi Damodar Acharya didn't waste time to showcase the Parivar's success. Her product line didn't need to be praised, just presented.

This time, she went with a single one-line exhortation: 'We did it! *Hum ho gaye kaamyab!*'

And with that, as choreographed, the 5400 reincarnated people walked on to the stage as the crowd cheered them on.

'These bodies aren't theirs.'

'That's the way things are now, Anvesha.'

'The families of these bodies must be watching this. Mothers, wives, sons and daughter. They loved these bodies but now they are owned by . . . invaders,' remarked Anvesha. 'How must they feel?'

'The prisoners gave them their consent,' I argued.

'You know what I'm talking about, Druvan. It couldn't have been easy,' she said.

'It's not.'

Despite knowing that these men and women whose bodies were now being used would have been dead anyway, it was still distressing to watch.

How would I feel if I saw Anvesha on the stage, but she couldn't recognize me? How would I feel if it housed someone else's soul? That her body would now have a different lover?

Our discomfort melted away a little when the camera cleverly panned on the faces of the people who had new bodies. Many of them were crying, their mouths wide in big smiles.

'The time has now come to meet your families!' said Vidhi Damodar Acharya to the cheering crowd. 'Put on the earphones and meet them again. People whom God has willed to live again.'

Thousands of necks craned downwards at the iPads they were carrying. The anxious relatives typed in the registration numbers or names of their relatives and pressed enter.

'Let's search Amruta?' Anvesha said.

I typed the name 'Amruta Swaraj' in the search bar. Two video thumbnails and a few pictures capturing the left, right and straight profile of a young man appeared on the screen. He was slightly dark with a sharp jawline and bright eyes. His hair was cropped short and he was standing ramrod straight.

'Namaste. I'm Amruta Swaraj, age twenty-four, and now in the body of Kaiz Baloch. I thank Kaiz and his family for allowing me to use his body. I promise to take care of him, his family and myself. I will never forget this debt. I want to thank the Parivar for giving me another chance.'

We clicked on the other video of Kaiz Amruta Thakur. It was addressed to her mother, Sanyukta Swaraj.

'Mumma,' Amruta's eyes welled up. 'I'm back. Please make kadhi-chawal for me, okay?'

The video ended.

'You're crying,' I pointed out to Anvesha.

'It's actually you who's crying,' replied Anvesha. 'I'm pretty good at holding back my tears.'

There was a section of babies as well for those who had chosen the Reincarnation plan. It was only accessible to the relatives.

We looked at the relatives stand. It was drowned in shouts of Maa, Mumma, Papa, Daddy, and thousands of names. The relatives in the stands tried committing the new faces to memory. The reincarnated waved back at the crowd. There was collective crying, chanting that coursed through the crowd in waves. A few started chanting, 'Parivar Zindabad! Parivar Zindabad!'

This was the closest to a religious miracle anyone had ever experienced.

Tearing ourselves away from it all, we tapped on the other names on the iPad. When Faisal spoke from the body of Arun Pandey, we noticed the familiar tilt of the head, the same accent from before, and the twinkle of the eye. Same with the other six. Everyone had retained their ticks from their previous souls. It was uncanny.

Vidhi Damodar Acharya then raised her hand. And with that, the entire garden fell silent. It was so quiet, we could hear the light buzzing of the drones over us.

'The Parivar is fortunate to be a part of this celebration,' she said. 'But the Parivar also knows of the difficult road that lies ahead, and we will not rest till we can give joy to every citizen. The Parivar recognizes the hurt and the confusion of the people whose loved ones gave up their bodies and is thankful for their contribution to the society. Their crimes are now fully paid for and God will see that! Keep your heads high because this . . .'

she pointed to the 5400 people who had been saved from death, their families spared the grief, 'is a worthy sacrifice!'

There was applause all around. Vidhi said, 'This is for the dead, the worthy, the ones who redeemed themselves! Once criminals but now heroes! Jai Shri Krishna!'

'Such a player,' remarked Anvesha.

When the applause died, she continued, 'There is another announcement the Parivar wants to make today. The Parivar has been a *bhagidar* in the grief of the people who didn't make it through the selection process. We apologize and ask for your forgiveness. There are multiple constraints that we would like our junta to recognize. Going forward, we know we wouldn't have enough bodies for soul transference for everyone.'

The silence returned.

'. . . but then, our scientists have found another solution to prolong life that the dying can opt for. Today, for the second time, the Parivar will change the world.'

She took a long pause.

We ran our fingers around our wrist where the Roohnium wristlet was strapped on for the past three months. Initially, we had waited for the afterlife we had been scared of, the pain that would come from straddling another dimension—hell's physical manifestation—while we were still in this body. The pain didn't come. Kanika, Hasan and the others were shocked. We were perfect subjects, a perfect fit, the souls tailor-made for the Soulmate programme.

We were worried about would happen when it was time to take it off. But when they took it off, nothing transpired. The only pain I felt was when Anvesha's soul phase-shifted. 'It was nothing,' she said for days after. When I scampered through her memories in our shared brain, I couldn't find anything. Had she been that noble? And if we were a perfect fit, had I been this awesome?

Sameer burst into the room.

'It's time,' he said to us.

The guards came soon after, created the now-familiar security cordon around us and led us out of the room, into the lift and up to the stage. The lift opened to the all-glass area of the stage where the Parivar stood at a distance.

It was now just the family on the sprawling stage which spread out interminably in whichever direction we looked. This was a goddamn mountain which had had its head cut off cleanly.

The glass enclosing we were in was sound proof, so we couldn't hear what Vidhi Damodar Acharya was saying, but on the screens we could see the shock on people's faces.

Sameer held out his hand, looked at us and started opening his fist. 1. 2. 3. 4. 5. He pointed to the stage.

'Go, walk to the cross and stand there. Speak normally if asked. The microphones will pick up your voice. GO. GO. GO.'

The security cordon melted away. The glass doors slid open and a chilly breeze hit us. As we started to walk out towards the cross twenty paces away from us, it felt like we were walking in the clouds.

'COME!' Vidhi Damodar Acharya's voice boomed from the heavens above.

She was pointing at us. We walked past the family who bowed ever so little to greet us.

While we walked, Vidhi Acharya spoke, 'Reincarnation is still a developing technology and as we all know, we ran into some speed bumps. But starting today, we found an alternate route that might be attractive to some people.' She raised her voice. 'We are calling it the Soulmates programme. It's now open to each and every citizen of the country! No limits! If you are dying, you have a chance at rebirth!'

A deafening applause filled up the gardens. She raised her hand to quieten the crowd down.

'The only criterion for the dying is that they should have someone healthy who would share their body with them for the rest of their life. It could be a parent, a child, a lover. The relationship should be pure, untainted, unsullied!'

On the stage, we took our position on the white markings. Anvesha was nervous, I could feel it. That's something we found we could do, now that we were in the same body. I could also sense when she was about to cry or laugh; how she felt about things. Not the exact thoughts, that would be strange, but I could tap into her soul and scamper through her vibe, her memories, how it made her feel. For the first time, 'I know you inside out' wasn't just a phrase but the truth. We could access the same parts of the brain. I could feel creative, conspiratorial, like her, and she could access my strength in mathematics. It was weird.

Vidhi Damodar Acharya walked towards us and stopped a few paces from us. She cleared her throat.

'Welcome to the first success of the Soulmates programme!'

Just as we had been taught, we raised our hand to wave at the crowd.

She continued, 'Presenting to you—Druvan-Anvesha. Soulmates for life and beyond! One body, two souls! The new era of humanity!'

She looked at us to speak.

'I'm Druvan,' I said. My lips moved again but it was Anvesha moving them. 'And I'm Anvesha.' We both spoke together. 'And this . . . is our new body.'

Vidhi Damodar Acharya continued, 'We tested our technology on many people—lovers, parents and children, husbands and wives. It failed each time till we found Druvan and Anvesha, the first true soulmates of the world. Their relationship was untainted, pure and that's the one reason why their souls could co-exist. Their love is the reason for their survival, their love is the reason they beat death and their love is the reason why they will be immortal! For giving us the breakthrough, the Parivar will always have a body available for Druvan-Anvesha for the rest of eternity. Druvan-Anvesha will be the first immortal couple in the history of mankind!'

Shock ran through the crowd. As it died, a deafening applause coursed through the air. Soon, a chant started from a little group of young people.

Druvan. Anvesha. Druvan. Anvesha. Druvan. Anvesha. Others joined in, found a tune, a beat, and our names rang through the Parivar Gardens. Druvan-Anvesha. Druvan-Anvesha.

I could feel her well up.

'I always told you we were soulmates.'

'Technically, you're wrong. We are body-mates. When you share a room, it's called roommates,' she whispered.

'Look up!' I said. 'What does it say?'

On the biggest screen, the words lit up: The Soulmates programme—now open for people who think they are soulmates.

'Soulmates,' she said.

'For life and beyond,' I said.

'Creepy but okay,' she whispered.

'I love you, Druvan-Anvesha.'

'I love you, Anvesha-Druvan.'